SAUSAGE
HALL

CHRISTINA JAMES

SALT

CROMER

PUBLISHED BY SALT
12 Norwich Road, Cromer, Norfolk NR27 0AX

© Christina James, 2013

The right of Christina James to be identified as the author of this work has been asserted by her in accordance with Section 77 of the Copyright, Designs and Patents Act 1988.

First published by Salt Publishing, 2013

Printed in Great Britain by Clays Ltd, St Ives plc

Typeset in Paperback 9 / 12

ISBN 978 1 907773 82 2 paperback

1 3 5 7 9 8 6 4 2

*For Emma, with love. I hope that you
will visit Sutterton one day!*

ONE

I lie dozing on my sun-lounger on my private patch of beach in Marigot Bay. I am sheltering under a large umbrella that Derek, my steward, has angled adroitly to protect both Joanna and me from the sun. Derek would do anything for us. The heat is pouring through the canvas, but it's diffused by the fabric: bearable, pleasant.

Joanna has placed her own sun-lounger almost at right-angles to mine, but she isn't stretched out. She is hunched at one end of it, legs tucked under her, head and face covered by a great pink hat that resembles a plaited bucket. She has wound a pink chiffon scarf around the crown. She sits with her back to me. I can't tell whether she is reading the book that rests on her bare thighs or simply brooding.

It has taken all my ingenuity to get her here. I won't let her spoil this now. I don't want to be contaminated by the darkness of her thoughts. I've worked hard for this holiday – I've worked hard for everything – and Christ knows I deserve a break. I'm even working now, in a way. When Sentance came up with his idea of using the boats for luxury cruises, I knew I couldn't trust anyone else to test it out. The experience on board, anyway. I draw the line at staying in that hotel he's done the deal with. Four star – it should be OK, though I'd have preferred five. But still. My grandfather bought this beach house years ago and as a family we've barely used it. Work-life balance, that's what we've never managed to achieve.

Opa was a brilliant businessman, but not exactly imaginative. He called the beach house Laurieston, the same as our house in Sutterton. Sutterton: while I'm lying here it's difficult to believe it actually exists. Sometimes I think I hate the place, with all the problems it brings: the farms, the packing sheds, the factories, the staff. Especially the staff.

I stretch across to the little table that Derek has placed within reach and grasp my glass of piña colada. It is so chock full of ice cubes that they have hardly melted. I take a sip. The drink is so cold it makes my teeth ache. We could stay here, Joanna and I. She could spend the rest of her days here. How long does she have? Six months, a year? I need to talk to that quack again. Squirming bastard. He never gives me a straight answer.

My mobile rings. At first, I don't realise it's mine. Joanna and I both use the traditional telephone ringtone. It's a sign of quality, of class. I can't bear the vulgar tunes most people choose. Vivaldi's *Four Seasons* or *You'll Never Walk Alone*. Phones should sound like phones. I've told Archie that, too. Miraculously, on this point he seems to agree with me.

Joanna turns, shoots me a dark look from under her hat.

"Your phone's ringing," she says. "If you're going to ignore it, can you switch it off?"

"Sorry." I lean my head out and peer under the sun-lounger. The mobile is lying on a folded towel and I grab it; seeing who the caller is, I realise I must take the call.

"Sentance," I say, "I thought I told you not to disturb me."

"I'm sorry, Mr Kevan. But you said except in an emergency."

"Are you saying there *is* an emergency?"

"It's not exactly . . ."

"Oh, for God's sake, cut the cackle, man. Why have you called?"

"It's your house. Jackie Briggs was walking past it early this morning, on her way to that ice-cream van cleaning job that she has, when she saw a man standing on the conservatory roof. She went to fetch Harry. He called the police, who called me. Harry managed to hold on to the man until they arrived. Jackie thought that there were two of them, but if she's right the other one did a runner."

"So they didn't get in, then?"

"Yes, they did. We don't think they took much. The guy that was caught was carrying a rucksack. He'd only managed to lift a DVD player, a camera and some small items of jewellery. Oh, and a Toby jug, for some reason. The other one may have nicked more. Jackie went round the house to see if she could spot anything else missing. She couldn't think of anything. But you'll know better yourself, when you come back."

"The house has been made secure?"

"Yes. There was just one pane of broken glass in the conservatory. I've had it repaired. The police are going to keep an eye out until you get here, in case the other guy tries to return. If you don't think that's enough, I'll go and stay there tonight myself, if you like."

"Well done. It's all sorted, then. I don't think you need to put yourself out, but thanks, anyway. Tell the police I'll deal with it when I come home."

Sentance falls silent. I can read him like a book, even when he's invisible and on the other side of the Atlantic. He hates to be the bearer of bad news. It's not that he's overflowing with fellow-feeling; it's more the case that he's afraid I'll shoot the messenger. I've already dragged out of him more disagreeable information than he thinks is good for him. Craven little sod.

"Well, what else is there? I can tell there *is* something."

"The two policemen that came insisted on going round the house with Jackie, to make sure everything was all right. They found the cellar door open. They asked her what was down there and she said she didn't know; she said she's never been down there. They left her at the top of the steps and went down for a poke round themselves. They found some stuff in there."

"What do you mean, *they found some stuff in there*? Of course there's stuff in there. My wine's stored there, for a start. I hope that nobody's touched that. And my lathe. And quite a lot of old furniture. Which *stuff* did they mean?"

"It looks like passports," says Sentance in a hushed voice. He says it so quietly that at first I think the word is passe-partout. Then it dawns on me.

"Passports? Whose passports?"

"I don't know. They didn't know, either. But they said it looked as if someone had been . . . making them. As in forging them, I mean."

"How did you find this out? Were you there, too?"

"Yes." Snivelling little creep, trying to distance himself from it.

I sigh wearily.

"I've got no idea what this is about. I'll deal with it when I get back."

Again there is silence.

"You don't think that's a good idea?"

"It's not what I think, Mr Kevan. I'm just trying to warn you. The police have asked me how to get hold of you. I've stalled them so far, but in a minute I'm going to have to give them this number. When I do, I know they're going to tell you to come home straight away."

TWO

Detective Inspector Tim Yates dragged on a pair of latex gloves and tipped on to the sheet of plastic he'd draped across his desk the contents of the Ziploc bag that Detective Constable Ricky MacFadyen had just handed to him. The bag contained what appeared to be five United Kingdom passports. He picked one up and carefully turned over its pages, one by one. The stationery that had been used to produce it was either genuine or a very good fake. The passport itself was obviously counterfeit, since it contained no name or photograph. Putting it down, he worked through the other four red-covered booklets. Each was identical to the first.

"What do you make of these, Ricky?"

MacFadyen shrugged. He'd been called out very early to the house in Sutterton where the passports had been found, having been awoken from a bare four hours' sleep after celebrating the birth of his friend Charlie's daughter the night before. His hangover was relatively mild, but the effort required to keep his eyes open intensely painful. He stifled a yawn.

"Somebody's obviously working some kind of racket. It's a pity they didn't get a bit further with what they were doing with these. We might have had more of an idea of what they're up to. Aliases for criminals, most likely. Generally, criminals only need fake passports if they're planning on travelling abroad with false names. If that's what they're for, there's something big going on."

"I'd say it's definitely big, given the quality of these. I'll need to get them checked over by a Home Office expert, but they look pretty good to me. I know something about this Kevan de Vries, the character whose house they were found in, but I've never met him and had no official dealings with him or his company. I understand he's on holiday in the Windward Islands. Thornton, who does know him personally, has spoken to him on the phone, told him he needs to come home immediately. I understand he cut up pretty rough about it."

"I've not met him, either, but I should think most people in the area know something about the de Vries family. Kevan's grandfather came here from Holland in the 1930s. He was part of a group of Dutch bulb-growers and market gardeners who all settled in the Fens at around the same time. I think they got grants from the Dutch government to move here. There were too many farmers in the Netherlands, so the authorities offered sweeteners to get rid of a few."

"Sounds like a forerunner of EU interventionist policies!"

"You could say that. Seems a bit Stalinist to me, shipping people out of the country – like collectivisation in reverse – even if they came here willingly and got paid for it. Anyway, old man de Vries did all right. He was easily the most successful of the lot of them. He practically owned Sutterton and land stretching for many miles around it when he died. By then he was much more than a farmer. He'd built canning plants and freezer plants; food-packing plants, later, when the supermarket chains started to want pre-packed produce. And acres of fields of tulips. He turned into a local tycoon."

"All above board?"

"As far as I know. My great-uncle worked for him for a while. Said he had a reputation for being a bit of a slave-driver, but he paid quite well. That made him a better employer than many round here, then or now."

6

Tim nodded.

"So has Kevan de Vries inherited all of his grandfather's empire? Or is Kevan's father still alive?"

"I don't know the answer to that. I'll find out. I don't actually remember hearing much about Kevan's father. Kevan's listed as the MD and CEO of de Vries Enterprises, whatever that is. It may not include all of the companies. I'll check that as well."

"Tell me in detail how the passports were found."

"There's a woman called Jackie Briggs who cleans at Laurieston House, Kevan de Vries' home. She's actually called the housekeeper, but I think that's a bit jumped-up for what she does. She lives close by and has to pass it on her way to another job that she has, cleaning the inside of ice-cream vans."

"That a de Vries business, too?"

"I don't think so. She cleans out ambulances as well, apparently. She has to finish cleaning the ice-cream vans before the drivers start their rounds, so she gets to the depot early. She was passing Laurieston House at about 6 a.m. this morning when she saw two men there. One of them was emerging from an opening in the conservatory roof; the other was standing in the garden. She knew the de Vries family were away, so she went to fetch her husband, who called the police. The bloke on the roof had only just jumped to the ground when the husband turned up and caught him with a rugby tackle. He was still holding on to him when the police arrived. The other one had scarpered, of course."

"Anyone we know?"

"Terry Panton. Local kid. He had a bag of stuff he'd taken from the house. Nothing of great value. He's already on probation for breaking and entering. He'll have to do time now."

"A petty thief, though? Not likely to be a passport forger?"

MacFadyen gave a short laugh.

"Hardly! He hasn't got the brain. Besides, why would he want to plant the passports there, if he was involved in some way?"

"I've no idea; and you're probably right that he knows nothing about them. A bit unfortunate for Mr de Vries, if he's engaged in some kind of scam, to be exposed by a bungled burglary."

"You say *if* he's engaged. Can there be any doubt that he's mixed up in this in some way?"

"My intuition says that he must be; yours too, probably. But stranger things have happened. He wouldn't be the first rich man unwittingly to play host to someone's little sideline. Talking of which, what did you make of the Briggs woman?"

"She seemed pleasant enough. A bit flustered, a bit in awe of the situation. And worried about her husband. Panton gave him a nasty bite when he was trying to get away from him."

"Vicious little bastard! So you think she's straight up?"

"I'd say so. She seems quite loyal to the de Vries family. She was concerned they might have lost something valuable."

"But she didn't think they had?"

"No. Something that struck me was that she didn't like the bloke who showed up when we were looking round the house with her. Sentance, his name was. Some kind of senior de Vries henchman. Oily so-and-so."

"That's interesting. And you say she didn't come down into the cellar with you when you found the passports?"

"No."

"What about this Sentance character?"

"Oh, he came all right. He wouldn't let us out of his sight."

"He saw the passports?"

"Yes."

"How did he react?"

"He said that he was sure that Mr de Vries would be able to give us an explanation."

"Did he? I wonder what kind of explanation he was thinking of."

THREE

Tim Yates was not surprised that Superintendent Thornton had instructed him to meet Kevan de Vries off the plane when it landed at Gatwick Airport. Thornton liked nothing better than to be able to demonstrate the importance of his position by organising the transatlantic telephone conversation that had taken place with the high-profile businessman, but he was less keen on getting up at 3.30 a.m. in order to apprehend him.

The flight from St Lucia was scheduled to touch down at 7.00 a.m. Tim and DC Juliet Armstrong had arrived at 6.45 a.m. to find a notice flashing on the arrivals board. De Vries' flight was estimated to land 45 minutes late.

"Let's go and find some coffee," said Tim.

Juliet nodded ruefully. "I'd rather have had another three quarters of an hour in bed," she said.

"Likewise, but at least we haven't missed him. I doubt very much whether he'd be the type to hang around waiting for us if *we'd* been late."

They found a table at the airport's Costa Coffee shop where they could sit and nurse their giant cappuccinos (Tim's choice). Juliet took the opportunity to talk more about the task ahead of them.

"Did Superintendent Thornton give de Vries our names?"

"I believe so. Which means that he's expecting us, at least. I wish I had more idea about exactly what Thornton said to him. I know that de Vries was very shirty when Thornton said we'd have to ask him to cut short his holiday. Thornton doesn't stand up to people he thinks are influential. If de Vries was uppity and Thornton didn't show him who was boss, that's going to make our job more difficult."

"We're not arresting him, though, are we?"

"Not as such. We're going to ask him to come with us voluntarily. We'll drive him and his wife back to Sutterton. We'll show him where we found the passports and listen to his story. Depending on what he says and how convincing he is, we may want him to accompany us to the station to charge him. On the other hand, we may just ask him to stay in the area until we've got to the bottom of it. Either way, he's bound to want to involve his solicitor."

"Did Superintendent Thornton ask Mrs de Vries to return with her husband?"

"I don't know. I'm guessing he didn't, as he probably thinks it's unlikely that she's involved in the forgery. Apparently she's been an invalid for some time. But she wouldn't want to finish the holiday on her own, would she?"

"She may do. I think we'll find that they weren't just taking their ordinary annual leave. De Vries is in the process of setting up a new business venture. For some years he's owned a small fleet of ships to import bananas from the Windward Islands. He's now decided to get more mileage out of it by offering a kind of upmarket package holiday that consists of a luxury cruise on each ship's outward journey, followed by a stay in a four-star hotel in St Lucia and the flight home. Along with some business acquaintances, Kevan de Vries and his wife were testing the outward cruise, so it was a business trip as well as a holiday for them. If they were looking after guests, Mrs de Vries may feel that she has to stay with them."

Juliet opened her shoulder-bag and took out a neatly-folded sheet of newsprint torn from the *Spalding Guardian*.

She smoothed it out and passed it to Tim. *Kevan de Vries takes a busman's holiday*, the headline proclaimed. Beneath it were a short article explaining what Juliet had just outlined and a grainy picture of Kevan de Vries shaking hands with the captain of the *Tulip*, one of the de Vries vessels. The newspaper was dated the previous Thursday.

"They'd only been gone for five days when the burglary happened," said Tim. "They must only just have arrived in St Lucia."

"Don't tell me you're beginning to feel sorry for them! I got the distinct feeling that Kevan de Vries was going to be one of those people you'd decided you didn't like before you'd even met him!"

Tim put down the wooden stick-spoon with which he'd been trying to scoop up the foam from his coffee and gave her a look of lingering mock incredulity.

"Surely I'm not as prejudiced as all that?" he said. Without waiting for an answer, he continued, "I wasn't really thinking about their holiday at all. I was thinking that anyone, including the burglars, could have seen that article and known they were away. The same goes for the people who had legitimate access to the house. Servants and employees wouldn't have needed to read the papers to find out, though. They'd have known anyway."

"Meaning you think it likely the passports were planted and Kevan de Vries is innocent?"

"Meaning, whether he's innocent or not, he and his lawyer can make a good case for his having known nothing about them, unless we can find a completely foolproof link between them and him. They were clean of prints, as you know." Tim looked at the news clipping again. "Short bloke, isn't he, unless the captain's a giant? Thornton gave me a photo of him – quite a good one, I think – but it's only of his head and shoulders. Somehow I'd assumed he was much taller. He seems to be quite powerfully built."

Tim reached into his inside pocket and drew out a brown manila envelope with *Kevan de Vries* inscribed on it in Superintendent Thornton's large, flowing hand. Juliet took it from him and studied the picture inside carefully. It was of a man in his early- to mid-forties. He had broad, almost Slavic features and a high colour. His receding blond hair had been allowed to grow quite long at the front, and was swept sideways across his forehead. As Tim had noted, he had broad shoulders. His white shirt collar seemed to be almost painfully tight, his neck bulging slightly above the dark tie. His expression was not exactly disdainful; rather, it suggested a kind of supercilious amusement.

"Where did this come from, sir?"

"Thornton got it from the Rotary Club, I think. His social pretensions come in useful on occasion."

Juliet grinned. "At least it saves us from the indignity of having to stand at the barrier waving a piece of cardboard with 'Kevan de Vries' printed on it."

"Yes. I doubt if he'd have liked that, any more than we would."

FOUR

The parting with Joanna is tough. I expect her to cling to me in tears and beg me to take her with me, but, after some initial pleading, she decides to punish me with silence. Not complete silence: Joanna is far too adult and generous-spirited to sulk like a child, but we have no real conversation after she's accepted I'll travel back to Lincolnshire alone. She makes me promise several times to call Archie and arrange to visit him as soon as I land. She retires to bed some time before I am ready to leave. I listen at her door for several minutes while Derek hovers in the hall, waiting to take me to the airport. I'd hoped to creep in to see her face in repose, perhaps to kiss her, but I can hear her breathing regularly in what must be an unfeigned deep sleep and decide it will be selfish to risk waking her. I know that sleep alone gives her respite from the pain.

The first class section of the plane is almost empty. I decline all food and drink and tell the stewardess not to disturb me. I accept her offer of a blanket and try to sleep. I must have dozed off fitfully, because I am awoken by the plane's speaker system. It is the captain, relaying a message about a slight delay.

I'm sitting up now, fully awake. For me sleep is an effective analgesic, if only a temporary one. At first awakening, I am troubled with no specific cares, just a vague feeling of tension and anxiety. Then all the old problems crowd in to populate my thoughts, all the weary heartache associated with Joanna's illness and Archie's disabilities, all the grinding weight of running de Vries Industries and the irritations of having to deal day in, day out, with unsavoury characters like Sentance. And finally, this new set of difficulties sitting on top of them. It's the first time I've had any kind of brush with the law. What the hell has been going on? Whatever it is, it sounds unlikely that it was precipitated by Joanna's and my absence. I can believe that the burglars knew we were away and saw their opportunity, but whoever was responsible for the passports must have been working on them for months. Whether or not they've been dumped in the cellar recently, whatever racket they represent must have been carefully planned. I wonder if Sentance is involved in some way, and dismiss the idea. He has too many irons in his own grubby little fire, all of them dead certs as far as he is concerned, for him to be willing to jeopardise his cowardly hide for a riskier scam, dancing his grisly attendance on Joanna as he does.

I release the seat-belt and stand up briefly to brush down my suit, which is horribly crumpled. I long for a shower and a shave. I've eaten and drunk nothing since leaving St Lucia and I have no need to visit the lavatory. My mouth feels dry and there's an unpleasant metallic taste that seems to come from the back of my throat. The stewardess, who has been nodding off on her seat at the top of the gangway – it faces the first class passengers – snaps her eyes into life and smiles at me glassily.

"Are you all right, sir? You may have heard that there's been a bit of a delay. We should land in Gatwick in about forty-five minutes, even so. May I bring you a breakfast tray?"

I wave my hand impatiently.

"No food," I say, "but I'd like some coffee, if you don't mind. And some water."

"Of course."

She disappears behind the curtain that leads to her pretend galley. I smooth my trousers and sit down once more, re-engaging the seat-belt. I close my eyes again briefly. I realise that I have been dreaming about Joanna and the first time we met. Childhood sweethearts, almost. Opa had over-ruled my mother and insisted that I should attend Spalding Grammar School, rather than be sent away to one of the grander boarding schools that she'd favoured. Joanna was a High School girl. When we met, we were both in the Sixth Form. Her mother was a widow; her father, before he died, had been a farm labourer. I knew that Mother never liked Joanna, though I only caught her out in showing it very occasionally. I suspect it was because she thought Joanna's background too humble for me. Opa loved her, though, if anything because of her origins rather than despite them. He said that her family had come from the soil, the same as our own, and that it was something in which we should all take pride.

We met at a social event arranged by her school. It was a bit pretentious, truth be told. She and I belonged to that heady period when teachers thought that to provide a generation with enough learning to get them into university would transform the world into their oyster. Some also realised that the new cadre of working-class undergraduates they were creating would require coaching in the social skills and, accordingly, they organised occasions contrived to provide them. I had no need of such aid, because both Opa and my mother encouraged the South Lincs county set to come to bridge rubbers, swimming parties and tennis parties at Laurieston, so by the time I reached the sixth form I'd had more than my share of exposure to pretentious small talk. I'd gone along to the wine and cheese evening organised by one of the teachers at the High School, even so. I'd just split up with my girlfriend and thought that the High School do would be as good a place

as any to find another; and if not, I could take advantage of
the free wine.

Joanna had been standing near the door with a little
gaggle of her friends, all prefects. They weren't wearing
school uniform, but all still sported their red prefects' sashes,
wrapped around their wrists so that their authority could be
recognised. She was standing slightly outside the circle that
they'd formed, so she was the first to see me when I came in.
She had long, blonde hair and an elfin face, with huge blue
eyes. Her colouring was Dutch, but she was too willowy to be
a Dutch girl. She took my ticket, smiling. I realised that she
was just about the same height as I was myself. The wine and
cheese party was being held in the gym at the High School.
A disc jockey had been hired and a small square dance area
created in the centre of the parquet flooring. The music
wasn't loud: in fact, it was rather schmaltzy and plaintive for
such an event – I seem to remember that Simon and Garfun-
kel tunes were played for most of the evening. The wine was
adequate rather than plentiful, but none of us was used to
drinking it, so it made us feel heady quite quickly. However,
there were so many teachers dotted about, observing everyone carefully, that it would have been impossible to get properly drunk. It was evidently intended to be a very decorous
occasion.

A few pairs of girls and one couple – I recognised Nigel
Asher, from the year below me – were dancing desultorily on
the parquet square.

"Dance?" I said to Joanna.

She shrugged and allowed me to lead her to join the other
dancers. Neither of us was good at dancing, and when the
tempo increased she drew away from me, laughing, and
shouted that she'd had enough. I followed her to the far side
of the room, where one of the refreshments tables had been

laid out, and there we stayed, sipping wine and talking. I spent the whole evening with her.

The arrival of the stewardess bearing coffee and water on a small tray dispels my reverie. She hands it to me carefully and I thank her.

"Not a problem," she says, in that irritatingly chirpy way that people in the service industries have recently adopted. I think it's supposed to indicate that they're there solely for their clients' convenience, but to me it suggests the exact opposite. "We should be landing quite soon, now. The captain has managed to make up some of the time that we lost."

I nod thanks to avoid exposure to more of her semi-reflex comments. I sip the coffee, which is both bitter and weak and scaldingly hot, as if it has just been re-heated. Suddenly, I feel apprehensive. Somehow I have to summon the energy to deal with the police enquiry. I'm quite aware that this DI Yates is likely to take some convincing that I know nothing about the wretched passports. What I have to do at all costs is to stop him prying further into my affairs. If I co-operate in every respect, perhaps he'll confine himself to the passport matter. If not, I have the option of trying to make Thornton dance for his supper, I suppose, though I feel about as well-disposed towards him as I do towards Sentance. I know that I'm going to have to put up with quite a lot of Sentance over the next few days.

I sigh and look bleakly out of my porthole window. I'm surprised to see that we're diving fast towards the runway: the plane is on the point of landing. It hits the tarmac with the slightest of thuds and I feel the pilot apply the brakes. The stewardess begins to broadcast her routine patter through the speaker system.

As soon as the seatbelt sign has been switched off, I rise and take my overnight bag from the locker. I didn't bring a suitcase: there are plenty of clothes at home. Just a shirt and a change of underwear in case I was delayed; and my laptop, of course.

I'm first off the plane. There's a short hold-up while I have to wait for some of the passengers from an earlier flight to go through passport control, then I'm through to the barrier where friends and relatives wait. I've always found this stage of travelling particularly irksome. People who've only been away for a week or ten days on some package holiday are greeted as if they've just returned from six months working in a space station or fighting in Helmand Province. There's a whole gaggle of such greeters here now, their spirits over-buoyed, craning their necks to get the first sight of whoever it is that they're looking for. Behind them stands a row of chauffeurs and car hire firm operatives, waiting patiently, some holding discreet little cards bearing the name of the person they're meeting. It occurs to me that I have no method of recognising this DI Yates. I'm assuming that since he's a detective he won't be sporting a uniform.

I pass through the barrier and come to a halt to one side of it, looking around me as I do so. A man advances briskly, a woman in his wake. I have no doubt that this is he, though he's younger than I expected. Not much more than thirty, I'd guess, the woman perhaps a few years older. He's tall, with thick, curly red hair and an open expression. The woman's quite dumpy, with well-developed calves and thick ankles. He's smartly dressed in a lightweight suit, but she's somewhat lacking in dress sense. She wears a brown chain store dress that's seen better days, flat shoes and dark tights, despite the heat. Her hair's curly, too, but dark. It's shoulder-length, without much styling. And her eyebrows are also heavy and dark. She wears spectacles with thick plastic frames. I can't see her eyes clearly. A pity, as it would help me to gauge her intelligence. From the way that she's trailing after him, I'd guess that she doesn't have too much self-esteem.

The man walks up to me and holds out his hand.

"Mr de Vries? DI Yates, South Lincs police. This is my colleague, DC Juliet Armstrong. Thank you for returning so promptly."

I take the hand and clasp it. I know my grip is strong – I've made business colleagues wince on occasion – but DI Yates's is a match for it. He holds on for some seconds longer than I deem necessary. I try not to scowl at his comment and attempt a pleasantry in reply.

"Hobson's choice, wouldn't you agree, Detective Inspector?" I nod at the female, who throws me a brief smile. I deduce that it shouldn't be too hard to get her on my side.

I hear someone clearing their throat close to my shoulder. I spin round and find myself staring at Sentance's unctuously insincere countenance. I feel myself prickle with rage. How dare he show up here after I told him not to come?

"Would you like me to take your bag, Mr Kevan?"

"Certainly not. You're not a lackey, and I have no need of one. What the hell do you think you're doing here?"

I step backwards so that the two detectives and Sentance are all within my range of view. Sentance continues to hover, simpering. The police are looking puzzled, the woman slightly shocked. I realise that I have no option but to introduce him.

"This is Tony Sentance, the Finance Director of de Vries Industries. What he thinks he's doing here is anybody's guess."

Sentance inclines his head briefly in their direction and addresses himself to me.

"I thought you might need me to fetch the car, Mr Kevan. I left it here in case you needed to make a quick business trip, as you instructed. I thought you might feel too tired to drive safely."

"Very thoughtful, I'm sure, but as you see my travelling arrangements have already been catered for. I think it unlikely that I shall be travelling back to Sutterton with you."

I turn to DI Yates.

"I assume that you're expecting me to ride with you and your colleague?"

"That was our intention. But if you wish to accompany Mr Sentance, I'm sure that . . ."

"I don't wish to accompany Sentance. I will travel with you, as arranged. My time is limited, as I'm sure is yours. We can probably make some progress during the journey – clear up the preliminaries, etcetera."

Sentence appears to be quite unruffled.

"Should I leave the car here, then, and join you all? As you know, I was present when the pass . . . when the original search took place at Laurieston."

"I think that will be quite unnecessary, thank you. Since you've kindly turned up to collect my car, I suggest that you complete your self-appointed task and make yourself useful by delivering it back to Laurieston. How did you get here, as a matter of interest?"

"I asked Harry Briggs to drop me off. By chance, he had to deliver something to Maidstone, so it wasn't too far out of his way." I might have known that Harry Briggs would have wormed his way in somehow.

"Indeed."

I notice that DI Yates is listening intently, and that he has absorbed this detail. I steer his attention back to Sentance.

"You'd better drive the car back to Laurieston and leave it there. I probably *shall* need it over the next few days. I could take Joanna's car, but, since you've taken it upon yourself to restore mine to me, I may as well go along with it."

Sentance extends his hand, which I ignore.

"Welcome back, Mr Kevan," he says, his sang-froid not slipping, though I think I detect a flicker of discomfort in his voice now. "It's good to see you, despite the unfortunate circumstances. I've told Jackie to open up the house." He pauses. I don't respond. "I'll see you there, then, shall I?"

"There's no need to meet me again today. You can drop the car off and go home. There'll be time for us to talk tomorrow. Let's go, shall we?" I say to the police. I turn my back on Sentance and walk away, with DI Yates following quickly on my heels, the female detective once again some paces behind.

FIVE

Despite Kevan de Vries' assertion that he would welcome conversation during the journey in the police car, he remained resolutely taciturn during the three-hour drive to Sutterton. This suited Tim very well. He knew he and Juliet would at least have to provide polite answers to any reasonable comments or queries that de Vries might make, which could only mean duplicating their effort when they came to question him formally. He was curious as to why de Vries had been so adamant that he didn't want to travel with Sentance. Tim wouldn't have taken much persuading to let them drive together, if de Vries had really pushed for it. If he'd wanted to have an off-the-record discussion with Sentance, he would surely already have talked to the man on his mobile by now. De Vries seemed to loathe the sight of his employee.

Juliet, who was sitting in the back of the car with de Vries, observed that he was extremely fatigued. Part of this could be accounted for by jet-lag, but she thought she glimpsed something more deeply etched in his face than the tiredness that comes from a temporary assault on the body clock. De Vries' face was tanned, either because the Windward Islands sunshine had worked quickly or because he habitually spent a lot of time outside, but beneath the weather-beaten tint she discerned a greyness in his skin, a tautness and fragility – though it seemed an odd word to apply to such a stocky man – that suggested either underlying illness or some chronic anguish.

On several occasions, she saw his head jerk forward, his eyes half-closing as he fought back sleep.

As the police car slowed to negotiate the large roundabout that, together with the village green, formed twin hearts at the centre of Sutterton, de Vries sat up straight and struggled to smooth down his clothing. He was wearing a pale summer jacket and chinos, both crumpled by many hours of travel. He passed the back of his hand across his forehead and rubbed his eyes vigorously.

"Are you all right, Mr de Vries?" Juliet asked quietly. Tim studied his passengers in the driving mirror. He sensed that Juliet was beginning to like the man, or at least to sympathise with him. He sighed inwardly. Juliet's 'instincts', which had at one time come in for a bit of stick from her colleagues, had now been proved correct on too many occasions to be ignored. However, if she suspected that de Vries was innocent, Tim was certain that on this occasion she'd be proved wrong. He'd bet his life that de Vries was guilty of something. It wasn't necessarily what they wanted to question him about at the moment; Tim conceded that he seemed to be too confident about that. But he'd met businessmen like de Vries before; their activities opened out of each other like corridors in a labyrinth. Somewhere at the heart of the labyrinth there would be something nefarious going on, even a whole parallel universe of illegal activity being matched against what was above board. The big imponderable would be whether the police would be able to muster the acumen and resources simultaneously needed to expose it.

They were drawing level with Laurieston House now and Tim had slowed almost to walking pace. The grounds of the house were bounded by wrought-iron railings, on the other side of which grew thickets of laurel. Only a few glimpses of the double drive could be seen from the road.

"Fuck!" said de Vries suddenly.

Juliet followed his line of vision. He was looking through one of the gaps in the laurel hedge. A gleaming maroon Bentley had been parked on the gravel sweep, just to the right of the front door.

"Is something wrong?" asked Juliet.

"The little shit!" de Vries muttered, almost to himself. Then, in a louder voice. "I apologise. I'm very tired. I hadn't expected to see Sentance here just yet. And he hasn't gone straight away, as I asked – that's his car parked further up."

"He doesn't have to join us if you don't want him to, sir," said Tim. Privately he was thinking that Sentance must have stepped on the gas to have beaten them to it. He didn't seem like too much of a risk-taker, but evidently getting there first had been more important to him than breaking the speed limit, even though he was chancing being quizzed about it by two police officers.

"I don't want to cause any awkwardness."

"As you wish, Mr de Vries," said Tim. Strange that such an arrogant man was wary of offending the sensibilities of an employee whom he disliked.

SIX

I don't believe in giving way to my temper, but I could explode when I see that Sentance has ensconced himself at Laurieston before I arrive with the police. I know the man has no finer feelings, but I should have thought common sense alone would have told him to stay away today. He's already fucked things up for us once. Why can't he just make himself scarce?

The coppers seem OK, for coppers. The woman is full of concern for me. Even the guy has said I don't have to involve Sentance if I don't want to. It will look peculiar, though, if I make a point about sending him away. I can't make out what the little twat thinks he's doing. Probably just revelling in it all. I'll make sure that the smile is wiped from his face before too long.

The copper parks at the side of the house, on the smaller drive that leads to the old stables and the garage. I get out of the car. My legs are numb and I stumble a little. The female copper has already climbed nimbly out at her side and she's beside me in a trice now, grabbing hold of my arm. It's hard to bring myself to tolerate this: I almost make the mistake of shaking her off.

"Are you all right, sir?"

"I'm fine," I say, walking rapidly across the gravel so that she's forced to let me go. The male copper catches me up. He has long legs. He lopes along beside me, at pains not to outpace me.

Jackie Briggs opens the door. At least Sentance has the sense not to rile me further by welcoming me into my own house. I notice that she's quite dressed up: she's discarded her overall and is wearing a sort of pinafore dress with a striped shirt underneath it. There's a big rather vulgar brooch on her collar. Her best outfit, no doubt. It dawns on me that she won't be allowed to do any cleaning until the police have finished whatever it is they're doing.

"Good morning, Jackie."

"Good morning, Mr Kevan," she says, in her fluttery way. "I'm really sorry you've had to come back before your holiday's finished. Should I make you some tea?"

"I'd prefer coffee. Black coffee," I say, walking past her. As I expect, Sentance is hovering further down the hall. I leave it to her to decide whether she wants to offer anyone else refreshments, which I can see makes her uncomfortable. She disappears into the scullery.

I open the morning-room door and gesture to the police to go in. Sentance hot-foots it towards us, his feet clattering on the tiles in his haste. I hold up my hand.

"I'd rather see them on my own, Tony, if you don't mind."

"But I . . ."

"You've already spoken to the policeman who came here about the burglary, I believe? Presumably you told him everything you know?"

"Yes, but . . ."

I turn to DI Yates.

"Do you need Sentance to take part in this discussion?"

"Not if you'd prefer him not to be there, sir." He looks across my shoulder at Sentance. "Would you mind waiting until we've finished, Mr Sentance? We may need to speak to you again before we go."

Sentance shrugs as if it's of no importance and follows in Jackie's footsteps. I catch sight of that glowering look on his face, though, before he turns away. It hits me with some force that I must make the effort to get rid of him. I'll do it as soon as Joanna . . .

I follow the police into the morning-room and shut the door firmly. It's only six days since Joanna and I left, but already it has a sour, shut-in smell, not helped by the heavy drapes which have been drawn across the windows. Jackie's idea of decorum, I suppose. It's as if someone's died, rather than that a foiled burglary's taken place. I stride across to the curtains and fling them back, letting in bright shafts of sunlight.

The police choose to roost awkwardly in front of the fire-place. I point at one of the sofas and myself take the chair nearest the window, so that my face is in shadow and I can observe them better than they can see me. DC Armstrong moves and perches on the edge of the sofa. She has to twist her neck awkwardly in order to look at me. DI Yates is more canny. He remains standing. This puts me at a disadvantage, but I'm too weary to get to my feet again. They both look discomfited.

"Well?" I say. "Shall we get on with it?"

"Certainly," Yates agrees, smoothly enough to renew my mistrust in him. "As you know, we're here about two incidents: the attempt made to break into this house yesterday morning and what appear to be counterfeit passports found by the policeman who searched the house after the burglars were apprehended."

I nod.

"First of all, do you have any idea why this house might have been targeted for a burglary?"

"I should have thought that was obvious. We're a wealthy family and my wife and I were known to be away from home. I asked Jackie and Sentance to keep an eye on the place and

I also told the local bobby that the house would be empty. I realise now that wasn't enough. Next time I shall put in a security guard – if there is a next time."

"How many people knew you were on holiday?"

"After that article appeared in the Spalding Guardian, just about the whole county, probably. Before it was published, only my senior office staff and Jackie and her husband. And my son Archie, of course, but he's at boarding school, so even if he told his friends – which is unlikely – I doubt it would have travelled further. Nine-year-old boys aren't much interested in the travel arrangements of their friends' parents, in my experience."

"No, indeed." DI Yates manages a thin smile. He probably disapproves of kids being sent away to be educated. If he but knew it, so do I.

"How long is it since you told Mr Sentance of your holiday plans?"

"What? Why do you want to know that? I really couldn't say. It's more than a holiday; it's also a business trip. Sentance was in on it from the start."

"I see. And Mrs Briggs?"

"You'll have to ask her. My wife deals with the domestic side of things. I didn't speak to Jackie about it myself – I don't see her very much, actually – but I'm guessing that Joanna told her a couple of weeks ago. Longer ago than that, possibly."

He nods.

"How many people have access to this house, Mr de Vries?"

"Quite a few. I use it for business meetings on occasion, with my senior managers as well as business partners."

"Do you allow anyone to use any of the rooms independently of your permission, or when you're absent?"

"Not as a rule. Sentance comes here when we're away sometimes, to deposit mail and that sort of thing. He has a key. I wouldn't expect him to conduct meetings here or invite people in off his own bat. In fact, I'd take a dim view of that, as I'm sure he knows."

"How many people have keys altogether?"

"Myself and Joanna, of course. Sentance and Jackie. I believe that Joanna gave one to her mother. There's a spare that I keep in my desk. Oh, and Archie has one, of course."

"That's seven."

"Yes."

"Do you think that any of those people might have had an extra key cut?"

"They can't. There's a code on each key. It means that my permission is required before any new keys are cut."

"Your permission *or* your wife's?"

"No. Just mine. I do have some idea about security."

DI Yates pauses before he speaks again.

"I'm sure you do. We'll need to account for all of the keys in due course – make sure they're all still with the people you gave them to, I mean, and that none of them has lent one to someone else."

"I hardly think that's likely."

"Perhaps not; but the alternative is that we arrest you on suspicion of forgery." He moves closer to me. His voice is harder now. He's looking at me carefully. I return his stare. I refuse to be intimidated by a copper, especially in my own house. I decide that if this one oversteps the mark, I shall have words with that toad Thornton.

There's a knock at the door and Jackie comes in with a tray. As I'd guessed, it bears a coffee-pot and a teapot, several cups and a plate of biscuits. She puts it down on the low table that stands between me and DC Armstrong.

"Thank you." I say. She disappears quickly. I don't bother to offer the drinks.

"You were saying?"

"I said that the alternative is to arrest you on suspicion of forgery." He's watching me levelly, appraisingly.

DC Armstrong rises to her feet, closing in so that we form a misshapen triangle.

"Do you mind my asking why Mrs de Vries didn't come home with you?" She sounds gentle, but she's probing.

I return her gaze for several seconds.

"Not at all," I say, after the silence has become uncomfortable. "My wife is ill: seriously ill. She's been suffering from leukaemia for a long time now. We hoped that it had been stabilised by the drugs, but we knew that there was a chance that it would get out of control again. This time, they can't pull it back. She's tried everything that the quacks can think of, but it's been of no use. She's in palliative care, now. She's not in too much pain at the moment and, although she's weak, she can still enjoy some aspects of her life, provided that she takes it easy. Relaxation doesn't come naturally to her. It took all my powers of persuasion to get her to St Lucia. If you must know, she was very keen to return here with me, but I wanted her to stay there. I'd like her last weeks to be as tranquil as possible. I didn't think that having a posse of policemen traipsing around the house asking questions would quite cut it." I glare at her.

"I'm sorry . . ." she begins to say. I hold up my hand. The impertinence of the woman suddenly enrages me.

"Don't!" I say. "She wouldn't thank you. Nor do I. The grief is ours. It's private. You will allow us that, at least."

She looks down at her shoes.

DI Yates leaps to her rescue.

"Of course we won't intrude," he says, his voice still stern. "Can we get back to the passports now?"

The bastard has not only wrong-footed me, he's also implied that Joanna's illness is incidental, a little aside that's obscuring the real topic of business. But he's over-stepped: I shall definitely be on to Thornton when they've gone.

"What is it you want me to say? I've never seen them. I'm prepared to accept the word of your colleague that he found them here, but I don't know how they got here, or even what they look like. They were British passports, I take it?"

"Yes. What makes you say that, sir?" He screws up his eyes as he speaks.

"It was a logical guess, nothing more. Everyone knows how desirable a British passport is."

"Quite."

"How do you know they're forgeries, anyway? Are they very bad ones?"

"On the contrary, they seem to be excellent copies. At present we know they're fake only because there are no names in them. Passports are never issued blank, for obvious reasons. We've sent all but one to an expert to see if she can identify any other anomalies. We'll arrange to show you the one that remains in our possession. It's at the police station. We'll have to ask you to come there, eventually."

"Does this mean that I'm under suspicion of some kind of wrongdoing?"

"I'm afraid we can't rule that out at the moment, Mr de Vries. We'll be asking you to stay in the area until we've got to the bottom of this. Look at it as a formality, if you prefer."

"I see. Is that all you require of me?"

"Not quite. The passports were found as part of the routine post-burglary check to try to establish what was missing from the property. We weren't authorised to conduct a thorough search at that point. We'll need this authorisation now. My preference would be for you to agree voluntarily, but I can obtain a warrant if you wish."

"What do you mean by 'thorough search'?"

"We'll need to carry out a meticulous examination of the cellars. It will involve moving around the items that you have stored there. We'll also want to search the other rooms in the house. You or one of your staff may be present if you wish."

"There's not much point in withholding my permission, since you're clearly going to do it one way or another. I take it you'll allow me to stay here? You're not proposing to shunt me off to a hotel or something?"

"Thank you, sir. As you're being so co-operative, that shouldn't be necessary. We'll start with the rooms that you want to use. We'll also assign a policeman to spend the night here with you."

"To protect me, or to make sure that I don't try to destroy any evidence?"

Again that level look. Clearly he doesn't think this is a joke.

"A little of both, sir."

Suddenly I can't wait to be rid of them.

"Just remember one thing," I snap. "My wife has only a few weeks left. I wish to return to her as soon as I can. If I'm not back in St Lucia by the end of the week, I'll make sure that you both live to regret it. Is that clear?"

DC Armstrong looks guilt-stricken. She opens her mouth to speak, but DI Yates cuts in.

"It's not wise to threaten us, sir. We understand the situation and we'll do our best to release you as soon as we can."

I decide not to push it.

"As long as we understand each other," I say more quietly. "Now, do you want me to ask Sentance to come in?"

"Yes, please. There's no need for you to be present when we speak to him. In fact we'd be grateful if you'd allow us to see him alone."

I make no protest. It's humiliating to be dismissed in this way, but the prospect of having to listen to Sentance's insincere grovelling holds no appeal whatsoever.

SEVEN

Kevan de Vries stalked out of his drawing-room, slamming the door behind him pointedly. Tim Yates and Juliet Armstrong moved back to their original positions on the hearth-rug. Although the house had thick walls, they had agreed by means of silently-exchanged looks that it would be inadvisable to talk while they were waiting for Tony Sentance to appear.

It took Sentance slightly longer to present himself than they had anticipated. Tim had been about to go in search of him when a light tap on the door heralded his arrival. He entered immediately.

"Sorry," he said ingratiatingly, with a grimace that was meant to be a smile.

Tim had already taken a dislike to the man, although he and Juliet had engaged in only that one brief conversation with him at the airport and subsequently witnessed his brusque dismissal by Kevan de Vries in the hallway half an hour previously. Having the opportunity to observe Sentance at close quarters did not improve Tim's opinion of him. The man's face was almost mask-like in its glib plausibility, yet every so often the mask slipped to reveal some more naked emotion pushing its way up to the surface. At intervals, the right side of his temple, near the eye, twitched unprepossessingly. Whether this was owing to an underlying infirmity or Sentance's imperfect attempt to present an unruffled exterior was impossible to say. His gaze flicked uneasily from Tim to Juliet, around the room and back to Tim again, in the process alighting upon the tray that had been deposited by Jackie Briggs. He seized upon it as if it were a lifeline.

"DI Yates, DC Armstrong, I'm so sorry, Mr Kevan appears to have forgotten to do the honours. He has a lot on his mind, of course. May I offer you tea or coffee?"

"Thank you, but no," said Tim stiffly.

"I'd like some tea," said Juliet. "Should I help myself?"

"Oh, please, allow *me!*"

He removed a cup from the stack, set it on a saucer and seized the teapot. His hand shook a little as he poured.

"Milk and sugar?"

"Just a little milk, thank you."

Juliet held out her hand to take it. Once again, Sentance's grip was unsteady. Some of the tea spilled into the saucer. Both chose to ignore this.

"Won't you sit down?"

"Thank you, I prefer to stand," said Tim. "Please take a seat yourself if you like."

Tony Sentance smiled wryly and gave a funny little shake of his head. Tim had no idea what this meant, except that the man was apparently indicating that he would remain standing as long as Tim himself did so.

"Mr Sentance, I understand that you have a key to this house?"

"Yes, of course. I'm Mr Kevan's right-hand man."

"Do you often come here when he's away?"

The eyes swivelled to the floor, then to a spot above the fireplace that was roughly level with Tim's head.

"Not especially. Unless he asks me to."

"So he usually knows if you come into the house during his absence?"

"Certainly. And until recently Joanna's usually been here, even if Mr Kevan hasn't."

"So you may in fact have brought people here without his knowledge?"

Sentance's eyes swerved away again. They collided briefly with Juliet's, before fixing themselves on the teaspoon that he held in his hand.

"Only if Joanna didn't tell him." Not my fault, in that case, he was saying, loud and clear.

"How many times have you let yourself in since Mr and Mrs de Vries left for St Lucia last week?"

"None," he said guilelessly. "Jackie let me in after she reported the burglary to the police on Sunday, and again today. I didn't need to use my key on either occasion."

"And those are the only times you've been here since your employer left?"

"As I've just said." He gave a further irritating shake of the head.

"Who told you about the burglary on Sunday? I understand that Mrs Briggs had already let DC MacFadyen into the house when you appeared."

There was a pause.

"I'm not sure. I think that Jackie herself must have called me. She'd have known that Mr Kevan would want me here if anything was wrong. Or it might have been Harry. He's her husband," he added in a confidential tone, as if the relationship were a secret. He flicked Juliet a brief smile.

Tim was writing notes.

"Thank you," he said. "So you arrived and Mrs Briggs let you in. What happened next?"

"Jackie had been round the house with the cop... er... policeman to see if she thought anything was missing – besides what they found on that young tearaway, that is. I don't think she thought that there was anything. Then your colleague noticed that the cellar door was open. He said he'd like to check down there and asked Jackie if she'd go with him. She said she'd never been in the cellar, so she couldn't be of much help. She said that she doesn't like enclosed spaces. So naturally I said I'd be happy to accompany him."

"Did he ask you to?"

"No, but I knew Mr Kevan would want . . ."

"Precisely," Tim agreed, cutting him short. "Had you been down there before yourself?"

Tony Sentance shrugged.

"On a couple of occasions, I suppose. Mr Kevan keeps his wine there. I think I've been asked to help him choose . . . When we've had business meetings here, you understand."

"You only *think*, Mr Sentance? Don't you know for certain?"

"Well, of course I know I've been in the cellar; I was just trying to recall the exact circumstances."

"I see. How long ago would you say that was?"

Tony Sentance lifted his left forefinger theatrically to his lip and pressed it.

"You've got me there," he said. "Some time ago, undoubtedly."

"How long ago? Six months? A year? More than a year?"

"I'm sorry. I really can't be precise." Sentance looked affronted and slightly afraid, as if he suspected that he was about to be bullied.

"It is your job to be precise, though, isn't it?"

The supercilious smile returned.

"With figures, DI Yates. My forte is figures and balance sheets. Sometimes I think they are more real to me than actual events, if you understand me."

"I'm not sure that I do, sir. But I'll take your word for it."

Juliet divined that Tim was in danger of making Sentance

so defensive that he would clam up completely. She leapt in before the implication of Tim's last words could sink too deep.

"You know, of course, that DC MacFadyen found what we believe to be counterfeit passports in the cellar," she said. "Did he show them to you?"

"Just briefly. He was keen to get them into his plastic bags, in case they had fingerprints on them, presumably."

"Had you seen them before?"

Tony Sentance shrugged again.

"Yes and no, if you get my drift. From the outside, they looked just like ordinary UK passports to me. Naturally I wasn't allowed to touch them."

"Thank you." She smiled at him warmly.

"Do you have any idea how they came to be there?"

Tony Sentance sighed. Juliet thought that it was possibly more out of relief than exasperation.

"Your colleague asked me that, too. No, I don't know how they came to be there – any more than I know how most of the things Mr Kevan has in his house have come to be here. I think that's what all of you police keep on forgetting. This is Mr Kevan's house, not mine."

EIGHT

Upon reflection, Tim decided that he would, after all, obtain a warrant to search Laurieston House. There were several sound reasons for this: firstly, it was apparent that Kevan de Vries was of uncertain temperament and might decide on a whim to bar the police or to allow them in only to eject them later; secondly, Superintendent Thornton was jittery about the whole thing. He'd clearly prefer not to inconvenience de Vries at all, but if this couldn't be avoided, he wanted the process to be 'entirely above board', as he put it. Tim's debriefing with the Superintendent had taken place as soon as he had driven back from Sutterton to the police station at Spalding after the interviews with de Vries and Sentance. He had applied for the warrant immediately and was granted it later that afternoon. That counterfeit passports had been found on the premises had encouraged the awarding magistrate not to prevaricate.

Tim himself was anxious not to upset Kevan de Vries more than was necessary. This was not out of regard for Thornton's standing at the Rotary Club. Tim had already seen enough of those who frequented Laurieston House to know there was a lot more to the situation there than met the eye. He was beginning to think that his conversation with Juliet at the airport had been prophetic: he was no longer convinced that de Vries himself was guilty of forgery, or even that he was in any way involved with the fake passports. Yet he was equally persuaded that de Vries had something to hide and Tony Sentance had guilt written all over him. Whether or not their strange behaviour related to the forgery or indeed to the same or different events or deeds was impossible to guess. Even more curious was de Vries' dislike for Sentance, which was almost palpable. There could be only two reasons why he tolerated his oleaginous and evidently to him hateful henchman: either Sentance was performing some service that no-one else could fulfil, or he was exerting a hold over de Vries or a member of his family.

The de Vries family itself presented another puzzle. Tim could accept that de Vries had taken away his ailing wife to give her peace and quiet; he was less convinced that it was natural to leave a dying woman on her own on the other side of the Atlantic, even if she had servants to care for her. It stretched credibility that de Vries could fear that the police would pester his wife if she'd returned with him. It was much more likely that he'd wanted her to stay away for some other reason. If satisfactory answers could not be provided about the passports, Tim knew that he would have to ask her to return anyway. He was dreading this. He knew that he would receive little support from Thornton and that if the police put a foot wrong in their treatment of Joanna de Vries, her husband would make hay of it quite ruthlessly. Then there was the son. De Vries' reference to him had seemed almost impersonal. Again, it was impossible to speculate as to why. And why had the boy been separated from his mother during her last months?

Tim had been granted the warrant at about 3 p.m. He couldn't decide whether to pursue the search straight away or leave de Vries in peace until the next day. As so often when there was a delicate issue to address, he consulted Juliet.

"I think you should contact him again today. Mr de Vries himself told you that he wanted this sorted out a.s.a.p., so why waste time? If he's sleeping, the housekeeper or someone will tell you. Ricky may be there already, as you've asked him to stay there overnight; you could call him first, if you're worried."

Tim opened his mouth to speak. Against his will, it stretched into a colossal yawn.

"I'd forgotten about Ricky. Must be losing my touch," he said indistinctly.

"You didn't get enough sleep last night, more like," Juliet replied. "Neither did I. If we start the search today, will we be there late into the evening, do you think?"

"There's no reason why *we* should, if you mean you and me. We can send a couple of uniforms to help Ricky, since he's got to stay there, anyway. In fact, that's probably the best way of handling it. I don't want to irritate de Vries by showing up myself too often at the moment. He'll probably be seeing much more of me than he likes before all this is over."

"Is that your plan for the rest of the day, then, sir? To get Ricky in place and send two uniforms to support him?"

"Yes, I think so." Tim yawned again. "But there's something I'd like you to do, as well."

Juliet raised an eyebrow. Tim's sympathy for her fatigue was evidently less urgent than for his own. She thought back over the day's events, and knew with unerring prescience what he was going to say next. She decided to pre-empt him.

"Jackie Briggs?" she asked.

Tim grinned admiringly.

"Yes. How did you guess?"

"She was the only person present that we didn't question this morning, despite the fact that she was the one who raised the alarm about the burglars. And she seemed very uneasy. Was that why you didn't ask to speak to her then?"

"Up to a point," said Tim. "But I don't read too much into her uneasiness. It's obvious that the niceties of social distinction are alive and well in Sutterton, no doubt in all their subtle and preposterous gradations . . . and Jackie's near the bottom of the heap. There's all that 'Mr Kevan' business, for a start, even though the guy's only entitlement to respect stems from the size of his wallet. His grandfather was a small-time Dutch farmer, after all. I could hardly believe it when I first heard Sentance address him, as if he were an old retainer talking to the scion of an ancient noble household. And Sentance himself is obviously acutely aware of his own elevated position in the hierarchy. I wouldn't mind betting that de Vries is the only person that he kowtows to. De Vries said that he himself has little to do with the domestic staff, so Jackie Briggs is probably in awe of them both."

"What do you want me to talk to her about? The robbery?"

"Yes, of course. But get on to some more general stuff, if you can. Find out what it's like working in that household and what goes on there on a day-to-day basis. And ask her about any unusual visitors they've had recently, or anything else that's seemed odd to her."

"Like business gatherings in the cellar, for example?"

Tim gave Juliet a sharp look. It wasn't always possible to spot when her tongue was in her cheek.

"Yes. Oh, and see if you can talk to her husband as well. Find out what he knows. But see her on her own first."

"OK," said Juliet. "Got it. It should all be quite simple."

Tim jerked up his head to look at her again, but Juliet had already turned on her heel and was heading for the door. He yawned again and picked up his mobile to speed-dial Ricky MacFadyen.

NINE

Juliet had picked up from conversation with Kevan de Vries that the Briggs lived next door to Laurieston House. They could hardly be described as close neighbours, separated as they were by the extensive garden and second gravel sweep of the larger house, as well as its high boundary hedge. There was also a small stream running along the hedge on the Briggs' side. Mindful of Tim's instructions that she should initially avoid Harry Briggs, Juliet had consulted Ricky MacFadyen's report on the burglary, in the hope that Ricky would perhaps have noted a mobile number for Jackie Briggs. However, she could find no contact details for either Briggs except their joint address. She therefore had no option but to knock on the door of 1 Laurieston Terrace and run the risk of encountering Harry.

Situated at the side of the house, its door was a solid piece of Victorian craftsmanship. Two small twin panes of stained glass adorned its central panel. The shape that appeared, silhouetted, in these was too bulky to be Jackie's. Damn, thought Juliet.

Harry Briggs unlocked the door and peered round it. Juliet saw a thick-set man in his mid-forties. A large dressing on his cheek was held in place by two crossed pieces of sticking-plaster. His complexion was ruddy, perhaps because he spent much of his time outdoors, although the spider veins around his nose suggested a likely alternative cause. He gave Juliet an uncertain smile, exposing yellowing smoker's teeth.

"Yus?" he said. His voice was gruff and uneducated.

Juliet held up her identity card.

"Mr Briggs? DC Juliet Armstrong. I wondered if I might have a quiet word with your wife."

He opened the door wider. Juliet was rather surprised to see that he was wearing no shirt, but an old-fashioned string vest. His workman's navy-blue trousers were held up with leather braces. She remembered that farmworkers and men digging their gardens had sometimes dressed like this when she was a child, but she'd thought it old-fashioned even then. Beyond him, she could see a wooden banister that shone even though the hall was dark. There was a smell of lavender polish.

"She's not 'ere, m'duck. She cleans out ambulances of an afternoon."

"Is there an ambulance station in Sutterton, or does she have to travel to somewhere?"

"It ain't a station, really, just a garage. Down by the church."

"So I could find her there?"

He shrugged.

"I suppose so. She's meant to be working, mind."

Juliet took a dislike to the man, but did her best not to let him see it. She smiled again.

"I'd be grateful if you'd give me directions. I won't keep her long. Afterwards I'd like to come back and ask you a few questions, too."

He looked defensive.

"Aye, well, I'll be here for an hour or so. After that I'll be going up the Quadring Arms. My darts team's playing," he added, as if the statement needed justifying.

"I'll come back as soon as I can. I'd appreciate it if you'd wait for me. It's important."

"I told the other copper all I knew about that Panton bastard," he said. He put his hand up to his cheek.

Juliet remembered that Briggs had been bitten while hanging on to the young burglar.

"How *is* your face?" she asked sympathetically.

"I'll live," he said dourly. "Now, d'you want me to show you where Jackie is?"

He emerged from the house, his feet clad only in his blue socks, and brushed past Juliet as she stood on his doorstep. He made his way to the end of the path with a curiously shuffling gait, though Juliet reflected that this might have been because the uneven stone of the path was uncomfortable for his unshod feet. He opened the black wrought-iron gate and turned to Juliet, who had followed him.

"I won't come into the street, as I've no shoes," he said, "but if you walk up to the roundabout and turn right, you'll see the church. Before you get to the church, if you look across the road, you'll see a big sign with MediFen on it, and a kind of biggish lock-up. She'll be in there. She's probably got the door open, but if not you'll have to bray on it."

"Thanks," said Juliet. "I'll look forward to speaking later."

He threw her a hostile look, but she could tell that he'd taken the comment on board.

The afternoon was both still and warm. As Juliet embarked upon her short walk, she thought how perfect this village seemed. The jigsaw-style duck-pond and lush village green had probably remained unchanged for centuries. The postcard look was completed by the thatched cottage that stood beyond the green. No-one else was in sight. It could have been an enchanted place, marooned in the past as if in some fairy tale. Yet just beyond it she knew that the wheels of the massive de Vries empire were grinding ceaselessly away. Prosperity didn't seem to have brought much peace to the de Vries family. She looked across at the windows of Laurieston House as she passed, but could see nothing stirring beyond them.

She reached MediFen in less than five minutes. As Harry Briggs had said, a large sign had been erected to the left of what looked like a triple lock-up garage with up-and-over doors. The door of the middle section stood open. A white station wagon with 'ambulance' printed in day-glo green had been parked on the tarmac, the front of its bonnet flush with the frame. The rear doors of the vehicle were both open. A woman was kneeling on a mat on the ground, her head and the upper half of her body hidden inside it. A bucket and a 'Henry' vacuum cleaner stood beside her. Her rump was swaying slightly, keeping time with the exertion of her arms.

Not wishing to startle her, Juliet tried to make as much noise as possible as she stepped on to the tarmac.

"Mrs Briggs?" she said.

The swaying halted. Jackie Briggs paused for a few seconds before edging herself backwards until her head and shoulders had emerged. She sat back on her heels and looked up at Juliet, her eyes crinkling against the sunlight. Her face was flushed with effort. She was holding a cloth in her pink-gloved hand. Recognition dawned.

"You're the lady policeman who brought Mr Kevan home, aren't you?" she said. "I'm sorry, I don't remember your name."

Juliet smiled at the description.

"I'd hardly expect you to. It's DC Armstrong," she said. "I hope I didn't make you jump. I've just told your husband I was coming to see you. I thought he might have called you to say."

Jackie Briggs got to her feet. She had changed out of the smart pinafore dress that she'd been wearing that morning and was now clad in jeans and a T-shirt, over which she had placed a tabard-like sleeveless overall of pink gingham. Her figure was trim to the point of gauntness. She looked puzzled.

"There's no phone here," she said. "It's just a garage."

"You don't have a mobile?"

"No." She said it with some vehemence, as if denying a vice.

"Is there somewhere we can go to talk? Somewhere with a bit more privacy than out here on the street?"

Jackie Briggs smiled as she glanced to her right and left along the road.

"Not much chance of getting overheard here," she said. "The place is like a morgue during the day. There's only the house next door on this side, and the old boy who lives there is a bit dulally, if you know what I mean. But if you're worried, we can go and sit in the garage." She gestured at the open doorway with her pink-gloved hand. "There's a stool in there, and a kettle. I can make you some tea."

Juliet nodded thanks. Jackie Briggs peeled off her gloves and picked up her kneeling-mat and the vacuum cleaner. She deposited them inside the garage door and led Juliet deeper into the building. A stainless steel sink stood at its far end. There was a kettle on the draining-board.

"No tea for me, thanks," said Juliet. "Don't let me stop you if you'd like some. And do take the seat. I've been sitting down for most of the afternoon."

Jackie perched on the stool. She seemed quite at her ease with Juliet. She looked up at the policewoman expectantly. Juliet guessed that she was about forty-five, maybe a little younger. The shadows under her eyes and incipient crows' feet might have made her look older than she was. Despite her sharp features, she had a pleasant face, but she seemed very tired.

"Is it about the burglary?"

"Yes. And I'd like to ask you a few more general questions as well, just to get some idea of the background to it. But tell me about the burglary first."

CHRISTINA JAMES

Jackie Briggs wriggled to get comfortable and composed her face, solemn as a schoolgirl repeating a lesson.

"It was just after six o'clock on Sunday morning. I clean ice-cream vans for Mr Lusardi in the summer. Just the inside, like. He takes them to the car-wash for the outside. They've to be ready for when the drivers turn up at 7.30."

"You're a busy lady! Ice-cream vans in the morning and ambulances in the afternoon!"

Jackie gave a strange little laugh.

"You wouldn't want to hear what Harry says about that! I suppose it is a bit funny, doing both. But the ambulances are year-round; the ice-cream vans only from March to October."

"You're Mrs de Vries' housekeeper, as well?"

"That's what she likes to call me. I'm not a proper house-keeper: I don't live in and I don't do the cooking. To be honest, I'm more of a glorified cleaner, though better-paid."

"How do you fit that in with the ice-cream vans and ambulances?"

"Usually she doesn't want me until about 10 o'clock. She's not well, as you probably know, and she doesn't get up early. It gives me time to have a quick shower after I've finished the vans. And I'm usually done there by two. If there's time for some lunch, I nip home; if not, I come straight here. Occasionally she wants me to go back again in the evening, if she's having people round."

Juliet's heart went out to this woman. She seemed to spend her life on a continual treadmill of menial tasks. She made a mental note to find out why Jackie Briggs had to work so hard.

"Sorry, I side-tracked you," she said. "So you were going to do the ice-cream vans. Where are they?"

"Lusardi's. They've a dairy on the other side of the duck-pond. The vans are parked in the yard. There's usually someone in the dairy by the time I arrive, but if not I've got a key. The keys to the vans are hung on hooks in there. Anyway, on Sunday I didn't make it, because I'd just got level with the entrance to Laurieston when I saw something move out of the corner of my eye. It was lucky, really, because another few feet and I'd have been past the gap where you can see in. The hedge gets much thicker further along."

"Was the gate to Laurieston House closed?"

"No. It should have been. That's maybe the reason that I thought to look across. It's often left open during the day, but Mr Kevan likes it closed at night and when he's away, although Harry says that's advertising that he's not there. But he's the boss. What's odd is that I was sure the gate had been shut the previous day. It's Harry's job to see to it."

"Perhaps the burglars left it open?"

"Maybe. But not if they'd any sense. They'll have climbed over the back wall, more like."

"So did you go to look?"

"Yes. I walked a few steps into the drive. I could see a lad on the conservatory roof. He was kneeling, reaching down back inside for something. I couldn't see the other one, but he must've been standing in the conservatory, passing whatever it was up to him. I'd tried not to make any noise, but the gravel's deep and it must have scrunched under my feet. The lad on the roof saw me and leapt down. He ran off."

"He didn't come past you?"

"No. He headed for the back wall. As I said, that's probably the way they came in, as well."

"What did you do then?"

"I walked a few more steps towards the conservatory, which is when I saw the other one. He was standing on one of the cane tables in there, trying to make a grab for the skylight. That was when I went to fetch Harry."

"How soon was he able to get there?"

"Pretty much straight away. I just ran back to our door and opened it to shout him, and he came out. He didn't mess about." She spoke with some pride.

Interesting, thought Juliet. She'd had Harry Briggs marked down as a bit of a layabout; yet he'd been up at 6 a.m. on a Sunday morning.

"He was already dressed?"

"Oh, yes." She threw Juliet a look which plainly suggested that the question was eccentric. "He went belting over to Laurieston – I haven't seen him run so fast in years. He caught the second kid with a rugby tackle and held him until the police got here. The kid bit Harry's cheek – vicious little devil. He hung on, though." Her pride in her husband was even more apparent now. If Harry Briggs had his shortcomings, they weren't important to his wife.

"Did you follow your husband immediately?"

"Almost." Jackie Briggs flushed. "I expect it was the excitement, but I suddenly had to – *go*, if you know what I mean?" She looked embarrassed. Juliet nodded gravely.

"Could you describe the scene when you arrived?"

"Harry already had the lad on the ground. He was struggling, but Harry's strong."

"So you weren't there when your husband caught him?"

"No."

Juliet cast her mind back to the statement that Ricky MacFadyen had taken. Jackie Briggs seemed to have nothing to hide, but what she'd said then had certainly implied that she'd watched the whole incident.

"Was your husband's face already wounded when you reached him?"

"Yes. It was bleeding. I was worried about it. Fortunately, the police arrived quite quickly."

Juliet thought back again to Ricky's notes.

"Who actually called the police? Do you know?"

For the first time, Jackie's face assumed a shut look, as if she was worried that she'd said too much.

"I'm not sure," she said. "Does it matter?"

TEN

Sentance is hovering, bursting to speak to me, after I show the policeman and his sidekick out. God knows, we have enough to talk about and I need to get to the bottom of what he's playing at. I don't have the energy or the patience at the moment. I need to be rested and as calm as I can manage before I tackle him. I tell him to go home and come back later. I'll phone him when I want him.

I climb the stairs to the bedroom and think of phoning Joanna. I look at my watch and realise that in St Lucia it's still only 6.30 a.m. Joanna is probably already awake; she rarely sleeps well now. But on the off-chance that she's managing to rest, I decide to call her later. I know that I should speak to Archie, tell him that I'm home, but it will involve so much explanation – and no doubt tantrums when he knows that his mother isn't here, too – that I chicken out. I persuade myself that it will be better done later; that I should talk to his house-tutor first. I know the guy thinks it isn't a good idea to disrupt Archie's routine. One thing I must do is phone Jean Rook. I know that Sentance has already briefed her. No doubt she's champing at the bit to see me, too.

Jackie calls on the internal phone. She wants to know if I have all that I need and, if so, if it's OK for her to leave. She offers to come back later, to prepare supper if I'd like her to. I tell her that she's very kind, but there's no need. If there's nothing I like in the freezer, I'll go to the Quadring Arms.

She thanks me, tentatively suggests that I should try to rest. I agree, to get rid of her. I think that it will be futile to try, but take off my shoes and lie on the bed anyway.

I'm surprised to be awoken by the telephone. I sit up on the bed and seize it, glancing at the clock as I do so. I'm astounded to find that I've slept for almost four hours. My head is pounding.

"Yes?" I say. If it's Sentance, I'm going to fire him, whatever the consequences.

"Mr de Vries? It's DI Tim Yates of South Lincolnshire police."

"Not much of an improvement on Sentance," I mutter.

"I'm sorry, sir, I didn't quite catch that . . ."

"No matter, it wasn't intended for you. How may I help you, Detective Inspector?"

"DC MacFadyen's on his way to stay with you, as promised. I wonder if when he arrives you'd be happy to allow us to start the search? If so, I'd like to send a couple of uniformed police to help him. We have a warrant now. But do tell me if . . ."

"I told you that no warrant was necessary!" I'm furious. Does the man always exceed his brief in this way? I've gone out of my way to co-operate, to put myself in the best light possible. Now it's been rendered useless.

"I know, sir, and we were grateful. However, Superintendent Thornton . . ."

". . . is an interfering prick if he told you to do it anyway." The phone goes silent. I sigh.

"Do what you please," I say. "If sending your people here tonight helps to speed up my return to St Lucia, let them come by all means."

"Thank you, sir. DC MacFadyen will be with you within the hour. The uniforms may take a little longer."

I look at my watch. There's time for me to take a shower and make the calls as well, if I'm quick.

I strip and am about to head for the shower when the phone rings again. I see from the number coming up on the display that it's Jean.

"Kevan, what the hell is going on?" she demands, without preamble. She's almost shouting. It's not like her to lose her cool.

"I thought Sentance had briefed you."

"You know what I think about Tony Sentance," she said. "He did 'brief' me, as you put it, while you were in the air. In fact, he's just been back on the phone again, to 'advise' me of what he thinks I should be doing. Haven't you had even a moment to talk to me yourself since whatever this is about all started? Or does he decide on what you think now, as well as dropping grease all over your businesses?"

Her voice drips sarcasm. I feel my scalp tighten. Jean and I think as one about Sentance, which makes it impossible for her to understand why I appear to tolerate him, despite what she knows. No doubt he's just rattled her cage, as she says, but she and I both know she has another reason for blowing her top.

"I'm sorry, Jean. I didn't ask him to call you again today; I was going to do it myself, but I fell asleep. I've just woken up now. I'll give Sentance a blast next time I see him."

"Are you all right?" Her tone has suddenly changed.

"Just weary. Why?"

"You sound as if all the stuffing's been knocked out of you, that's all."

"Well, what do you expect? I don't have much to cheer about, do I? Look, Jean, the cops have been here once and they're coming back in less than an hour. I really need a shower before they arrive. I've got to call both Joanna and Archie, too.

I don't have any information about what's happened except what Sentance and the cops have told me, so I'll have to take their word for it. You probably know as much as I do. But I'd like you to be here when they return, if you don't mind."

"Of course I don't mind. I was about to suggest it myself."

"Thanks," I say as I begin put to down the phone. "I appreciate it. And your concern as well, Jean."

She gives a kind of strangled gasp. What she means is not intelligible from the other end of the telephone. I'm glad that at this precise moment I can't see her face. She recovers quickly.

"I'll see you shortly," she says.

ELEVEN

Juliet was walking back to Laurieston Terrace with Jackie Briggs. As she passed Laurieston House, she glanced up at the first-floor windows and saw a hand holding back the vertical blind. It was quickly released and the blind dropped back into place.

It was rather less than fifty minutes since she'd talked with Harry Briggs. She was not surprised, however, that when Jackie preceded her up the path and tried the door it was locked. From the moment she'd mentioned it, she'd been sceptical that Harry would wait for her to return. Jackie obviously thought so, too. She took out her latch-key with an apologetic look on her face.

"Harry!" she called out. "I'm back, love."

There was no answer.

"His mates must have called for him early," she said to Juliet, her expression wry. "I don't suppose he'll be back until late, but you're welcome to wait if you'd like. Do you fancy a cup of tea now?"

"No, I'm all right, thanks," said Juliet, quite shortly for her. "I need to get back to the station. I'll call your husband to make an appointment to see him tomorrow. Could you write down the number for me?" She handed Jackie her card.

"There's a spare card for you, as well," she added. "In case you remember anything else." She remembered to smile. "Thank you very much indeed. You've been extremely helpful."

She was almost back at the gate when a dark blue car slowed and turned into the drive of Laurieston House. Juliet quickened her pace. If it was Ricky MacFadyen, she'd like to take the opportunity for a swift word with him. But on closer inspection the car was much swankier than Ricky's VW Golf. The driver was a woman. She was attractive in a bohemian sort of way: she had longish unruly ash-blonde hair. The window was open on the driver's side and the hand that rested there was well-manicured, the nails long and polished a shade of dark red. She wore a large, square, very modern ring on her middle finger. It took Juliet a minute to place her, before recognition dawned. She'd last seen this woman a couple of years back, when she'd been Ronald Atkins' solicitor. She'd been quite a terrier then, Juliet seemed to recall, tenacious in defending her client's rights. Rook, that was her name. Jean Rook.

Juliet debated whether she should hang around until Ricky appeared and apprise him of the lawyer's arrival. On balance, she decided that it wasn't a good idea. If Kevan de Vries – or Ms Rook, for that matter – saw them conversing, it would only antagonise them. She could send Ricky a text message, though. Technological dinosaur that he was, he might not pick it up in time, but it was worth a try.

She had just finished texting Ricky when something shot out of the undergrowth, coming from the direction of Laurieston House. It was some kind of creature, more than a foot in length, long-haired and greasy-looking. Juliet looked down too late to see it clearly, but became suddenly aware of a stinging pain on the side of her left foot. She bent to examine it and saw immediately that the creature had bitten her and drawn blood. It was oozing through a tear in her tights.

Shaken, she stood for a few moments, supporting herself by holding on to the gatepost of Laurieston House. She took off her shoe and washed the worst of the blood from her foot in the little stream, opening up the tear in the tights to do the job as thoroughly as possible.

She walked back to her car. Within minutes her foot was throbbing. She debated whether to call in at A & E on her way home, but the fatigue that had been stalking her all day had now kicked in with a vengeance. She decided that her best plan would be to go home, bathe the foot properly, apply some disinfectant and then get an early night. She drove off unsteadily into what was still a shimmering summer's evening.

TWELVE

Tim Yates closed the door of his office quietly and sped nimbly down the stairs. It was 5.30 p.m. precisely. Today, he was particularly anxious to reach his house in Edinburgh Drive at a civilised hour and desperate not to get waylaid by Superintendent Thornton. He hoped to make a clean getaway via the back door of Spalding police station and the car park. He knew that Thornton was like a cat on hot bricks over the de Vries case and would probably order Tim to go straight to Sutterton in person if he found out that Ricky MacFadyen, a mere detective constable, and one for whom Thornton had no particular regard, had been assigned to the task. Tim scanned the car park, not without an element of conscious self-parody; he enjoyed pretending to be James Bond on occasion. It was deserted. He made a dash for his aging BMW and leapt into it. Unless Thornton called him back on his mobile, he reckoned he'd succeeded in effecting his escape.

He was therefore a little disappointed when he reached home to discover that Katrin's Fiat was not standing in the drive. He tried to parry a sudden stab of worry. She'd not been at work that afternoon and had told him she'd be back by 5 p.m. He hoped that she was OK. He let himself into the house and filled the kettle.

He had barely plugged it in when he heard Katrin's key in the lock. He heard her dump her bag on the hall stand, as she always did.

"Tim?" she called. She sounded excited.

He hurried out of the kitchen. He needed only to take one look at her face. He opened wide his arms and she rushed into them.

"It is definitely positive?" he asked, somewhat superfluously.

"Yes!" she said, her voice muffled from talking into the wool of his jacket. "Let me out, Tim, I can't breathe."

He released her, turned her face up towards his and kissed her several times.

"Well done!" he said. "I'm so happy."

"Me, too," she said. Less than a year ago she had believed that the news she had received today would never happen, that it was a physiological impossibility.

"What now?" he asked. "Do you want to call your mother?"

"No. It's early days yet and anything could happen." She put out her hand to touch the wood of the hall stand as she spoke. "But it's not just that. At the moment, it's our secret, something to hug to ourselves and hoard for a little while."

He smiled at the way she had put it.

"Would you like to go out to dinner somewhere? A quiet celebration?"

She paused to consider.

"No, not even that. I'm happy to stay here and have something simple to eat. An omelette, perhaps."

Tim's smile broadened. He was a good cook, although with a limited repertoire. Soufflé omelettes were one of his specialities.

"I'll make us one each," he said.

Two hours later they were half-lying on the sofa watching a documentary on the TV, their arms entwined, their empty plates relegated to a tray on the floor. The programme was about the future of the welfare state, but Tim was giving it less than half his attention. About ten per cent of his thoughts were engaged in running over the day's conversations with Kevan de Vries, including the peculiar interventions from Tony Sentance. He wondered which, if any, of several comments that had struck him as odd or out of place would prove significant. Overlaying this was a sort of general, non-specific feeling of euphoria, tinged with a little bit of apprehension. He was well aware that fatherhood would change his life irrevocably. He knew that, for a policeman, meeting the conflicting demands of parenting and career posed a particular challenge. He was determined that he would rise to it, though he knew that to do so with success would require a great deal of good management and self-discipline. Perhaps entail some job sacrifices, too.

Katrin was paying diligent attention to the documentary.

"Oh, for God's sake!" she exclaimed. Tim looked at the screen. Montagu Philpott, a civil servant employed at the Home Office, was explaining the 'right to reside' rule.

"Just listen to him!" said Katrin. "How is anyone supposed to understand that? I don't mean the basic rule, but all the exceptions he keeps coming out with!"

Tim tried to concentrate. He'd missed too much of the programme to be able to pick up the source of Katrin's indignation. As a Swiss by birth, she was often sensitive about immigration issues, even though she herself held dual Swiss / British citizenship.

Tim's mobile rang. He picked it up to see if he could recognise the caller's number. If it was Thornton's, he felt inclined to ignore it. But it was Ricky MacFadyen's number that came flashing up on the screen.

Tim disentangled the fingers of his right hand from Katrin's.

"Sorry!" he said. "I'm going to have to answer this."

She shrugged philosophically. It was one of the great joys of Tim's marriage that his wife did not object to the unsocial demands of his job. As a police researcher herself, she understood them very clearly. He pressed the 'accept' button.

"DI Yates? It's DC MacFadyen here."

Tim noted the speaker's formality and deduced that Ricky was not alone. Someone was listening as he made the call: probably somebody less in his confidence than the uniforms who had accompanied him to Laurieston House.

"DC MacFadyen," he responded, equally formal. "Any news?"

"Yes, sir. I'm sorry to bother you, but I think that you're needed here. And the SOCOs, too."

"That sounds ominous," said Tim. "What have you found? Let me guess: five illegal immigrants hiding in the cellar, still waiting for their passports!"

He regretted his flippancy as soon as he'd said it. He hoped that whoever was listening to Ricky didn't hear the comment. He didn't know why he'd made it: perhaps his subconscious hadn't moved on from the documentary.

"No, sir," said Ricky, still deadpan, after a short pause. "But I *am* in Mr de Vries' cellar; or was until I came up to get a signal. We found some loose flags and pulled them up. There seems to be something underneath them."

"What do you mean, 'something underneath them'? Don't you know what it is? What makes it such a cause for concern?"

"I *think* I know what it is, sir. It looks to me like the bones of a human foot."

THIRTEEN

Half an hour later, Tim had driven to Sutterton and was ringing the doorbell of Laurieston House. He was taken aback when it was opened by a tall woman wearing candelabra earrings, a short red skirt and a clinging black top. He was aware that the ageing bimbo look that she cultivated was misleading, probably deliberately so. He had encountered Jean Rook on previous occasions and knew that she was a force to be reckoned with. So Jean was de Vries' solicitor. On reflection, Tim was not surprised. Jean Rook was based in Peterborough, which was quite a distance from the de Vries empire, but she was sharper than any of the solicitors he knew in either Spalding or Boston. Whatever else he might be, Kevan de Vries was not behind the door when it came to showing some nous.

"Ms Rook!" he exclaimed. "It's a pleasure to see you again."

He glanced over her head at Ricky MacFadyen, who was standing some way along the passage, almost at the same spot that Tony Sentance had occupied that morning.

"Sorry!" he mouthed. Tim understood at once why their short phone conversation had been so strained.

"I'd like to return the compliment," Jean Rook said coolly. "But first we'll wait and see whether it's warranted, shall we? Talking of warrants, may I see yours?"

Tim nodded gravely and handed it over, congratulating himself on his foresight as he did so. He had a sneaking admiration for Jean Rook, obstructive though she could undoubtedly be. It took some chutzpah to stand there and imply that he was likely to cause unreasonable trouble when human bones had apparently been discovered in her client's cellar.

"You'd better come in," she said. "Kevan's just getting himself a bite to eat. I'd be grateful if you'd talk to me about how you propose to take this forward, so that when he's ready I can advise him accordingly."

Tim sensed that she was trying to bounce him into making a quick decision, probably so that she could then raise some objection to it.

"First things first," he said. "I need to see for myself what's been found. Could you show me?" he directed the question at Ricky MacFadyen.

"I can show you myself . . ." Jean Rook began. Under her customary veneer of somewhat combative sang-froid, Tim thought that he could detect a hint of nervousness.

"That's kind, but if this is a crime scene, we need as few people as possible to disturb it until Forensics have done their stuff. Have you been down there already?"

Jean Rook gave an exasperated sigh.

"No, your colleague wouldn't let me. Your two plods are down there, though. Presumably they know to tread carefully in their size elevens?"

Tim gave her a courteous little nod. Without admitting defeat, she was backing down. It would therefore be counter-productive to precipitate an outright confrontation. He followed Ricky down into the stale-air cool of the cellar. The stone steps were broad and smooth, the sequence of brick-lined rooms into which they led well-built and broad.

Ricky moved without pause through the first of these, which was a kind of underground ante-room or lobby. Beyond it was an archway – there was no door – that gave access to a much larger room with a vaulted ceiling. An assortment of furniture and filing cabinets had been stacked neatly on one side of it. A solid teak workbench ran the length of the opposite wall. Several stone flags had been lifted at one end of this and were piled up on the floor. There was the strong smell of damp earth newly released from long-term enclosure and a slight underlying whiff of decay. Or was that merely Tim's imagination going to work?

Two policemen were standing as still as sentries, one at either end of the work-bench. Tim recognised one of them.

"Hello, Giash," he said. "I didn't realise that you'd got this job. Apologies if I've kept you away from bath-time."

Giash Chakrabati grinned. "Not really my scene, sir. The au pair does all that. She washes both the children and puts them to bed if Padma's working."

Padma Chakrabati was a GP. She had recently given birth to the second of their daughters. Tim felt a passing pang of sadness for this child, left to the ministrations of an au pair so early in her life. He gave himself a mental kick. Who knew what domestic compromises he and Katrin might have to make? He realised that Ricky was talking to him.

"The passports were lying near to the end of that work-bench when I came here on Sunday," Ricky was saying. "I thought it might be an idea to search around that area a bit more. I noticed that there seemed to be a piece of yellow paper wedged between the back of the bench and the wall. I crawled below it to try to pull the paper from underneath, and realised that the flags on the floor just there were loose. We decided to lift a couple of them. That's what we found."

He indicated the patch of disturbed earth that had been uncovered. Tim bent down to examine it more closely. He could see quite clearly the ray of fine bones embedded in the soil. Ricky was right: it looked like the remains of a human foot.

"Have you talked to de Vries about this?" he asked.

"In so far as Jean Rook would let me. She interrupted almost every other word and finally said that she wanted to wait until you arrived. De Vries said that he needed something to eat at that point. He hasn't been cautioned."

"How did he react when you said that you'd found the bones?"

"Difficult to say. I'd have expected him to register surprise, though I didn't really see that in him. But he didn't seem to show any guilt or fear of the consequences, either. He didn't say much at all – 'Oh, really, I suppose that introduces another complication?' – or words to that effect. It was almost as if he had something else on his mind and this was just another minor irritation getting in his way. Either that or he's depressed. I've known people with depression behave in that same peculiar detached manner."

"What about Jean Rook? When did she arrive?"

"She got here before me. I think that de Vries asked her to come. He was obviously pleased that she was with him. She's been sticking to him like a leech. You've got no chance of talking to him on his own."

"I think that's the general idea. He told me that he was going to consult his solicitor and I agreed that would be prudent. He didn't mention that it was Ms Rook!"

"Bit of a handful, isn't she? But at least she's managed to stall that Sentence character."

"He isn't here too, then?"

"No. I understand that Mr de Vries sent him away this morning, told him to come back later. But Ms Rook spoke to Sentence on the phone and told him not to bother."

"Hmm, well, that might have been useful in different circumstances, but once we've established for sure that these *are* human remains, we're going to have to question him, as well as de Vries. Sentance has access to the house and he was here when the de Vries were away."

Ricky MacFadyen looked doubtful.

"I don't think these bones were left here during the past few days, sir," he said.

"Neither do I, Ricky. But Sentance has presumably had his key for years. Along with a few other people – Mrs de Vries, obviously, and apparently her mother, too. We're going to have to check out all the key-holders. Sentance seems the obvious person to start with, apart from de Vries himself."

FOURTEEN

"Get this cordoned off as a crime scene, Ricky," Tim said, "and call Patti Gardner." He turned to Giash Chakrabati and his colleague, who had been standing in the shadows next to Giash, and was about to give them an instruction when he noticed for the first time that the colleague was a woman PC and not one he knew. He'd assumed without paying attention that it was Gary Cooper, probably because Giash and Gary usually worked together.

"I'm sorry," he said to her now. "DI Tim Yates. I don't think we've met?"

"I'm Verity Tandy, sir," she said. "I've just transferred from Boston. I asked to come to Spalding because my partner's moving here. Sarge sent me with PC Chakrabati. He and PC Cooper are showing me the ropes."

Tim took a step back in order to examine her as well as the dim light allowed. She was of medium height and plump to the point of being obese, with blotchy skin and rather lank semi-curly hair that lay flat on her crown where it was greasiest. Somewhat uncharitably, he thought that a woman like her *would* be prepared to follow her partner, once she'd managed to hook one. He looked down at her feet and saw that they were surprisingly small and dainty. Presumably Jean Rook had been speaking metaphorically when she'd talked of 'plods' and 'size elevens', as Giash was neat and wiry, only just tall enough to have qualified for the force, his feet in proportion.

"Delighted to have you with us," he said briskly. He turned slightly so as to include Giash in the conversation. "Once Ms Gardner arrives, you can leave, unless she says that she needs you. I'd like you both to come back here first thing tomorrow, though. I shall want the building and its grounds isolated as a crime scene, with one of you on duty at the gate all the time."

"Yes, sir," said Giash. Verity Tandy nodded mutely. Shy or sulky? Tim couldn't tell which. On first impressions, he didn't mark her down as one of the force's bright hopes for the future.

He pounded back to the top of the cellar stairs. Jean Rook was waiting for him.

"Mr de Vries will see you now," she said, as if she were a courtier admitting Tim to the royal presence.

"Too damn right he will," Tim thought. Belatedly, he realised that he shouldn't interview de Vries and Jean while he was alone. It was a thousand pities that Juliet wasn't here. He could hear Ricky MacFadyen's footsteps advancing from the cellar. Ricky appeared at the door, brandishing his mobile phone. He was slightly out of breath.

"DC MacFadyen, when you've made that call I'd like you to join us. In the drawing-room?" The question was directed at Jean Rook.

"I suppose so," she said. She disappeared in the direction of the kitchen. Kevan de Vries emerged after a short interval and followed her into the drawing-room, barely acknowledging the two policemen. Tim waited for Ricky to make a short call to Patti Gardner, after which they entered the room together. Kevan de Vries and Jean Rook were seated on either side of the fireplace. It struck Tim with some force that they could have been mistaken for a married couple.

"Good evening, sir. I'm sorry that I've had to disturb you again today."

"That's quite all right, Detective Inspector; I told you to do so, although I hadn't quite envisaged *these* circumstances." He had recovered some of the mildly astringent urbanity that he'd displayed during the conversation at the airport. He glanced across at Jean Rook, as if for approval. She crossed her legs, tugged once at the hem of her skirt for form's sake and poised her pen over her notepad.

Tim and Ricky sat down awkwardly on one of the two-seater settees. Ricky also took out pen and notebook.

"Mr de Vries, you know why I'm here. As you're aware, I asked you if my officers could return this afternoon to begin a search of the premises, following the discovery on Sunday of what were apparently counterfeit passports in your cellar. Further searching has now yielded what appear to be human remains buried under the floor of the cellar. If that turns out to be correct, I must ask you if you had any prior knowledge of them? Can you shed light on how they came to be there?"

"I should have thought that it's obvious that I don't. I would hardly . . ."

"DI Yates, is this a formal interrogation? If so, don't you think you should caution Mr de Vries?" Jean Rook's tone was clinical.

"It's informal in the sense that I'm not accusing Mr de Vries of any crime. I'm merely asking him to help us with our enquiries, by supplying as much information as he can."

"So if you were to charge him formally, you would wish to caution him and go over the same ground again?"

"Yes, indeed."

"In that case, bearing in mind that he is still jet-lagged, I would like to suggest that you desist . . ."

Kevan de Vries held up his hand in a languidly weary gesture.

"It's all right, Jean. I'll answer the questions. As you're

aware, my intention is to return to Joanna as quickly as I can. If this helps, I'm happy to comply." He turned back to Tim.

"I really have no idea, and I'm as horrified as you are."

"Has the cellar been refitted during the time that you've owned this house?"

"No, not in my time, and as far as I know, not in my grandfather's, either. The cellar was just as it is now when I was a child coming to visit. That big old workbench was already there and the floor was flagged, just as you see it now. The only addition I've made is to have the third room – the one beyond the one where the workbench stands – turned into a wine-cellar."

"What about the furniture that's piled against the wall?"

"Some of it was removed from the main part of the house by my wife. She's kept a lot of my grandfather's things, but some of his stuff was just too big and heavy for our tastes. Some of it's been there much longer."

"You inherited this house from your grandfather?"

"That is correct."

"Did your father pre-decease him?"

Kevan de Vries gave a disdainful shrug.

"Who knows, Detective Inspector? He may still be alive. My understanding is that he disappeared from the scene before I was born. My grandfather had two daughters, my mother and my aunt. No sons. I fulfil that role."

"De Vries was your mother's maiden name?"

"It was her *only* name. I'm sure I don't need to spell it out further. I've always been happy to bear my grandfather's name. I'm proud of what he achieved."

"Quite. You're suggesting that the flagged floors and the workbench have been in the cellar since the house was built?"

Jean Rook opened her mouth to speak, but once again Kevan de Vries raised his hand to silence her.

"I'm suggesting that they were there when my grandfather

bought the house, which was when I was quite a small child. Obviously I can't say exactly how old they are."

"Who holds the deeds?"

"They're stored at my offices," said Jean Rook. "I assume that you're interested in knowing who the previous owner was?"

"Possibly," Tim said. "That depends on how long ago the bones were buried, if indeed they're human."

"I know who the previous owner was," Kevan de Vries volunteered unexpectedly. "It was an old lady. Her name was Mrs Jacobs. I believe that Jackie Briggs's grandmother acted as a sort of paid companion to her."

He was suddenly silent. He twisted his head to look back at the door. His face assumed an anxious look: anxious, but deeply absorbed. He didn't speak for several minutes. He cast his eyes about the room, not vacantly, but as if searching for something, or someone, not visible.

"Mr de Vries, are you quite well?" Tim asked at length.

FIFTEEN

Shit! Shit! Shit! I don't believe this. It's like some kind of grue-some joke. Bones in the cellar! God only knows what is going on. Jean thinks that Sentance is behind it all, but I can't see it. He's self-seeking, certainly, and probably dishonest, but I doubt he's a murderer. I don't think that he's got it in him, to be frank. I'm going to have it out with him, whatever Jean says about keeping him at arm's length. I suppose we'd better wait until they've put a date on the bones first, as that Yates says. But fuck it. If it had just been the passports, I thought I might have had a chance with Thornton. Got him to see that Yates is over-keen, let me go back to Joanna on compassionate grounds. He's not likely to let me go if he thinks I'm a murder suspect, though, is he? Fuck! Fuck! Fuck!

What am I going to say to Joanna? I promised I'd call her again this evening. She was upset enough when I told her about the search. She's going to be desperately unhappy about them digging up the cellar, pulling the house about. We'll have the whole 'I want to come home' thing all over again. I prob-ably won't be able to make her stay put this time, either. Espe-cially if she finds out that Jean's here. I'm surprised that she hasn't asked about Jean already. When Sentance started on about contacting my solicitor, she must have known who he meant.

Jean's been almost manic since she got here. I don't know what her game is, either. She's doing her job superbly well, as always, but there's more to it than that. She must know that there's no use her trying to rekindle old flames. I'm sure she'd have the good taste not to try while Joanna's still alive and, if she hasn't, she's surely got enough sense to know what I'd think about it.

There's a light tap at the kitchen door and I know that she's back. She tells me that the cops want to see me in the drawing-room. She'll be there too, of course. I surprise myself by suggesting that she should be a little less combative with them. God knows I don't want them in the house, but we're not likely to be rid of them unless we attempt some semblance of co-operation. She nods, but in her 'I'm the lawyer and I know best' way.

I sit through their so-called interview in a kind of dream, as if I'm viewing them through glass. I know, although they say they're not accusing me . . . yet, that I'm bound to be a suspect. I worry that they'll say that Joanna's a suspect, too. Jean keeps on retaliating like a terrier that's caught a rat bigger than itself. I cut her short on a couple of occasions, but politely, naturally. I suddenly find her outfit offensive. I think I understand the rationale behind the way that she dresses: she lures blokes like me into her web and hoodwinks the coppers into thinking that she's dim at the same time. She's getting too old for it, even so. She should try a bit more grace and dignity. God, am I weary with all of this! I honestly believe that if they charge me with murder now I won't have the energy to defend myself.

Yates starts talking about the deeds of Laurieston and who owned it before Opa. I'm transported back almost forty years, to a hot and stifling day in August. What year would it have been? I suppose the deeds will say. I think it was one of those two fierce summers in the mid-1970s. I was a small boy, holding Opa's hand, standing beside him in the porch as he rang the bell.

A tall woman with silver hair opened the door. She was dressed in old-fashioned clothes: a high-necked blouse made of some lacy material and a wide brown skirt that almost reached her ankles. I noticed that she walked with a limp. When I looked down, I saw that one of her ankles was very swollen. Her shoes were shiny brown lace-ups with suede panels inserted at the sides. I'd never seen shoes like them.

"You've come to see Mrs Jacobs?" she asked.

"Yes," said my grandfather. "I understood that her son would be here, too."

"Mr Gordon? He's not here yet. Do you want to see Madam on her own?" She uttered the word 'madam' in a curious way. When I thought about it afterwards, I realised that it was the opposite of respectful. At the time I was more taken with the name 'Mr Gordon'. I thought I'd like to be called 'Mr' followed by my first name, not my surname, just like Mrs Jacobs' son.

The tall woman opened the door wider and motioned to us to enter. My grandfather went first, pulling me after him. We stood in the hall while the woman knocked on what is now the drawing-room door, the room we're sitting in. A feeble voice said, "Come in."

"I'll just go first and make sure that she's decent," said the woman, her brown skirt swishing as she limped into the room and turned to close the door. "Sit down, if you'd like to." She indicated a high-backed wooden settle that had been placed against the wall. Opa lifted me on to it. I swung my legs and looked down at the floor tiles between my sandalled feet. They're still there now. They're made of tiny mosaic pieces in brown, blue, cream and dull red. They create an elaborate pattern of what I now know are stylised fleurs-de-lys, their bold cream swirls dramatic against the other, more muted colours.

After a while, when the woman hadn't returned, Opa came to sit beside me. He fixed his eyes on the wall opposite.

"Bless my soul!" he said. Being an ex-pat Dutchman, he liked to cultivate phrases that he thought were very British. He never managed to rid himself of his guttural accent, though.

I looked up to where his gaze had fallen. Ornamenting the wall were several rows of pictures, hung vertically in threes, framed in what as an adult I came to identify as passe-partout. They were in sepia. I'd never seen brown photographs before and I was fascinated by them. Opa clearly disapproved. I could see that the pictures were strange. They were all of the same man, a man with whiskers on his face, dressed in pale clothes and a hat like a white policeman's helmet. But what held both me and my grandfather transfixed was not the man himself, but his companions. In each of the photographs he was posing sometimes with one, sometimes with several black women. Some had bones or beads pushed through their noses, or ear-lobes distorted by the weight of heavy earrings. All wore elaborate many-tiered necklaces. Every one of them was naked to the waist. All were grinning at the camera. The bewhiskered man grinned, too.

"Extraordinary!" said my grandfather, more or less talking to himself. "Those photographs are probably valuable. Not to my taste, though. No. Not at all." He was emphatic about this, as if he'd been caught practising some vice.

The drawing-room door opened at that moment and the tall silver-haired woman limped out. Opa jumped to his feet. He motioned to me to stand and I scrambled off the settle.

"Mrs Jacobs will see you now," she said.

"Thank you," said Opa, with a short bow. "I'm sorry, I didn't catch your name."

"I'm Beatrice Izatt. Mrs. I'm Mrs Jacobs' housekeeper, or companion, as she prefers to put it."

He bowed again. Mrs Izatt lowered her voice.

"She's not too bad, today," she said, sotto voce, "but don't be surprised if her attention wanders, or she nods off while you're talking to her. If you can persuade her to let me show you around the house, I'll be happy to do so. If you can't, you'll have to wait until Mr Gordon arrives. She doesn't know that the house is to be sold, so don't alarm her. Just say that you'd like to see her lovely home. She won't think it's odd. People did that sort of thing when she was young and she spends most of her time living in the past now."

I felt rather afraid. I sensed that my grandfather was apprehensive, too. He took hold of my hand again and led me through the drawing-room door. Mrs Izatt followed us.

The room that we entered smelt fusty and was far too warm. It was also very dark. The heavy curtains had been drawn. The only light came from two little electric wall-lamps that had been fixed to brackets on either side of the bed. The bed itself was an enormous four-poster, around which smaller items of furniture had been crowded with more reference to usefulness than aesthetics. There were several small tables, a two-seater sofa and a commode. In the further reaches of the darkness gleamed a dressing-table mirror. The fireplace was as it is now, but not in use. An embroidered firescreen stood in front of it. Although the day was warm, one bar of the electric fire that stood in front of that had been switched on. I can see it as clearly now as . . .

"Mr de Vries, are you quite well?"

It is the red-haired policeman speaking. I'm brought rudely back to the whole mess of Joanna, Jean, Sentance and the bones in the cellar.

"Yes, of course. I'm sorry. I just drifted off for a moment."

"Kevan, if you're not up to this . . ."

"Stop trying to mollycoddle me, Jean. When I'm unable to cope, I assure you that you will be the first to know. You can then relay the message to DI Yates, even if he happens to be sitting beside me at the time."

SIXTEEN

Juliet Armstrong awoke in her neat small flat and consulted the clock on her bedside table: 7.45 a.m. She'd overslept. She turned over and groaned. Her mouth was dry and there was a pounding in her head. She sat up and felt the room lurch into a spin. She tried to swallow and was alarmed to find that her throat was so dry and swollen that it was difficult for her to breathe. It felt constricted, as if something malicious and scratchy, like a giant twig, had become lodged there.

Juliet had been a policewoman for more than ten years. During the whole of that time, she had never missed a day except to take annual leave or attend the occasional funeral. She was loath to break this record by calling in sick. She resolved to have a cup of tea and see how she felt before making such an extreme decision. She swung her legs out of bed and got slowly to her feet. She made a grab for the top of the chest of drawers as it disappeared into a blurred morass that jumbled together ceiling, carpet and door. Juliet collapsed to the floor, going down heavily, knocking her head on the side of the chest of drawers as she fell.

SEVENTEEN

"DI Yates!"

Tim had taken a detour to Laurieston House to call in briefly on Patti Gardner, but she'd arrived only just before him and made it clear that it would be some time before she could produce constructive results. Tim took the dismissal good-naturedly; in any case, he needed to get to Spalding while it was still early. He'd reached his car when he turned to see Jackie Briggs standing in front of him.

"The lady policeman said that you were interested in knowing more about Laurieston House. My grandmother was housekeeper to the old lady who owned it before it was sold to Mr Kevan's grandfather. She gave my grandmother her diary. I thought you might like to see it."

Tim took the notebook from Jackie Briggs and turned it over in his hand. Viewed as a tome likely to yield up the secrets of a modern forger, let alone a murderer, it wasn't encouraging. He was holding a thick-paged volume bound in heavy crinkled yellow leather, tied together with a pale pink bow. Towards the bottom of the front cover was a small oblong picture. It was an idealised domestic scene, the study of a tea-table adorned with floor-length napery, pink china and a vase of blue flowers. One of the flowers in the vase had been painted larger than the others and highlighted with a kind of line-drawn halo. Tim looked at the small picture more closely and decided that the book's owner had probably embellished the cover by pasting on to it a cigarette card.

There was no other writing on the cover. Tim opened the book carefully. It was not bound, but consisted of loose sheets and the front and back covers, held together with the ribbon. They creaked when he prised them apart. The first page proclaimed that the volume was *My Ladye's At Home Booke*, this printed in a pseudo-archaic font. Underneath it someone had written in copperplate script *Lucinda Jacobs, 1888*. The ink had faded to a dull brown. The inscription had been crossed out, and beneath it inscribed in a much more childish, unformed hand *Florence Hoyle: her booke*. This writer had aimed to copy the other's copperplate, but had not practised the dexterity needed to make the letters slope uniformly. The 'e's in Florence had been badly blotted and the 'y' of Hoyle was a deformed squiggle. Tim smiled wryly as he noted the mis-spelling of the word 'book', no doubt copied from the title page by a naive girl unable to recognise that it represented a rather twee marketing ploy on the part of the late Victorian manufacturer.

Tim turned another page. This and all the subsequent pages were set out like the guest books still in use at some small hotels. Each contained three columns, headed respectively 'Date', 'Observations' and 'Signature'. The 'Observations' column was twice the width of the others.

There were two blank pages before the journal itself began. It had been composed in the same messy handwriting and was therefore almost certainly the work of Florence Hoyle. The writing traversed all three columns, ignoring them and the guiding feint lines as if they had not existed. All of the entries were in the same faded ink.

Jackie Briggs was looking at him expectantly, hoping perhaps to be praised for having contributed something useful to the investigation. Tim smiled at her encouragingly before turning his attention back to the journal. His misgivings redoubled. The first pages seemed simply to be the semi-literate musings of an immature young girl.

Madam give me this book. She says she now has a better. Shes been learning me to read and rite better and wants me to try ard. I said I went to the bord school but she said I could do better. I will try to rite in it every day.

Madam ad visiters this evening. Cook and I was very bizy. Cook said that Madam as no bizness encurridging me to rite, that I'm a growing girl and need to get my rest when works finished. Ive stayed up to do it. I promist Madam.

My day off. Jenny Wilson and I begged a ride to Spalding on Mr Shearers cart. He was going to markit. I've not been to markit before as Madam needs me when Cook goes. But Cook said there was so much left from the visiters that she didn't need to go this week. Jenny and me bought ribbons. I went to see Ma in Gas Lane. Madam gave me wool for er and soop. Only Milly left with er now. Madam paid my half-years wage. I give it Ma.

Tim skipped a few pages. Although there was no evidence that someone had been correcting Florence's work, the spelling and style improved as she became a more practised diarist. The intellectual quality of the prose remained the same. Florence was concerned mostly with the trivia of her own life, and remarkably unobservant about the people whom she encountered. There were numerous references to 'visiters' in the first half-dozen pages, but Florence did not try to identify or describe them or say whether they appeared to have enjoyed themselves or what *Madam*'s reaction to them had been. He supposed that she must have been the ideal servant: hard-working, unquestioning, completely on-side and extremely incurious. But, for a diarist, these traits could hardly have been worse. He'd read diary accounts from the past by other uneducated people, some of which had been enthralling or full of insight: their authors' shortcomings in learning had been more than compensated for by the perspicacity and the freshness of their observations. Florence's prose, on the contrary, was lumpish and dull. He doubted that even the best education could have made her fascinating.

Jackie Briggs was still hovering.

"Did your grandmother ever describe Mrs Jacobs to you? Tell you what it was like to work for her, what she made of her character, and so on?"

"She used to moan about the old girl quite a bit. She always called her that: 'the old girl'. My grandmother was very quick-witted. She'd started work as a nanny and was later trained as a proper nursery nurse at Guy's Hospital. It gave her a taste for what she'd missed. She was the eldest of a large family and often kept off school to help her mother with the babies. I suppose she was fond of Mrs Jacobs in a way, but she despised her for not making the most of her opportunities. I think that she found the long winter's evenings in the old girl's company very boring."

"Florence was a maidservant before she married her employer?"

"Yes. Frederick Jacobs was much older than her – probably more than twenty years older. And she was at least fifteen years older than my grandmother. My grandmother was born in 1892, so Frederick must have been born in the 1850s or 60s."

"Did you know him?"

Jackie Briggs laughed. Tim realised that it was an absurd question.

"No, of course not. Florence was a very old lady when I was a child. Frederick must have been dead for many years. I was taken to see her a couple of times, but she was practically witless by then. Sometimes, though, she knew what was going on. She gave me a brooch from her jewellery box once. I've still got it."

"Curious that Frederick married out of his class, wasn't it, especially as Florence didn't dazzle with her wit?"

"I suppose it was; although by all accounts she was very attractive as a young girl. He wouldn't be the first man to have fallen for a pretty face."

"No, indeed."

"Do you know whether there were children?"

"One son. My grandmother always called him 'Mr Gordon'. He didn't want to keep Laurieston House after Mrs Jacobs became too ill to stay there. It was him who sold it to Mr Kevan's grandfather."

"Do you know what happened to him? Where he lived?" Jackie shook her head. "Is that book useful?" she continued, eagerly.

Tim frowned. He didn't want to disillusion her, and not just out of empathy. He suspected that there would yet have to be a lot more delving into Harry Briggs' doings, and that Harry's wife would be a much more co-operative source of information than Harry himself. Besides, she was so pathetically keen to know that she'd helped. Juliet could take a look at the diary. It wouldn't do any harm. She might even be able to spot something cryptic in its primitive style. If there was anything to be gained from it, she would find it.

"It's difficult to say," he said. "This throws some interesting light on what life was like in that house at the time. I've only read a few pages. There may be some more concrete information when I get further into it. Would you allow me to borrow it for a few days? I'll give you a receipt, of course."

Jackie Briggs beamed gratification.

EIGHTEEN

That afternoon, Patti Gardner was kneeling on the floor of the cellar at Laurieston House, carefully dusting away the earth from a skeleton with a brush. She paused to yawn: she and her team had been there until almost midnight the previous evening before calling it a day. She was wearing a white paper suit and a face mask, which stretched perilously as it was contorted by her wide-open mouth. She leaned even closer to the bones and examined them with a magnifying glass.

Tim Yates leant against the cold brick wall, watching her.

"Have you found something interesting?" he asked.

"That depends on what you mean by interesting. I can't be sure – I'll have to carry out some tests in the lab – but I'm beginning to think that these bones have been here for a very long time. And there are three skeletons, not one."

Tom whistled.

"How long?"

"If I'm right, probably longer than living memory. A hundred years . . . maybe more than that."

"So if it was murder, whoever did it would have died long ago?"

She sat up on her heels and shyly met Tim's eye. Aside from those occasions on which they were jointly engrossed in their work, their relationship had been strained since their brief fling before Tim had met Katrin. Tim didn't know whether Patti still carried a torch for him. Certainly she found the fact of their former liaison much more embarrassing than he did. As far as Tim himself was concerned, it was ancient history, water under the bridge. If there was anything to regret, it was simply that friendship between himself and Patti now seemed to be impossible. He still liked and respected her and found her evasive behaviour rather sad. He smiled encouragement now.

"As I said, I need to do some tests. But I think it's likely that the skeletons have been here much longer than anyone currently living in this house. What happens when a crime's so old that there's no chance of finding the murderer alive? Would the police still decide to investigate it?"

"Speaking personally, I'd always want to know what had happened, but unless the crime was a famous one, or there were surviving influential relatives of the victims demanding explanations, it would be left to the discretion of the senior investigating officer and his superiors. In our case, that means Thornton. Preoccupied as he always is with making his budget stretch far enough, I doubt if he'd authorise investigation into a cold case crime if there were no prospect of a conviction."

"A pity. Because that's probably what's going to happen. And, like you, I'd always hope to find the solution to a murder, no matter how old it is. Especially as there's another fascinating factor to this case: one that I am quite certain about, without conducting more tests."

"What's that?"

"At least two of the three victims were female. And all were of African ethnic origin."

Tim was incredulous.

"You're absolutely sure?"

"Yes. The shape of their skulls leaves no room for doubt. I'd say they were all from the same part of Africa and possibly related to each other. Lab tests might give me the answer to both of those questions, too."

"You mean that you can carry out tests to tell exactly where they came from?"

"Probably. Testing their teeth, in particular, should narrow down where they lived to quite a small geographical area. And DNA tests should be able to tell us whether they were related."

"Isn't it odd that several black women came here to their deaths a hundred years or so ago? There are very few black people living in the Fens even now. They must have been extremely conspicuous then. Perhaps we'll be able to find some historical record of when and why they were here."

"Perhaps. But they didn't necessarily die in this cellar; they were just buried here. And if they lived in the Fens for some time before that, they could have been held captive. If so, it's possible that no-one knew about them except the person or people holding them. I'm going to get the bones transferred to the lab as quickly as I can now," she added. "I assume that you have no objection to that? And that you'd rather we kept to ourselves their likely age until we're absolutely certain about it?"

"No objection, of course," said Tim. "And yes – the further we get with exploring their identity before we have to consult Thornton about whether to proceed, the better. Though even Thornton might have to think twice before denying budget to investigate the deaths of three black women, however long ago they happened. He'll be worried that some political lobbying group will take up their cause."

"I suppose that he might get extra funding from such a group, or from the government, to help to pay for the investigation if he allows it?"

"He might," Tim agreed. "I've no idea what his options might be. But you can bet that if there is any such money to get hold of, Thornton will know about it. It's one of the areas in which he excels."

"Said without a touch of irony!" laughed Patti, behaving naturally in Tim's presence for once. Tim also laughed, but stopped suddenly and frowned.

"Something else occurs to me," he said. "I should have thought of it before, given our reason for searching the cellar in the first place. Even in the nineteenth century, surely these women would have required passports?"

"That depends on where they were born. You're the historian, not me. But it's my understanding that there have been some black people living in this country since the Middle Ages. Mostly in ports, I believe, particularly in the South of England. And the numbers of ethnic Africans living in the UK obviously increased rapidly in the latter part of the twentieth century. But even if they come from a much earlier period, as I believe may be the case, you shouldn't rule out the chance that they might have been British citizens."

"I suppose not. I wonder . . ."

"What's that?" Patti exclaimed suddenly. "Tim, could you hold the light a little closer to here, please?" She pointed with her brush.

Tim grabbed one of the electric lanterns that Patti had switched on to augment the dim electric lights in the cellar and held it close to her hand. She exchanged the brush for a tiny trowel, which she used gently to lever something free from its prison of bone. She held it up, gripping it with the thumb and forefinger of her latex-gloved hand.

"It's a bead," she said. "A large, green bead. Made of malachite, unless I'm much mistaken."

NINETEEN

Tim bounded up the stairs to his office bearing Florence Hoyle's notebook. He was impatient for Juliet to arrive. Despite her regard for authority, he knew that she would find the prospect of working through the journal so fascinating that she would ignore Superintendent Thornton's instruction if he told them to abandon the ancient cold case, even if it meant studying Florence's musings in her own time. Unlike Tim himself, Juliet was not a formally-trained historian, but she shared his interest in human psychology and far surpassed him in her ability to draw accurate conclusions from documentary evidence and forensic detail.

Tim made himself a cup of tea. Through the glass of the kitchen cubicle he caught site of Andy Carstairs, red-faced, hefting his sports bag up the stairs. Andy had recently embarked upon a fitness campaign, although its effects had yet to be made manifest. Tim held up his mug and pointed at it. Andy grinned and nodded. Tim made more tea and carried both mugs through to the open area where Andy and Juliet, when they were both in the office, occupied facing desks.

"Have you made any progress with the fake passports?" Tim asked, after they'd exchanged a few pleasantries.

"I've been in touch with an expert in the Home Office. Her report came in yesterday. It appears that the stationery that we found at Laurieston House was authentic – the real stuff that is used for making British passports."

"Inside job?"

"Possibly, but the Home Office expert, a fearsome woman called Veronica Something (by the way, I doubt if she'd 've deigned to talk to me at all if she hadn't worked with Juliet in the past), thinks not. Apparently part of a consignment of the stationery was stolen about eighteen months ago. Intercepted en route, they say, though they don't really know how it came to be lost. You may remember the internal report about it. It was played down at the time because the Home Office thought that we'd be more likely to catch the thieves if it didn't make the press . . ."

"Didn't want to be caught with egg on their faces, more like," Tim interposed. Andy grinned.

"Whatever. I suppose that may explain why this Veronica is so prickly. Anyway, she thinks that the stuff used to make the passports may have come from that consignment. It's quite difficult to establish if she's right, but she's asked the manufacturers to carry out more checks."

"Underworld job, then?"

"Yes, but it had to be really, didn't it? The standard of those passports was excellent. They'd never have been spotted as fakes if they'd included the photographs and personal details of the holders."

"You're right. There can't be many forgers with that sort of capability. I suppose you've checked out all the ones known to us who might have the skill to do it?"

"I've started on it. I need the Met to help and they're a bit snowed under at the moment."

"The real question that we need to ask ourselves is how a set of high-class fake passports found their way into the basement of a rich Lincolnshire businessman's house in Sutterton. It's not the usual sort of place for forgeries like these to turn up."

"Agreed," said Andy. "Do you have any suggestions?"

"Though I can think of plenty, most of them too far-fetched, one of them seems more than just a possibility. They might just be intended for use in this country by people who shouldn't be here."

"Illegal immigrants, you mean?"

"It's a hunch worth looking at. If it's correct, someone would still be running a considerable risk to get them into the country in the first place. There'd have to be something in it for them. Cheap labour, for example. An illegal immigrant with a kosher passport wouldn't actually look illegal to a prospective employer. Quite literally, it would be the passport to a job."

"And the supplier of the passport takes a cut of their wages?"

"Perhaps. Or maybe *pays* their wages – at way below the national average. In return for services rendered."

"Kevan de Vries owns a lot of businesses. Most of them are run on low-tech manual labour."

"Precisely," said Tim. "I'd like you to start checking out the payroll of his businesses. All of them. Find out the workers' names, when they started work, where they live, how much they get paid. If Thornton allows it, you might get Katrin to help. She's good at that sort of thing." He looked at his watch.

"Where is Juliet? It's not like her to be late. Do you think I should call her? See if she's OK?"

"I'd give it until this afternoon," Andy replied. "She may just have had a heavy night." Tim grinned. Neither of them thought this likely. "Or overslept," Andy finished lamely. "There's bound to be an explanation. It doesn't seem fair to breathe down her neck so soon, especially as she's never been late before."

"You're right," said Tim. "I'll wait a couple of hours." He picked up the journal. "In the meantime, I'm going to see

Katrin. There's a job I need her to do. I'll mention the de Vries stuff while I'm there."

"Right," said Andy. "If your job's what I think it is, may I suggest you should be careful? It wouldn't be right to drag her into your defiance of Superintendent Thornton. Sir," he added. There was a silence. "I'll get on with studying the de Vries payrolls, then, shall I, until I hear whether she can help?"

TWENTY

Two days later, Tim was standing by the window of his office looking gloomily out on to the Sheep Market when his telephone rang.

"Hello, Tim, it's Patti Gardner here." He noted that the formality had returned to her voice. "I wanted to let you know that we were right about the skeletons. Carbon 14 dating suggests that the three women died around 1890, plus or minus ten years." Modest as ever, she had said 'we', not 'I'. Tim was grateful. He guessed that the reason for Patti's measured tones was in part because of the conversation they'd had about proceeding with the case. She knew that Tim would now have to request permission from Superintendent Thornton to proceed. How Thornton would react was anybody's guess. Of one thing Tim was certain: he'd want the business of the faked passports cleared up in double-quick time now, so that Kevan de Vries, if he appeared to be innocent, could be released as quickly as possible to rejoin his wife in Saint Lucia.

"Are you still there?" said Patti.

"Hmn? Yes, sorry," said Tim. "I was just trying to think this through."

"Do you want me to write a report that you can show Superintendent Thornton?"

"Yes – thanks – that would be great. And Patti?"

"Yes?"

"You know what you were saying about where they came from? Did you carry out those tests, as well?"

"I've taken some samples. I've had to send them to a lab in London: it's too sophisticated a technique for the equipment we have here."

"OK, thank you."

"Do you want me to wait until I've got those results as well before I send the report?"

"How long will it take?"

"Four or five days, probably."

"In that case, no. I can't stall Thornton for that long. But let me know as soon as the results come through."

"Of course. And I'll have the report with you later today. I'll email it, so keep on looking out for it."

"Will do."

Tim replaced the phone in its cradle. Not for the first time, he reflected fleetingly on his good fortune in being surrounded by so many efficient and industrious women. That in turn made him think of Juliet. Her neighbour had called the police station just before midday to say that he'd found her collapsed on the floor of her flat. She'd been rushed to the Pilgrim Hospital and had been there for almost forty-eight hours now. Although her condition was stable, they were no further forward in establishing what was wrong with her. He was about to pick up the phone to enquire again when it started to ring.

"DI Yates, is that you?" He recognised Ricky MacFadyen's voice immediately.

"Hello, Ricky. I'm glad that you've called, because I have some news. As Patti Gardner thought, the skeletons found at the de Vries house aren't modern. I've just been speaking to Patti, and she says that . . ."

"I'm sorry to interrupt you, sir." Ricky sounded agitated. "This is urgent."

"What do you mean? Where are you?"

"I'm still at Laurieston. I've stayed here, as you instructed, sir. But I've just taken a call from one of the officers from Boston who came here when the house was broken into, who'd been contacted by the police in King's Lynn . . ."

"Regular little jungle telegraph, isn't it?" observed Tim sardonically.

"Yes, sir," said Ricky, with impatient politeness. "Anyway, the message was that they've found the body of a young woman, half-buried in the woods at Sandringham."

Tim was all attention now.

"Thanks for letting me know. Of course you're right to tell me about it. But surely it's a case for the Norfolk Constabulary to pick up on? Why did they want to inform you – or us?"

"The girl was found naked. But there was a bundle of clothing on the ground beside her. It included overalls and overshoes marked with the de Vries logo."

"I see." Tim was still thinking about the implications of this when Ricky started speaking again.

"Laundry marks on the clothes suggest that she was employed in the de Vries canning factory at Sutton Bridge. But she's been dead for a while and none of the workers from there has been reported missing."

"I agree that that's odd and, as you know, I tend to mistrust coincidences. The de Vries name turning up again is certainly a coincidence, but not much of a one, given that my understanding is that the de Vries empire employs several thousand people. And, at a pinch, we could claim that Sutton Bridge is on our patch, although as you know we don't often penetrate that far. But aside from the fact that we're working with Mr de Vries on these other matters, I fail to see why Norfolk needed to tell you so urgently about the dead girl. What are their thoughts? Illegal immigrants, or home-grown slave labour?"

"They say they've got an open mind about it. Could be either of those, I suppose; though I'd put my money on illegal immigrants. They're keener on getting on than people who've already fallen through the cracks in our society. Smarter, therefore, and more industrious."

Tim nodded assent, realising as he did so that the gesture was invisible to Ricky.

"But I still don't see what the panic's about, given that we're holding Kevan de Vries ourselves. If he's involved in this new case – which he very well may not be – he's already here for questioning. I'm assuming that he can't hear you, by the way?"

"No, sir, I'm making this call from my car."

"Thank God for that," said Tim. "Well? What's spooking them? Am I right in thinking that it does have something to do with him?"

There was an uncomfortable silence.

"Yes. Well, when I told PC Bedford at Norfolk that we were now only holding de Vries on the passports charge, and that Superintendent Thornton was keen to allow him to get back to his wife . . ."

"So you told him that the skeletons were probably too old to have been put there by anyone still living?"

"Yes. I . . ."

Tim sighed exaggeratedly.

"Really, Ricky, I would have expected more discretion from you. You realise that I haven't told Thornton himself that yet? I'd better do it now, and at the double, too. I'd intended to wait until Patti's report came through, but, as you say, the matter is now urgent. I take it, by the way, that Norfolk want to make sure that de Vries is detained until they can get to him for questioning?"

"Yes."

"Well, that shouldn't be a problem, should it, as you're on the spot? They ought to know that they'll have to run the gauntlet of his solicitor, though. They'd better not put a foot wrong, or Ms Rook will crack down on them with all the civil liberties charges in the book. No doubt you'll be able to manage to convey that piece of information satisfactorily, given your obvious communications skills."

TWENTY-ONE

The girl laid out on the mortuary slab was emaciated rather than slim. She had brown eyes and very blonde, curly hair which clung flatly and without sheen to her forehead. The mortician lifted the cloth that was covering her and Tim saw that she was naked.

"I understand she was found like this, without clothes."

"Yes. Her clothes had been tossed in a bundle into the bushes nearby. They're in a plastic bag on the counter."

"So she was entirely naked? No underwear?"

"I believe not. I wasn't first on the scene, but there are photographs if you want to check." Professor Salkeld removed one of his latex gloves with a slapping sound and tossed it on to his workbench. He walked across to the desk in the corner of the morgue and removed from it a blue plastic folder. He handed this to Tim, who opened it and withdrew a set of matt photographs, each with a scale measure running down its left-hand side. Most were pictures of the girl lying on the ground, taken from different angles. A couple of others showed the clothes in the undergrowth.

"As I think you'll find," said the Professor grimly, "there was no underwear – either on the body or with the other clothes. Just jeans and a white T-shirt and the de Vries overall and rubber clogs."

"Anything in her pockets that might help to identify her? Any jewellery, keys, purse? Anything at all that's personal?"

"Nothing. Not even a comb or a packet of tissues."

"What conclusions have you drawn? Can you tell us the approximate time of death, or what killed her?"

"She's been dead for several days – I can't be more precise than that. I'm not yet sure about the cause of death – I may not be able to establish it with certainty – but my guess is that she was either strangled or asphyxiated. I could be wrong about that, you understand, and I'll need to check the body for toxins. So long after death, though, the tests may not be completely accurate."

"Anything else?"

"As you can see, she's painfully thin. There could be a number of reasons for that: she may have been suffering from some underlying illness, or simply an eating disorder; or perhaps she was too poor to be able to eat properly."

"Surely not that? Even if she only worked on the floor of a food-packing shed, my understanding is that the de Vries companies pay relatively well. They don't allow their employees to starve."

Professor Salkeld shrugged.

"I'm only telling you what I see. I have no idea of what this woman's circumstances were when she was alive; I can merely make suggestions about what may have caused her physical condition at the time of her demise. She was a woman, not a girl, by the way. I know that your colleague told you that she was a teenager, but I think that the officers who first attended were misled by her size. She may have been the weight of a young adolescent, but other factors – in particular, the maturity of her skull and the state of her teeth – tell me that she was at least twenty-five and possibly a couple of years older than that."

"Are there any marks or distinguishing features on the body?"

"Yes, two." Professor Salkeld moved to the foot of the trolley where the corpse lay and lifted the sheet so that its feet were exposed. "As you can see, she'd had a tattoo in the shape of a chain bracelet etched on her right ankle." He folded the sheet down again, then reached underneath it to take one of the dead girl's hands in his own. "And although she bit her nails, she also painted them. Bright turquoise, although some of it's now chipped off. I'd have expected it to be against the rules for an employee in a food factory, although that would depend on what her actual job was."

He passed the hand to Tim with the same deference that he always adopted towards the cadavers in his care. Tim took it from him with equal reverence. As always, he was shocked by the profound coldness that death brings to the flesh. He bent to examine the short, slender fingers. The bitten nails were rather grubby, the turquoise varnish lurid and peeling. He was struck with some force by the pathos of the woman's forlorn attempt to introduce some colour and no doubt what she believed to be sophistication into her life.

"There are no overt signs of abuse? Bruises, cuts, lacerations, anything under the nails, evidence of forced sexual penetration?"

"There are one or two minor bruises, but they're probably of no significance. If she was indeed a factory worker, they're the sort of small injuries she would have incurred all the time – knocking her limbs against machinery, that type of thing. Nothing under the nails, but, as you see, she had none to speak of. There is one thing that concerns me, however: her anal sphincter is extremely loose, and there are signs of inflammation in the surrounding tissue. Again it's not conclusive, but this could be evidence of deviant sexual behaviour. If so, whether it took place with or without her consent is impossible to tell."

"Have you swabbed for semen?"

Professor Salkeld regarded Tim over the top of his rather smart Armani spectacles with a look that spelled mild amusement tinged with a hefty dose of sardonic irony.

"Yes, now you mention it, it did occur to me to do that. But you're quite an expert on these matters yourself, I believe, so you'll know that my chances of obtaining a semen swab that would allow me to identify her sexual partner so long after death are almost nil. The chances are that she engaged in both vaginal and anal intercourse in the hours preceding her death, but – with apologies for sounding like a gramophone record stuck in one groove – I can't be definite about it. I'll carry out some tests on the clothing as well – this may yield better results. But, as I've said, the underwear is absent. It's likely that her attacker was forensically aware and deliberately removed her undergarments from the scene in order to prevent detection."

"Thank you, Professor, you've been as helpful as always." As had often been the case in the past, Tim felt abashed by the Professor's gentle mockery. He stood like a schoolboy in the presence of an eminent master.

Professor Salkeld inclined his head slightly in a courtly acknowledgment of the compliment.

"Of course I'll let you know if I find anything else, especially anything that might help you to identify the poor woman."

TWENTY-TWO

I know that I must brace myself to call Archie. Joanna calls him twice a week and she'll certainly tell him that I'm here. Not only that, but I can't talk to Joanna herself again until I can say we've spoken. Last night she was very agitated about the police, even though I didn't tell her about the skeletons.

My hands tremble as I search for the number of Archie's school. It's in Sleaford. Chosen, as Joanna has pointed out many times, so that visiting would be easy. As she would doubtless say if she were here now, I could hop in the car and be with him in less than an hour. I'll be expected to indicate to the school what the purpose of such a visit might be. Mindful of this, I decide to talk to his housemaster first: Hamish Maitland. I find his number on a short typed list that has been pinned to the kitchen notice-board. Joanna's handiwork, no doubt; or possibly Jean's.

The number turns out to be his direct line and, miracle of miracles, he is sitting beside his telephone.

"Hamish Maitland? It's Kevan de Vries. Archie de Vries' father. I've just called to . . ."

The voice at the other end cuts me short in mid-sentence.

"Mr de Vries! I'm so glad to hear your voice. I've been meaning to call you myself."

His slight Scottish twang is irritating, as is his teacherly assumption of superiority.

"Oh? Why is that? Nothing wrong, I hope?"

"Well, now, that depends on what you mean by 'wrong'. As I'm sure ye know, Archie didn't take kindly to your own and his mother's departure for abroad. No tae put too fine a point on it, he's been quite difficult since you left. Nothing that we can't handle, which is what we're here for." He allows a sort of pregnant silence to elapse, which I find infuriating. I leap quickly into the vacuum.

"I'm glad that we're agreed on that," I say as smoothly as I can. "Your fees are not cheap, as we both know, but until now I've been convinced that Joanna and I are receiving good value for our money."

I, too, let a meaningful silence into the conversation. Much to my surprise, the sarky little rat shows that he's prepared to take me on.

"Yes. Well, Mrs de Vries is a different matter. Archie's very upset about her . . . condition, as any wee lad would be, even without the challenges that Archie faces. I've a huge amount of respect for your wife, Mr de Vries, and the way that she is facing up to . . ."

"Facing up to her death, you mean? Do go on."

He falters, but only for a few seconds.

"What would really help," he concludes in the bland, non-specific manner I've come to associate with his kind, "would be if yeself and Mrs de Vries could be a little more . . . co-ordinated – in your relations with Archie."

"What the hell is that supposed to mean?" I demand, my patience now threadbare. "Why can't you just spit out exactly what it is you want to say, instead of talking in these dishonest insinuating riddles all the time?"

This time the silence is much longer; so long, in fact, that if I couldn't hear the man's laboured breathing at the other end of the phone, I'd be inclined to think that he'd cut me off.

"Very well, Mr de Vries, since you want it in the raw,

you shall have it. I was just trying to spare the feelings of all concerned." I can picture him, the paunchy little runt, steepling his fingers and telling himself to keep calm as he gets the better of me, disciplining himself not to show his glee. But I'm too weary and now too concerned about both Archie and Joanna to pursue his cat-and-mouse game any further.

"The truth of the matter is that we've had to keep Archie mildly sedated since his mother's departure. I wasn't there myself when she took her leave of him – neither, I believe, were ye yeself – but something that she said has persuaded him that he won't be seeing her again. Naturally, I've tried to talk him out of this. I've told him that, although she's very ill, she'll be standing by him; that you're a family and you'll all work through this thing together. That *is* correct, isn't it?" I can imagine his piercing little piggy eyes winkling the truth out of me and for the first time am glad that ours is not a face-to-face conversation. There is another long pause, before I steel myself to reply.

"It's true as far as I can make it so. But – and perhaps I should have told you this before – Joanna's illness has destabilised. That's the official term: the ones that the doctors use. What it actually means is that the leukaemia has taken rampant control of her body, to the point where there's little that they can do for her. All that they – and I – can do is make her as comfortable and tranquil as possible and help her to wait for the end. As it happens, I was called to St Lucia on business shortly after we received this diagnosis. It was my decision to take her there, to help her to shed all the cares that she has here and to find some peace. I make no apology for saying to you that Archie is the biggest of her worries and therefore the one that I most hoped to release her from during her last few weeks on this earth. You may criticise me all you wish," I conclude defiantly, hoping that the nasty little man can't hear the catch that's come unbidden into my voice.

"I'm very sorry to hear that, very sorry indeed." He sounds genuinely sympathetic, but there is a steely quality to what he's saying that tells me that he has a sting in his tail.

"But what?"

"Beg pardon?" It's a phrase that riles me, but I make myself humour him.

"I accept your sympathy, and I'm grateful for it, as I'm sure Joanna would be if she were listening. But I sense that you still have a point that you wish to make, perhaps your original point when we started this conversation?"

"Indeed. Well, it seems a little unkind to say so now that you've explained matters in so much detail, but the fact is that Mrs . . . his mother spoke to Archie yesterday and he's been pretty much unreachable ever since."

"What did she say to him?"

"I don't know exactly. I was in the room, but I didn't put the phone on speak; I considered that too much of an invasion of his privacy, particularly as we'd been reducing the medication over the past few days and he seemed to be coping well on the lower doses. But I'm certain she told him that you'd come home."

"Why do you say that?"

"Because he kept on saying, 'Why hasn't he come to see me?' He said it several times."

"And that sent him into one of his spasms, did it?"

"I wouldn't call the manifestations of Archie's illness 'spasms', but I realise it's not appropriate to discuss the details of that now. No, actually it didn't. He was pale and upset, but still quite rational. It was something else that tipped him into hysteria. Something that she said about the house."

"Which house? This one?"

"I assume so. He wasn't specific, but there aren't many houses with which he's intimately acquainted, are there?"

"I suppose not. I can't think what Joanna can have said, though. She's usually so careful with his feelings; and besides, I haven't told her about the . . ."

"I'm sorry?"

"Nothing. Nothing that need concern you, or Archie. I was just thinking aloud. So is Archie back under heavier sedation again? Or is it possible for me to speak to him now, or arrange to visit him?"

"He has been prescribed tranquillisers – quite strong ones – but not so strong that they've knocked him out completely. He's still able to study a little. But I wouldn't advise talking to him at the moment. He's not confident on the telephone, as you know, and, if I may say so, your having attempted to contact him so belatedly after your return is only likely to confuse and anger him further. I can't stop you from visiting him, of course, but I'd like to offer my professional opinion that just the one visit this week will be all that we can expect him to cope with."

"What are you talking about now? Who else has been to see him? He's not supposed to receive visitors without our written permission."

"No-one else has seen him, yet," Maitland says, silky smooth again now that he has firmly repossessed the upper hand, "but it is my understanding that your wife will be coming here tomorrow. As one of his two legal guardians, she has no need to supply written permission for herself, as I'm sure that you'll agree."

"Joanna? But I've just told you that our plan was for her to stay in St Lucia until . . ."

He is merciful enough not to make me finish the sentence.

"Quite so, Mr de Vries, which brings me back to the point I

was trying to make much earlier in our conversation. I take it that you were unaware of her plan to return, and her reasons for not telling you are certainly not my affair. However, your son's welfare is very much my business. A little more communication between yourself and your wife would help Archie a great deal. Certainty is what the boy needs, or as much certainty as we can supply. A complicated and confusing succession of strange adult stratagems and being told half-truths can only lead him into despair. I hope that you will forgive me for being so blunt?"

"Eh? Oh, yes, of course. You're only doing your job," I say, with as much irony as I can muster. "Goodbye, Mr Maitland, and thank you for spelling out the situation so clearly. I'll find out exactly what my wife's plans are before I contact you again."

I put down the phone and lay my head on the desk, willing the tears not to come. Who is now leading whom into despair? It seems to me that it is not just Archie who is staring into the abyss, but the whole of our crazy 'privileged' family.

TWENTY-THREE

Tim had booked an appointment with his boss and was now standing a short way down the corridor from Superintendent Thornton's office, rehearsing what he was going to say. As far as he knew, Thornton had not yet been informed of either the age or the racial origin of the skeletons that had been found in the de Vries cellar, which at least gave Tim a bit of a head start. But unless the Superintendent were to be spooked by the race issue – which Tim realised would only happen if he were himself to talk it up – he was nevertheless convinced that he'd be told to drop the case. That Norfolk police had asked Thornton to make some of Tim's and Ricky MacFadyen's time available to help with the Sandringham murder investigation was bound to set alarm bells ringing in Thornton's head, even though he had smiled sweetly at this suggestion and agreed to it with no outward reluctance. South Lincs CID was under-manned at the best of times; with Juliet out of the picture for the time being and Tim and Ricky now operational on their own territory on only a part-time basis, Thornton would be left with little more than a skeleton staff (Tim smiled grimly at this unintentional pun). One solution to the dilemma would be for the Superintendent himself to second a couple of detectives from another force: from Peterborough, say, or from North Lincs. But any practical measures of this kind were likely to be eclipsed in Thornton's head by rapid calculations made on the cash register that always resided there. As the Superintendent was well aware, if he could charge out some of his own officers' time without replacing it, he would be quids in.

PCs Gary Cooper and Giash Chakrabati passed by on their way to the canteen, staring a little at Tim as they did so. He raised a hand in greeting and smiled in a way that he hoped was normal for him. Nevertheless, he realised that if even these two uniformed officers, who had on many occasions proved themselves staunch allies, were thinking that his behaviour was strange, it was high time that he stopped lurking in the corridor. He marched up to Thornton's door and tapped firmly on it.

"Come in!" said Thornton in the imperious, schoolmasterly manner that always set Tim's teeth on edge. Today, though, he would refuse to be rattled.

As soon as he entered the room, he realised that the Super-intendent was in the throes of a very animated telephone conversation.

"I'm sorry, I'll wait outside . . ." he began.

"No need, Yates, I asked you in and quite frankly I have no more time to spend on this than I have done already," his boss barked, directing his comments at the handset that he was holding rather than at Tim himself. "So we'll hear no more about it, shall we? The idea is quite outrageous!" He slammed the phone down and sat glaring at Tim, his eyes black and unblinking. Not a good start, thought Tim. Should I humour him or pretend that nothing's happened?

Superintendent Thornton spoke first, removing from Tim the need to choose a course of action.

"How long have you been married, Yates?" he demanded crossly.

"About three years, sir," said Tim. It suddenly dawned on him that he'd walked in on what Ricky called a 'domestic' between the Superintendent and his wife. He had to concentrate very hard on composing his facial muscles to prevent himself from grinning. Mrs Thornton was a mysterious woman, seldom seen at police functions or even out shopping in Spalding itself. On the rare occasions when she was mentioned, Thornton always made it clear that she was too much of a lady to get involved in any of the social activities in which he himself deigned from time to time to participate with his colleagues, and that he wholeheartedly approved of her decision not to follow a career of her own. "Wife in the home," he would say smugly, "that's the best situation. Never mind if she's bored: she'll come to appreciate it eventually." Coming as he did from a family whose women had worked from time immemorial and married now to a wife who took her own career very seriously, Tim had never been able to think of a polite reply to such comments. It amused him that the impeccable Mrs Thornton appeared at present to be crossing her all-powerful, breadwinning husband.

"Three years!" muttered the Superintendent. "Just wait until it's thirty-three, and see how you like it."

"Nothing wrong, sir, I hope?" said Tim blandly.

Superintendent Thornton cast a single penetrating look in Tim's direction and shut down his expression as quickly and completely as if he had donned a mask. Tim hoped that the glee he'd felt about Thornton's ruffled nerves had not been too obvious.

"Nothing that I can't handle," he said huffily. "Let's get to the point of the matter in hand, shall we? I doubt if you can afford to waste the day on irrelevant pleasantries and I'm quite sure I can't. What do you have to tell me about the Sutterton case? I'm assuming you've made some progress; otherwise you wouldn't be here. I shall tell you now that, although I've accepted the request from Norfolk for your partial secondment to help them with the death of that young girl at Sandringham, it's up to you to fit in both cases as best you can. Norfolk, of course, is convinced that the two are linked in some way, but I see no reason to agree with them. Unless, of course, you intend to supply evidence that Kevan de Vries is a serial killer. Is that what you think, Yates? Eh? Because I can assure you that if you jump to unfounded conclusions about him and he decides to press charges, you'll be entirely on your own!"

He shot Tim one of his sparring partner looks. Trust my luck, Tim thought, cursing inwardly. I want him to do me the favour of pursuing an ancient case and he's in just about the worst mood I've ever seen him in.

"No, sir," he said deferentially. "In fact, rather the opposite. I'm about to receive a report from Ms Gardner that will indicate that Mr de Vries could not have killed the three women whose skeletons were found in his cellar."

"Oh?" said the Superintendent, immediately contrary, "and what makes you – or Ms Gardner – quite so certain of that?"

"The bones are at least a hundred years old, sir. Whether or not they've been in Mr de Vries' cellar for all of that time is impossible to say. But, since he himself is some years shy of his fiftieth birthday, we can hardly lay their deaths at his door."

"Oh. No. Of course not. Well, that's something of a relief, isn't it? We won't have to prosecute a leading local figure and you won't have to waste your time on solving an old murder."

Tim cleared his throat. The Superintendent shot him one of his cat-seeking-mouse looks.

"I rather hoped that you would allow me to proceed with the de Vries investigation, sir. Time permitting, of course."

"Proceed? Oh, yes, I suppose you mean the farce with the passports. Well, it's still on the books and it needs resolving somehow. I'm inclined to take Kevan de Vries' word for it when he says he has no knowledge of them and allow the poor man to get back to his wife. But I agree that you still need to make some sort of effort, to show willing, even if you won't get to the bottom of it."

Tim could hardly believe that this was the same man who, however reluctantly, had ordered Kevan de Vries to travel back from partway round the world just a few short days ago to answer questions about the crime that he was now describing in such a phlegmatic fashion. It was as if the gravity of that offence had been erased by the prospect that de Vries might have committed the even more serious crime of murder and that now he had been absolved of that Thornton had decided without proof that he was probably innocent of all wrongdoing. Although it was apparent that the Superintendent was in a morose and unyielding mood, Tim felt unable to let such an assumption pass.

"With respect, sir, it is hardly a farce. As you know, forging passports is not just a serious offence in itself; it's often evidence of other organised crimes."

"Don't preach to me, Yates. You have my permission to continue with the passport enquiry and to enlist MacFadyen's help if you think he can be useful, as long as you're able to fit in the Norfolk investigation as well, and attempt at least some semblance of continuing to keep your finger on the pulse here. And I expect you to either bring a charge against Mr de Vries or to have released him from all restrictions by the end of the week."

"Yes, sir. Thank you. However . . ."

The Superintendent glowered.

"However," persevered Tim, "I don't just mean the passports. The skeletons, I understand, were women from Africa; they were black. There may be . . ."

Superintendent Thornton's face registered such a sequence of expressions that Tim, with some degree of amusement, was convinced he could follow his superior's probable train of thought.

"You'd better ask the Home Office what it wants you to do with them. My guess is that they'll suggest a decent funeral with the minimum of fuss. I'd prefer it if the press weren't to get hold of the story, but if they do make sure that they don't get hung up on the race thing. I assume that you agree with me?"

Superintendent Thornton scrutinised Tim's face, his eyes narrowing.

"Now that you mention 'the race thing', sir. Don't you think it might be safer to try to pursue this as a cold case enquiry, even though we know we won't secure a conviction? As you've already spotted, we could be accused of not caring enough about what happened to the victims because they were black."

"You aren't telling me that despite the fact that we're absolutely strapped for personnel at the moment, you're proposing to continue an investigation into a Victorian crime? Don't be ridiculous, Yates. Of course I don't think we should pursue it. I know about your interest in history." The Superintendent made it sound like an addiction or a grubby vice. "You should ask yourself whether you're allowing it to cloud your judgement."

"Yes, sir. You're probably right. I just thought that I'd point out that if we ditch it too precipitately it could cause a controversy and therefore considerable embarrassment to the force. I know that you take care to be sensitive about such matters. I've always considered you to be a role model for political correctness." Tim realised too late that he was now laying it on with a trowel. He'd probably gone too far to delude even Thornton that he was making such an observation in earnest.

"Oh. Yes, well, I do my best."

The Superintendent rose to his feet and walked distractedly towards the window, where he paused and stood looking out for some minutes, his hands clasped behind his back. When he turned round again, Tim could see that his words had struck a chord. The belligerent demeanour that Thornton had displayed previously had turned to one of uncertainty.

"I think you're probably being over-cautious, Yates, and as I've said I strongly suspect that your own agenda is creeping in here. However, there may be a grain of sense in what you're saying. You'd better consult the Home Office about that, too. Explain your concerns and ask them how we should proceed. Then if they make the decision to drop the case and there's trouble, we can point the finger at them. Not that I'd say so in so many words to anyone but yourself, you understand."

"Quite so, sir," said Tim, trying not to grin.

"Let me know what they advise."

"Yes, sir. Certainly."

Tim turned to leave. He was halfway out of the door when the Superintendent called him back.

"Oh, by the way, Yates . . ."

"Yes?" Tim answered, a little irritably. He'd got the answer he wanted and had hoped to escape before Thornton could change his mind again.

"Do you know how Armstrong is? Have you been in touch with her or the hospital?"

"I'm going to see her this evening, sir. The last time I phoned the hospital, they still hadn't got the results of the tests. I understand that she's still very poorly."

"Pity. It would have to happen at this juncture, wouldn't it? We could do with her back here double quick, as you know. Try to make some discreet enquiries as to when she might be well enough, will you?"

Tim resolved through gritted teeth not to lose his cool.

"I'll pass on your good wishes, shall I, sir?"

"Yes, you do that. And don't forget what I said about freeing up Kevan de Vries, will you?"

TWENTY-FOUR

Tim wanted to carry out further searches at Laurieston. Something had been niggling at the back of his mind since the discovery of the skeletons: something that had struck him as odd or not quite right. It was something he couldn't quite put his finger on; he'd racked his brains to try to think about exactly what it was, but no answer came to him. He'd therefore decided to try to confront his unease from a different angle, by thinking about how he might have followed up the discovery of the skeletons if they'd been part of a contemporary murder enquiry.

The answer was blindingly obvious: he and his colleagues would then not have been satisfied with merely raising the flags in the immediate area where the skeletons had been found. They'd have taken the whole cellar apart. Now he thought about it, that in itself might explain his half-formulated worries. What was it that Kevan de Vries had said? That his wife had stored some of his grandfather's furniture in the cellar, but that there might be other stuff down there that was much older. He remembered the huge bank of jumbled artefacts, several items deep and high, that had been stacked against the wall opposite to where they'd found the skeletons. Some of them had been covered over with pieces of old carpet and sacking. It would be a daunting task to shift that lot, but suddenly he knew that that was what they must do. At least it shouldn't be too difficult to get Kevan de Vries onside for this new search: if Tim were to explain that it was designed to shed further light on how and when the skeletons had come to be placed in the cellar, he was certain that de Vries, who now knew with certainty that he could not himself have been accused of involvement with these deaths, would be delighted to have the spotlight shifted from himself. Even Jean Rook would be exercised to find a reason to object to it.

He would call Kevan de Vries once he'd made sure that Giash Chakrabati – and, he supposed, Giash's unprepossessing new mate, who seemed to be glued to him at the moment – could make themselves available to help him. First of all, however, Tim had a more pressing engagement. He was going to the Pilgrim Hospital to see the consultant in whose care Juliet had been placed. He hadn't yet managed to visit Juliet, but reports he'd heard about her state of health were not good. Giash's temporary sidekick – what was the woman's name? Verity something – had apparently tried to see Juliet when she'd been back to Boston on a brief jaunt with her former colleagues and, according to her, had been told that Juliet wasn't well enough to receive visitors. Whilst Tim didn't exactly doubt the accuracy of this, his first impressions of the woman had not been favourable and he doubted her intentions in making such an overture. As far as he knew, she and Juliet had never met. She might not, therefore, have tried very hard to get into the ward, or perhaps not tried at all, but just claimed to have made the attempt to curry favour with her new colleagues. Or perhaps Juliet herself had decided that she couldn't be bothered with her. What worried Tim much more was that Juliet had not contacted him and that, when he'd (twice) tried to call her, he'd been told she was sleeping.

Even more worrying was that no-one seemed to have much idea of what was wrong with her. After his conversation with Superintendent Thornton on the previous day, Tim had asked to speak to the consultant, a Mr Wu, by telephone. At first Mr Wu had sounded hostile and claimed that he couldn't discuss Juliet's case with someone who wasn't a relative. When Tim had explained that she had no close relatives and that the only relations of whom she was herself aware lived in New Zealand, and furthermore that he was a policeman and Juliet's boss, Mr Wu had been much more forthcoming, deferential even, but was still unable to offer any but the vaguest reassurance. He'd as good as admitted that Juliet's condition was causing concern, but that they were no closer to diagnosing it. That Juliet had a high fever and had been drifting in and out of consciousness ever since the man who occupied the flat adjoining hers had heard the thud as she collapsed on the floor, and had broken in when he could not obtain an answer, did not help.

Tim regarded himself as a cut-and-dried sort of person. He disliked it when professionals failed to give answers to the questions that he put to them. He suspected the consultant to be guilty of incompetence, indifference or both. Furthermore, he needed an outlet for his increasing anxiety about Juliet. If this Wu weren't doing his job properly, Tim was resolved to find him out. Mindful, however, that Juliet herself – or Katrin, if he'd been prepared to worry her with it – would have advised him to be both cautious and polite, in the first instance he'd merely made an appointment to see the consultant. He'd be better able to gauge what kind of care Juliet was getting if he could see it for himself.

Tim didn't like hospitals. The Pilgrim Hospital, which he'd visited several times in the line of duty and which had also been at the centre of the one distressing period of his marriage, held little for him but unpleasant memories. He detested its seventies concrete architecture and resented its plundering of history for a name that was hardly suitable, since the seventeenth-century pilgrims to which it referred had mostly run away from or been forced out of Boston. His mood therefore became increasingly truculent as he approached the building and was not helped by the amount of time that it took him to find a parking space.

He had omitted to ask Mr Wu how he might be reached. He therefore concluded that he had no option but to present himself at the reception desk in Outpatients and say that he had an appointment. It was only after he'd embarked upon a baffling and increasingly cross-purposed conversation with the burly porter who seemed to be doubling up as reception-ist, and who told him bluntly that he wouldn't get anywhere without 'your hospital letter', that it dawned upon him that almost everyone who turned up there would have had an appointment of some kind. Irked by his own stupidity, he decided that the best way out of the impasse would be to show his identity card and say that he had arranged to see Mr Wu on police business. Not strictly speaking true, but near enough.

The porter-receptionist asked him to wait and turned his back on him while he made a telephone call. It was conducted sotto voce and Tim could not hear much of what the man was saying, but after he'd put down the receiver he gave Tim a thumbs-up. Tim thought that this looked promising, even if it was an unorthodox way of managing a reception desk.

"Mr Wu's registrar will come down to meet you," he said. "Mr Wu is expecting you; you're quite correct." Tim felt and quelled a further surge of irritation. He stood to one side of the desk and waited as patiently as he could.

An earnest young woman wearing a white coat appeared after a very short time. She was walking rapidly down the cor-ridor towards Tim, looking from side to side as she went, obvi-ously trying to spot someone. When her eyes focused on Tim, she attempted a polite smile. She held out her hand as she reached him.

"Detective Inspector Yates? I'm Louise Butler, Mr Wu's registrar. Mr Wu's asked me to meet you, as giving directions to his office can be quite tricky."

"Thank you. I appreciate it."

She turned on her heel and headed back the way that she'd come, walking so swiftly in her high-heeled patent leather pumps that Tim had to lengthen his stride to keep up. She headed for the lifts, pressing all the buttons until one arrived.

"Juliet Armstrong is a colleague of yours?" she asked, as the lift doors swung shut and it began its laborious ascent.

"Yes," said Tim. "I'm very concerned that I haven't heard from her, even though she's ill. It's quite out of character for her to ..."

The lift juddered to a halt and the doors opened again. A couple of porters were waiting to enter with their charge, a man reclining in a full-sized hospital bed on wheels.

"Room for a little'un?" said one.

Louise Butler smiled at him.

"We've only one more floor to go. We'll get out of your way," she said. She sprang out of the lift and headed for a door marked 'Stairs', with Tim loping in her wake. She ascended the two flights of stairs so rapidly that Tim was quite breathless by the time they'd completed another sprint and finally come to a halt outside a door marked 'Dr Wu'. She knocked at it tentatively.

Dr Wu did not answer, so she poked her head around it and then looked over her shoulder at Tim.

"Do come in," she said. "Dr Wu, this is DI Yates."

Tim found himself in a small square room containing a large desk that faced the door. There was a tiny window behind it that would barely have admitted enough light to allow its occupant to see the words that he was writing so furiously upon a large lined pad of paper, had its deficiency not been over-compensated for by a yellow striplight that ran the length of the room. It bathed the figure seated at the desk in its harsh glare.

Dr Wu put down his pen and looked up. He held out his hand to Tim, but did not rise to greet him. Tim saw that the doctor was a fairly thick-set Asian man, probably a Chinese national, who had a mop of straight black hair and a very pock-marked face. Like all the hospital doctors Tim had met, he seemed weary. Tim thought he also detected the faint aroma of cigarette smoke clinging to the doctor's clothes, though he could have been mistaken.

Tim was about to clasp the proffered hand when the doctor let his own fall. He proceeded to wave it about in an agitated fashion.

"Ah, Dr Butler, don't go! I'm sure that DI Yates will want to know about the care you've been taking of our patient, and especially your diagnosis."

Louise Butler was close to the door and had evidently been planning a hasty exit. She halted now and turned to face both Tim and the doctor, nervously fiddling with one of the buttons on her white coat in a childlike gesture. Dr Wu beamed at her.

"Dr Butler is very talented, DI Yates, and also a very unas-suming lady. But you should know that she has suggested a diagnosis for Juliet Armstrong's condition that, in my opinion, will turn out to be the correct one. We're just awaiting the results of some tests as we speak."

Tim looked at the callow young woman with new interest.

"You think you know what's wrong with Juliet? What is it?"

"As Dr Wu said, we're still awaiting tests, so we can't be sure . . ."

"Leptospirosis," said Dr Wu, cutting in. "DI Yates under-stands that we're not certain, but," – he turned from his subordinate to Tim – "that is what Dr Butler *thinks* is wrong and, now she's told me why, based on her observations of Miss Armstrong since she was admitted, I'm bound to say that I concur. In fact, I'm jealous of her perspicacity: I should have thought of it myself."

Tim was beginning to lose patience again. He disliked jargon, whether it came from computer programmers or the medical profession. He always suspected the person using it of being less than above board.

"Come again?" he said. "I apologise for my ignorance, but I'm afraid that I'm none the wiser."

Dr Wu grinned. Tim felt his face redden. He was about to ask the doctor to stop playing games when Louise Butler spoke. She was suddenly much more confident.

"You may know it as Weil's disease," she said. "It's the more commonly-used name for it."

"I *have* heard of Weil's disease, but I don't know much about it. Isn't it something to do with rats?"

"Correct," said Dr Wu. Tim noticed for the first time that he spoke with a vaguely American drawl. "It's actually much more common than people realise, and very unpleasant. It's transmitted by water that's been polluted by rats' urine. In certain circumstances, it can be fatal."

"How did Juliet come into contact with it?"

It was Dr Butler who replied.

"She's been able to tell us the answer to that now, I think. She's much more lucid, because we've managed to lower her fever. I went to examine her this morning. She said that her ankle was troubling her. When I looked at it, I could see some puncture marks; the area around them was inflamed. It probably didn't swell up at first, which is why it went unnoticed. Juliet told me that some creature rushed at her when she was following up an inquiry in Sutterton earlier this week. She thought that it might have been a rat. She'd hardly been in a state to remember it before."

"Was that when I sent her to interview Jackie Briggs?"

Louise Butler smiled.

"She didn't disclose the details of her inquiry. She'd probably think it unethical." She regarded him sympathetically. "I don't think you should beat yourself up about it, anyway. It's hardly the sort of hazard you'd have expected to have to safeguard her against."

"But if this disease is transmitted by rats' urine, how did she get it from a bite?"

"She says that she rubbed water from the stream on to the bite, to soothe it. The water must have been infected."

"Shouldn't you be treating her for this now, instead of waiting for the results of the tests? Has any harm been done by the delay in diagnosing it? What is the treatment for it, anyway?"

"Steady on!" said Dr Wu. "One question at a time, please."

"It's OK," said Louise Butler. Then, turning to Tim, "I understand how anxious you are about her. We can't give you any absolute assurances yet, but, if it is Weil's disease, we've actually caught it quite early. It can take more than a week to manifest itself, but Juliet got the symptoms very quickly. We have started the course of antibiotics used to treat it already and we should have the results of the tests by lunchtime, in any case. We're therefore hopeful that there won't be long-term damage in her case. If untreated, it can damage the internal organs, especially the liver and kidneys, but it is unlikely to have spread to those organs so soon: it usually takes about a week to do so."

"Is it OK for me to see her?"

"Yes, if she agrees to it. She's quite weak. She's had a high fever and very bad headaches, and she's been unable to eat since she was admitted, though she's been on a drip. The antibiotics may make her feel worse at first, as well. They certainly won't improve the muscle aches that she's been experiencing."

"Poor Juliet! This is just terrible. Will you ask her if she'll see me? I assume she's in a ward on her own?"

"Certainly. Yes, she's been isolated for the moment. If the diagnosis is correct and she responds well to treatment, we may move her into a small shared ward in a few days' time."

"It's not infectious?"

"Not if the proper hygienic precautions are taken. It's passed on through urine-infected water, as Dr Wu said, not from person to person. In the past, it was believed that humans infected each other, but it's almost certain that they were in fact infected by sharing a joint source of polluted water."

"We've just found out that my wife is pregnant. Does that mean I ought not to come into contact with Juliet?"

"You should be fine, but just to be safe, we'll fit you out with scrubs and a face mask. That's if she'll see you, of course. And you must promise not to worry her about work."

"I won't! How long is she likely to be here?"

"We'll probably keep her in hospital for at least a week. She's unlikely to make a full recovery in less than six weeks, though."

"That won't please my boss!"

Dr Butler gave him a curious look.

"I'll go and tell her you're here. Perhaps you wouldn't mind waiting in the ante-room, so that we can leave Dr Wu in peace."

Tim turned to look at Dr Wu, and saw that he had started writing his rapid notes again.

"Certainly. Thank you, Dr Wu, you've been most helpful."

The doctor looked up, momentarily startled, as if surprised to see that Tim was still there.

"Always a pleasure," he said in his American drawl, obviously selecting at random from his collection of courteous comments. He turned back to his task immediately. Tim followed Louise Butler out of his office.

It was a quarter of an hour before Dr Butler returned.

"I apologise for the delay, DI Yates. Juliet feels up to seeing you now." She offered no explanation for the length of her absence. "I'll take you to the nurse's station to get fitted out with a gown and mask. The nurse will show you where Juliet is and she'll return after five minutes to tell you that time's up. I'm afraid that five minutes is the most that we can allow at the moment."

"Thank you. I'm grateful," said Tim. "Will you stay, too?"

"No, I have some rounds to make and I also want to check on the lab to make sure they've prioritised those tests. So promise me – no talking shop!"

"Scout's honour!" said Tim. Once more he followed Dr Butler's swift-moving form down a couple of corridors to an area fronted by a desk console.

"This is DI Yates," she said to the nurse seated there. "He's come to see Juliet Armstrong. Could you tog him out, please? Goodbye, DI Yates," she added. "I'm sure we'll meet again soon."

Tim took her hand, which was surprisingly small and limp. After a token shake, she extracted it and walked rapidly away.

The nurse in whose charge he had been left was dumpy and businesslike. She provided Tim with a green gown that, once he'd put it on, almost swept the floor, and handed him a barrier mask and a hairnet. He donned these as well.

"Follow me," said the nurse. She led him the short distance

to a pair of doors. Close to the nurse's station, they were situated at the opposite end of the corridor to the main ward. The nurse opened one of them carefully and held it for Tim as he entered the small room to which they led.

"Your visitor, duckie," said the nurse. "Doctor's instructions are that he can stay five minutes, tops. I'll be back to fetch him then. But you can kick him out before that if you want to!"

She threw Tim a triumphant look as she swept out again.

Juliet was lying back against the pillows, the head section of which had been raised so that she was almost in a sitting position. She was very pale and her normally springy dark curls clung limply to her forehead.

"Juliet?" She raised her head a little more and attempted a lop-sided smile. Tim could now see that her right arm was wired to a drip. She was also attached to some kind of monitoring device. A cradle had been placed over her legs, the bedclothes forming a tent across it.

"God, Juliet, you've scared us. I feel scared now, just looking at you."

Juliet managed a small gurgle of laughter.

"You look pretty scary yourself."

"What? Oh, the get-up, you mean."

"Why are you wearing all that? The nurses haven't been bothering with special clothes."

"It's because Katrin..." Too late, Tim realised that he'd have to continue. "She's pregnant," he concluded. "We haven't told anyone yet, so I'd be grateful if you'd keep it to yourself."

"Oh, Tim, congratulations!" said Juliet. Despite her illness, she was making a valiant effort to sound enthusiastic. Nevertheless, Tim thought that she looked – how? Sad would be too definite a word to use: wistful, maybe. He frowned. He'd never

126

have supposed that Juliet might have hankered after children. He thought that she was devoted to her career.

"Thank you. But it's you who I'm concerned about at the moment. Dr Butler tells me you think you were bitten by a rat when you went to Sutterton."

"Yes. It just came out of the laurel hedge. I barely had time to be startled before it lunged at my foot and then disappeared. I washed it in the stream there. Apparently, it was the worst thing I could have done!" She pulled a rueful face.

"They're not entirely sure that you have got this Weil's disease yet, are they?"

"No, but as good as. They'll know for sure by lunchtime. I wouldn't mind betting that they're right, though. Since I've been taking the antibiotics, I've begun to feel a bit better, even though they make me feel slightly sick."

"I feel responsible, for sending you to Sutterton in the first place."

"Don't be ridiculous! It was my job. You could hardly have anticipated such a bizarre thing happening to me, anyway."

"That's more or less what Dr Butler said. I'm quite impressed with Dr Butler. She seems to know what she's talking about."

"Oh, she does!" said Juliet. "And she's taken such good care of me while I've been here."

"I'm not so keen on her boss, though – Dr Wu. He seems a bit of a charlatan to me."

Juliet giggled softly.

"It doesn't surprise me that you haven't taken to him. I think he's all right, really. He's allowed Dr Butler to take responsibility, even though she's only a registrar."

"Some people might attribute that to laziness."

"And some might say that he's just good at delegation!" Juliet's dark eyes were snapping now. Tim was pleased to see that she was well enough to feel annoyed with him.

"Point taken. Superintendent Thornton sends his regards, by the way."

"Thanks. No doubt he's told you to find out exactly when he can expect me back at work."

"No . . . he . . ." Tim faltered. Juliet laughed again. "He *is* concerned about you," Tim finished lamely.

"I'm sure he is – as concerned as he is about his payroll and his crime quotas, at least. I've been told I won't be back at work for about six weeks, but you can tell him that if I'm able to return earlier, I certainly will."

"You're going to have to do as you're told on this occasion," said Tim as sternly as he could. "And Thornton's going to have to part with some of his precious reserves and get some secondments."

"Is Ricky still the man on the ground in the de Vries case?"

"I've promised not to talk shop with you. But yes, he is. Why do you ask?"

"He needs to keep an eye on Harry Briggs. I'm sure he's not on the level. His wife's OK – a bit naïve, and far too trusting of Harry – but I'm convinced that he's up to something."

"What makes you say that?"

"I went to their house to ask for Jackie. She was out doing one of her jobs – I caught up with her eventually – but Harry was at home on his own. He was cagey with me and as offhand as he thought he could get away with. I asked him to wait until I came back from talking to Jackie. I wanted to check his statement about the burglary. He said he'd be there for another hour before he went out to join his darts team, but when Jackie and I returned to the house forty-five minutes later he'd already gone."

"Perhaps he just doesn't like coppers."

"Perhaps. But I think that there's more to it than that. I

don't know if Ricky checked him out, to see if he's got a criminal record . . ."

"Dr Butler said not to talk about work," said the nurse, bustling in. "I'm afraid it's time for you to go now, in any case, DI Yates. Perhaps you'd like to call and see if it's convenient for you to come again tomorrow?"

"But . . ."

"No buts. Juliet needs to take some more pills now, and then she needs to rest. Perhaps you might manage some soup later, love. What do you think? If you'd wait outside, DI Yates, I'll be with you in a minute," she added, turning her bulky rear towards him as she bent to plump up Juliet's pillows.

"Goodbye, Tim," Juliet said, smiling at him over the nurse's shoulder. "Thank you so much for coming. You really have cheered me up."

TWENTY-FIVE

Tim was woken several times in the night by Katrin as she got up hurriedly to go to the bathroom. As dawn was breaking, she finally managed to fall asleep. He was worried enough to work from home until she awoke at around 10.00 a.m. Eventually, she emerged from the bedroom, pale and shivery. Her creamy skin had taken on a greenish tinge and there were purple shadows under her eyes.

"I've called Holbeach and told them you're not well," Tim said. "I'll make you something to drink and then, if you don't need me, I'm going to have to go." He moved across the room to embrace her. "I wanted to check you were OK before I left."

Katrin allowed herself to be embraced, but she stiffened nevertheless. Noticing it, Tim released her so that he could meet her eye.

"Is something wrong? Apart from feeling unwell, of course?"

"You know that I don't want to tell anyone just yet that I'm pregnant. If I start taking days off, they'll begin to put two and two together pretty quickly."

"Don't worry. I told them you've got summer 'flu and that you've had a very disturbed night. It's the truth, more or less. Besides, you're much more likely to be able to keep it a secret if you take a few days off now. From my recollection of those two pantomime dames in your office, they'd be willing to pin anything on to the first symptoms of pregnancy: a broken arm, toothache or cholera would all do the job equally

130

well. You can bet they've been observing you closely for months."

Katrin laughed in spite of herself.

"OK, I'll stay here today, on condition that you agree that I may do some more work on Florence Hoyle's journal. But I'm not promising to take several days off. Unless I feel really dreadful tomorrow, I shall be back at my desk again."

"Well, take it easy. But do some more work on the journal if you feel up to it. You'll probably feel better if you've got something to do. Besides, I'm looking forward to hearing what you make of it."

"Don't raise your hopes too high. So far, although I agree with you that Florence's relationship with both her husband and her mother-in-law is a bit odd, I can't find anything to link any of them to your skeletons – except, perhaps, the periodic appearance of a mysterious Mr Rhodes in their lives, who I think may be the famous Cecil Rhodes."

Tim whistled.

"You mean the Victorian colonialist?"

"Yes. But don't jump to any conclusions yet. I have no proof that it is *that* Rhodes that Florence speaks of. I need to establish that it was possible for *the* Cecil Rhodes to have visited Lincolnshire at the dates that she specifies and even then I'd need to find a concrete link between him and Frederick Jacobs before I could be convinced. And even *then*, I'd still need to find a reason for them to have abducted black women and brought them to Sutterton to kill them."

"I don't believe in coincidences, as you know. One thing that is sure is that Cecil Rhodes must have come into contact with plenty of black women in his time."

"I agree; but why would he have brought them to Spalding, to the country house of an obscure English landowner?"

"Ask me another."

"There's no point in asking you! But I will try to get to the bottom of it. Let me finish reading the journal first. Then I'll find out more about Cecil Rhodes and see if he had any specific links with Lincolnshire."

"Perfect!" said Tim, kissing her first on the lips, then on the forehead. "I can't wait to hear more. Let me know if you find out anything significant before the end of the day. But do take it easy. Promise me."

"I promise," said Katrin, smiling as vivaciously as she could manage. She was beginning to feel queasy again and was quite anxious for Tim to leave so that she could make dry toast before she took a shower. She was glad that he'd already forgotten his offer to make her a drink. She waved to him from the window as he set off in the BMW, then headed for the kitchen.

An hour later, having eaten two slices of toast, drunk some weak tea and taken a quick shower, she was seated at the kitchen table, once again immersed in the journal. Certain passages had struck her as quite poignant and she wondered if they'd been constructed as artlessly as at first appeared. There was one entry in particular that she'd read over several times. It appeared to chronicle the conception of Gordon Jacobs, Florence and Frederick's only child, which was not only in itself a strange thing for someone who was striving to be a lady to have written about towards the end of Queen Victoria's reign, but also suggested that Florence's sexual relations with her husband occurred so infrequently that she was able to pinpoint the date. This in turn led Katrin to suspect that the journal entry had been written retrospectively. Once again, Lucinda Jacobs seemed to have played a leading part. The entry was dated July 1896, almost four years after Florence and Frederick had married.

Frederick has been very melancholy for some weeks. I've tried to cheer him up and divert him in all sorts of ways, even learn-

ing to play chess, though not well. He's taken to sleeping in the blue room, because he says he has no wish to disturb me. Before I retired last night, I asked him if there was anything that he wanted. He repeated that there was nothing, and that I should go to bed. Mamma was still in the drawing-room, looking very displeased. I asked if she felt well, and she said yes, quite, and bid me goodnight. She rose to kiss me and called me a dear child, I think to reassure me that she wasn't cross with me.

While I was washing my face I heard raised voices coming up the stairs. I think that Mamma was being angry with Frederick, but she was speaking in a low, rapid voice and I couldn't hear the words. Frederick bellowed something back at her once or twice. It's not a very polite word to use, but it's the best I can think of: he was really shouting.

They were quieter after a while. I heard Frederick say goodnight to Mamma as I was getting into bed. I sat up in bed for a few moments, and was about to blow out the candle and lie down when there was a light tap at the door and Frederick came in. He said that he had changed his mind about wanting company for the night and asked if he could stay. Of course I said yes.

In the same ink Florence had written above this entry *My dear son, Gordon Cecil George Jacobs, was born on 23rd April 1897.*

Had Florence added this note for herself, or for posterity, and if so who had she expected might read it? And what of the boy's names? Either Florence or Frederick had probably chosen George because their son was born on St George's Day. Was Cecil Frederick's choice? And was there anything significant about the child's first name, other than that, presumably, they had liked it?

The next entry was of yet more interest. It was dated 10th September 1896.

I have been quite unwell, so I have written nothing for some time. I'm beginning to feel better now. It is as Mamma had supposed all along: I am with child. She is very happy about the baby. Even Frederick seems quite pleased, though I know he finds my condition hard to cope with. He says that he hates to see me suffer, but although he is too gentlemanly to say so, I sense that he is affronted by my nausea and by my increasing plumpness. He used to say how much he admired my boyish figure.

Mamma says that Fredrick should be taking better care of me, and that I need sea air. She has booked The Grand Hotel in Brighton for all of us. We are to leave on Monday. I am quite excited, as I have seldom seen the sea. Frederick has agreed to escort us, although he says that he may not remain for the whole week. Mr Rhodes is in London and they have business there. Mamma says that London is not far from Brighton if Frederick takes the train, or that Mr Rhodes could stir himself to visit Frederick at The Grand. Frederick says that unfortunately some of the business needs him to be in Lincolnshire, and that he may have to return to Laurieston in our absence. I can tell that Mamma is extremely annoyed about this, though she has said nothing out loud. I am a little upset that Frederick always puts Mr Rhodes first, but even more that he and Mamma seem always these days to be at odds with each other. To be fair to Frederick, at the moment I would not be good company if he were to spend every day with me; I'm no longer sickly, but I'm still weak and tired.

Katrin felt a sudden wave of nausea sweep over her. She just made it to the bathroom. The intensity of these bouts of vomiting was beginning to frighten her now. Afterwards she returned to the kitchen table and tried to take up the journal again, but was suddenly overcome with exhaustion. Angry with herself for succumbing, she knew that she was able to do nothing but lie down and rest. She returned to the bedroom and huddled under the quilt. She was asleep within seconds.

TWENTY-SIX

I knew that Joanna would not want to see me at the airport; equally, I knew that I had to be there to meet her. I was waiting for her at Gatwick early in the morning, exactly as the two plods had come to meet me. I have no idea what their feelings were as they hung around waiting for my delayed flight: boredom, possibly, irritation or just a weary *déja vu* sense of wanting to get on with it? Of one thing I am certain: they could not have been dreading their encounter with me as much as I was dreading mine with Joanna.

I've not had much time to think over the past three days, but what few minutes there have been have been devoted to her. I've had to face up to my cowardice, for I'm forced now to admit to myself that I dread seeing Joanna *in extremis*. My departure for the UK was, of course, inevitable and not of my own choosing, but I cannot deny that I left St Lucia gladly and not without a sense of relief. Joanna as she is now is not the woman that I married. I shall be loyal to her as long as she lives, but I can't deny that I no longer love her. The most terrible thing about a lingering death is that it claims the mind long before its ravages have exhausted the body. If she'd been cut down by a flash of lightning or crushed by a bus, the agony would have been so much easier to bear. As it is, I'm forced to keep on struggling with a hollowed-out shell, an angry cypher. Joanna as she is now seems to be beyond much feeling or sensitivity: she is a living corpse.

So I'm standing now at the barrier, once again jostling with the excited cretins who are frantically welcoming home relatives to whom they rarely speak for the rest of the year, watching for my frail and vengeful wife to appear. I'm a little concerned that already half a dozen or so first class passengers have sprinted through to the exit, most to be welcomed, not by embarrassing relatives, but by the more restrained greetings of the corporate employees or hire car chauffeurs who lead them discreetly away, taking charge of their luggage as they go. I know that Joanna can be quite awkward about our wealth – she makes a parade of never having forgotten her farm-labourer roots – but surely even she would not dream of travelling economy in her condition? I continue to watch and wait, and resolve to ask an airline official for help if she isn't with the next tranche of arrivals.

A wheelchair comes round the corner, pushed by a blonde stewardess, handsomely discreet in the dark-blue uniform worn by British Airways staff. She is striking and at first my attention is drawn to her expertly made-up face and blonde coiffure. Then I notice that her charge is gesturing quite agitatedly. I look more closely and see a face grimacing with anger. The woman in the wheelchair is gaunt, almost skeletal, but she, too, is elegant in her way. Her hair has been professionally styled into a smooth chignon. She wears a cream linen trouser suit with a black silk shirt. Of course I see at once that it is Joanna, horribly changed during the brief five days since I left her, yet still retaining the distinctive bearing of my wife and some of the vestiges of her former beauty.

The stewardess has evidently now been told who I am. She passes through the barrier and halts beside me.

"Mr de Vries?" she asks, with a saccharine smile. "Your wife has had a difficult journey, but I think she is beginning to recover now."

She turns and bends down to meet Joanna's eye. I'm sure that she just wants to get the hell out of here, escape perhaps to a warm bath or the embrace of her lover, but that is not the impression that she gives. Joanna fixes me with a venomous stare and treats me to the full vent of her fury.

"What the hell do you think you're doing here? And who told you I was coming? If you can't be bothered to look after your son, I'll thank you to leave me to do it by myself."

The stewardess looks alarmed. She glances between us, trying to gauge the situation. Eventually, she decides to consult Joanna.

"Are you happy for me to leave you with Mr de Vries, or would you like me to call someone else to look after you?" she asks, studiously ignoring me now.

"I am quite capable of looking after my wife, thank you, and you need have no fears on her behalf," I say, as smoothly as I can. Inwardly, I am livid. How dare Joanna suggest to this woman that I may not be a suitable person to take charge of her?

Joanna herself seems to acknowledge that she's gone too far. She sits back wearily in the wheelchair, half-closing her eyes.

"It's OK," she says, slowly opening them again. "You can leave me with him. Inept and self-centred as he is, I don't think I'll come to any harm with him. And if I do, quite frankly, what difference will it make?"

"Oh, for God's sake . . ." I begin. But I see that the stewardess is regarding me warily, as if I'm a monster. In the interests of getting out of the situation as quickly as possible, I tone it down.

"Thank you so much for looking after Joanna," I say. "We're both very grateful to you." I fish in my pocket for a £20 note and present it to her. To my surprise, she hands it back.

"Thank you, that's very kind," she murmurs, "but I was just doing my job. It was a pleasure to look after Mrs de Vries. Goodbye, Joanna, I hope that we'll meet again." She gives my wife a searching look.

Joanna laughs harshly.

"I think that's unlikely, unless our paths cross again very soon," she says. "But it is a pious thought, and I thank you. It has been a pleasure to have met you. I mean that," she adds, less urbanely. The stewardess looks troubled.

"Well, goodbye, then," she says, holding out her hand. Joanna gives it a little squeeze. The woman walks away, her heels clacking on the polished floor surface. She has no valedictory words for me.

"What the fuck was all that about?" I say. "And why are you in this wheelchair? Have you suddenly got worse? Why have you come at all, when you're so ill? You know that we agreed that you'd stay in St Lucia."

"Ever the charmer, Kevan, aren't you? I'm not too delighted to see you, either. To answer your questions, I don't know what you mean by 'all that'; I'm in the wheelchair because my medication made me quite ill on the flight and I was judged incapable of walking off the plane under my own steam – wrongly, in my opinion, if you want to know; I don't know whether I'm worse or not – how would you expect me to be able to tell? I'm here partly because Archie is distressed because he doesn't know what is going on; partly, as I'm sure you're aware, because I want to secure his future; and we didn't agree that I should stay in St Lucia – it was merely an instruction that you chose to issue to me. I have now chosen to disregard it."

She looks up at me, her classic features yellow and haggard and contorted with a concentration of hatred of which, until recently, I should not have believed her capable.

I take the handles of the wheelchair with trembling hands. I know that I must de-fuse the situation somehow.

"Would you like to go for coffee?" I say.

"I'd like you to take me to see our son – my son, if you prefer," she snaps back.

I'm aware that two women who have been waiting by the barrier are eyeing us curiously. I push Joanna to a quiet part of the concourse and crouch down so that I can speak to her properly. I take her hands in mine. She does not try to withdraw them.

"Look, Joanna, I'm sorry that I haven't been to see Archie yet. This police case is more complicated than you realise – I haven't told you more, because I didn't want to worry you with it. I did try to see Archie, though not as soon as I got here, as I promised you I would, and I'm sorry for that. I spoke to that housemaster of his and he told me that you'd already been in touch with Archie and that he'd had some kind of relapse. You probably know that, too?"

I look into her face, force her to make contact. She nods. I realise that her unhappiness about this is all-consuming.

"He told me not to disturb Archie. He said that you were going to see him yourself and that would be about as much as he would be able to cope with. That's how I knew you were coming home. Of course, once I'd found out, I checked the flights. You wouldn't expect me not to meet you, would you?"

Joanna crumples.

TWENTY-SEVEN

Andy Carstairs was growing very red in the face. He was talking to Miss Nugent, the personnel officer at de Vries Industries, and getting precisely nowhere. Miss Nugent's office was situated in a single-storey building to the rear of the de Vries canning factory in Spalding. The factory had been erected in Marsh Rails Road in the 1940s, on the eastern extremity of the town. At the time, there had been no buildings beyond it, but now a complex of light industrial businesses and market gardens stretched all the way to Wardentree Lane, beyond which lay the large village of Pinchbeck.

Margaret Nugent was a large-boned lady in her fifties. Although she had been working in her office when the receptionist announced Andy's arrival, she was ostentatiously clad in the white lab coat and white trilby hat that the office workers were required to don when they walked through the factory. She rose to greet Andy without offering to shake hands. She gestured at a small plastic chair that had been placed in front of her desk, before seating herself again. She made a point of continuing to write something in the margin of the document placed in front of her. Eventually she reached the end of the document and signed it with a flourish.

"Now," she said, regarding Andy with unfriendly, watery blue eyes. "What is it that you wanted?" She made no attempt to call Andy by his rank or make other reference to his status of policeman.

Andy sat in the plastic chair as bidden and immediately felt at a disadvantage. The chair was much lower than her own, with the result that, although he was taller than she, he still had to peer up at her in order to look her in the eye. Its round plastic seat, as well as being extremely uncomfortable, was also very small. Andy was uncomfortably aware of his thighs and buttocks as they bulged untidily beyond it on both sides. If not actually designed to humiliate, it was surely an item of furniture selected to discourage those to whom it was assigned from spending more time in Miss Nugent's office than was absolutely necessary.

"Thank you for taking my call earlier, Miss Nugent," Andy had said, hoping to disarm her with chatty friendliness. "It's good of you to see me at such short notice. Now, can I just confirm once again that you are personnel officer for all of the staff at de Vries Industries, not just the people who work at this factory?"

Miss Nugent inclined her head.

"That is correct. As the company has grown, I've had some assistance: Moira, the receptionist whom you've now met, does some work for me when she's on the desk and I can call on help from the typing pool. But it makes sense for one person to be in charge of all the staff, because it's easier to move people around between the businesses, or ask them to change shifts."

"Are you saying that you personally know everyone who works for Kevan de Vries?"

She scrutinised him for some seconds.

"More or less. Not all the casual seasonal labour, naturally, but I can put names to faces for most of the regular staff."

"So you're in charge of the staff at the food-packing plant at Sutton Bridge?"

"I wouldn't say I was *in charge* of them. They have their

own line managers, or they *are* line managers. I'm responsible for seeing that they get paid and for their welfare. The three 't's: tea, towels and toilets. That's what personnel managers are supposed to be about, isn't it?" She smiled bleakly at her own joke. Andy gave her an enthusiastic smile in return.

"As I mentioned on the telephone, I'm here in connection with a suspected murder. The body of a young woman has been found in the woods at Sandringham. She was wearing an overall and overshoes belonging to de Vries Industries. We don't yet know her identity. We have a working theory that she was employed at the food-packing plant because Sutton Bridge is much closer to where she was found than any of the other de Vries operations. But of course we could be jumping to the wrong conclusions entirely."

Miss Nugent looked at him steadily without speaking. He found her passively-hostile intransigence intimidating.

"Miss Nugent?"

"Yes?"

"I wondered if you had any comment to make. Something that could help us."

"What sort of comment?"

"Well, for example, have any of the staff at Sutton Bridge been reported missing, or unexpectedly failed to turn up for work?"

"Not to my knowledge. But I wouldn't expect such details to be reported to me unless the person concerned was a persistent offender, or in need of formal disciplining."

"Do you pay staff for unexplained absences?"

"Not *unexplained* absences. Sickness benefit is paid according to statutory obligations. Staff may request days off unpaid. And then there is their annual holiday entitlement."

"So you'd know if someone had failed to turn up for work

but was neither off sick nor on holiday – nor taking the day off unpaid?"

"I'd know at the end of the month, when I receive the weekly time-sheets. If the supervisors had filled them in correctly and not tried to cover the absence out of some misplaced idea of loyalty, that is."

"Does that happen much?"

"Not as far as I can prove. But sometimes I have my suspicions, naturally."

Not for the first time while they'd been talking, Andy wondered why Miss Nugent had chosen a career in which 'staff welfare' was supposed to play a prominent part.

"Do you have a picture of this woman?" she asked with sudden avidity.

"Not yet. I'm hoping to have one sketched by an artist shortly. It will be based on the face of the corpse, but remove the distressing details. For public circulation."

Miss Nugent looked at him stonily. Andy thought to himself that he might have produced the head from a plastic carrier bag and laid it on her desk and she would still have looked as unmoved.

"I'm not sure how I can help you. But I'll check with the supervisors at Sutton Bridge."

"Thank you. What about the clothes she was wearing?"

"What about them? I doubt that we'd want them back. We operate strict rules of hygiene here."

"I didn't think you'd want to use them again! But if I bring them to you, will that help you to help me? Would you be able to say what tasks the victim was engaged in? Or identify the clothes in some way, say when they were issued, that type of thing?"

There was another long pause.

"I'll have a look at them, but I very much doubt that it'll

help. We buy the overalls in bulk from a Chinese supplier. They come embroidered with the de Vries logo, but we don't mark them ourselves. They come in all sizes, from an 8 to a 22. All the workers wear the same ones, regardless of the jobs that they do. And everyone is issued with them. The only staff who don't have them are the office workers who never go into the plants, but there are only a few of those, as many of the lower grade office workers choose to supplement their incomes with the odd evening shift from time to time."

"What about the senior managers and directors?"

"Senior staff have white coats like this one, and are issued with white hats. When we're in the plants we wear the same white rubber shoes as the rest of the staff."

"And seasonal staff?"

"Seasonal staff are also required to wear the overalls; it would be a contravention of the hygiene rules if they didn't. But they're only issued with two each and I try to give them older stock if possible – I mean, overalls that have been handed in by leavers."

"Any particular reason for that? Or is it just that they aren't as valued as the regular staff?"

"That's a very inflammatory suggestion, Mr... I'm sorry, I don't remember your name."

"Detective Constable Carstairs," said Andy, accentuating the first two words.

"Yes. Well, all of our employees are equally regarded, but, in the case of some of the gang women, there have been instances of the overalls – and, especially, the rubber shoes – not having been returned. We stop an appropriate amount from their wages if we find out in time, but this is a further precaution to protect company profits."

"Are you saying that there's a black market in de Vries factory clothing?"

CHRISTINA JAMES

Miss Nugent shrugged.

"How should I know? Personally, I can't imagine why anyone would want to keep one of our overalls once they've left our employment. The shoes, I agree, might come in useful for working on the land or, I suppose, for wearing when carrying out household chores."

"But there's a possibility that this clothing might come into the possession of someone who's never been a de Vries employee?"

"Notionally, yes."

"That could make the job of identifying the victim much more difficult. Miss Nugent, as I'm sure you're aware, murder enquiries are time critical. We've already lost the precious first few days after the victim's likely date of death because the body has only just been discovered. We need all the co-operation that we can get if we are still to catch whoever did it."

"That is quite understood. But, as I've already said, I'm afraid that I probably can't be of much help."

"No, you're *probably* right," said Andy. Miss Nugent blinked a little at this forthright statement and sat up straighter in her chair. "I probably need to speak to someone more at the coal face, if you'll allow me," he continued smoothly. "How many supervisors are there at the Sutton Bridge plant?"

"Eight, I believe. They're not all there at the same time: that plant operates two shifts per day, from 6 a.m. to 2 p.m. and from 2 p.m. to 10 p.m."

"So it might be possible, say, to meet them all together just before or just after 2 p.m.?"

"In exceptional circumstances, I suppose so. But I'm not a director. You'd need a director's permission to halt work at the plant in that way."

"Permission from the Operations Director, I suppose?"

"No. No – we don't have one as such. It would be permission

145

from my own boss. He's the Finance Director, but I report to him as well as the two financial controllers."

"Could you let me have his name and contact details?" Andy had already guessed what her reply would be.

"Certainly. It's Mr Sentance. Tony Sentance."

TWENTY-EIGHT

Tim called Giash Chakrabati as soon as he reached his office.

"I want to carry out a further search at Laurieston House, now that Ms Gardner's finished there. I'll contact Kevan de Vries again, as a courtesy, but I can't see any reason for him to disagree to it. Assuming there aren't any hitches, will you be able to meet me there at 11 a.m?"

"Yes, sir. And PC Tandy, too?"

"I was assuming that you'd bring her. She's detailed to accompany you everywhere at the moment, isn't she?"

"Yes, for the next month. If you don't want her to come, though, I'm sure she can spend the afternoon on desk work."

Tim hesitated. He'd taken a dislike to the new female PC, which he knew to be unfair. He didn't want her to pick up on it, as he knew that would cause problems later if he had a legitimate reason to get rid of her and she could claim that she'd been discriminated against.

"Er . . . no, no, that's OK. There'll be some heavy lifting to do and quite a lot of stuff to move, so we'll need her help as well. You'd better both bring overalls. Get some for me, too, if you can, will you?"

"Of course," said Giash. "We'll see you there."

"Don't attempt to go in until I get there. I'm wary of putting a foot wrong where Kevan de Vries is concerned. I don't want that solicitor of his coming down on me. I've had dealings with her before."

"OK. We'll park near the green in Sutterton, if you'd like to give us a call when you arrive."

Tim's next task was to phone Kevan de Vries. He tried the landline of Laurieston House. A female voice answered. He knew immediately that it wasn't Jean Rook.

"Could I speak to Mr de Vries, please?"

"I'm afraid he's not here at the moment," said the woman, her voice fluttery. She had a slight Lincolnshire accent. "Can I take a message?"

"Is that Mrs Briggs? It's DI Yates speaking."

"Oh, hello. I think Mr Kevan's gone to the airport, to meet his wife. I'm not sure when he'll be back."

"His *wife*? I thought that she'd decided to stay in St Lucia."

"I think she's changed her mind."

"I see." It was on the tip of Tim's tongue to ask her for more details, but he realised that this would be unprofessional of him. Jackie Briggs probably didn't know the reasons for her employers' actions, and if she did she would consider it disloyal to discuss them. "Shall I call Mr de Vries on his mobile?"

"That would be best," she said. She put the phone down precipitately. Tim cursed. He would have to search through his notebook for the number now. He knew that if it had been Juliet, she would already have programmed it into her own mobile.

He found the number without too much trouble. His call was answered immediately.

"Yes?"

"Mr de Vries? It's DI Yates. I'm still investigating the skeletons that were found in your cellar. I'd like your permission to carry out a further search, if that's OK with you? It's a forlorn hope, I know, but there may be something else down there that can throw more light on who those women were and how they died. I'm not suggesting that you or your family are implicated in any way, as you know."

There was a sigh at the other end of the phone, followed by some seconds of silence before Kevan de Vries replied.

"Have you talked to Miss Rook about this?"

"No, sir. Technically speaking, we don't need to, as we already have a warrant. This is a courtesy call, more than anything."

"I see. When do you want to do it?"

"From eleven o'clock today, if convenient."

"Of course it's not *convenient*," Kevan de Vries shot back, "but, as it happens, if you must go poking about in there again, I'd prefer it if you were to do it now. My wife has returned from St Lucia. I've just picked her up at the airport – you're lucky she isn't with me at this moment. I certainly don't want her peace of mind to be disturbed any more than it is already by having you and your men clodhopping around the house."

"I understand. Thank you, sir." Tim congratulated himself on the pragmatic politeness of his reply. Not so long ago, he would have retaliated to such rudeness in kind. He felt Juliet's invisible presence, standing like a guardian angel at his elbow. He hesitated about whether to enquire after Joanna de Vries and decided that he should. "I hope that Mrs de Vries is no worse?" he ventured.

"Who knows the real answer to that? Physically, she's slipping away inch by inch. Mentally, she's much more agitated than when I left her. You may not be surprised to hear that your investigation is a contributing factor."

"I'm sorry about that, sir. When will you arrive home with her?"

"Probably early this evening. I'm taking her straight to see our son. You've caught me just as I was returning to the airport terminal for something. She's waiting for me in the car. I don't want her upset by your calls."

"I understand, sir. Thank you for agreeing to the search. How shall I gain entry to your house?"

"Jackie Briggs should be there at the moment. She can let you in. Where are you? Are you in Sutterton now?"

"No, I'm in Spalding. I can be there in twenty minutes. There'll be some colleagues helping me: the same officers who assisted DC MacFadyen earlier in the week."

"Jackie should still be there when you arrive, but just to make sure I'll give her a call. I know that she has several jobs in the village. I'll ask her to leave the key with Harry Briggs if she's finished her work at Laurieston and plans on going out again. You know where their house is, I take it?"

"Yes, sir, thank you." Inwardly, Tim cursed again. He didn't want Harry Briggs clinging to him like a leech while they were carrying out the search. He suspected that Harry might alert Tony Sentance to their presence, as well. Still, it was unlikely that Jackie would keep the visit to herself, even if she was able to wait until he arrived.

"And DI Yates?" Kevan de Vries' tone was suddenly devoid of its former hauteur. He sounded almost supplicatory.

"Yes, Mr de Vries?"

"Could you do me an immense favour, and make sure that you and your colleagues have left for the day by the time that I come home with Joanna? It shouldn't be before six this evening, but if it's earlier I'll call you while we're en route. It's essential that I try to keep her as calm and tranquil as possible. I hope that you'll be able to complete whatever it is you're doing by the end of the afternoon, but if not and you have to return tomorrow, so be it. At least it will give me a little time to explain to her. She doesn't know about the skeletons yet, you see."

"Of course," said Tim. "We'll try to make it as easy as we can. Thank you again for co-operating with us."

As Tim pressed the red button to finish the call, he reflected that, unpleasant and difficult though it might be, it would be interesting to meet Joanna de Vries. He was sure that the miasma of tension and unhappiness that seemed to descend upon Kevan de Vries every time he mentioned his wife could not be explained solely by her illness. De Vries was also unique among the parents of Tim's acquaintance in never seeming to express anything but irritation and anxiety when he talked about his son. Were they just a dysfunctional family, or was there a more tangible reason for the tangle of misery that had swamped their household?

TWENTY-NINE

I'm sitting in the car outside Archie's school. Joanna is visiting Archie at this moment. She has forbidden me to accompany her. She's enlisted the support of that smug little runt of a housemaster, who's just been out to the car to shake my hand and assure me that, regrettably, he agrees with her that my presence will make Archie too agitated. I've refused his invitation to wait in the reception area with its plush tea machine. I suppose that he thinks that he's just about been polite enough to persuade me to continue to pay his inflated fees. If he stopped to think at all, he'd realise that, however much I might despise him, I have no option but to continue sending Archie to the school, even when Joanna is no longer with us, unless Archie turns against the place. Archie himself pulls all the levers in that respect.

Joanna's illness and her bizarre relationship with Sentance have not only imprisoned me completely, they've also wrong-footed me. I might as well be wearing a strait-jacket for my sins. If only I could get her to talk to me civilly, I wouldn't feel so trapped. I don't expect to receive any of the vestiges of love that she has left in her: I've come to recognise that the huge reservoir of affection and generosity with which she used to be filled has gradually seeped away with her pain. Mortal illness is more hideous than I could ever have imagined. The small stock of concern and fondness that she has left is all for Archie. Her son. She makes a point of emphasising that. Archie is *my* son. He's *my* heir, if he's ever well enough to shape up to it, but I'm not allowed to be his father. Except for Opa, fathers seem destined to fail in our family.

I'm mildly irritated by what that detective's up to, but I know there's no point in crossing him. I want him out of my hair as quickly as possible and now that he knows that Joanna has come home she's removed my excuse to push him to hurry himself. I'm certain that Jean would have tried to stall him when he asked to search the house again, but I know there's no point. It would have irritated him and he'd have got what he wanted in the end. Jean should confine herself to getting to the bottom of this passport business. I'll tell her that next time we speak. Perhaps she's working on it now: she seems to have gone to ground for the past forty-eight hours. She doesn't know that Joanna's back. Not that Joanna would consider that Jean is entitled to know her movements.

As if I've summoned her with my thoughts, my mobile rings and I see Jean's number flash on to the display.

"Jean. How are you?"

"I'm fine, Kevan. What about you? Briggs tells me that Joanna's returned to the UK."

"It's not up to Briggs to pass around information about my family. Why have you been in touch with him, anyway?"

"I rang you at home and he answered. He was there with Jackie. He said that she was there because the police were about to return. What exactly is happening? And why don't you want me to know that Joanna's back?"

"If Jackie's still at the house, I don't see why she's asked Briggs to be there too. I shall have to speak to her about that. The police are still working on their investigation into the skeletons – it's nothing to do with me or Joanna. I gave them permission to search further, therefore. It's best that they think that I'm co-operating as much as I can. And I have no objection to your knowing that Joanna's here: of course I don't. But, equally, you will be aware that Joanna herself won't be delighted to see you. I suggest that you continue your work on the passport business from your office as much as possible, now that she's going to be at Laurieston again."

"If you say so, Kevan. I know that we no longer have a . . . *social* relationship. You should have told me about the police, though. I could have stopped them from being so precipitate in their demands."

"I agree that they only gave me short notice, but it actually suits me to get them to do as much as they can while Joanna isn't there. I've explained this to them. She'll be upset enough about it as it is."

"You haven't told her, then? About the skeletons?"

"No, not yet. She's with Archie at the moment. That's why she came home: because he appeared to be going into a relapse again. She didn't want to stay at St Lucia on her own, anyway."

"So he provided her with the perfect excuse to do exactly as she wanted?"

"Don't go too far, Jean. What Joanna wants and how we arrange our lives is not your affair. What I particularly want *you* to do is find out where the police have got to with their enquiries into the passports. They're not the only ones who want to get to the bottom of that. I want my name off their radar as soon as you can possibly manage it. I can try to use my influence with Superintendent Thornton if you think it will do any good?"

"It might come to that, but I'll try other avenues first. I've met DI Yates before, on a case I worked on a couple of years ago. He's shrewd, and also quite self-aware. It might backfire if we try to go over his head too soon."

"Well, I'll leave it to your good judgement. I'm sure that you'll get the result that we want, one way or another. Christ!"

"What's the matter?"

"Joanna's coming back to the car. That little toad of a housemaster has got his arm round her. She looks as if she's been crying."

Jean ignores this.

"Do you want me to go to Laurieston and stay there with the police?"

"Certainly not. I'm intending to keep Joanna away from there for the whole of the afternoon, if I can, but if we should arrive back early and you're there as well as the police, it will only make matters worse."

"Charmed, I'm sure. Well, I'd better leave you to it, then. I'll call you again tomorrow."

"Thanks." I switch her off, relieved. Another couple of minutes and I would have had to ask her to terminate the call.

THIRTY

Almost as soon as Tim had swung the BMW into the sweep of Laurieston House, Giash Chakrabati's patrol car pulled in behind him. Tim smiled to himself. Giash was ever obliging, always efficient. He had a subtle touch, too. He'd have made an excellent addition to Tim's team of detectives, but, on the one occasion that Tim had broached this, Giash was adamant that he enjoyed being a uniformed policeman. When Tim had asked why, Giash said (with a meaningful look) that he didn't like internal intrigue. Tim had been about to probe further when Giash took his mind off it by adding that he thought that it was important to have Asian policemen on the streets, particularly in Lincolnshire, a county that until recently had known few ethnic minorities but in which they were now gathering apace. Local prejudices still ran high.

He got out of the BMW quickly and crunched his way across the gravel before Giash could emerge from his car, bending to tap on the window on the driver's side. Giash pushed the switch to lower it.

"Thanks for coming so quickly, Giash," said Tim. "I'd like you to stay here until I've announced myself. I'm not sure who's going to be there to meet us and I'd like to gauge the situation before we all turn up on the doorstep. If Mrs Briggs is on her own, I don't want to alarm her too much."

"Should I come with you, sir? She may be happier to see another woman."

Tim looked across Giash and noticed Verity Tandy for the first time. She looked more prepossessing than last time they'd met. Her hair appeared to be newly washed and she'd pinned it up into a kind of topknot. She was also smiling, which made her white and rather flabby countenance more engaging.

"Good morning, PC Tandy. Thank you – that's a nice idea. I think I'd rather be on my own at first, though."

Verity Tandy shrugged, the smile disappearing rapidly. It was an inappropriate gesture to make towards a superior, but he decided to overlook it. Perhaps she was just shy, as Juliet had suggested, and had had to screw up her courage in order to make the suggestion.

"I'll give you a call when I've done the preliminaries," he said to Giash, who nodded.

Tim scrunched back across the gravel – as on the previous occasion, he wondered in passing why it was so deep – and disappeared into Laurieston's cavernous porch. He was about to pull on the old-fashioned bell when the door was flung open. A powerfully-built, short and stocky man was standing there. He was looking rather sinister, as if he had been in a fight, because there was a large and none-too-clean dressing stuck on his cheek; it dominated his face. He was wearing work clothes which were serviceable without being shabby. He extended a grubby hand, on the back of which sprouted clumps of coarse black hair, as if he were a dog with the mange.

"Detective Inspector Yates?" he asked, with somewhat forced cordiality. "I'm Harry Briggs, Jackie's 'usband. Come in. She's expecting you."

Tim's hackles rose at the effrontery of the man. He was increasingly doubtful that his original assessment of Kevan de Vries had been correct. First Tony Sentance and now Harry Briggs seemed to be treating their boss's home as if they owned it. Under his suave, apparently controlling exterior, was de Vries actually a pushover? Or did he let these people domineer him for some other reason?

Tim was spared the handshake, because at that moment Jackie Briggs emerged from the recesses of the hall and ducked around her husband. Tim noted that she was wearing the pinafore dress that she'd been dressed in at their first meeting, when he and Juliet had escorted Kevan de Vries home from the airport. Clearly she thought it a suitable outfit in which to receive visitors, or visiting policemen, anyway. The shirt she'd chosen today was short-sleeved, but as on Monday it was pinned at the throat with the same large, old-fashioned brooch that she'd used then to fasten the collar tightly up to her neck. The result was almost a parody of primness.

"DI Yates," she said in a high, uncertain voice. "Mr Kevan said that I should expect you."

"Good afternoon, Mrs Briggs. It's good of you to have waited for me. Mr de Vries said that he'd ask your husband to take over if you had other business to attend to. I hadn't expected to see both of you here, though."

"Oh, Harry's come because I popped home to change after I'd finished the cleaning. I was hardly respectable!" She gave an affected little laugh, as if she'd said something risqué. "I've only just got back again."

Tim nodded at Harry Briggs.

"Thank you, Mr Briggs." He turned back to Jackie. "If you're able to stay, we won't need to keep your husband any longer."

She opened her mouth to reply, but before she could say any more Harry Briggs jumped in.

"I'll stay now I'm here," he said gruffly. "Jackie doesn't like it down the cellar. She gets claustrophobic."

"There's no need for either of you to accompany us . . ."

"I think I'd better," said Harry, more overtly hostile now. "I've had a word with Mr Sentance, and he thinks I should.

I can help with some of the moving, if you like. How many of you are there, three?"

"Yes. My two colleagues are waiting outside."

"D'you want me to fetch them in?"

"That's not necessary," said Tim. "I'll get them myself in a bit. They're just . . ." his voice trailed off. He had no need to offer Harry Briggs an explanation and realised belatedly that to do so would only weaken his own position. He wondered why Briggs had involved Tony Sentance. He supposed it was nothing to do with him, but it offered yet another example of these two men's apparently working behind their boss's back, in cahoots with each other. He fixed Briggs steadily with his eye.

"Mr Briggs, if you have instructions from Mr de Vries to remain here while we're on the premises, of course I'm in no position to object. But, much as I value your offer of help, I'm afraid you'll have to allow us to do our work in the cellar on our own. There's a risk of contaminating the evidence, otherwise."

"What evidence?"

"That's what we're here to find out. It's nothing that need concern you. I'm pretty certain that the bones that were found down there had already been here for many years before you were even born."

Jackie Briggs laid her hand gently on Briggs's arm.

"Why don't you come with me to make some tea, Harry?" she said appeasingly.

Harry Briggs moved as if to shake her off, but thought better of it. He disengaged himself quite firmly from her grasp and turned back into the house without another word.

"You'll have to excuse Harry," she said to Tim, giving him a wan smile. "He was shaken up by that young hooligan on Sunday. He's not been himself since. He's ever so polite normally."

"I understand," said Tim, smiling more readily himself. He liked Mrs Briggs, but he would stake his life that her husband was not the solid gold citizen she was at pains to suggest. Whether she really believed her assessment of his character or had introduced it from a misplaced conviction of loyalty was impossible to gauge. Tim remembered, even if Briggs had no other pressing work to take him elsewhere, that Jackie herself was holding down three jobs. "Thank you, Mrs Briggs. I know that Mr de Vries wanted one of you to stay here, but since your husband clearly doesn't intend to leave, don't let us keep you from your other work."

"What? Oh, you mean my other little jobs. It's OK. I did the ice-cream vans this morning, and there's only one ambulance at the garage today. I can go down there after you've left."

She continued to hover. Tim broke the impasse by moving back towards the front door.

"I'll fetch my colleagues now," he said. "And, as you kindly suggested, some tea would be very welcome."

Jackie Briggs smiled relief. She turned to head for the kitchen, slightly ungainly in heels that were higher than she was used to.

Five minutes later, Tim and Giash Chakrabati and Verity Tandy had descended into the cellar, bearing hot mugs of tea with them. Giash produced overalls and plastic overshoes from the holdall that he'd slung over his shoulder. "Hairnet, anyone?" he asked.

"I don't think we need to go that far," said Tim. Verity Tandy looked stern. "If you think I'm going to mess up my hair, you can think again. I spent ten minutes doing it like this this morning."

"Very nice, too," said Giash. She beamed. Tim noted with approval that Giash had an easy way of being around Verity.

Her prickliness seemed to dissolve under his influence. "How are we going to tackle this, Boss?" Giash injected just enough irony into the appellation to make it funny rather than creepy.

"I think we should move that old red carpet that's been hung over this pile of stuff here to see exactly what there is beneath it. We'll have to be careful, because I don't want it to fall on the area that Ms Gardner's marked out, where the skeletons were dug up. It's filthy, too, and likely to generate a dust cloud. We'd probably be best off wearing masks. We'll finish this tea first."

Giash duly fished three masks out of his bag and handed them out. They drank the tea and put them on.

"Go over to the far end, Giash," said Tim, "and see if you can get a purchase on the carpet over there. I'll lift it from this side. PC Tandy, if you could just stand between me and the cordoned-off area, to make sure that I don't step on the soil where the paving has been removed."

Tim and Giash worked in unison to shift the carpet. As Tim had expected, it weighed a ton. As they lifted it, clouds of dust rose with it. The carpet itself smelt foul – worse than musty, there was some underlying stench that Tim couldn't quite define. Between them, they managed to hoist it into the air and then double it back on itself, so that there was just room enough to lay it on the floor to one side of the excavation.

Underneath it was a mishmash of furniture and large-ish artefacts – as well as two wardrobes and a Dutch dresser, Tim could see brass pots, an old-fashioned push-chair, an enamel portable bidet, an old treadle sewing machine and several iron bedsteads.

"I'm not sure how we're going to work through these with that carpet sitting there," he said. "There's not going to be space to take them out and examine them."

"If we fold the carpet again, you could pass me some of the smaller items and I'll take them into the next room," said Verity Tandy.

Tim thought about it and nodded. He was impressed: he had not expected an intelligent contribution from her.

They devoted half an hour or so to passing to Verity the more portable items. Tim carried the treadle sewing machine through himself and Giash moved some small tables. By the time they'd finished, the centre of the floor in the middle room was completely covered with small pieces of furniture and other household goods.

"Work through that lot and see if you can find anything interesting," Tim said to Verity. "Some of those things have got drawers in them, or other places that could conceal stuff."

She seemed almost over-pleased to have been given this task.

"Certainly. What sort of 'stuff' am I looking for?"

"Documents, I suppose. Or anything else that might give us a clue. Anything unusual, that you wouldn't expect to find here."

Giash grinned.

"That either gives her plenty of scope, or not much at all. I'm not sure what she could *expect* to find in a place like this. Almost anything seems possible."

"Point taken," said Tim. "Just use your discretion, will you, Verity? I'm sure you'll pick up on it if you find something that could provide a link to the skeletons, or whoever put them here."

He turned away from her too soon to see how pleased she was that he'd called her by her first name.

"What does that leave for us, now?" he asked Giash.

"A whole load of furniture. It's not all from the same period. The mahogany pieces look to me as if they're Victorian. The dresser and some of the other things – that table, for example, and those high stools – date from later. They look continental – Scandinavian possibly. The mahogany stuff is English, I'm sure. I'm not sure what era those hideous red button-backed chairs belong to."

"Quite an authority, aren't you? But you're right – there are two lots of furniture down here. That fits with what Kevan de Vries said: that some of it belonged to his grandfather, some of it to the old lady who owned the house before him."

"So the earlier stuff could have been in the house when the skeletons – or the people to whom they belonged – first came here?"

"Yes, but it probably wasn't in the cellar then. It's worth working through it, nevertheless. I'm guessing that whoever put it down here will have gone through all the drawers and cupboards at the time – I certainly would have – but not everyone is curious about the past. And even if they did look, they may have missed something."

"There's something funny about all of this," said Giash.

"Well, I agree with you there. It's not every day that you find three skeletons and five forged passports in a place like this. But I assume you're referring to something specific that you've just noticed?"

"Yes. Two things, in fact. One is that this furniture is remarkably free of dust. The other is that some of the earlier stuff is in front of the later stuff: so it must have been moved at least once."

Tim was unconvinced.

"You may be right, but I'm not sure it's of any significance. That carpet was doing its job pretty well. And whoever brought the second lot of furniture down probably had to move what was already here in order to fit it all in."

Giash shrugged.

"Just a thought," he said.

"We don't need to bother with the tables, stools and small chairs," said Tim. "They won't tell us anything. We'll move them out of the way and look through the drawers of these cabinets and dressers first, and then move *them* as much as we can to get to those two wardrobes at the back."

"OK."

Giash began stacking the chairs in a pile in the far corner. One of the tables was gate-legged and folded up neatly. He lifted it quite easily and placed it beside the chairs. The other was made of metal, hideously topped with turquoise formica. He dragged it across to the corner as far as it would go.

"Let me move those chairs out again," said Tim. "We can probably stack them on this, if we can push it right up against the wall."

"OK," Giash said again. "I'll help you." He divided the pile of chairs into two and, taking one of them, leant back against the wall so that Tim could remove the ones that he'd left on the table.

"Ouch!" he said. He put the chairs down on the floor in front of him and drew his hand across the back of his head. When he examined it, he saw that whatever it was he'd bumped his head against had drawn blood.

"Are you all right?" said Tim.

"Yes, I think so. I've just cut the back of my head on some-thing. It's stinging a bit, but I think that it's just a slight graze."

"Let me see," said Tim. He'd meant that Giash should let him look at the wound, but instead the PC stepped to one side so that Tim could get closer to the wall. It was very dark in this part of the cellar – the low wattage light bulb did not reach into the outer shadows – but they'd brought a torch. Tim shone it on the spot where Giash had been standing. He saw that a vicious-looking hook had been driven into the masonry there;

it was rusty with age, though the metal wasn't flaking, as if it might have been used fairly recently. Turning the torch beam along the wall, Tim could make out two similar hooks, forming a row with a couple of metres between them.

"Good God!" he said. "I wonder what those were for."

Giash turned round to see for himself and touched his scalp gingerly. It was still bleeding, though not copiously.

"I think you need to get an antiseptic wipe for that," said Tim. "You'll have some in the car, won't you?"

"I'll go for you," said Verity, suddenly appearing from beyond the archway that led to the second room. "I'll put a dressing on it, too."

She made for the stairs. They could hear the scuffle of her footsteps in their plastic overshoes as she climbed them. The scuffling ceased as she reached the top of the flight and opened the door that led into Laurieston's hallway.

"Hello," said a voice. "I think we met briefly on Monday?"

"Good afternoon, Mr Sentance," said Verity. Standing out of sight in the cellar below, Tim guessed that she'd deliberately raised her voice in order to warn him and Giash of Tony Sentance's arrival. "Can I help you, sir?" she added, still speaking very distinctly.

"That's sweet of you, but I'm really looking for your boss. DI Yates, I mean. I'm assuming that he *is* your boss?"

"Not directly, sir, but I'm assisting him at the moment. Shall I tell him that you're here?"

"If he's down there, as Jackie's led me to believe, I can announce myself perfectly well. You may run along on whatever errand he's sent you on."

Tim smiled in spite of himself. He'd have given a lot to have seen Verity's expression at that moment. If she deemed Sentance's patronising comment worthy of a reply, Tim did not hear what it was. It was evident that Verity had continued on her way, because Sentance's heavy-soled brogue shoes could first be heard and then seen clattering down the steps. He reached the bottom as Tim emerged from the shadows to greet him. Tim saw his face for a split second before he composed it into an ingratiating smile. He might have expected to read anger there, or perhaps an exasperated kind of languor. Instead, what he had observed fleetingly but very clearly etched into Tony Sentance's countenance was unmistakably fear.

"Good afternoon, Mr Sentance. We weren't expecting you."

"Harry Briggs told me that you'd asked if you could come here again and, since Mr Kevan is otherwise engaged this afternoon, I thought I'd come to check that everything was all right."

"You didn't come at Mr de Vries' specific request, then?"

"I . . . no. I've not spoken to Mr Kevan today. He's preoccupied, but I know if he'd thought of it, he would have asked me to be here."

"Why is that?"

"Good grief, is that blood on your hand?" said Sentance, directing the question at Giash and, Tim thought, hamming up his feeling of concern quite considerably.

"PC Chakrabati has grazed his scalp on a hook in the wall. It's just a surface wound, but we'll dress it to be on the safe side. That hook's a murderous-looking thing, though. You don't happen to know why it's there, do you?"

Tim had waited for Sentance to come out with his customary mantra: that Laurieston was not his house, so he could not be expected to know the whys and wherefores of what had gone on there. He was therefore mildly surprised when Sentance said in an unusually co-operative voice:

"As a matter of fact, I do."

Tim looked at him. Evidently not a master of timing,

Sentance was obviously trying to achieve a bit of éclat; probably, Tim reflected, to steer the conversation about whether Kevan de Vries wanted him there or not.

"Well, go on," said Tim. "Enlighten us. We're all ears!"

"Very well. I think that Mr Kevan may have told you that his grandfather bought this house from an old lady. Her name was Mrs Jacobs. Jackie lived in the village at the time – has always lived in the village, in fact – and she, like Mr Kevan, just about remembers the old woman. Mrs Jacobs had a housekeeper, a Mrs Izatt, who was also Jackie's grandmother. Jackie says that she didn't get on particularly well with Mrs Jacobs, who I gather was in any case a bit gaga by then, but of course she talked to the old girl in the evenings and found out quite a lot about her early life and this place. Mrs Jacobs' husband was much older than she was. He didn't actually have this house built. His mother bought it for him when he was a young man, presumably after she herself was widowed. It was almost new then. Apparently the dowager Mrs Jacobs – if I may call her that – had an eye for a bargain, and bought this house from a butcher who had built it for himself and then gone bankrupt. I've reason to believe that this is true, because the older locals here still call this place 'Sausage Hall'. I suppose the nickname's been passed down through the generations."

"That's fascinating," said Tim. "Thank you." Giash – who had been quite bored by all of this – threw him a sidelong look and realised that there was no shred of irony implied in his words. Tim delighted in historical details of this kind.

"So you're saying that these hooks were probably put there by the butcher?"

Sentance tried to look unassuming.

"It stands to reason, doesn't it?"

"It's certainly a possible explanation," said Tim. "Do you know anything else about Mrs Jacobs' husband?"

"Only that he was a gentleman farmer who never actually got his hands dirty – not on English soil, anyway. He spent much of his youth exploring, I believe. That's why he married so late."

"Did he have any children? Any descendants that we might possibly be able to trace?"

"I believe there was a son, whose name was Gordon. He was in late middle age when Mr Kevan was a boy, so if he were still alive, he'd be very old now. It's unlikely, I think. Why don't you come upstairs for some tea? We can wait until Mr Kevan comes back, then. If he knows any more, I'm sure that he'll be happy to talk to you about it."

"Thank you, but we've had tea already and Mr de Vries particularly asked me to have finished for the day by the time he returns with his wife." Tim looked at his watch. "We've got less than two hours left now, so if you'll forgive me, we'll press on."

"Oh, but let me help you put those things back where they came from. We can have it shipshape again in no time at all."

"I'm afraid we haven't finished yet," said Tim. "We want to move all of the furniture out to look at it, even those big wardrobes at the back. As you see, we have some way to go." Nice try, he thought. But why was Tony Sentance so keen on getting them out of the cellar? He should guess that that would only make them the more determined to examine it properly.

"Gosh, you *have* got your work cut out. I think you're being a little ambitious, but I'll leave you to it. Give me a shout if you need me. I'll be waiting in the kitchen with Jackie. I hope your head gets better soon," he threw over his shoulder at Giash, as he began to plod up the stairs again. He almost collided with Verity on her way back down, clutching the first aid kit from the car. There was some awkward manoeuvring on the stairs as these two large and ungainly people squeezed past each other, which Tim secretly relished. Then Sentance was

168

gone, but within easy reach, as he had himself pointed out. Knowing that he was now at Laurieston made the house feel very oppressive indeed.

THIRTY-ONE

Joanna shakes the hand of the housemaster. He opens the car door for her and she gets in in her usual way, seating herself first and then swivelling round her legs with her customary elegance. She has not allowed illness to compromise her standards. I feel a rush of pity and tender love for her. My lip trembles, but then I see the odious little man looking across her. He is grinning – whether at my discomfort or because he has just uttered some valedictory witticism, I can't tell. If he did speak, I wasn't listening to him. I turn on the ignition and rev up the engine. Reluctantly, he slams shut the door for Joanna and stands back. As we draw away, I look back in the mirror and see that he is waving like a maniac.

I give Joanna a sidelong glance. Her face is long, her cheeks sunken, her eyes somehow smaller and more receded into their sockets. Her expression is set, to show me how angry she still is, but what she most conveys is her sheer exhaustion. Of course, we've both known for some time that Joanna has only a few months left, but it suddenly dawns on me how close she now is to death. She barely seems strong enough to last the night, perhaps too fragile even to take the journey back to Laurieston. She is living on willpower alone; the skull beneath the flesh is gaining ground by the hour.

"You look tired. When we get home, you must rest. Spend tomorrow in bed. The flight has worn you out."

"Rest isn't going to help me now. In any case, I don't feel

any worse than I did when I was lolling around in St Lucia. I'm glad to be back. Nothing's more important than making sure that Archie is as OK as he can be. I must have been mad to allow you to persuade me to go away in the first place."

"It was a joint decision," I remind her, "and one based partly on what we thought would be best for Archie. If you remember, we didn't think it would be good for him to see you . . ." I pause, searching for words that will not devastate.

"On my way out, you mean?" Her tone is bleak, her look savage.

"I was going to say, looking ill." I know this sounds feeble and insincere. I look at her again. She's staring straight ahead, unseeing. I feel for her hand. She snatches it away.

"Concentrate on the road, will you? Hideous as this illness is, I don't want to die in the wreckage of your bloody car."

"How is Archie?"

"Tearful. Confused. Resentful."

"Resentful of what?"

"Not what, whom. You, mostly."

"He has no reason to resent me, unless you've encouraged him to." I'm desperate not to pick a quarrel with her, but I know I can't let this pass.

"He found out that you'd come home without going straight to see him, as I asked. And he knows you tried to make me stay in St Lucia."

"I see." I decide not to pursue this, but I wonder if it's just Joanna who's been telling Archie these things. If someone else has been unsettling him – or her – I swear I'll find out who it is.

We travel on silently for several minutes. I look at the clock on the dashboard. It's earlier than I'd planned. Unless we take a detour, we're going to be back at Laurieston before the police leave. I glance at Joanna again. She's clearly long past the state where she might find pleasure in stopping somewhere for tea and she'll notice immediately if I don't take the direct route. I realise that even if we manage to avoid the police, they'll probably have left some evidence of their visit, or someone – Mrs Briggs or Briggs, or Sentance, if he comes poncing round – will let something slip. I realise that I'm going to have to tell Joanna about the skeletons. I drive until we reach a lay-by and pull over.

"Why are you stopping?" Her voice is sharp.

"There's something I need to tell you. It will help to explain to you why I was unable to see Archie."

"Oh. You have an excuse?"

"It's not an excuse, and that's not the reason I'm telling you. You're right: I should have made Archie the priority. I was disorganised. But I want to tell you about this . . . other thing, anyway."

She looks sceptical and doesn't reply, but she seems to be waiting for me to continue. I see that she will listen to me.

"You know that the reason that I had to come home was that the police had found forged passports in the cellar?"

"Of course. And you gave me to understand that you had no idea how they could have got there."

"I didn't – I don't. It's not about that. Naturally, they asked for permission to search the cellar more thoroughly. As a matter of fact, they produced a warrant, though I'd have let them do it anyway. I was keen to show that I had nothing to hide and at that stage I was still doing all I could to come back to be with you in St Lucia by the end of the week."

"I hope they enjoyed themselves in the cellar. I've never been brave enough to sift through all that junk myself." I detect a glimmer of humour in her statement which makes my heart lurch. I have no idea how she will react to what I have to say next.

"The thing is, they found something else down there."

"What was it? A body?" She gives a short laugh.

"Not exactly. A skeleton. Three skeletons, actually."

"Skeletons? You mean that three people have died in the cellar?" She is shocked, incredulous.

"No-one knows how they died, or whether they died there or somewhere else. If they were murdered, the murderer almost certainly won't be caught, because the skeletons appear to be old – perhaps almost as old as the house."

"You mean they've been there all the time . . ." – she takes a deep breath – ". . . all the time we've been living there?"

"It looks like it."

"My God!"

She is suddenly paler, her eyes swerving skittishly. I lean across awkwardly to embrace her and she doesn't resist. I half-bury my face in her hair. I'm comforted because she allows it and at the same time it cuts through me like a knife that this may be one of my last opportunities to breathe in her scent.

"Try not to get upset about it," I murmur. "I know it's unpleasant to think of them lying there, but they'll have just been bones for many years before we were even born. Looked at logically, it's no worse than living in a deconsecrated church or chapel, with coffins in the crypt."

She struggles free.

"Don't be ridiculous!" she spits the words so fiercely that her saliva sprays my cheek. "Those aren't just bones. They're malevolent, they belong to evil spirits! I understand now what's made me ill. I thought I was imagining it before."

"Joanna, darling, you're not making sense! Try to tell me what you mean."

She's staring at me now, her irises huge and black.

"I've heard them down there, banging around. I heard a scream once, and crying. They've haunted us; they've put a curse on us. That's why Archie's ill. That's why I'm dying."

I trust Joanna. Mentally as well as physically, she is but a cypher of the woman that she once was, but she's not mad. Although it's impossible for me to draw the same conclusions as she has, I don't doubt that something real must have disturbed her.

"What have you heard? When did you first hear it? Tell me about it. Why have you never said anything before?"

"Please don't bombard me with questions. I can't cope."

"I'm sorry – take your time. But you must tell me. Don't you see, I'm furious that you haven't felt at peace in your own home. Do you want some water?" I add, seeing that her face, which had been deathly pale, has now turned a hectic shade of red. She nods.

There's a small bottle of mineral water in the pocket of the car door. I lift it out and unscrew the cap before I hand it to her. She takes it from me, sips at it weakly a few times and replaces the cap. I take her hand again. She is calmer now. Her hostility has evaporated.

"I can't remember when it first happened," she said, "but it was a long time ago – Archie was only a toddler. It was Archie who heard the noise first. He'd been in the hallway, playing some game with his trucks. I was in the kitchen with Mrs Briggs when he came running in. He was crying. He said that he'd heard 'nasty noises' coming from the cellar. I said that there couldn't be anything there, that I'd take him down to the cellar and show him. I wanted to put his mind at rest."

"Did you succeed?"

"I managed to soothe him, no thanks to Mrs Briggs. I'd expected to get some common-sense support from her, but she was as frightened as he was. She advised me to 'let well alone' in the cellar. She said that she'd always thought of it as an evil place and that wild horses wouldn't drag her down there. I asked her what she meant and she was evasive – unlike her, as you know. She said that she'd always had a thing about that cellar, ever since she was a girl."

"But surely you weren't swayed by such rubbish?"

"Not on that occasion, no. Archie had calmed down and, although I was annoyed with her for reinforcing his fear of the cellar, I decided that it would do no good to drag him down there against his will. It would probably have given him nightmares."

"Where was I at the time?"

"I don't know: not at home. I think you were probably away somewhere – I mean properly away, not just for the day. That must have been why I didn't mention it to you."

"But it happened again?"

"Yes. Several months later. It was after you and I had started to worry about Archie's behaviour. I was in the drawing-room when he came tearing in, sobbing hysterically. It took me a good five minutes to placate him enough to get him to speak to me. He said that he'd heard rattling in the cellar and someone crying for help. I held him until he'd stopped crying. I was afraid for him: he'd already seen Dr Johnston then and we were waiting for the results of the tests. I was hoping against hope that they'd be normal. I wanted to keep him as placid as possible."

"Were you on your own this time, or was Mrs Briggs in the house with you again?"

"I think I was alone. If Mrs Briggs was there, she must have been in the kitchen. But I don't think so, because I know I didn't discuss it with her."

"Did you talk to anyone about it?"

"Only Tony."

"Tony! How did he get involved?"

"He happened to be in the house. You know he often calls to collect things from the office when you're away."

"Oh, so I was away again, was I?"

"Yes."

"And did it again slip your mind to mention it? Or was it Tony's suggestion that you shouldn't?"

"It was Tony's idea, but you're making him out to be sinister, or at least interfering. He wasn't, at all. He was still in the office after I'd put Archie to bed and I looked in on him to ask if he'd like some tea. He'd heard the noise that Archie had made and he also knew of Dr Johnston's concerns."

"You told him about those?"

Joanna sighed.

"I know you don't like Tony, Kevan, but if it weren't for him we wouldn't have Archie. Naturally he feels responsible for him. I felt it was only fair to tell him that Archie might have a . . . disorder."

"Why? So that we could ask for a refund? A discount for damaged goods?" I took one look at her stricken face and immediately wished I could have bitten the words back again.

"I'm sorry," I said. "I didn't mean that."

"Tony offered to come down into the cellar with me, so that I could see for myself that Archie was imagining things. Between Archie and Mrs Briggs, I'd developed a thing about the place myself by then, but when I followed Tony down there I could see that nothing had been touched for a very long time. Everything was as I remembered it when I'd cleared out your grandfather's furniture soon after we came to live here."

"So did Tony oblige you with some words of advice?"

"He did, actually. He said that our best chance of 'curing' Archie was to say nothing about the episode unless Archie himself mentioned it. If he did, I was to say I'd looked in the cellar with Uncle Tony and there was nothing to be frightened of; that he'd probably heard a trick of the wind, or something like that."

"I see. Did he suggest I shouldn't be told about what had happened?"

"Not in so many words, no."

"What is that supposed to mean?"

"He thought that the whole matter should be played down; that dwelling on it could only harm Archie. Why can't you accept that?"

"Assuming that I do accept it, what about the other occasions? The ones when you say you heard the noises yourself. When did they happen?"

"More recently. About the time that I first became ill again – or just before it, I'm not sure. The first time was late one afternoon. Archie was away at school and you were on one of the boats. I'd made myself a cup of tea and taken it into the drawing-room. I was very tired. I must have drifted off to sleep. I was woken up suddenly by an unearthly low moan and the beginnings of a scream – as if someone had started to scream, and been suddenly silenced."

"What did you do?"

"I was afraid, but I knew I couldn't let it rest. I opened the door of the drawing-room and listened, but all was quiet again. I moved across to the cellar door and stood with my head against it, still listening, but there was no sound. I was thinking about going down there again when Tony came downstairs and asked me if I was all right. He said that I looked ill."

"Just how often does Tony come to work in the office when I'm not there?"

"Not all that often. Perhaps once each time you're away. You know he brings papers for you to look at when you return. He sorts them into piles for you so that you can deal with them as quickly as possible. Surely that's helpful?"

"Oh, amazingly helpful. And he just happens to be on the

premises every time something strange happens! What was his take on it this time?"

"He said that I was over-tired from worrying about Archie and that I'd probably projected Archie's irrational fears on to my subconscious."

"And you believed that?"

"It seemed to make sense."

"Was that the last time you heard the noises?"

"No, I've heard them twice more: both times when I was completely alone. But I was taking the new medication by then, and I thought that this, combined with the reason that Tony had suggested, could probably explain them."

"In other words, you decided that you might be hearing things?"

"Yes."

"So how does knowing about the skeletons change your view?"

"Because, despite all I've told you, I've had the feeling all along that there's something really evil there. I've never been down into the cellar again since that time I went with Tony. It's always scared me. And, although I know it sounds superstitious, I've been convinced that whatever the evil thing is, it's been sapping my strength, just as it's undermined Archie's sanity."

I embrace her again, looking over her head at the march of the flat fields beyond. I have no doubt that someone has sapped her strength and frightened both her and Archie. I am equally convinced that it is a living person, or people, and not the ghosts of three unfortunate Africans who died more than one hundred years ago.

THIRTY-TWO

The following morning, Tim found himself in a bit of a quandary. He'd had misgivings about being escorted off the Laurieston premises so firmly, if not discourteously, by Tony Sentance the previous day. Sentance's arrival in the cellar, coupled with Verity Tandy's discovery, when she'd returned with the first aid kit to dress Giash's wound, that the latter was nastier than they'd thought and probably ought to be examined by a doctor, had more or less halted their activities for the day. Against Giash's protests, Tim had encouraged her to take him to A & E in the patrol car while Tim himself had tried to get as much work done in the cellar as he could before 5 p.m., but in practice it had proved impossible for him to move the remaining large items of furniture on his own. In any case, Sentance had returned within fifteen minutes to tell him that he'd had a text message to say that Kevan and Joanna de Vries would be home shortly, considerably earlier than the time de Vries had originally suggested. Tim had wondered who had sent the message. Sentance had implied that it had come from Kevan de Vries himself. Having twice witnessed de Vries' barely-disguised disgust for his henchman, Tim had doubted this, but been willing to believe that Sentance was not exaggerating when he said that Joanna would be both distressed and annoyed if she were to encounter Tim or any of his team at her homecoming. De Vries himself had indicated as much. Tim had recognised that he would have to complete the cellar search at another time.

He'd therefore looked carefully at everything they had so far done, taking particular note of where they'd placed the various items, and been on the point of going home when Sentance, still hovering, had offered to give him a short tour of the garden. He'd said that he wanted to show Tim from the outside of the house how the burglars had forced their way through the conservatory window. Tim had shrugged, but agreed – in his mind, the burglary was something of an irrelevance, unimportant except for its role in exposing the two much more serious crimes that had been discovered at Laurieston. However, he'd wanted to keep Sentance onside for as long as he could. He'd had no doubt that there was an ulterior motive behind the offer and initially assumed it to be a pretext for getting him out of the house so that he could have left without meeting Joanna de Vries should she and her husband have arrived home. On further consideration, however, he realised that this could not have been the reason: if he'd left when he'd intended, Joanna would not have seen him anyway. Watched closely by Sentance, he'd closed the cellar up and meticulously and pointedly re-taped it against intrusion and then followed Sentance into the garden.

When he thought about it, Sentance had managed to place them by Tim's car just as Kevan de Vries had driven in, his face turning into a vicious scowl as soon as he'd seen them. Tim had wanted to meet Joanna, but de Vries had surged past them and stopped right beside the door, after which he'd quickly shepherded his wife inside, shielding her from Tim's gaze.

He could only conclude that Sentance wanted Joanna to be aware of his presence, while at the same time attempting to ingratiate himself with de Vries by appearing to be responsible for removing an offending policeman from the scene. But what would Sentance have gained from such manouevrings? Were they just a further move in his perennially manipulative power game, or did he have a more pressing imperative?

Whatever the answer, by acquiescing to Sentance's demands, Tim had put himself in a tricky position. He would need to go back to the cellar to complete the search, accompanied by at least one of the two PCs, but, because Sentance had adroitly steered him away from de Vries yesterday, he'd had no opportunity to request more time from the businessman, or even to establish that his wife was now in full possession of the facts. Although Tim didn't particularly like de Vries, he felt desperately sorry about his wife's illness. This, together with a certain half-acknowledged fear of Jean Rook, made him almost shy about bothering de Vries again. He felt, however, that he must bite the bullet; he'd ring de Vries and suggest that he would need to complete the search, but, out of consideration for Mrs de Vries' feelings, leave the couple alone until tomorrow, as long as they both agreed to leave the cellar alone and let no-one else down there, either. In the meantime, he'd place Ricky close by but away from the house and let things be whilst he himself turned his attention to Norfolk; he consulted his watch, and saw that it was almost 9 a.m. Not too early to make a discreet call to de Vries on his mobile, surely?

He reached in his pocket for his Smartphone, congratulating himself that he'd taken a leaf from Juliet's book and had now remembered to save de Vries' number in its memory, when the large, rather old-fashioned squat grey phone that sat on his desk began to ring.

"DI Yates."

"Ah, Detective Inspector, it is Stuart Salkeld here."

"Professor Salkeld! Good morning to you. You're up and working early!"

"I could say the same to you, but in fact your surmise is

correct: I have been at work very early this morning. I've been in the lab since 6 a.m. I started the post-mortem on the young woman whose body was found at Sandringham yesterday evening. There were several things that I found disturbing about it. I couldn't stay too late, as my wife had roped me into attending one of her social functions – she's a big wheel in half a dozen charities, as I think I may have mentioned before, and one of them in particular is the bane of my life – so I came back here today as soon as I could. What I suspected turned out to be correct."

"Do you mean the cause of death?"

"No, though I can tell you what I think that was: asphyxiation, as I originally thought; I'm almost certain of it now, though I can't vouch for it one hundred per cent. But that's not what's been worrying me. Last night, when I turned her body on to its front, I found some inflamed marks on her back. They could have been caused by post-mortem lividity, but I didn't think so. Today I've examined them further. They look like welts, inflicted with a whip or maybe a belt. And they're definitely ante mortem."

"A sex game gone wrong?"

"Possibly. Her anal sphincter is quite loose, and the area around it appears to be discoloured, which could indicate that non-consensual anal intercourse has taken place, though as you know she'd been dead for some time when she was found and all kinds of pigment changes occur to the flesh quite rapidly after death."

"If the welts weren't caused by kinky sex, what other explanation could there be?"

There was a short silence.

"I hesitate to suggest this, as I've had no first-hand experience of it myself. But there was an article in *The Lancet* recently by a doctor who works for Médecins sans Frontières, somewhere in Africa, I think. It described the injuries that had been inflicted by militia groups on some of the remote local communities in – I can't remember the country: Sudan, possibly. The article included photographs."

"And you think the marks on the girl's body are similar?"

"Yes, in a word. I'm going to ask a colleague – someone who has treated such injuries – for a second opinion."

"Poor kid!" said Tim.

"Yes. A cynic might say that she's been murdered either way, and that there can be nothing worse than death by another's hand. But a violent and perhaps terrifying death preceded by hours or days of suffering: that is barbaric."

"I'm in complete agreement. Thank you, Professor, for letting me know, and for all the work you've done on this."

"I don't really expect thanks for bringing such news," said Professor Salkeld, gruffly. "I'll send through my report, once I've got the second opinion, shall I?"

"Please. There's one other thing before you go: you say that it's possible that the girl was raped. Did you manage to obtain evidence that might convict her attacker?"

"DNA from sperm or other bodily fluids, you mean? Unfortunately not. There was no trace of sperm in either the vagina or the rectum. As I told you before, I wouldn't necessarily have expected to find it after so much time had elapsed: but it's also likely that the perpetrator was forensically aware. We haven't analysed her clothing yet, but, as you know, she was discovered without underwear. The only items of apparel found near the body were her jeans and T-shirt and the de Vries Industries overall and rubber clogs. Naturally, if there is evidence that can be extracted from these, we'll find it."

"Thank you again, Professor."

Never one to waste words, the Professor rang off without bothering with a farewell.

Tim looked at his mobile again. It was now several minutes past nine and definitely not too early to call de Vries. He still hesitated. Somehow, the conversation with the Professor had sapped his energy and certainly given him less of an appetite to return to Laurieston. He'd been adamant that the cold case should be investigated and he'd successfully compiled a list of reasons that had obliged Superintendent Thornton to agree with him. Now, however, he was forced to confront his own priorities as dispassionately as he could. There could be no question that unearthing the facts behind an ancient crime, for the committing of which no-one could now be brought to justice, was not as important as apprehending the tormentors of the young woman and possibly preventing them from inflicting a similar fate on others. On the other hand, his warrant had given him only temporary access to the de Vries cellar and the enquiry there had been triggered not by the skeletons alone, but also by the passport forgeries, a crime that was both current and unsolved. Forging passports was serious and not infrequently linked to murder. Irrespective of his investigation into the fate that had befallen the skeletons, it was surely his duty to see that the cellar had been thoroughly searched. Which crime should he focus on? That at present his team was so desperately depleted only served to compound his dilemma. Buying himself a further twenty-four hours was definitely the best way forward.

"Ah, Yates. I should have thought that with all you've got on your plate at the moment there'd be precious little time for daydreaming."

Tim looked up sharply. Superintendent Thornton's bulky frame was filling the doorway of his office.

"Good morning, sir. As a matter of fact, I was just myself considering what's on my plate, in order to work out my priorities."

Superintendent Thornton gave him a ferrety look.

"I'm glad about that, Yates, because as a matter of fact it touches on what I want to talk to you about. The de Vries case, in particular."

Tim stonewalled the look.

"Which aspect of the de Vries case, sir? It so happens that everything that I'm doing at the moment is related to de Vries Industries, one way or another."

"Don't play games with me, Yates. We both know that I'm talking about that passport affair. That's the reason that we brought Mr Kevan de Vries back to the UK in the first place, isn't it? Those skeletons are nothing to do with him and neither is the death of the girl in Norfolk."

"How do you know that, sir?"

"Know what?"

"That Kevan de Vries was not involved in the death of the woman whose body was found at Sandringham. What makes you so sure that he wasn't?"

Superintendent Thornton blustered a little while he searched for the right words.

"Well, I... well, it stands to reason, doesn't it? There isn't even a record of that girl working for one of the de Vries companies. And even if she turns out to have been a casual worker of some kind, which I understand is being investigated, it's unlikely that Kevan de Vries would have associated with a girl like that, isn't it?"

"A girl like what, sir?"

"Oh, come on Yates, you know what I mean. Do I need to spell it out? A barely literate little factory worker, that's what I mean. Not exactly in his social class, is she?"

"I suppose not. It's mere under-privileged girls ... women ... like her – and men, for that matter – who keep the wheels of the de Vries Industries turning. You're probably right: it's likely that Kevan de Vries has no interest in them as individuals." Tim could feel his colour rising.

"Now, don't get on your high horse with me. You're sidetracking me, apart from anything else. That's not what I came here to talk about. I came to ask you to get on with the passport enquiry, and to put it before everything else that you've got on at the moment."

"I see. May I ask why?"

"It comes from higher up than me. It's a discretionary request. Because of Mr de Vries' personal situation. I'm sure there's a reasonable explanation for why those passports were found at his home and we don't want to cause the family any more distress, do we? We've already ruined their holiday and intruded on Mrs de Vries' last illness."

"Has Jean Rook been talking to you?"

"I . . . no. That is, not on purpose. I happened to bump into her when I was in court yesterday..."

"Ha!"

"What's that supposed to mean? It was a chance encounter, I assure you."

"On your part, I'm certain, sir."

"Yes, well you can't possibly know what her intention was, can you? You weren't there. Unless I was taken in, I can assure you that she was very surprised . . ."

Tim decided to cut this as short as he could.

"I should tell you that Ms Rook has been quite obstructive so far, sir. I appreciate that you haven't had the opportunity to realise this, because you've seen little of her in connection with this case. If you want my candid opinion, she's much more to Kevan de Vries than his attorney, or has been at some point in the past."

"That's nothing to do with us."

"No, it isn't," said Tim. "I agree completely. And if Ms Rook has made representations to you about her anxiety over distressing Mrs de Vries when, as you say, she's terminally ill, I think we should take what she says very seriously."

"Exactly," said Superintendent Thornton. "That's what I told her myself."

"Furthermore, I agree with you when you say that the case involving the passports is the only one in which we can reasonably suppose that Kevan de Vries may have played some part."

"Quite." The Superintendent clasped his hands together, almost as if he were about to rub them in glee, then dropped them to his sides again. He frowned. "Did I say that? I'm not sure that it was what I meant."

"I'd just like a little more assistance with a couple of things," Tim continued, apparently without guile. "Then I'm sure we shall be able to leave the de Vries family in peace."

"Oh?" Superintendent Thornton turned out not to be naïve enough to swallow this without some resistance. "What might that be?" he asked.

"I'd be grateful if you'd use your influence to get the Home Office to expedite their help with the passport investigation."

"Yes, of course." Superintendent Thornton preened a little. He liked to be seen as an influential man, an important senior policeman. "Focus on this now, will you? I know you're helping Norfolk with the murder as well and of course that's important work, but they'll see the sense of putting your own patch in order first."

"Er . . . I did say there were two things. Both requiring your influence."

"What's the other one?" Thornton rapped out the question. Tim saw that, despite being susceptible to flattery, his boss was running out of patience.

"Kevan de Vries is a personal friend of yours, isn't he, sir?"

"Well – I probably wouldn't go so far as to say that," said the Superintendent, casting down his eyes in a gesture of cod modesty which almost prompted from Tim an outburst of unseemly laughter, "but we do socialise. At the Rotary Club, you know."

"So I'd heard," said Tim. "I wondered if perhaps you could ask Mr de Vries if PC Chakrabati and I could just spend a few more hours searching his cellar tomorrow? I know we still have a warrant, but, as you say, the situation is a delicate one. If he would just agree to let no-one into the cellar in the meantime, that will show him how sensitive we . . . you are."

"Jean Rook won't like it."

"No, sir, but she needn't know unless Mr de Vries chooses to tell her. And, as you've said yourself, we spend too much of our time being dictated to by the legal profession."

"Did I say that?"

Tim nodded briefly.

"And the search is in connection with the passport enquiry? You're not still chasing phantom Victorian murderers?"

"It should help us to conclude the passport enquiry, as you wish." It fleetingly crossed Tim's mind that if his grandmother had still been alive, she'd have feared that he'd be struck down by a thunderbolt as he spoke.

"Very well, I'll see what I can do."

"Thank you, sir."

THIRTY-THREE

Katrin had slept too heavily, but at least her night had been unbroken. She'd not jerked awake suddenly at 2 a.m., that most dismal of times for insomniacs, with her limbs aching, or, worse, been forced to sprint for the bathroom, assailed once more by nausea. She squinted at her alarm clock and saw that it was almost 8 a.m. She thought she was well enough to travel to work today, but she wouldn't attempt to arrive at her usual time. That would mean rushing her shower and skipping breakfast, a regimen that she'd frequently adopted in the past but acknowledged would be foolish now. 'You must learn to take care of yourself,' Tim had said. It was an over-worn phrase that she'd heard many times – 'Take care' was even a form of farewell – but now she began to understand that the platitude concealed some good advice for those who cared to listen. She'd call the office in a few minutes, tell them that she'd work from ten until six. It would be the first time she'd taken advantage of the flexi-hour system that had been introduced some time before. She'd probably be making use of all sorts of other working concessions that she'd previously scorned when she returned to work as a mother. Perhaps it was no bad thing. 'Work-life balance' – wasn't that what people called it? – when you still fulfilled your work commitments conscientiously but without letting them claim time that should be spent with your family. Tim, especially, could do with a little more of that. It was the first time it had occurred to her that the baby could be a positive influence on their working lives. She determined to keep hold of the idea. It would be much more helpful than that pained word 'juggling' that she'd heard working mothers use to describe their days full of tasks. Hard work had never frightened her, whereas her own expectations of herself tended towards the unreasonable.

She stretched out in the bed and wiggled her toes luxuriously. She would lie here, resting, for another fifteen minutes and she would not feel guilty. She resolved not even to think about work, but her thoughts were already straying to Florence Jacobs' journal. But that wasn't proper work, she told herself defensively: reading it had been a useful diversion from the nausea, though she could hardly claim that it had gripped her like a novel. It provided a disheartening insight into the mind of an average woman a century or so ago. As she'd read deeper into the journal, however – if the experience of absorbing such a banal document could be said to count as 'deep' – she'd become increasingly suspicious of its naiveté. The earlier entries that Florence had made before her marriage, when she could be seen to be struggling with their composition, struck a genuine note, but as Florence's social standing, and with it her grasp of writing, improved, the sentiments that she expressed seemed to become ever more jejune. Florence had been a pretty servant. Katrin imagined that she'd been quick and nimble at her work, probably with a ready smile, and anxious to please. She was uneducated, of course, but it was hard to believe that she could have been 'slow'. The dowager Mrs Jacobs was unlikely to have chosen a half-witted girl for her future daughter-in-law.

Katrin sat bolt upright in the bed. The dowager Mrs Jacobs had arranged Frederick's marriage to Florence. Reading between the lines, she had probably insisted upon it. Although this was implicit in the journal entries, it was the first time

Katrin had thought properly about its significance. Florence had stopped writing the journal immediately after Mrs Jacobs' death. Was it possible that Mrs Jacobs, not Florence herself, was the author of the journal? Katrin discounted this idea immediately. The cover of the journal bore a sample of Lucinda Jacobs' fine copperplate hand, so different from Florence's childishly laborious script. Lucinda could have influenced what Florence wrote, though. When trying to build up a picture of Florence's domestic situation, Katrin had never quite been able to envisage Frederick and his role in her daily life. Lucinda, on the other hand, featured in all her activities and was consulted – or made her view known – on practically every aspect of them, including when and whether Florence should pay visits to her own family. Had Florence's almost total deference to her mother-in-law's wishes been willing, or had she been coerced? If the latter, the diary could merely be a faked record of her actions, feelings and thoughts. Was it Lucinda Jacobs' attempt to leave a sanitised account for posterity?

She was sorry that Tim had left before she'd woken up that morning, because even before she'd had these thoughts she'd wanted to talk to him about the journal. He'd come in quite early the night before and she'd planned to discuss it then, but she'd felt shivery and sickly and he'd insisted that they should not talk shop, so they'd watched an old film until Katrin had fallen asleep on the sofa and Tim had persuaded her to go to bed. She'd intended to wake early enough today to ask him if she could send the journal to Juliet Armstrong. Katrin didn't know whether Juliet would be well enough to look at the journal, or indeed whether she'd want to be bothered with it, but guessed that she of all people might be able to unravel its mystery. Tim would know the answer, or could at least tell Katrin how to contact Juliet to find out.

Katrin always hesitated before she rang Tim at work. It was partly because she also worked for the police, partly because it was her instinct not to claim privilege as his wife. However, this was police business – sort of, at any rate. She picked up the phone and dialled his office number.

"DI Yates."

"Tim, it's me. I've finished reading Florence Jacobs' journal."

"What, this morning?"

"No, I'd finished it before you came home yesterday. I just didn't feel up to talking about it."

"You're OK now, though?"

"Yes, I slept better than for a long time."

"Good. What did you make of the journal?"

"I'm not sure. I think there may be more to it than appears. That it was written for a purpose that I can't quite see, perhaps."

"That's interesting, but if you can't tell what it is, it's unlikely that I'll be able to, especially as I haven't read it."

"No, but two heads are better than one and I haven't been able to do as much background research as I intended. I was thinking about showing it to Juliet. Do you think she'd mind? You said she was getting better."

"Well, you certainly can't go to see her. They don't know what's wrong with her yet. It might be infectious."

"I know that, but you could ask her. Or give me her number if it's possible to ring her."

There was an unexpectedly long silence.

"Tim?"

"I'm not sure. There's been a new development in the Norfolk murder. And Thornton's told me to concentrate on the passport case, to get de Vries off his back."

"I'm not asking you to commit time to this yourself and the

work I've done on it so far has been in my own time. The same would go for Juliet, if she feels up to it. Officially, she's not allowed to work."

There was another, shorter, silence.

"OK, I'll see what she says," said Tim, speaking more slowly than usual. "But I'm going to have to ask her to keep quiet about it – which she may not be happy about. You, too."

"I'm not sure that I understand why."

"We're very short-staffed and Thornton doesn't see the old case as a priority. He never has done. As you know, I disagreed with him and succeeded in making him let me carry on with it for a while, but it was against his better judgment. Now he says that pressure of work no longer allows us to focus on it, at least for the time being, and for once I'm inclined to agree with him."

"As I've said, you'd only be agreeing to help from two people who'd be working on it in their own time. I don't see what harm that can do. You're suggesting that you might come back to the case later – I know you're interested in it – but by then I'll have forgotten the detail of the journals and the work will have been wasted. I hardly ever see Superintendent Thornton, so that won't be a problem. Will he visit Juliet in hospital?"

Tim gave a short laugh. "I think that's unlikely."

"Well, then, she's not going to be actively deceiving him, is she? But of course you must mention the need for secrecy, as you say."

"I expect you're right. I wouldn't want to be less than above board with her, but provided she knows that Thornton would disapprove – I can just see him asking her to follow up on some of the passport queries from hospital if she feels well enough to work – and is still happy to do it, that's fine. Good idea, in fact. When you send her the journal, could you include some rough notes on your thoughts?"

"Of course."

"Thanks. Are you going to work today?"

"Yes. I'll aim to get there for ten. You've just reminded me: I need to call in."

"I'll leave you to it, then. Take care."

"You, too," said Katrin, slightly irritated at having that phrase crop up again. She put the phone down.

THIRTY-FOUR

Andy Carstairs had taken the drive along the A151 and A17 from Spalding to Sutton Bridge quite slowly. He was thinking about what he was going to say to the eight supervisors when he arrived at the de Vries food-packing plant. As Miss Nugent had suggested, he'd asked for permission to interview them from Tony Sentance and had been surprised at the alacrity with which her boss had agreed. Theirs had been a telephone conversation, not a face-to-face meeting, so Andy had not been able to see Sentance's expression, but were it not for what he'd heard about the man, he would have believed he was a public-spirited member of the community doing his best to aid the police with their enquiries. Of course, if Sentance had something to hide, he wouldn't have been the first crook to adopt super-helpful tactics as a smokescreen. Andy was convinced that he was playing some sort of game, and was more than a little irritated that so far neither himself nor Tim Yates had been able to penetrate what it was about. Hence the slow drive. He entertained a strong suspicion that Sentance planned to allow him one showcase meeting with the supervisors and ensure that it drew a blank. There would then be no reason for further visits to the packing plant.

The de Vries plant at Sutton Bridge was situated on a bleak and windswept site about half a mile before the outskirts of the town when approaching from the Spalding direction. Andy had typed its postcode into his satnav; otherwise, he might have driven past it. The buildings were half-concealed behind a line of tall conifers; there was a high wire fence in front of that. Access to the factory was gained via a narrow lane that led through the fence and the trees. There was a barrier across the top of the lane, beside which a small porter's hut had been erected. Andy had seen open prisons with more lax security.

He drew up behind the barrier. The porter came out immediately; he was a burly man with a black beard and dressed in what Andy had come to recognise as the ubiquitous de Vries Industries overall, with a name-badge pinned to it: Roberts. Curious, thought Andy: the boss goes by his first name, though crucially prefixed with his title, and, if this bloke is typical, his staff use only their surnames.

"Can I help you, sir?" The man was friendly enough, but there was an edge to the question, as if he were unable to imagine what legitimate business Andy could have in this place.

Andy flashed his ID.

"DC Carstairs, South Lincs police. I'm conducting routine enquiries. I've come to speak to some of the people who work here. Your Miss Nugent said that she'd make the arrangements."

Roberts put on a show of consulting his clipboard.

"Ah, yes," he said. "Miss Nugent has booked a parking space for you, sir. When I've raised the barrier, drive straight through and bear left. You'll see half a dozen car park spaces immediately in front of the main building. One of them should have been reserved for you – there'll be a bollard in front of it. Just move it out of the way, if you would, sir, and take the space. Or I can call the receptionist and ask her to come out ..."

"Thank you," said Andy briskly. "No need to bother anyone

else. I'm surprised that you've only six parking spaces, though. How does the workforce manage?"

"Most come in works buses, sir, but there's another car park, round the back of the building, that shop floor workers can use if they want. The spaces at the front are for management only. And visitors, of course."

"Thank you," said Andy again. He closed the window again as Roberts stepped back to raise the barrier. He'd been wrong about the place's similarity to an open prison: it was more like a feudal estate. He wouldn't mind betting that the workers had to sit in a separate part of the canteen from 'management', too, or perhaps the latter ate their lunch in a different room altogether.

Still driving slowly, he passed between the trees. Outwardly, the food-packing plant was an agreeable two-storey brick building fronted by a tarmac drive. A narrow strip of lawn grew between the building and the drive, with a paved path leading to the front door. Miniature box hedges lined the path and there were circular flower beds cut in the lawn. No flowers were growing in these at the moment, but they too were edged with box. Andy was surprised at this attention to detail, until he remembered that de Vries Industries produced flowers as well as vegetables. He supposed that it would be bad for business to leave the grounds looking scrubby.

The parking spaces had been laid out at the end of the drive and set at right angles to it. No vehicles had been left there. Nevertheless, as Roberts had indicated, the space furthest from the building had been 'reserved' with an orange bollard. Getting out of the car to move it, Ricky noted that at its head the space was labelled with the word 'Visitor' on a little plaque. A similar plaque had been placed on the two adjoining spaces. The others were labelled: 'E M Nugent', 'A J Sentance' and 'K P de Vries'. Excellent, thought Andy: so none of them had chosen to attend in order to try to stage manage the interviews.

He was rather annoyed, therefore, when an Audi saloon with Tony Sentance at the wheel came around from the rear of the building and parked in its designated spot.

"DC Carstairs! Dead on time, I see!"

He took the outstretched hand reluctantly. It was dry and hard, the grip almost painfully vice-like.

"We've got the afternoon shift supervisors to come in early, so all eight are waiting for you in the canteen."

"Thank you, but there was no need to alter your normal arrangements on my account. I'd actually have been very happy to have seen the supervisors individually or in pairs, as their own arrangements permitted. I don't want to turn this into a big deal." He didn't add that he'd have less opportunity to gauge if they were telling the truth if he saw them all together.

Sentance eyed him cagily.

"Oh, but surely it is a big deal, isn't it? A poor young woman has lost her life, after all."

"Indeed," Andy agreed, uncharacteristically taciturn. There was a short, awkward silence.

"Well, if you'd like to follow me . . ."

Sentance led the way through the grandiose revolving glass entrance door, past the receptionist and along a narrow corridor that managed to be scrupulously clean yet dingy at the same time. Andy saw that the gloss of the reception area petered out quickly in the parts of the building to which most visitors did not penetrate.

"Here we are."

Sentance held open one of a pair of swing doors. Painted a light lemon yellow, each had a porthole-style window cut into it so that the occupants of the room beyond could be observed

from the corridor. Andy concluded that this was probably for
no more sinister a reason than to allow would-be diners to see
if there was a free table. Even so, he could imagine Sentance
prowling the corridors, checking up on the staff. He probably
thought it was his right to do so.

"This is DC Carstairs," Sentance announced, once they
had both entered the room. Andy couldn't be sure, but he
suspected that the announcement had been made with just a
shade too much of a flourish, as if inviting humour. One look at
the row of faces in front of him told him that, if so, the gesture
was ill-judged. The supervisors, uncannily alike in their de
Vries overalls, were sitting in a row on two tables that had been
pushed together. To a man (or woman) they were regarding
him with little-concealed hostility.

"Would you like to make some introductions?" said Andy
as lightly as he could, turning to his host.

"Of course. But, first of all, may we offer you some coffee?
Or tea?"

"That won't be necessary, thank you. I don't want to take up
more of your time than I have to."

Sentance shrugged. "It would have been no trouble, I
promise you." There was another awkward silence. "Well, if
you're sure, I'll get on with the introductions."

After this ponderous start, Andy was taken aback at the
speed with which Sentance proceeded to acquaint him with
his subordinates. He worked along the row, pointing uncer-
emoniously at the supervisor he was presenting.

"This is Alan, and Dulcie, Molly, Fred, Geoff, Wayne, Eric
and Douglas. Eric's been with us the longest – thirty years, isn't
it, Eric? But we've all put in a good few seasons." He chuckled
for no apparent reason. Perhaps the joke was that he'd just
associated himself so democratically with the workforce.

"Nice to meet you," said Andy, nodding. The two women

managed frosty smiles. The men's expressions remained flint-
ily expressionless. He turned to Sentance: "Thanks for the
introductions. First names are fine for now, but I'll need surnames as well, if you wouldn't mind providing me with a list
before I go. And mobile numbers, unless anyone objects?" He
looked at the group of supervisors again.

"I don't have a mobile," said Eric.

"I'd like your landline number, in that case." Eric gave a
surly half-nod. Sentance officiously wrote something in his
diary.

"Now I'd like to show you all some photographs," Andy continued. "There are quite a few of them, so you might be better
off sitting down properly. Then you can pass them around
more easily. I should warn you they're a bit upsetting – they're
of the girl whose body was found in the woods at Sandringham
– though she's been tidied up as much as possible."

The two women slid off their table first. Slowly, the men
also got to their feet. Andy noticed that they were all pretty
hefty. There was quite a bit of scraping of furniture on the
tiled floor as they converted the two tables from an oblong to
a square and dragged across chairs. Eventually they were all
seated. Sentance chose not to sit with them; he moved over to
the windowsill immediately opposite and perched on it. He
watched intently as Andy drew a sheaf of photographs from
the manila envelope that he was carrying and passed the first
one to Dulcie, who was sitting nearest to him.

"I'd be grateful if you'd all look at each one of these carefully before passing them to the person on your right: I don't
want anyone to miss any of them. This is a picture of the spot
in the wood where the girl was found. I realise that the police
tape may make it look unfamiliar, but do any of you recognise
it?"

The photo was passed around solemnly. Andy walked

around the table while the group was looking at it, so that he could see each of their faces. No-one showed a spark of recognition, but he had to acknowledge it was a picture of a fairly anonymous spot, made strange, as he'd said, by the scene-of-crime tape.

"Have you all been to Sandringham at some point?" There were some nods. To Andy's amusement, two of the men half-raised their hands, as if they were primary school children answering a question in class.

"Has anyone not been there?" No response.

Andy continued with the next picture, which was of the girl lying at some distance from the camera.

"I don't expect you to be able to recognise her from this. It's just to show you how she was found."

This photograph also was passed around the supervisors, finishing with Sentance, who officiously returned both photographs to Andy. No-one offered any comment.

Andy was exasperated by their apparent lack of interest; it gave him a dark sense of pleasure to anticipate their shock at what he would show them next. He held out a sheaf of several photographs, all turned face down, to Alan, who was stationed at one corner, furthest away from Sentance. As Alan held out his hand to take them, Andy kept hold of the sheaf for a moment before releasing it, saying as he did so:

"As I said, you may find these upsetting. I apologise for having to put you through looking at them."

Alan was a ponderous individual with a square, beefy face and black hair combed back to reveal a widow's peak. He turned over the top photograph, looked at it for a moment, then put it to the back of the pile, imperturbably turning to the next one, and the next. Andy had intended him to pass them on as he looked at them, but decided against intervening. After perhaps three minutes, Alan squared up the batch of photos as if they were a bunch of charge sheets, turned them over again and passed them wordlessly to Dulcie.

"Just a moment," said Andy. "I'd like Alan's reaction first."

Alan stared at him and still did not speak.

"Well?" said Andy. He realised that he shouldn't have allowed Sentance to introduce the supervisors by their first names alone. It put him at a disadvantage when he was questioning them. He shot a glance at Sentance, but the Finance Director was giving nothing away. He was still balanced against the windowsill, examining the fingernails of his right hand, his head bent forwards so that Andy could not see his expression. He had crossed his legs and was tapping one foot gently on the floor. Whether this was a sign of nerves or impatience was impossible to tell.

"Well what?" asked Alan with surprising truculence.

"Do you recognise the girl, sir?" said Andy, with elaborate patience.

"No, I don't think so. It's difficult to tell when she's so mangled up."

"Quite. Dulcie, perhaps you'd take a look now."

Alan looked at his watch and folded his arms. Dulcie was a buxom woman with frizzy sandy hair which was escaping from her cap. She was coarse-skinned, her face almost chapped, as if she'd been working out in the fields in a high wind. Or she could be a drinker, Andy thought. She threw him a timorous smile and turned over the pile with a slightly shaking hand. She was nervous, but it might only have been because he'd warned her that the pictures were unpleasant. Like Alan, she stared at the first one for a while, then moved it to the back of the pack. When she came to the second, she drew in her breath sharply and let the photo fall. It hit the others awkwardly, slewing them across the table-top. Two of them fell to the floor. Dulcie immediately scraped back her chair and plonked down heavily on her hands and knees to retrieve them. When she re-surfaced, her face was scarlet.

"Are you all right?" said Andy. He noted that Dulcie's colleagues had remained curiously impassive.

"Yes – it's just . . . The bastard. Look what he did to that poor girl. That was unforgivable. He could've . . ." She began to whimper.

"I'm afraid that you've distressed Dulcie, Detective Constable." Sentance's voice cut smoothly across Dulcie's babbling. "Molly, could you fetch Dulcie a glass of water? And perhaps you'd like to take her to the ladies' rest room for a few minutes, until she feels more herself?"

Molly, who was sitting next to Dulcie, nodded and stood up, hatchet-faced. She took hold of Dulcie's arm and made a rough if unsuccessful attempt to yank her to her feet. Dulcie remained seated, her face now covered with both her large workwoman's hands.

Andy stepped forward quickly and patted Dulcie on the shoulder.

"Dulcie, I'm very sorry that you're upset. I tried to warn everyone, but it's difficult to be prepared for something so horrific. Mr Sentance is right: you must rest until you feel better. But I'd appreciate it if you'd just tell me first whether you knew the girl?"

He couldn't be sure, but Andy thought that he noticed Molly tightening her grip on Dulcie's arm. Dulcie slowly moved her fingers from her face and met his eye. Contrary to the impression she'd given, no tears swam in her own, but her countenance was troubled, even haunted. Something more than an unpleasant photograph was frightening her: she seemed beside herself with fear. She gave a quick glance to her right. Sentance stared back at her, his face intent, but shuttered against all emotion.

"No, I don't think I knew her," she said. "But we get a lot of casuals here and it's hard to remember them all."

"What did you mean when you said 'he'?"

"Pardon?" Her pale blue eyes had blanked.

"You said that the killer was a 'bastard' – I'm sure everyone would agree with you. Then you said 'Look what he did to that poor girl'. What did you mean when you said 'he'? Were you thinking of someone specific?"

"Really, DC Carstairs, where do you think this is leading? It's a natural assumption that this crime was committed by a man, isn't it? It's unlikely that a woman would have overpowered the girl, and in any case women don't . . ."

"I'd be grateful if you'd let Dulcie herself answer."

Sentance sighed and opened wide his arms in a 'be my guest' gesture. Dulcie flicked another fearful glance in his direction, then fixed her eyes on the table. She did not raise them to meet Andy's again.

"Mr Sentance is quite right," she said, her voice rising squeakily as she gasped for air. "I just jumped to the conclusion that it was a man, that's all."

"And you didn't know the girl?"

"I've said, haven't I?" She rose to her feet, Molly still gripping her arm. "I need to have a sit down somewhere quiet now. I'm sorry."

The two women left the room.

"Highly strung," Sentance observed reflectively, as if talking to a fellow director. "But a good worker."

"Can we continue?"

"Of course."

Andy gathered up the photographs and passed them to Fred. They were silently examined by all the remaining male supervisors in turn. Each said that he didn't know the girl and none of them betrayed any feeling. When the photos reached

Sentance, he riffled through them perfunctorily before handing them back to Andy with a half-flourish. Andy had known from the moment that Dulcie had clammed up that he would get no further with the supervisors. He didn't even bother to ask if Molly could return to speak to him. He thanked the supervisors politely and allowed Sentance to escort him to the door.

"As you see, we're just like a family here," said Sentance unctuously.

Andy ignored the remark. He held out his hand to shake Sentance's briefly.

"Thank you for arranging for me to visit," he said. Sentance gave a half-bow. "I'd like the full names of all the supervisors, please, with their addresses and how they may be contacted by phone, both during the day and at home. And e-mail addresses for those who have them. By the end of the day, if possible. I'd appreciate it if you'd e-mail them to me."

He handed Sentance his card, who took it wordlessly.

"Just like a family!" Andy muttered to himself, as he trudged to his car. "They say that blood's thicker than water and this *family*'s certainly seen some blood. I'd say that this lot were in it up to their eyebrows. It's proving it that's going to be the problem."

THIRTY-FIVE

Katrin was sitting at her desk in her office in Holbeach. Florence's journal was lying in front of her, meticulously wrapped in plastic. She'd read it from cover to cover, looking back over certain passages more than once, and still failed to unlock its mystery. She was convinced there was more to it than the vapid ramblings of a Victorian maidservant who'd married above her station.

She picked it up again, weighing it in one hand as if for inspiration. Part of her didn't want to send it to Juliet: she'd prefer to crack the mystery herself. But she knew that Juliet's elliptical approach to solving problems often worked. Sometimes her brain was like a searchlight, illuminating what was obvious to her but everyone else had failed to see.

Katrin sighed and put the journal down again. She was tired and slightly bored. What she'd really like would be to take the journal to Juliet herself and spend an enjoyable few minutes chatting to her. But that was out of the question, obviously.

For the first time, she thought about how she might arrange for the package to be delivered to the Pilgrim Hospital. If Tim had been planning to visit Juliet that day she might have sent it with him, but he'd told her that he'd be in Norfolk until late. Katrin decided that if Juliet felt well enough to take a look at the journal, she'd send it by courier. The research unit had one that they used regularly. A non-emergency delivery shouldn't be too expensive.

She picked up the phone and dialled the number that Tim had given her. As she'd suspected, it wasn't a direct line, but after she'd jumped through a few hoops she could hear Juliet's voice.

"Hello? Juliet? It's Katrin. How are you feeling?"

"Not too bad, thanks." Juliet sounded quieter than usual, but cheerful. "How are *you*?" Katrin experienced a flash of annoyance.

"Oh, so Tim's told you, has he?"

"He didn't have much choice, did he? He had to find out whether it was safe for you to visit me."

"I suppose so. And as you probably know, I've been told that I can't. Visit, I mean."

"Well, pity from my point of view, but you're well out of it, to be honest. Tim said that you've got something you'd like me to look at?"

"Yes. It's a journal. It's late Victorian. It was written by the wife of an earlier owner of the house that Kevan de Vries and his wife live in."

"You mean Laurieston House? I've been there. It's close to where I was bitten by the rat."

"Oh, yes, I should have remembered that. What do you think, anyway?"

"About the journal? I'd love to see it. It looks as if I'm going to be here for a few more days, and I'm just about comatose with boredom. Do you have any tips or clues that you'd like to give me before I read it?"

"I'd rather you came to it fresh, really. I can tell you that the woman who wrote it had been a maidservant, so she wasn't well-educated. She writes in quite a naïve manner. She also seems to be heavily influenced by her mother-in-law, who lived in the house with her – unlike the husband, who was often away. But you'll see all that for yourself."

"OK, fine. How are you going to get it here? Will Tim bring it?"

"I think he's in Norfolk today and I'd like you to have it as soon as possible. I thought I'd send it by courier. It will reach you all right, won't it?"

"It will if you say that it has to be signed for. Why is Tim in Norfolk?"

"He's helping with a murder investigation, but I don't know the details. Before I forget, though, he asked me to ask you to keep it to yourself, if you decided to take the journal. He seems to think that Superintendent Thornton will take a dim view of it if he knows you're working on it. He wants the de Vries case putting on the back burner, apparently. Tim thinks he'd prefer you to be doing something else, if you're up to working at all."

"If I didn't know the Superintendent, I'd be outraged by that remark. It's none of his business what I do while I'm signed off sick. But Tim's probably right and, as you know, I'm quite good at keeping the peace, so in the unlikely event of Thornton's calling me or coming to visit, I'll keep quiet about it. He can't put the de Vries case 'on the back burner', though. It's about forging passports. Thornton surely knows that he has to get to the bottom of that."

"I don't know any more than you do. I'm sure Tim'll fill you in next time he sees you. I'm really pleased that you feel well enough to read the journal – though promise me you won't tire yourself out in the process. Take your time."

"I will. *You* promise *me* to take care of *your*self, too."

"Of course. And we must meet as soon as you're out of quarantine. I'm really looking forward to seeing you. It'll be fun to discuss the journal then, if you haven't already made it give up its secret."

"What secret?"

"I don't know. But I'm sure there is one. There, I've hinted more than I meant to, now."

"Don't worry: you've just whetted my appetite. Will it come today?"

Katrin looked at her watch.

"If I can get the courier to collect it before two, it should be with you later this afternoon."

After Katrin had put down the phone, she thought that there'd been something unusual about the conversation with Juliet. Thinking back over it, she realised that, although she'd sounded weak, Juliet had seemed upbeat, almost ebullient. Even in good health, she was usually demure, her voice less inflected than most people's (Katrin hesitated to use the word 'colourless').

THIRTY-SIX

After his fruitless visit to the De Vries packing plant, Andy
Carstairs had pulled into the petrol station just along the
road from there to fill up; he was just easing away from the
pumps and looking back to find a gap in the traffic when he
saw a familiar Audi turn out of the packing plant entrance and
head off in the direction of King's Lynn. Without a second's
thought and in response to instinct, Andy turned right after
him. He knew that he must keep his distance: if Sentance
suspected that he was being tailed, Andy had no doubt that
he'd either speed off or head for somewhere other than his
present intended destination, wherever it was. Sentance had
now crossed the swing bridge that spanned the River Nene
and was driving along the A17 where it became a high straight
bank leading out of Sutton Bridge towards King's Lynn. The
bank was flanked on both sides by low-lying ploughed fields.

Andy briefly pulled into a lay-by to make himself less
obvious to Sentance, letting his engine idle, before setting off
again. He could see quite a long way ahead: he'd taken his eyes
off the road for only seconds and now it was deserted. He was
surprised that Sentance had managed to cover the ground so
fast, but equally certain that he had vanished. Cursing, Andy
stepped on the accelerator, gathering speed so rapidly that he
almost missed an opening on the left hand side of the bank,
some five hundred yards further down the road. Backing up
cautiously, he saw that the agricultural track which passed

through a gap in the crash barriers and turned steeply down the side of the embankment was angled in such a way that it wasn't possible to see from his driver's seat what lay at the bottom. Andy knew that it would be too risky to drive straight into it. He could see nowhere in the immediate area where he could hide the car, so he drove on further, until he reached a farm track on the other side of the road. There was a ruined barn standing at the bottom of the slope, roofless and over-grown with creeper. Andy manoeuvred his car in behind the barn, praying that it would not sink into the mud. Jumping out, he ran back up towards the road, crouching low, and giving one backward glance when he reached the top of the bank again. He noted with satisfaction that the car was com-pletely concealed from view.

He was hastening back towards the spot where he had seen the opening, when he heard a car engine roaring somewhere ahead. He was still some yards from the opening and had just time to leap over the crash barrier to his left and crouch behind it when Sentance's car suddenly emerged, paused momentar-ily and then raced away, back towards Sutton Bridge.

Andy couldn't be certain, but he thought he'd caught a fleeting glimpse of someone seated next to Sentance in the passenger seat. If he was correct, it was someone slight: a very small woman, or a child, perhaps; someone who could barely see over the top of the dashboard. He eased himself to his full height, rubbing his back where it ached from the unnatural position that he had adopted, and debated what to do next. To continue his pursuit of Sentance would be impossible: it would take him at least ten minutes to run back to his car. By that time, Sentance would be back at the Sutton Bridge plant or well on his way to . . . Sutterton?

Andy didn't feel like giving up. Sentance must have had a reason for taking that detour. If Andy was right about the passenger, Sentance must have picked her – or him – up while he was off the main road. To Andy's knowledge, there were no buildings down there along the bank. Had the person, whoever it was, been waiting for him at the gap, concealed from the road? If so, how had he or she arrived there? And did the bank conceal some kind of shelter, or had they just stood around in the mud?

Andy knew that he'd have to investigate further. He also realised that there might be someone else – perhaps more than one other person – still lurking there. He debated whether he should spend time on fetching his car, which would offer him at least some protection if he encountered hostility. If he did so, he would not only lose precious minutes, but also scare off anyone who had no right to be there. He decided simply to cross the road and take a look down.

What he saw when he did so was an area at the very foot of the bank where four shipping containers, no doubt for use at crop harvest time, stood end to end on a bed of aggregate.

There were no lights on the containers and there was nothing to suggest that they were used for anything other than – he supposed, since the rest of the field had been ploughed – agricultural purposes. The presence of so many containers in such a remote spot was still strange. Andy knew that they'd have to be examined more closely, but he had no time to do it today. He had to get back to Spalding to see Tim. He'd ask the Boston police to investigate in the morning. It was unlikely that Sentance would return there tonight.

THIRTY-SEVEN

After dinner, at which I eat little and Joanna even less, we spend a silent evening which for me is further jaundiced by Joanna's silent recriminations. I do not complain and know that I have no cause to. Joanna's cross is weightier than mine and at least some of the resentment that she shows towards me is justifiable. I sit in my armchair next to the fireplace; she, on the sofa. I am idling with my mobile phone, tapping away at messages that are less urgent than I am making them seem; she is pretending to read a magazine. Her head lolls forward every few minutes before it jerks upright again and she carries on her charade of being engrossed in some frothy trash that I am certain lies a million miles distant from her true thoughts. I know she's exhausted. I lean across to touch her knee. I have to summon all my restraint not to burst into tears when she flinches away from me. I move my hand from her knee and grip the side of her hand, which is still clutching at a page of the magazine.

"You should be in bed," I say. "Let me take you up."

She shakes her head.

"I'm not ready yet," she says in a distant voice. "It's too early. Let me hang on to some semblance of normality while I'm able to."

"It's half-past nine," I point out, "and you haven't slept properly since you landed. When I came home on Monday, I slept for most of the afternoon. You're tougher than I am, but you don't have to prove anything to yourself. Or to me."

She does not reply, but gives me a withering look and returns to the trash. She has only turned the page once all evening. I wish she would let me in, to tell me what she is thinking, but I know that there's no point in asking. I'll probably never be close to her again. Once more, I have to fight back the tears, despising my own self-pity as I do so.

It occurs to me that she won't go to bed because she doesn't want me to join her there. The thought fills me with such an intense sorrow that I feel my heart constrict with pain. Her well-being is my paramount concern and I know that I must find a way of making her take rest. I say with a brightness that sounds false even to my own ears:

"Well, I think that I'll turn in myself, anyway. I've found today pretty tough and no doubt we'll be hearing from our policemen friends again tomorrow. I've got to take a call from India in the early hours, so I'll sleep in the guest room. Then I won't disturb you."

She doesn't look up as I leave the room. I hope against hope that she'll go to bed herself as soon as I'm out of the way, now that I've removed her concern about sleeping with me. I make a brief sortie into the kitchen to pour myself a large glass of Scotch, then lumber upstairs with it, exaggerating my footsteps so that Joanna can hear. I leave the hall and landing lights switched on.

The guest room, which has blue wallpaper and a shimmering blue satin eiderdown, has always struck me as a cold and cheerless place. It has an en-suite bathroom which I enter as soon as I've placed the Scotch on the bedside cabinet. I take a pee, then clean my teeth, using one of the new toothbrushes that are always stacked in the bathroom cabinet for the use of forgetful guests. I return to the bedroom, strip off to my shirt and pants and haul myself into the queen-sized bed. As I suspect, it is unwelcomingly cold; the smooth white sheets envelop me and inflict the kind of freezing shock that you experience when jumping into an outdoor swimming pool. I prop myself on one elbow and knock back the Scotch as rapidly as I can. It scalds the back of my throat and, after a minute or so, brings me out in a sweat. I switch off the lamp on the cabinet and lie down, drawing the bedcovers up around my ears. I thrash around for a while, trying to get comfortable, and eventually curl into the foetal position, facing the window. I fall into a doze. I can hear the cars passing on the Boston road. I think I hear one of them slowing, followed by the crunch of the gravel in the drive, but I'm sure that by this time I'm dreaming. I feel my bones relax as I sink deeper into sleep.

I'm awakened by a crashing noise and a sharp cry or scream. I sit bolt upright in bed and fumble for the lamp, knocking the whisky glass to the floor as I do so. I slide my legs to the floor and stand, swaying, for a few seconds, listening, as I pull myself from sleep and get my bearings. I look at my watch. It is 2.30 a.m. I hear no further sounds, but I don't find this reassuring. I seize the guest dressing-gown from the back of the door, wrap it around me and hurry out to the landing. The lights are still burning on the stairs and in the hall.

I turn back from the top of the stairs and hasten to our bedroom, tripping on the ties of the dressing gown as I go, my heart filled with dread. When I reach the door, I am about to burst in when I remember that if Joanna is sleeping there I must not alarm her. I knock gingerly on the door, then a little louder. When there is no reply, I inch it open carefully and creep across to the bed. It is empty and immaculate, still pristine with the clean sheets with which Mrs Briggs insisted on making it yesterday morning.

"Joanna?" I whisper, inanely. Obviously she is not there and therefore will not reply, yet somehow I feel I owe it to her to call her name, to let her know that I am intruding on territory that I have ceded to her. I think about checking the master-bedroom en-suite, then realise that it would be futile. Joanna has not come to bed. I hope against hope that when I go downstairs I will find that she has fallen asleep on the sofa.

I know I should be racing down the stairs, but instead I step slowly and with reluctance. Inside my head, I'm silently screaming that I can't bear it if ... anything has happened: that cowardly platitude that I've heard people use for every kind of unpleasant experience, but especially death ... DEATH, not 'passed away' or 'passed on' or 'sadly, has left us', I gibber to myself.

When I reach the foot of the stairs, I see that the cellar door is swinging open, the police tape that had been stretched across it drifting free. For some reason I slam it shut with a loud bang, as if this is of no significance. I stride on, now no longer trying to be quiet.

The lights in the drawing-room have been switched off. I snap them on quickly. Joanna is no longer here. Her magazine lies on the hearthrug, tossed into a pyramid as if it had accidentally fallen from her knee when she stood up. The cushions on the sofa have been rearranged: two are balanced one on top of the other on the sofa's padded arm, as if placed there to form a pillow. The other two are lying on the floor, next to the magazine. I remember that Joanna has always hated the over-abundance of pillows and cushions found on the beds in hotel rooms and deduce that she intended to spend the night here. There is no time for me to grieve over this: I know I must find her quickly. I pray that she hasn't gone out into the night on her own. I wrench back one of the heavy curtains and see that her car is still standing in the drive. Surely she wouldn't attempt to leave the house on foot?

I return to the hall and for the first time take in the significance of the severed tape. Joanna and I promised Superintendent Thornton that we would not attempt to enter the cellar if he would leave us without a police guard for the evening and I see no reason why Joanna would have gone back on her word. The cellar has for a long time given her the creeps, in any case – she made that clear when we were travelling back from Sleaford in the car – and I'm certain that she wouldn't venture down there now that she knows about the skeletons. Not of her own free will. That thought grips me.

I open the cellar door and see for the first time that the light suspended over the stone staircase has been switched on. I tell myself that the police forgot it. I look over my shoulder, suddenly fearful that the noise I thought I heard when roused from sleep was not part of a dream, but the sound of an intruder. I push the door back as flat against the hall wall as its hinges allow and secure it with the kitchen doorstop. I edge on to the first step of the cellar stairs and look over the banister. Although I shout out with the shock of it and for several seconds what I see dances in a black and yellow dizzy haze before my eyes, within the deeper reaches of my mind I know I knew as soon as I awoke that this was what I was going to find.

Joanna is lying spread-eagled to one side of the foot of the staircase, face down, her neck resting at an unnatural angle, her arms and legs splayed. Of course, although I rush down the steps, kneel beside her, raise her into my arms and cradle her head while trying to find a pulse in her neck, I have realised from first seeing her that she is dead.

THIRTY-EIGHT

Ricky was the first to arrive on the scene. Though he had agreed as a courtesy to leave Kevan and Joanna de Vries on their own for the night, Tim had asked Ricky to stay as near to Laurieston House as possible. Accordingly, he had taken the solitary room available for hire above the Quadring Arms. It was a scrupulously clean room, but as ascetic as a monk's cell and with a very hard mattress on the narrow single bed. Ricky had therefore been dozing uncomfortably when his mobile rang. It was Tim, informing him tersely that an accident had been reported at Laurieston House, a message that had just been relayed to Tim himself from Spalding police station.

Ricky's car had been locked in the stable yard at the back of the pub for the night. In order to retrieve it, he would have had to knock up the landlord, who lived in a small adjoining cottage. It would be a three-minute walk at most to cross the green and cover the few yards along the main road, which Ricky deduced would be the swifter option. He dressed swiftly and ran down the pub stairs to the small entrance lobby. In passing, he noticed that two pairs of chairs had, rather quaintly, been placed in front of the entrances to the kitchen and the bar, as if that would deter overnight residents from entering them.

With the key that the landlord had given him, he quickly let himself out through the front door of the pub and sprinted across the green, his way guided by a night sky bright with stars and a gibbous moon. As he neared Laurieston House, he saw that the downstairs lights were on at 1 Laurieston Terrace, Harry Briggs's house, and wondered if Kevan de Vries had summoned Briggs to help. He ran as fast as he could up the driveway to the house, his movements impeded somewhat by the depth of the gravel. As he rang the doorbell, he thought he could hear the siren of an ambulance sounding far away in the distance.

Kevan de Vries opened the door almost immediately. He was wearing a towelling dressing gown whose belt had come adrift, so that it hung loose to reveal a crumpled shirt beneath it. De Vries was both bare-legged and barefoot. His long comb-over was ruffled and lop-sided, either displaced by sleep or because de Vries had been raking his hands through it. His face was sallow and haggard, his eyes sunk deep into their sockets with ugly shadows beneath them. His expression was one of utter despair. Until he spoke, Ricky thought that he might have completely lost his reason.

"I thought you were the ambulance. Where's the ambulance?" he demanded. "What are you doing here?"

"The ambulance is on its way. I've just heard it," said Ricky, as soothingly as he could. "Would you mind letting me in, sir? DI Yates asked me to come. He said there'd been an accident."

"I suppose that's correct. It's Joanna – my wife. She's somehow managed to fall down the cellar stairs. I've checked for a pulse and can't find one. I called 999 for an ambulance. I suppose the operator sent for you as well?"

"I'm not sure about that, sir, but I'm here now. Let me see her."

"Of course. She's . . . but you know your way to the cellar, don't you? It's because of you people that all this business with the cellar started."

He continued to speak, but Ricky was barely listening. He brushed past de Vries and sped down the cellar steps. Kneeling beside Joanna de Vries, he tried to find a pulse in either her wrist or her neck, but he knew it was just a gesture and that the action was futile. It was clear to him that she'd been dead for some time. The body was already cooling. They needed to get Professor Salkeld here as soon as possible. He called Tim, who sounded considerably more awake and less irritable than when they had spoken ten minutes before.

"What exactly has happened?" Tim asked. "I couldn't get much from the Boston switchboard. Some garbled story about a fall."

"That's correct," said Ricky. "It's Mrs de Vries. She seems to have fallen down the cellar steps – or even over the banister, judging from where she's lying now. I'd say that her neck is broken."

"You're quite sure that she's dead?"

"Positive. There's absolutely no chance that she can be revived – the body's getting cold. There's an ambulance on its way, though."

"What was she doing in the cellar? I asked Superintendent Thornton to tell de Vries that no-one was to go down there – and I left it carefully taped."

"You did, sir. I don't have an answer to that. I'd 've said that would be the last place she'd want to go."

"Where's de Vries now?"

"Upstairs somewhere. He didn't want to stay here with me. I'm not surprised, poor bloke."

"Yes. Well, don't let him leave the premises. I'm coming straight there myself. And don't let the paramedics move the body or, it goes without saying, attempt to take it away. I'll try and get Stuart Salkeld there – though he won't thank me for wrenching him from his bed at this hour."

"I was going to suggest contacting him myself, sir. That's partly why I called you."

"Yes, well, perhaps you'd like to call him and get his customary earful when his sleep's been disturbed. But on second thoughts I'd better do it myself. If you call him, he probably won't come at all."

"I'll see you shortly, then, sir. Good luck."

Ricky terminated the call, a gleam of amusement in his eye despite the circumstances. DI Yates had a few failings, most of them venial ones, and among the most endearing was his belief that he and only he could persuade difficult colleagues to co-operate. If he only knew, Ricky ruminated, how often Juliet Armstrong had smoothed his way to success.

THIRTY-NINE

Tim arrived at Laurieston House about three quarters of an hour after Ricky MacFadyen. An ambulance was already parked in the drive, dwarfing Joanna de Vries' small Fiat. There were lights on in all the downstairs rooms and, Tim noted, in both the downstairs and upstairs rooms of 1 Laurieston Terrace.

Jackie Briggs opened the door to him. She looked close to tears, as if she had been crying. She was dressed in a black jumper and trousers, which accentuated her gauntness. A coincidence, Tim wondered, a macabre fluke that had happened when she'd pulled on the first clothes that had come to hand when she was awakened? Or had she gone home to change when she'd realised that Joanna de Vries was dead? She shouldn't have been there at all, strictly speaking: the fewer people who were admitted to the house now, the better. He could quite understand, however, that Ricky had found it impossible to exclude her once she had turned up, especially if Kevan de Vries had asked her to come. Somewhat incongruously, he saw that she was once again wearing her old-fashioned piece of costume jewellery, the brooch with the big stone. She'd pinned it to one side of the neck of her jumper.

Ricky met him in the hall.

"The two paramedics are waiting in the kitchen, sir," he said. "I knew you wouldn't want them to remove the bod . . . the deceased."

"Where's Mr de Vries?"

"He's in his bedroom. He said he'd come down to see you when Ms Rook arrived."

"He's called his solicitor? He's been a bit quick about it, hasn't he?"

"I suppose so. He called her soon after I came – from the phone in the hall."

"Was that before or after the paramedics got here?"

"Before – but only just. They'd arrived before he'd put the phone down."

"What did he say to her?"

"He was quite terse. I think he said, 'Jean, you'd better get over here as quickly as you can. I think that Joanna's just died.'"

"That was all? And he only said that he 'thought' that she'd died? Don't you think it was strange that he was having the conversation at all if he wasn't sure that his wife was dead?"

"I honestly don't think there was anything sinister about that, sir. When you see the deceased, you'll realise that he could have been in no doubt that she was dead. I suppose that the way he put it was just a kind of softening of the reality of it."

"How did he seem to you, when he let you into the house?"

"Distressed, but not hysterical. I asked him if I could check on his wife. He told me that I knew where the cellar was and said I could go down to look at her if I liked, but that he'd appreciate it if I didn't touch her. As I went down the cellar steps, I called back to him that I was a qualified first-aider and he said, quite quietly, that she was beyond my help."

"So you went down immediately?"

"Yes, but I didn't stay long. It was clear that what he'd said was correct. Despite what he said, I felt her neck for a pulse, but it was obvious that she was dead."

"And when you came back up, he was calling Jean Rook, and then the paramedics arrived?"

"Yes. Do you want to see the paramedics now?"

"Yes, but I'd like you to stay here, if you would. I want to know immediately Jean Rook arrives. I don't want her to get to de Vries on her own before we see him."

"He's going to insist that she's there with him."

"I know. And although that's a nuisance, it's his prerogative. I just want to make sure that Ms Rook doesn't have the chance to prime him on what to say. I think it's odd that he wants his solicitor present if he's asking us to believe that this is an accidental death."

"You don't think it is?"

"I don't know. What do you think?"

"I doubt that Kevan de Vries has murdered his wife. I can't think what motive he could have had, for one thing; and, for another, he seemed to be devoted to her. She'd have been more likely to murder him, if you ask me."

"Why do you say that?"

"Just a hunch – not based on much except their body language when I saw them last night; I know you told me to stay clear, but I thought I'd just call in to see that all was well and he invited me in for a moment to see that they were both fine. I noticed the way she shrank away from him when he tried to put his hand on her arm. Once she gave him a really hostile look."

Tim wasn't convinced. He realised that they were wasting time by straying ever deeper into the realms of speculation. He was, however, struck by Ricky's initiative and decided not to reprimand him for disobeying his instructions. He might very well have done the same himself.

"I'm going to find the paramedics. They're in the kitchen, you said?"

Ricky nodded. As Tim edged past the open cellar door, he added: "It goes without saying that you're not to let anyone down there. I've asked Stuart Salkeld to come as quickly as he can. I don't want anyone else in the cellar before he arrives. I'll wait for him, too; I don't intend to go down there myself just yet."

The two paramedics were standing awkwardly by the kitchen range. Between them and the door, Jackie Briggs was seated at the large deal kitchen table, her head in her hands, sobbing quietly. The older of the two, a large middle-aged woman with straw-yellow hair done up in a high ponytail, seemed as if she was herself close to tears. Her colleague was a man in his thirties who looked fit and strong, as if he probably worked out regularly. His expression had been impassive when Tim entered the room, but became more animated when he saw the policeman. Tim guessed that they hated getting caught up in the emotion of occasions like this – and that they probably didn't have to, very often. In most situations they drove away, bearing with them a sick person or, less frequently, a corpse.

"I'm Detective Inspector Yates, South Lincolnshire Police," said Tim. "Thank you for waiting. I'd like to ask you a few questions. Then we can probably let you go." He took out his notebook. "First of all, I'd like your full names."

"Sharon Julie Kerensky."

"Richard Venables."

"Thank you. Are you able to give me the time at which you arrived at this house? The more exact you can be, the more it will help me."

"O three seventeen," said Richard Venables. "Sharon logged it just before we parked the ambulance."

"You went straight to the cellar?"

"Yes. We found a woman lying to the left of the staircase.

We ascertained immediately that she had died. There were no vital signs."

"Did you move her?"

"Sharon lifted her arm to try to take her pulse."

"You didn't try to turn the body? Didn't attempt CPR?"

"There was no point. She was already cooling. I reckon she'd been dead for at least an hour."

"That was the other question I was going to ask you. So you reckon you arrived an hour or so after death?"

"At least," Richard Venables repeated.

"Did anything strike you as odd?"

Richard Venables gave him a quizzical look.

"I'm not sure what you mean, sir. It's odd enough finding a fully-dressed woman lying dead in a cellar in the middle of the night, isn't it?"

"Sorry, you're right, of course. I'll put it another way. Did you think there had been an accident, or did you think that she might have been attacked in some way? Pushed, for example? Or fallen as the result of a struggle?"

Venables shrugged.

"I can't say that I did. I assumed she'd fallen. I suppose it crossed my mind to wonder what she was doing in the cellar at all, especially when I noticed the police tape when I came back up again."

"You didn't notice it when you first arrived?"

"Too busy concentrating on the job. We never think about anything besides getting to the patient quickly, even if we've been told they've got no chance. Sometimes people are wrong about that."

Tim nodded.

"Thank you. What about you, Ms Kerensky? Was there anything about this that struck you as different from similar situations you've witnessed?"

"I can't say that I've ever seen a patient in a cellar before. I've seen fall victims, though. I'd say that the way she fell – awkward, like – wasn't unusual. Unlucky, but not unusual. My guess is that she broke her neck. Poor woman," she added. She put her hand to her mouth. Tim hoped that she wouldn't cry and, in the process, noticed that Jackie Briggs had raised her head and was watching them. She seemed to have mastered her tears. Tim caught her eye and was certain in the split second that elapsed before she looked down that he glimpsed some kind of recognition there.

"Are you OK, Mrs Briggs? Did you want to tell me something?"

"No," said Jackie Briggs tremulously. "It's just that cellar. It..."

There was an urgent knock on the kitchen door before Ricky MacFadyen appeared, evidently in a hurry.

"Ms Rook is just arriving, sir," he said to Tim. "She'll be coming through the front door any minute now."

Jackie Briggs scraped back her chair and rose to her feet.

"I'll go and let her in," she said.

Five minutes later, Tim and Ricky were seated on the small sofa that faced the fireplace in the drawing-room of Laurieston House. Jean Rook was sitting in one of the fireside chairs. Jackie Briggs had placed a tea-tray on the coffee table that separated them, but no-one had troubled to set out the cups and saucers. Nobody spoke. All were waiting for Kevan de Vries to appear. Jean Rook had tapped out two or three rapid messages on her Smartphone. Tim did not doubt that she was communicating with de Vries, but knew that there was little he could do about it. De Vries was not under arrest, after all.

Jean Rook stood up suddenly and walked across to the door. It opened a minute or so later. Kevan de Vries entered the room, somewhat hesitantly. He was casually dressed in an open-necked blue shirt and pale chinos. His hair clung damply to his forehead, as if he had just taken a shower.

Jean Rook embraced him rather ostentatiously. Tim noted that de Vries accepted the gesture courteously, but quickly disengaged himself from her grip. Ms Rook took hold of his arm and guided him to the armchair at the opposite side of the fireplace from where she had been sitting. He sank into it wearily. Now that Tim could get a proper look at the business-man's face, he was shocked at de Vries' harrowed, stricken expression. The man was literally grey with grief.

"Would you like tea?" his lawyer asked, addressing herself only to de Vries.

"No. Thank you, Jean. But do pour some for my guests."

"Thank you. Not for me, either," said Tim. "But it is kind of you. Mr de Vries, may we say how sorry we are for your loss?"

Kevan de Vries met his eye. Tim could detect no gleam of the spirited irony that he had registered at their previous meetings, but he thought he could still discern some residual contempt.

"Well, I can't say that your interference improved the last few days that she had left to her, but you weren't the direct cause of her death, at any rate."

"I'm not sure that I understand you, sir."

"Oh, I think that you do. Hounding me first of all to come back from St Lucia and then digging up the cellar and finding bones there. How do you think that made her feel?"

"I agree that the recent events that have taken place at this house have been unfortunate for someone as ill as your wife was, and I'm sorry for that. I know that this may sound insensi-tive, but it wasn't a problem that I could make go away. But I'd like to be able to comprehend what you mean when you say that we weren't 'the direct cause of her death'. Do you believe that someone else was involved besides your wife? That there was more to her death than an unlucky accident?"

"I . . . don't know." Kevan de Vries shielded his eyes with his hands.

"I'd like you to describe what happened as clearly as you can, sir. Where were you when your wife fell?"

"I was in bed. I'd been in bed for several hours. I left Joanna sitting on the sofa in here. I'd suggested to her that it was time for bed."

"What time would this have been, sir?"

"It was early – before 10 p.m. Joanna was still exhausted from her flight and the visit that we made yesterday to see Archie. I was tired, too. I thought that if I went up to bed first it would encourage her to go as well."

"I'm not sure that I follow . . ."

"You don't have to answer questions about your domestic arrangements if you don't want to, Kevan," Jean Rook interceded, her voice metallic with disapproval.

"I've got no objection to answering, Jean." He looked at the floor as he continued. "Joanna was annoyed with me. I knew that she needed to go to bed and I thought it would encourage her if I volunteered to sleep in one of the guest rooms. I told her that was my intention."

"So you left her down here by herself, despite the severity of her illness?"

"What else could I do? What would you have recommended, Detective Inspector? That I dragged her to bed against her will, or perhaps called the local police to ask them to make her?"

"Point taken," said Tim. "Was she taking medication for her illness?"

"Yes, she was taking something called Fludaribine in pill form, and I think some other drugs as well, to help with the pain. They'd stopped giving her blood transfusions. I didn't get involved with her medication: it was something she kept to herself, but I know that she always followed her doctor's instructions scrupulously. She was trying to stay alive as long as possible for Archie's sake."

"You don't think she might have become confused, or forgotten to take the medication because she was tired?"

"I think that's very unlikely. As I say, she was committed to keeping going as long as she could."

Tim nodded sympathetically.

"So you went to bed in one of the spare rooms. Did you sleep?"

"Yes, after a while. It wasn't a deep sleep, but I think I was dozing on and off."

"Did Mrs de Vries in fact go to bed?"

"I don't think so. When I was awoken I went to our bedroom to see if she was all right, but the bed was empty."

"It didn't seem to you that she might have slept in it for a while and then got up again?"

"No. I thought the bed was as Mrs Briggs had left it after she'd changed the sheets yesterday morning."

"You said just now that you were 'awoken' in the night. What was it that woke you?"

"I heard a crashing noise. And what I thought was a scream – or someone crying out."

"And you were still in bed in the spare room?"

"The Blue Room. Yes."

"What did you do then?"

"As I've just told you, I went to our bedroom to check on Joanna. When she wasn't there..." Kevan de Vries' face suddenly contorted horribly. His chest heaved as he failed to suppress a series of deep sobs.

"I think that it's time that you concluded this interview, Detective Inspector, don't you?" said Jean Rook viperishly.

"You can see that Mr de Vries is very upset and not in a fit state to be questioned."

"Jean, just leave it, will you?" Kevan de Vries was almost screaming the words. "*I'll* tell *you* when I'm not fit to carry on. Is that understood?"

Jean Rook crossed her legs and gave a curt nod.

"Somehow I knew," de Vries continued in a voice so low that Tim could barely hear the words. "I knew when she wasn't in bed that something must have happened to her. I ran downstairs. At first, it didn't occur to me that she could be in the cellar. I rushed in here, but she wasn't here, either. It was when I went out again that I saw that the cellar door was ajar. The police tape that you'd sealed it with had been cut."

"Do you think that your wife cut it herself?"

"That's not a question that Mr de Vries can answer, Detective Inspector." Jean Rook had evidently recovered from her recent humiliation by de Vries and was back on the attack again.

"It's all right, Jean." Kevan de Vries raised his head and met Tim's eyes again, but this time he didn't look away. "Since you ask, I can't imagine why she would have done it. Joanna resented your presence in her house, as you know, but in my experience she's always been pretty law-abiding. Besides, the cellar gave her the creeps, even before all of this happened."

Tim sat bolt upright. Ricky MacFadyen looked up sharply from the notes he was writing.

"Do you realise what you're implying, Mr de Vries? If your intuition is correct, and Mrs de Vries did not cut that tape, then you're saying that, at some point between the time that you went to bed and your wife's death, someone else must have been in the house besides her and yourself."

Kevan de Vries shrugged.

"It sounds far-fetched, I know. But you must admit that this whole bloody episode has been surreal. You couldn't make it up! I have no idea who cut that tape, but of one thing I am certain: Joanna would have had to have had a damned good reason for venturing into the cellar in the middle of the night. And the only one I can think of is that someone either cajoled or threatened her into going down there."

"Do you have any evidence that supports this theory, besides your own knowledge of how your wife would be likely to behave?"

"No, but . . . Yes, wait a minute. Some time before the scream, I thought I heard the sound of car tyres on the gravel in the drive."

"But you didn't get up to investigate? Look out of the window?"

"No, the Blue Room is at the back of the house. But in any case I thought I was dreaming. I was certainly half asleep. I might have been dreaming, for all I know. I couldn't swear that I heard it."

"And if you thought you heard someone, that didn't make you fearful of your wife's safety – or your own, for that matter?"

"I've told you, I was half asleep." De Vries was defensive now and getting angry.

"You heard what Mr de Vries said, DI Yates. I must ask you not to bully him."

"I apologise," said Tim. He paused for a moment. "Mr de Vries, can we go back to the point where you said that you came out of this room, went into the hall and saw that the police tape had been severed. You said that the cellar door was slightly open. Was the light on in the cellar?"

"Yes, I think so. I'm pretty certain that I didn't turn it on myself."

"So what happened next? Did you open the door wider and go rushing down the cellar steps?"

"No. I opened the door, of course, and went in. I stood at the platform at the top of the cellar steps and looked over the rail. I saw Joanna immediately. She was lying almost directly below me, face down." Kevan de Vries covered his eyes again.

"I'm sorry that this is distressing for you, sir, and I'll be as brief as I can. Did you go down the steps at that point?"

"Yes, of course I did."

"Were you hurrying?"

"I'm not sure. I don't think so. I was dreading what I was going to find when I reached her. It was quite obvious to me from the way that she was lying that she was dead."

"Did you notice anything else at all that might suggest that she hadn't been alone in the cellar?"

"What do you think? She was my only concern from the moment that I saw her. If there'd been a whole army of people with her, I doubt that it would have registered."

FORTY

It was early: breakfast had yet to be served at the Pilgrim Hospital. Juliet was sitting up in bed. There was still a drip in her arm, pumping in antibiotics. It had been fitted as soon as she'd been admitted to hospital and although it had been swapped from arm to arm several times, it was beginning to feel unbearably sore. The area around the cannula was puffy and red. She dreaded each change of the shiny bag of clear liquid. The staff nurse had told her cheerfully that the antibiotics were very strong and that some people were sensitive to them, before wheedling Juliet into putting up with it for just one more day.

The burst of optimism that had buoyed Juliet through the second stage of her illness was beginning to fade. She wasn't allowed to shower while the drip was in place and washing her hair was next to impossible. Her long, thick curls, always difficult to manage, had insinuated themselves into a hideous frizz, whilst the hair on the crown of her head was greasy and flat. She was beginning to feel dehumanised. Fiercely proud and always a little uncertain about her appearance, she could have wept when she looked in the mirror. She hoped that Tim wouldn't visit her today. But it wasn't just Tim that she minded seeing her looking like a freak: she knew that she'd be acutely embarrassed when Louise Butler came back on duty. She pushed the thought to the back of her mind. It, too, made her feel uncomfortable.

She changed her position, hoisting herself further up in

the bed whilst trying not to move her pinioned arm, and with her free hand reached across to the bedside cabinet to pick up Florence Jacobs' journal again. Katrin was right: there was something distinctly odd about the way in which it'd been written, almost as if it was a parody of a young woman's thoughts. Slowly, she flipped through the journal, taking care not to damage its stiff pages. It was a bulky tome, and quite heavy: it wouldn't have been practical for a woman who travelled much, though evidently it had accompanied Florence on her rare excursions to seaside resorts. Of course, it hadn't been intended as a journal: originally it had been a guest book. That in itself was odd. Mrs Jacobs had showered gifts on Florence and ensured that her clothes and jewellery were fitting for her station as a gentleman farmer's wife. Why, then, did she choose to palm her off with a second-hand guest book in which to write her journal? Did Florence like the guest book? If not, she certainly had the means to buy herself a proper journal.

"Breakfast!" shouted the cheerful ward orderly who pushed his clanking trolley round the wards each day.

Juliet wasn't hungry, but she'd been told that if she didn't eat the antibiotics would make her sick.

She managed a thin smile.

"What is there?" she asked.

"I got Krispies, cornflakes, muesli and toast." He consulted a clipboard, to which he'd fastened a sheaf of menu slips. "You didn't order hot, did you?"

"No. Is there any brown toast?"

"Sorry, just white. Want some?"

"I'll have muesli, thanks."

He put the clipboard on the bed while he poured out the cereal. Juliet put down the journal beside it and pulled her swivel tray towards her. She gave an involuntary kick as she did so and sent the clipboard and the journal skidding across the bed on to the floor and scattering the little bundle of menu slips.

"Sorry!" she said.

"No problem. I'll get them in a minute." He placed the cereal on her tray. "Tea?"

"Yes, please."

He bent down, retrieved the journal and handed it back to her and she watched as he dived for the menu slips.

"Can I just rest these on your tray for a minute? I need to make sure I get them in the right order."

"Sure."

He shuffled the pieces of paper around as if they were playing cards. They'd been inscribed with handwriting in many shades of blue, some of it flowing, some laborious and childish, some crooked and crabbed, painfully fashioned by arthritic fingers.

"Cheers!" he said, as he squared the bundle on the tray and clipped it back to his board. "See you later!"

He trundled off, the wheels of the trolley squeaking excruciatingly as he went.

Juliet picked at the muesli without enthusiasm and took a sip of tea. She flipped over a few pages in the journal again. The handwriting changed slightly over time, as she and Katrin had both noticed. What was strange was that the ink didn't. She didn't know much about how ink was made at the end of Queen Victoria's reign, but she guessed that it was unlikely that the same exactly uniform colour could be obtained over a period of many years. Even modern ink varied a little in colour from one purchase to the next. Now that she thought about it, another curious thing about the journal was that, after the first couple of pages, it contained no crossings-out or blots. The subsequent pages followed on from each other, immaculate.

The more she thought about it, the more she suspected that the journal had been written during a much shorter period of time than it tried to convey. The author had made some attempt to indicate that Florence had gained more proficiency in writing as she'd grown older, but the whole thing was a clumsy production from the point of view of authenticity. In particular, the author had made the assumption that a poorly-educated girl was also half-witted.

The author? It leapt to Juliet's attention that the author of the journal was probably not Florence Jacobs. If it *was* her, then she'd probably written it under duress. If it wasn't her work, who else might have concocted it? Lucinda Jacobs? Frederick Jacobs, even? Could either of them have had a motive for creating such an elaborate forgery? If so, what might it have been?

Juliet made a valiant attempt at finishing the muesli. When she pushed the bowl away, there were only a couple of spoonfuls remaining. She drank the tea and lay back on her pillows. Despite the throbbing in her arm, she drifted into a fitful sleep.

FORTY-ONE

It was 6 a.m. by the time Professor Salkeld's car drew up at Laurieston House. Patti Gardner had arrived an hour earlier, but could not start work before Stuart Salkeld had examined the body in situ. After a short exchange with Tim and Ricky, she chose not to join them, but said she would wait in the kitchen. They remained in the drawing-room with Kevan de Vries and Jean Rook. The silence was sepulchral. Almost two hours had elapsed, during which no-one spoke more than a few words. Jean Rook had suggested that de Vries try to get some rest, but he had rebuffed her quite brutally, Tim thought; it was plain to see how much the woman was annoying him. Emotional intelligence was not Jean Rook's strong suit, but that was hardly news to Tim.

He sprang to his feet with some relief when he heard Stuart Salkeld's car crushing the gravel, seizing a legitimate opportunity to escape from the tense quiet. Ricky also stood up, evidently struck by the same thought.

"It's OK, I'll go," said Tim. "I need to have a quick word with Stuart before he starts." He turned before he reached the door. "Mr de Vries, I think that that's Professor Salkeld just arriving. He's the pathologist. Would you like to meet him before he goes to examine your wife?"

Kevan de Vries rose and started pacing the room in obsessive fashion, backwards and forwards between the hearth and the bay window, muttering something under his breath.

"Mr de Vries, are you all right? I asked whether you would like to meet Professor Salkeld, the pathologist?"

"I don't think that will be necessary, unless he wants to see me. It's Archie I need to worry about now." He glanced at his watch. "I must see him. Somehow, I have to explain to him that Joanna's . . . gone. If I leave now, I should get to the school before the boys have breakfast."

"You're in no fit state to drive," said Jean Rook swiftly, her tone almost hectoring.

"For God's sake, Jean . . ." Tim suddenly wondered why de Vries had invited the solicitor there at all. She'd done nothing but irritate him since her arrival and, as de Vries was not being charged with anything, her presence seemed superfluous. Had he expected to be charged? If so, of what? His wife's murder?

"Ms Rook has a point, Mr de Vries," Tim said out loud. "It would be irresponsible of us to allow you to drive at the moment."

"I'll take you," Jean Rook announced.

"No, Jean, you won't. If you all insist that I should be accompanied, I'll ask Sentance."

Simultaneously Tim and Ricky remembered what they had heard from de Vries the previous evening. They looked at each other. Sentance had a lot of explaining to do and de Vries was behaving oddly. There was a great deal to fathom besides Joanna de Vries' death. Allowing them to spend time alone together would be foolhardy while there was still the possibility that they had been engaged together in some kind of crime.

"DC MacFadyen will accompany you, sir," said Tim. "His car's just nearby. That will be the quickest solution."

Kevan de Vries shrugged. "If you say so. As long as I get to Sleaford before Archie's lessons begin, I really don't care."

"Will you bring him back here?" asked Jean Rook.

De Vries ignored her, speaking to Tim as if the question had come from him.

"That depends very much on your pathologist friend," he said. "How soon is he likely to be able to move Joanna? I can't bring the boy here while his mother is lying in the cellar. I take it that your professor will want to move her," he added. "He won't be leaving her here for the undertakers to deal with?" His face twisted into an ugly grimace. For the first time Tim was able to see the depth of the man's grief. He felt a lump rise in his own throat. How would he himself have managed to bear it if the circumstances had been reversed and it had been Katrin lying dead in the cellar instead of Joanna de Vries?

He laid a friendly hand lightly on de Vries' sleeve. De Vries did not try to shake him off.

"Let's ask him, shall we, sir? I think I heard Mrs Briggs let him in. He's probably waiting just outside for us."

Tim opened the door and the three men stepped out, closely followed by Jean Rook. Stuart Salkeld was standing in the hall, saying something to Jackie Briggs. He came forward to greet Tim and held out his hand to Kevan de Vries. Tim was relieved to see that he appeared to be on his best behaviour.

"I'm sorry for your loss, sir," he said, without introduction.

De Vries inclined his head and at the same moment Professor Salkeld caught sight of Jean Rook.

"Ah, Ms Rook," he said, his tone swiftly changing from one of respect to the Teflon-coated inflection of irony that he reserved for those he didn't like. "I didn't realise you were here. Just putting us on the right track, are you?"

"Ms Rook is Mr de Vries' solicitor," Tim said quickly. "She's here at his invitation."

"I see." There was a dangerous gleam in the pathologist's eye.

"Mr de Vries has a question for you," Tim ploughed on.

"He'd like to know whether you will be removing his wife's ... remains ... to the morgue, once you've completed your in situ investigation, and, if so, when that is likely to be. He wants to fetch his young son back from his boarding school at Sleaford," he continued. He watched a half-formed witticism die on the professor's lips.

"It's hard for me to say," said Stuart Salkeld gravely. "But unless circumstances are very peculiar indeed, I'm not likely to be here for more than an hour or two. And yes, I shall be removing her. I take it that you don't want your son to see her?"

De Vries shook his head. Again, he seemed overpowered by grief.

"I'll let DI Yates know when we're ready to remove her," the professor said. "He can call you. Will you be able to stay at the school with the lad until then?"

"I expect so." He looked at Ricky MacFadyen, clearly impatient to leave.

"I'll just fetch my car, sir. I won't be gone five minutes," said Ricky.

"Well," said Jean Rook crisply, shooting de Vries an affronted look for the first time since her arrival in the early hours of the morning. "If that's all you want from me, Kevan, I'll be on my way. I've got to get through a day's work, somehow, and I'm desperately in need of a shower. You can always call me later if you need me."

Kevan de Vries looked at her blankly for a moment, as if he did not recognise her. He passed a hand across his face as if the action would help to gather his thoughts.

"There is something that you can do, Jean. Can you get hold of Sentance and ask him to meet me here later today? Not when I come back with Archie, but this afternoon."

Jean Rook did not try to contain her anger.

"You want to see Sentance? Today? But why?"

"I have a business to run, Jean, and I'm only too aware of the responsibilities that go with it. But I may want to take Archie away for a while. I'll need to see Sentance before I go. I'll need to see you again, too: to discuss Joanna's will, and my own, for that matter."

"But you won't be going away before the funeral?"

"I rather think I will. I believe I'm correct in thinking that Professor Salkeld might want to hold Joanna's . . . Joanna for some weeks?"

"That's not beyond the bounds of possibility, sir, but we'll try to be as quick as possible."

"I'm sure you will, but even if you release her quickly, we won't be able to have a funeral for some time. Joanna has donated her body to medical research."

"I'm not sure you'll be able to go away just yet," said Jean Rook, looking meaningfully at Tim. "Aren't you still supposed to be helping the police with the passports' issue?"

Tim was amazed at the woman's cold-blooded cheek. She'd been fighting tooth and nail to free de Vries from the passport investigation until now. Presumably Joanna de Vries' death had put a different complexion on it. But even Tim himself would not have hassled the man with such a reminder on the day of his wife's death.

"We can discuss that later, sir," he said quietly. "We'll try to get it cleared up as quickly as possible, to leave you free to concentrate on your son. Talking of which, DC MacFadyen should have had time to bring his car round now. You said you wanted to leave as soon as possible."

"Thank you," Kevan de Vries said. He headed for the door, turning just once after he had opened it.

"You won't forget about Sentance, will you, Jean?"

"Of course not." She was businesslike again.

"Well, I'll be getting on," said Professor Salkeld. "Did you say Patti Gardner was here? If so, she can probably help me."

"She's in the kitchen," said Tim. Patti materialised at almost the same moment. She and Stuart Salkeld disappeared into the cellar, leaving Tim alone with Jean Rook. She returned to the drawing-room to retrieve her briefcase.

"Goodbye for now, Detective Inspector," she said when she was back in the hall. "I'm quite certain that we shall be meeting again soon."

"I don't doubt it," said Tim. "In the meantime, there is a favour I'd like to ask of you."

"Oh?" she raised an eyebrow archly. "Do tell me what it is."

"*We* need to speak to Tony Sentance again. We'll be trying to get in touch with him today, naturally. But if you manage to reach him before we do, would you let him know?"

"Certainly."

Tim was not convinced by her tone.

"If we don't manage to contact him, we'll have to come here to meet him this afternoon. I'm assuming that he won't refuse Mr de Vries' request."

"I think that's unlikely. I'll be sure to tell him you want to see him."

"Thank you."

She turned on her heel and made for the door. Tim noticed a ladder in her sheer black tights. It was running high up her thigh. For a moment, it made her seem vulnerable.

He shook off the thought. He was about to return to the cellar himself when he saw Jackie Briggs standing in the kitchen doorway. The look on her face was unfathomable.

FORTY-TWO

Later that day, Katrin was sitting at her desk, trying to concentrate on the de Vries company accounts that Superintendent Thornton had now asked her to obtain and examine, when her phone rang. The shrill ring cut through her reverie. She'd been so deeply preoccupied with Florence Jacobs' journal that it took her a couple of seconds to lift the receiver.

"Hello, Katrin, is that you?"

"Juliet! I didn't expect to hear from you again so soon. How are you?"

"Improving, I think. Still tired, that's all." Once again, Katrin detected an unwarranted chirpiness in Juliet's manner.

"Did you get the journal all right?"

"Yes, it came exactly when you said. I started reading it yesterday evening."

"You can't have finished it yet?"

"God, no, I'm a slow reader at the best of times and I'm finding Florence's handwriting harder than I expected. Besides, I want to think about what I'm reading as I go: it'll save more time in the long run than rushing through and then having to read it again. But I wanted to ask you something."

"Go on."

"You've surely noticed all the references to a Mr Rhodes. Do you think Florence could mean *Cecil* Rhodes?"

"Yes, I said as much to Tim, but it seemed a little far-fetched, somehow. I wanted you to mention it yourself without my suggesting it. Frederick Jacobs was an obscure gentleman farmer, not an African colonial."

"Perhaps, but the journal refers to his frequent absences. He seems to have been a very reluctant 'gentleman farmer' and an even more unpromising husband."

"I agree with you there."

"What do you know about Cecil Rhodes?"

"Not all that much. My grandfather spent some time in the country he was pleased to call 'Rhodesia' just after the war. He used to annoy me when I was a teenager with his bigoted pronouncements about black people not being fit to rule themselves. I've no idea why Rhodes was allowed to call the country after himself."

"Perhaps you might make time to find out? I'd be really grateful if you could do a bit of research into him. It's virtually impossible for me to get internet access here. Could you look him up and get back to me? Perhaps print some stuff out for me? I'd particularly like to know if he had any Lincolnshire connections and if he could have been the man Florence talks about in the journal."

"We've come to the same conclusion about what we need to find out! However, I'll need to have the journal back again, to check specific dates."

"I'll make sure you get it back as soon as I've finished reading it. There's no need to check actual dates just yet: what I want to know is whether Rhodes came back to this country in the 1890s and, if so, whether he could have included, or could've had reason to include, trips to Lincolnshire while he was here."

"I meant to do this for myself – you've confirmed my own feelings exactly."

"Not overloading you, am I? I should have asked how busy you were first. Have you got a lot on at the moment?"

"Nothing particularly urgent. Superintendent Thornton's asked me to work through the de Vries company accounts. I'll need to try to finish that today."

"Has he? That's interesting. Perhaps he doesn't really think that Kevan de Vries is the sterling character that he keeps on trying to sell to us."

"Well, he hasn't given me a reason and I've deliberately not told Tim about it. I don't want the Superintendent to think that I run to Tim with every piece of information that I think he might find interesting."

"Even though you do?" Juliet's voice took on a teasing tone.

"I'm not going to answer that. I'll see what I can find about Rhodes and either call you back or post some stuff to you."

After Juliet had rung off, Katrin immediately googled Cecil Rhodes. She started with Wikipedia. She knew she'd probably need to supplement and verify anything that she could glean about him in the online encyclopaedia, but it was a start. She took a long look at the photograph of 'The Right Honourable Cecil Rhodes'. He was an unpleasant-looking man: jowly and self-satisfied, she thought, as well as mealy-mouthed, and quickly looked across to the text.

Rhodes was the son of the vicar of Bishop's Stortford, and the family's roots were in the countryside, where Cecil Rhodes always felt at home: tree planting and agricultural improvement were among his lifelong passions, though his earliest ambition was to be a barrister or a clergyman. His father was prosperous enough to send one son to Eton College, another to Winchester College, and three into the army. Cecil, however, was kept at home because of a weakness of the lungs and was educated at the local grammar school. Poor health also debarred him from the professional career he planned.

Instead of going to the university, he was sent to South Africa in 1870 to work on a cotton farm, where his brother Herbert was already established.

Bishop's Stortford, she thought. Not a million miles from the Fens. She googled the distance between Bishop's Stortford and Sutterton. The search engine came up with how long it would take by car, as well as the distance in miles: one and three quarter hours. She supposed that travel time would have been doubled in late Victorian England – although there would probably have been a train service to take Rhodes at least part of the way. She carried on reading the article, noting that it was very pro-Rhodes: in fact, almost reverent in tone.

There was some suggestion that he was a misogynist, a trait that he would have shared with Frederick Jacobs if they'd met. The article even contained veiled hints that Rhodes had been homosexual. It didn't state this directly, though, just as the journal wasn't explicit about Frederick's sexuality. There was still nothing to link the two men, though.

Katrin flipped through several paragraphs about African colonial politics. She could barely understand them – the article was too brief to provide a proper context – but, although whoever had written it continued to describe Rhodes' activities with adulation, she found the great white man's outlook on life and the long list of his 'achievements' distasteful. Even allowing for the massive changes in attitude to colonialism and the subjugation of non-Europeans that had taken place in the eleven decades since his death, Rhodes' ambition and his cruel treatment – not to mention trickery – of African 'natives' was indefensible. The hubris of his eventual success in naming Rhodesia after himself could not be disguised by hagiography.

Skimming the details of Rhodes' frequent conflicts with black Africans, Katrin started to read more thoroughly when the account turned to his relations with British politicians and

Queen Victoria. By dint of the most shamelessly crass flattery, he'd had the old Queen eating out of his hand (no surprise there!), but Joseph Chamberlain, the British colonial secretary, appeared to have seen through him. Katrin was just struggling through the detail of why Chamberlain thought that Rhodes was in breach of the law when a couple of dates caught her attention. Rhodes was in England in 1892 and again in 1896. She'd have to wait until she got the journal back again before she could verify it, but she thought that at least the latter of these dates coincided with one of Frederick Jacobs' periodic run-ins with his mother about 'Mr Rhodes'. She was certain that Frederick had been frequently absent from home in the mid-1890s. Was it possible that he'd spent some of that time in Africa?

She scrolled back to the top of the article again. Cecil Rhodes seemed to be close to his many brothers and sisters, but there was no record of their having lived in Lincolnshire. The sisters looked as if they might yield more promising clues than the brothers, who seemed to have dispersed themselves to all corners of the Empire as soon as they were able; reading further, she saw that one of the sisters had spent time with Rhodes in Africa, too. *"Rhodes left nothing to his sister . . ."* the article said.

She carried out a further search for the sister and found nothing more of interest. She moved to the next page of the search engine, then on to the third. Halfway down the page she read: *"Mrs Rhodes' sister, Sophia Peacock, lived at Sleaford Manor . . ."* Excited, she clicked on the link. It took her some minutes to find the extract that she was looking for; infuriatingly, the link led first to the title page of a digitised text entitled *Makers of the Nineteenth Century*. Impatiently, Katrin ploughed through it until she reached the quoted passage:

Mrs Rhodes' sister, Sophia Peacock, lived at Sleaford Manor in the Belvoir country, where she often had one or more of the vicar's children to stay, her special favourite being Frank, whom she practically adopted. Cecil was often there for the holidays, and found himself in a circle of relations and acquaintances. His aunt Sophy was always a good friend to him, and she was one of the few to whom in those early days he confided his plans and aspirations. Some Willson cousins lived two miles away at Rauceby; the Finch Hattons at Haverholm close by, and the family of Mr. Yerburgh, rector of Sleaford, were close friends, and Frank had Eton companions to stay there.

There's the link! Katrin was exultant. Rhodes had had an aunt in Sleaford and spent a chunk of his childhood there. How far was it from Sleaford to Sutterton? Eighteen miles, or 26 minutes by car, Google informed her. It was close enough for Rhodes and Frederick Jacobs to have had friends or acquaintances in common and therefore opportunities to meet socially. There was something else about the paragraph that tugged at Katrin's memory as she was reading it. She worked through it again, more slowly. Rauceby! The hospital was familiar to her as a now defunct former refuge for the mentally ill. Although it was now no longer in use, she'd visited it on one occasion, when it had been opened to the public, and in common with others had shuddered at the padded cell, the facilities for electric shock treatment and other barbarisms that had seemed more fitting props for the Middle Ages than the twentieth century.

She half-remembered that, before it became a 'mental hospital', in the late nineteenth century it had been a sanatorium – an isolation hospital for sufferers from tuberculosis. She knew from the Wikipedia article that Rhodes had been a delicate child. Had he been diagnosed with tuberculosis? Frederick

Jacobs was also frequently ill – or at any rate as an adult used indisposition as an excuse for not fulfilling his farming duties. Had he also been sent to the Rauceby sanatorium when he was young?

Eton was another possible line of enquiry. She knew that Cecil himself had not been sent to the school like his brother, ostensibly because of his poor health, but possibly also because his father's finances could not stand the strain of paying two sets of fees. But his elder brother Frank, the Etonian, was Aunt Sophy's favourite and he and Cecil, who were close, both stayed with her. Perhaps Frederick was originally one of Frank's school friends?

Katrin accessed several more promising articles, but could find nothing to link the two men directly. Still, she felt exhilarated. She'd discovered enough coincidences and common interests for it to be probable that they were acquaintances, colleagues, or even friends. She'd need to dig deeper by consulting more scholarly material about Rhodes: an authentic biography that mapped his life in detail. She might even be able to find more about Frederick Jacobs; in old Lincolnshire directories, for example. She'd need to visit the county archives and a big library.

Katrin cut and pasted the snippet about Aunt Sophy, added it to the Wikipedia article about Rhodes, saved it and printed the whole lot out for Juliet. She scribbled a few sentences to Juliet, addressed an envelope and consigned all the documents to the post tray. Juliet would receive it the following day and would no doubt agree with Katrin's deductions. But neither of them could get further until she unearthed more information. Finding the opportunity for this would be the next challenge. Katrin sighed as she forced herself back to the de Vries accounts. She knew that, however diligently she worked on these for Superintendent Thornton, he wouldn't allow her to pursue her Rhodes leads in work hours. As Juliet was still in hospital, she'd probably have to sacrifice a day's holiday to the cause.

FORTY-THREE

The whole nightmarish episode with Archie was even worse than I expected it to be. I asked the little twat of a housemaster how best to break it to him and with sickening coyness he offered to break it to Archie himself. I told him in no uncertain terms where to get off, which meant that I was probably not in the best frame of mind when Archie was eventually brought to me. I blurted out that Joanna was dead very clumsily. But to be honest, there was no good way of doing it, no chance ever of softening the blow. If the little housemaster had any inkling of how to 'take into account Archie's condition', as he so unctuously put it, he didn't pass it on to me.

What happened next was only too predictable. Archie flung himself at me, kicking, biting and sobbing. I let him carry on for as long as he could. I felt that I deserved it, even enjoyed it in a weird way, as if accepting some kind of just retribution. The housemaster just flattened himself against the wall and watched. He seemed not so much terrified as totally effete. That wasn't really a surprise, either.

Eventually Archie tore himself away from me and hurled himself into a corner. He knelt on the floor with his back to both of us and began to rock backwards and forwards, banging his head rhythmically against the wall.

FORTY-FOUR

Tim watched as Professor Salkeld supervised the removal of Joanna de Vries' corpse from Laurieston House. It had been put into a body bag and strapped to a stretcher, but even though it was thus tidied out of sight he found the spectacle both macabre and unnerving. He was convinced something was badly amiss in this house and he wasn't just thinking of the accidental death of a terminally-ill woman.

Stuart Salkeld had said very little since, together with Patti Gardner, he'd re-emerged from the cellar, so Tim was surprised when he came clambering back out of the ambulance. Patti was standing in the open doorway of Laurieston House, smoking a cigarette. Salkeld edged past her, sniffing appreciatively at the smoke that she was exhaling.

"DI Yates? A word, if you have time."

"Of course."

Tim led him back into the drawing-room. It seemed as if days, rather than hours, had passed since he'd sat here with Kevan de Vries and Jean Rook, tensely awaiting the professor's arrival.

Professor Salkeld fixed Tim with his bright blue eyes and began talking in his usual terse fashion, wasting no time with preamble.

"I don't think she died of a broken neck."

"She couldn't have been pushed, then?"

"Oh, she could have been pushed, and fallen awkwardly,

too. But I've yet to establish the cause of death. I'll need to perform an autopsy to be sure, but I suspect that it was an aneurysm of the brain."

"So she passed out and then fell?"

"If I'm correct, yes."

"And you're saying that no-one else was there? But, if that's the case, I don't understand why she . . ."

The professor cut in.

"Still good at jumping to conclusions, I see! I'm very far from saying that no-one else was there. In fact, I think it is quite impossible that she was alone."

"What do you mean?"

"As you correctly observed, the head was lying at a very awkward angle in relation to the body. I think that someone lifted her up after she fell, perhaps tried to revive her and, when they realised it was hopeless, dropped her again, probably none too ceremoniously, perhaps because they panicked."

"And left the house?"

"So it would seem. Or left the cellar, and quite precipitately, at any rate."

"But Kevan de Vries was the only other person . . ."

"That's your problem, not mine. I refuse to speculate."

"Indeed. Might it be possible to find fingerprints on the body, if the person who lifted her wasn't wearing gloves?"

Tim found to his surprise that his question triggered one of the longest speeches that he'd ever heard Stuart Salkeld make.

"Fingerprints are created from oils that come off the perpetrator's skin. It's hard work getting good ones under most circumstances, but usually easier when they occur on hard or smooth objects. Human skin has neither of these properties. Therefore, although it is certainly possible to get fingerprints off a body, the oils are similar to those of the victim and tend to mix, which can make them smudge. A lot depends on how much skin can be tested for the prints. They're not going to be easy to find and it is important to know where to look for them."

"Well, I'd be grateful if you'd do your best. Would you like Patti to come with you, to help?"

The professor threw Tim a withering look.

"Much as I respect Ms Gardner's forensic prowess, I'm quite capable of carrying out an autopsy on my own." His tone was severe, but Tim detected a hint of the underlying irony that was often present in the pathologist's pronouncements. "However, if Ms Gardner would like to accompany me, I've no objection to taking a pupil." Professor Salkeld glanced at his watch. "We need to get away now, though. The sooner I do the autopsy, the better; and that wee lad will be coming home soon, won't he?"

The professor gave a deep sigh. Tim had noticed before that he could drop his guard completely when there were children involved.

FORTY-FIVE

Jean Rook had not succeeded in reaching Tony Sentance by telephone, so she'd rung Tim to say that she'd left messages for him to meet them at Laurieston House. She'd suggested to Tim that if Kevan de Vries and Archie came home in the meantime, the police might take Sentance to the shoe-box-sized police station which was all that Sutterton could boast and talk to him there. She was being super-helpful now, a development that Tim mistrusted. Ms Rook was not renowned for co-operating with the police.

Tim had not been able to reach Sentance, either. He reasoned that the man was more likely to obey a summons that came indirectly from 'Mr Kevan' than directly from a policeman. It was strange that even de Vries could not raise him. Tim called Ricky to tell him that the coast was clear if de Vries wanted to bring his son home. He thought he might leave it up to de Vries himself to choose whether Sentance was interviewed at his house or not when he finally showed up.

Jean Rook had said that she'd asked Sentance to come to Laurieston at around 1 p.m. She'd left messages for him at the various de Vries factories and offices and, since it was his habit to call them all at around 11 a.m. each day, he would have received her message by mid-morning at the latest, which would give him plenty of time to reach Sutterton by lunchtime as long as he hadn't travelled further afield than the Norfolk plant.

Tim still had almost two hours to kill, therefore. He debated whether it was worth returning to Spalding to see Thornton and decided that it wasn't. Nevertheless, the Superintendent had been uncharacteristically quiet since he'd been informed of Joanna de Vries' death, which made Tim a little uneasy. He'd decided to go out to his car so that he could call his boss in privacy when the crunching of the gravel outside announced another arrival. Tim noted that the noise it made was quite loud. Such a sound could possibly have woken Kevan de Vries in the early hours, especially if he was a light sleeper.

The door opened slowly. Kevan de Vries entered, holding tightly the hand of a young boy. Tim could just glimpse Ricky MacFadyen standing behind them in the driveway at a respectful distance. De Vries was visibly annoyed.

"DI Yates. I saw your car in the drive. I didn't expect you still to be here."

"I'm sorry, Mr de Vries. I thought that you knew that DC MacFadyen had received a call from me; about ten minutes ago, I think it was."

Ricky was hovering in the doorway now, wearing an uncomfortable expression.

"Indeed. But I thought that the purpose of the call was to indicate that you were about to leave."

"No, sir, it was to let you know that . . . it was safe for you to come home." Tim glanced at the child, who was staring up at him impassively. He had a pinched, sallow little face and a peculiarly remote look in his eye. Tim supposed that he must be very distressed, although his state of mind was unreadable. "But forgive me," he went on. "It was not originally my intention to disturb you further – though I'm afraid I shall have to leave a PC on guard for the time being. I'm still here myself because Ms Rook has been trying to get hold of Mr Sentance."

I understand that she's asked him to come to your house at around lunchtime."

"Oh, God, Sentance. I'd forgotten that I'd asked Jean to call him. But I hadn't expected to share the meeting with you, DI Yates."

"I won't intrude on your meeting, sir. If you wish, I'll take Mr Sentance somewhere else to talk to him."

There was a small, sharp cry. It reminded Tim of the mewling of a hawk he'd seen at a country fair. It had been caged and shackled prior to taking part in a falconry display. He glanced at the child and saw that his face had turned white and was horribly contorted into a grimace of . . . what? It would be the most natural thing in the world for the boy to show sorrow, even uncontrollable grief. Instead what he was conveying, and most powerfully, was a mixture of disgust and anger.

Tim hated the 'Does he take sugar?' approach to communicating with children, so he decided to risk talking to the boy directly.

"Are you all right? Archie, isn't it? I'm sorry . . ."

"I don't think that Archie's in a fit state to talk now, DI Yates. I'll take him to Mrs Briggs and come back to you when he's settled."

"Of course."

As they brushed past him, Tim thought that he saw the child try to pull away from de Vries and that the father responded by tightening his grip on the boy's hand. He was rather surprised to see de Vries knocking on the kitchen door before he opened it – and, now he thought of it, Jackie Briggs had not come running out to see Archie when they had arrived. He supposed that some kind of master-servant etiquette must be at work.

Now that they were alone in the hallway, he turned to Ricky, who had just closed the front door.

"Strange kid," said Tim.

"You can say that again. I know that anger's supposed to be a part of grief, but he seems to be eaten up with it. I haven't heard him say a word yet, either."

"Does anything else strike you as odd about him?" said Tim, lowering his voice. Ricky twigged at once and followed suit.

"Just about everything about him strikes me as odd. What were you thinking of in particular?"

"Do you know how old he is?"

"I think he's nine. Small for his age, isn't he?"

"Yes, there's that, for a start. And then there are his parents."

"What do you mean?"

"Think about it. Joanna de Vries was tall and blonde and probably, from the photographs here, on the plump side before she got ill. De Vries himself is shorter, granted, but very stocky and also very blond. How did they manage to have a child like him?"

Ricky shrugged.

"Stranger things have happened. I've read about white women who've unexpectedly given birth to black babies and traced it back to a black ancestor that they didn't know about from four or five generations before."

"Yeah, right," said Tim. "And I can think of a simpler explanation for that, too. But I'd take your point about Archie if I hadn't found out something else about him as well."

"What's that?"

"Officially speaking, he doesn't exist."

"Come again?"

"No British birth certificate has been issued to a boy named Archie or Archibald de Vries during the past twenty years. I've had the records at Somerset House checked."

"Perhaps he's adopted?"

Tim shook his head.

"There's no record of that, either, or that the de Vries are registered as foster parents."

"Maybe they did adopt, but just didn't change the boy's name? They call him Archie de Vries, but his real name is still the one on his birth certificate?"

"It's possible, but I don't think so. A man like Kevan de Vries would want to make sure that his son took his name and he'd carry out all the correct legal processes necessary, if only to ensure that there would be no arguments when it came to inheriting his wealth."

"Then I don't understand."

"Joanna de Vries was diagnosed with leukaemia a long time ago, just a few years after her marriage, in fact . . ."

"You're right, Detective Inspector, she was. May I ask what bearing that can possibly have on your investigation into her death?" Kevan de Vries had reappeared silently while they were talking. He'd snapped right back into the cautious urbanity that he'd displayed on his first meeting with Tim. Tim detected an undercurrent of menace in his tone, nevertheless.

FORTY-SIX

Juliet was fingering Florence's notebook, which had been restored to her by the breakfast orderly. Its fall to the floor had knocked the corners of the boards. With her forefinger, Juliet traced the outline of the flower that had been affixed to its padded cover. She encountered a small tear in the thick paper that was almost concealed by the flower. Curious, but not wishing to damage the journal further, she held it up to scrutinise it. The harsh yellow overhead lights in the ward made it difficult to inspect, but, by turning on her bedside lamp and holding the journal close to its gentler, paler light, she was able to see through the tear that the padding under the cover consisted of some dark, ochre-coloured paper. She could see only a tiny piece of it – it measured perhaps half a square centimetre – but on this small section she could clearly see writing, or at least a few inked strokes that had evidently been formed by a pen.

Juliet found herself immediately thrust into a dilemma. She realised that the ochre paper might have no significance at all; it could just be scrap that the manufacturer of the notebook had used to pad out the cover. On the other hand, it might help her to understand what had happened at Laurieston House when Florence Jacobs had been its nominal chatelaine. But neither she nor Katrin owned the notebook. It was the property of Jackie Briggs. She couldn't inflict further damage on the cover to extract the ochre paper without asking Jackie for permission. She decided to call Katrin.

"I'm happy to call Jackie Briggs and ask her if she minds," said Katrin. "But I can't do it today. You obviously haven't heard from Tim yet. Joanna de Vries was found dead in the cellar at Laurieston House in the early hours of this morning. Tim's there at the moment, with Kevan de Vries and his son. I think that Mrs Briggs is helping to look after the boy."

"That's terrible news! I feel so sorry for the child. And his father: Kevan de Vries isn't the sort of person you take to immediately, but I've never been entirely convinced that he's a villain, either. But how did Joanna de Vries die? Was it suicide? It's strange that that cellar has claimed yet another life. It's as if it's jinxed."

"Tim said something like that when he called me. I think he was actually repeating something that Kevan de Vries said to him. I don't think they know how she died, yet. Stuart Salkeld's taken the body away to do a post mortem. It could have been an accident. But Tim says that what's most odd about it is that she was in the cellar at all. Apparently it always gave her the creeps."

"I'm not surprised! The whole house gives me the creeps. But she couldn't have known about the skeletons in the cellar until recently. I wonder why she didn't like it before that?"

"I don't know – but not everyone enjoys poking about in damp cellars, though I must admit I've always wanted to live in a house that had one, myself. I've just had another thought about the journal."

"Go on."

"It would still need Jackie Briggs's permission – but why don't we take it to the Archaeological Society and ask if one of the people who carries out restoration work there can get the ochre paper out from under the cover? They're likely to damage it far less than we will. They'll probably be able to stick the outside paper back to the cover so it looks just the same as it did before – they might even re-pad it."

"You're a genius!" said Juliet. "How should I return the journal to you? I don't suppose that Tim will be coming to see me today, given what you've just told me. I think they may discharge me tomorrow, so it could wait until then. But I don't know if they'll allow me to see you. There may be a slight chance that I'm still infectious. And I'm impatient for us to solve this mystery, if we can."

"Me, too. Great news that they're going to let you out. With regard to the journal – Tim told me that there's a new WPC in his team, who's still living in Boston. Perhaps she could pick it up. I think her name's Verity something."

"Verity Tandy. I've met her once and she left a message for me when I was first brought here. I didn't feel up to answering it at the time. But I agree, she's worth a try."

"How are you feeling now?"

"It's difficult to say while I'm in here. It's such an odd experience being in hospital: de-humanising, almost. And I've been pumped full of antibiotics, which certainly hasn't helped. I think I'm probably just a bit weak still. And bored. But having Florence Jacobs' journal to mull over has certainly helped in that respect. But how do *you* feel? I should have asked before."

"Still quite sick, but it's not unbearable. The journal's helped me, too. But work is boring at the moment – I've been looking at all sorts of financial and personnel records from de Vries Industries, for Superintendent Thornton. I don't know what he thinks I might find, but so far it all seems perfectly above board. I'd better get back to it now."

After Juliet had put down the phone, she lay back on the pillows for a while, looking at the drip in her arm and the inflamed red skin that surrounded the cannula. It was late morning. In the distance she could hear the clanking of trolleys, the signal that the first of the ward lunches were being served. She knew that Louise Butler would visit while on her rounds later in the afternoon. She'd make an effort to get out of bed after lunch, ask one of the nurses to help her wash her hair. She told herself that it was because, if she were to be discharged tomorrow, she wanted to leave the hospital looking presentable.

FORTY-SEVEN

Kevan de Vries had offered Tim the use of the drawing-room at Laurieston House so that he could wait for Tony Sentance to appear while de Vries himself disappeared into the kitchen. Tim could hear him speaking to someone in low tones and a woman's voice joining in. Both seemed to be cajoling a third person rather than conducting a conversation with each other. He guessed that de Vries and Jackie Briggs were trying to comfort or reason with Archie.

Tim paced around restlessly for a few minutes, before remembering once again that he had yet to contact Superintendent Thornton. Although he doubted that if he spoke in normal tones it would be possible for de Vries and Jackie Briggs to hear what he was saying, he felt uncomfortable about talking about de Vries while taking advantage of the man's hospitality. He therefore decided to make the call from the garden.

He slipped out through the front door and turned right past the bay window to a spot where he'd noticed a wrought-iron bench placed close to a weeping willow tree. It was damp and spattered with bird droppings, but he found a cleanish section near to the willow and sat down. He'd just taken out his mobile when it began to ring. He peered at the number. It wasn't one that he recognised.

"I want to speak to Detective Inspector Yates, please."

It was a woman's voice. She had a strong local accent and sounded agitated.

"Speaking. Who am I talking to?"

"My name is Dulcie Wharton. I work at the de Vries plant at Sutton Bridge. I've been trying to contact a DC Carstairs, but I don't have his number."

"I can give you it if you like."

"There's no time. I'll get caught. I'm in the office but I can't stay here. I found your card on Mr Sentance's desk."

"Can you tell me what it's about?"

"It's about that girl. The one who was murdered. I can't stand by and tell you nothing. It might happen again ..." There was a sudden silence.

"Hello? Mrs Wharton? Are you still there?"

"Yes... there was someone walking past. I've got to go."

"Call me again when..."

The phone went dead.

Tim called Andy's number immediately.

"Hello, Tim?"

"Where are you?"

"Heading back towards the station. I'm almost there."

"I've just been called by a woman named Dulcie Wharton, at the de Vries plant in Sutton Bridge. She said she'd really wanted to speak to you, but didn't have your number. She sounded frightened."

"I remember her. She was one of the supervisors I spoke to – the only one who got upset when I showed them the picture of the girl's body at Sandringham."

"She said 'she couldn't let it happen again'. Does this make any sense to you?"

"No more than it does to you, but I think we should take it seriously. I was convinced the supervisors were in cahoots over something and that Tony Sentance was masterminding it. Dulcie was the only one who wasn't quite toeing the line – and the others made pretty sure of shutting her up. The other woman among them hustled her out of the room very sharpish when she got emotional."

"Do you think she's in danger?"

"She could be, but my guess is that she won't put herself at any further risk. You've probably got as much out of her as she's prepared to give. What do you want me to do? I can go back to Sutton Bridge and ask to speak to the supervisors again, if you like."

"You'll have to be careful not to expose her. You could insist on interviewing them separately, and see if she'll tell you any more. I'd like to come with you, but I'm still at Laurieston House, waiting for Tony Sentance to turn up here. I'll let you know when he's arrived. You can head for Sutton Bridge now, but don't go into the plant until I call you. Then at least you won't have him getting in your way again when you start the interviews."

The call was interrupted by the impatient pip-pips that signified 'caller waiting'.

"I think that Superintendent Thornton's trying to get through. I'd better go."

"Yates? Where the hell are you? I've been trying to get hold of you all morning."

"I'm sorry, sir. I was just about to call you when . . ."

"Are you with Kevan de Vries?"

"Not exactly, sir. I'm at his house, waiting for Tony Sentance to show up. He's with his son at the moment."

"Is he quite happy to have you there?"

"I wouldn't say he was happy about anything at the moment, sir. But he seems prepared to let me interview Sentance here. My understanding is that he wants to see him as well. At the moment, no-one seems able to locate him. Jean Rook's trying to track him down."

"My God! Is she there, too?"

"Not at the moment, but . . ."

"Well, just try to handle all this delicately, will you, Yates? I want de Vries treated with kid gloves. The man's just lost his wife, for God's sake! Don't outstay your welcome, whatever else you may think you need to do."

"No, sir."

"And keep me informed. Are you making any progress with the passports? That's what you really ought to be doing. Once you've spoken to this Sentance, I want you back on that job. Concentrating on it, Yates, if that isn't too much to ask."

Superintendent Thornton didn't wait to hear Tim's reply. Tim thought that it was just as well: if he'd had the patience to listen a little longer, Tim would have had to tell him that he'd sent Andy Carstairs back to Sutton Bridge. He replaced the phone in its case and stood up. The call from Dulcie Wharton had been troubling.

Jean Rook's car swung through the double gates and drew in smartly beside his own. She shot out of it immediately. Tim observed that she was more elegantly dressed than when he had seen her in the early hours of the morning. However, her face was pinched and drawn, her eyes almost wild. She hurried towards him as fast as four-inch heels on deep gravel would permit. Intrigued by her unwonted lack of composure, Tim also began to walk. They met by the bay window.

"DI Yates! I'm glad you're still here."

"Well, that makes a first," said Tim drily. "Is there something wrong, Ms Rook?"

"I think that Tony Sentance may have left the country. There's evidence that he's helped himself to a significant sum of money from de Vries Industries."

"We should go into the house. We can't talk properly here."

Jean Rook glanced fearfully at the bay window and caught her breath.

"Kevan's watching us. We'll have to let him know, now."

Tim was puzzled.

"Is there any reason why he shouldn't know? Aside from sparing his feelings, I mean?"

"Yes . . . No. It's very complicated."

Tim had never expected to see Jean Rook so agitated. He grasped her elbow lightly.

"Let's go in," he said.

FORTY-EIGHT

Archie is resting in bed. Jackie and I finally persuaded him to go upstairs with us after she gave him some of the sedative that the doctor left, disguised in chocolate milk. Even though he's a child and incapable of making choices about his own health, I feel bad about tricking him with the drugs. He's taken too many drugs in his life, most of them, I suspect, of no benefit to him whatsoever. I leave Jackie sitting beside his bed, holding his hand as he dozes. I grit my teeth, knowing that now I have to run the gauntlet of another interview with DI Yates. Sentance will be here soon, too. And Jean, I suppose. I must think clearly. What I have to do now is close this whole thing down as soon as possible so that I can take Archie away. We can start again together. I'm determined to make him trust me and I'm equally resolved to make him happy. It's strange that for so many years I was desperate to create an heir, obsessed with the thought that if Joanna couldn't conceive there would be no-one to take over the business. De Vries Industries! Why would I wish them on anyone, let alone my own son? I'll divest myself of them as soon as I can and move away from the murk of this Fenland village, the sinister gloom of this house. Archie and I will find somewhere glorious to live in the sun.

I stand for a few moments on the landing, and listen. Jackie is humming to Archie, a wordless crooning to soothe him. He makes no sound. I hope that he is already asleep.

I'm mildly irritated when I enter the drawing-room to discover that DI Yates is no longer there. I'd assumed that the man would have had the courtesy to tell me if he was leaving, but there's no telling, of course. He strikes me as less uncouth than most of the policemen I've met, even so. I glance across the room and see that the small attaché case that he carries is lying on the sofa. Unlikely that he's left completely, then, but where has he gone? I suppose that he may have returned to the cellar, even though he told me it should be left sealed until the forensic woman can come back. I'm about to retrace my steps when I see him outside, standing close to the bay window. He's talking to someone. I crane my neck a little and see that it is Jean. She's looking agitated, which is out of character. I shouldn't have involved Jean in any of this. It cuts too close to the bone with her. And I know she's an inveterate schemer. God knows what might be going through her mind, now that Joanna's died.

She catches my eye momentarily and looks away. The detective takes hold of her arm. He seems to be persuading her to come into the house, which in itself is odd: she doesn't usually need any encouragement. I decide to stay put and wait for them to show up.

A couple of minutes later, there's a knock at the door. It's the detective's notion of being polite, I guess; I doubt if Jean would have bothered if she'd been on her own.

"Come!" I say, taking an ironic pleasure in sounding like my pompous headmaster when I was at the Grammar School.

They enter the room together. Yates is looking puzzled and Jean is decidedly flustered. I note that she's more appropriately dressed than usual, in a sober black suit with a skirt that reaches the knee. Out of respect for Joanna? More likely she wants me to believe this is her reason.

"How is your son?" the detective asks.

"He's upstairs with Mrs Briggs. With any luck she's

managed to get him off to sleep. He's very distressed, as I'm sure you could see." I turn to Jean. "When did you say that you asked Sentance to come here? There are several things that I want him to deal with as quickly as possible."

Jean looks at me without speaking. It's a look I can't read: stricken, or mutinous? It's hard to say, but I don't think I've ever seen her like this before.

"What's the matter?"

"It's Tony Sentance," she says eventually. "I think he's disappeared."

"What do you mean, disappeared? As in *absconded*? If so, why would he? I don't understand."

I see that the detective is watching me very closely. Does he know I'm hamming it up a bit? But it's Jean who speaks next.

"Kevan, I'm not sure what's happening. I think Tony's involved in more than we realise. There's quite a lot of money missing – I think maybe even . . ."

"Forget about the money, Jean. It's not important. As long as Archie and I have enough to live on in comfort, that's all that concerns me. And if I never have to clap eyes on Sentance again, so much the better. You'd better make sure all the bank accounts are closed against his signature, so that he can't take any more."

"I've done that already."

It's impossible not to admire the woman. I shoot her an appreciative glance before I turn back to the policeman.

"DI Yates, as it seems we are both unable to see Sentance this afternoon, perhaps you wouldn't mind leaving me in peace? I'd really rather spend the rest of the day with my son, if it's all the same to you. Perhaps you'd care to come back when your Professor Salkeld has established why Joanna . . . the cause of death."

"I'm sorry, sir, but I'm afraid I do have to continue with

my enquiries. It's become a matter of urgency. We don't have any proof yet, but we suspect that Tony Sentance is somehow involved in the death of the girl whose body was found in Sandringham woods a few days ago. One of my officers is on his way to interview the supervisors at your Sutton Bridge plant again now. If our suspicions are correct, the passports that were found in your cellar may be linked to her murder as well. We still don't know the girl's identity, but she was probably from one of the Eastern European countries. Forged passports can be used to get people into the country as well as out of it."

"Well, I'm sorry, but it's nothing to do with me. I've told you before that I know nothing about the passports and I don't have any relevant Eastern European connections."

"I see," says DI Yates. "In that case, I'll leave you in peace, as you request. If, when you've thought about it, you can come up with any ideas about where Tony Sentance is, or where he might be heading, I'd appreciate your letting us know. There's a possibility that another girl may be at risk. I shall put checks on all the ports and airports. I think it's likely he'll be trying to leave the country. And we shall get to the bottom of this, sir. I'm sure Ms Rook will be able to tell you about the penalties for obstructing the police and perverting the course of justice."

There is another uncomfortable silence. The last thing I want is some little slut's death on my conscience. Much more importantly, nothing must hinder me now from taking Archie away from here. But Sentance, a murderer? A dishonest and avaricious little crook, certainly. But I'd never have thought him capable of murder. I doubt he'd have the guts, for one thing.

"Kevan, I think you should tell DI Yates about Archie now."

Jean's voice breaks in on my thoughts. I am incredulous when I take in what she is saying.

"What are you trying to say, Jean? Everything that you know

about my family and my business is confidential. Besides, I don't know what you're talking about."

Jean looks at me with stricken eyes. For an instant, I think I see real devotion there, before she brings down the shutters.

"For God's sake, Kevan, stop incriminating yourself unnecessarily by sticking to a few stupid lies. All you're succeeding in doing is convincing the police you're mixed up in whatever it is that Tony Sentance has been up to. DI Yates has already been checking up on Archie. He's failed to find any proper record of his birth. Now, do you want to tell him the truth? Because if you'll take my advice, it will be your best option if you really care about Archie's future."

I suddenly feel quite weak. I sit down on the sofa.

"Are you all right, sir? Would you like me to fetch you some water?"

"No, thank you. I'll tell you about Archie. Just give me a minute."

"Please, take your time."

I draw a few deep breaths. Will this nightmare never end? Surely they can't take Archie away from me now. I start at the beginning, or as close to it as I think they need to know.

"Joanna and I married young. She was bright, but she chose to marry me rather than go to university. From the financial point of view, she didn't need to develop a career, though I think she always rather regretted not doing. Like my mother, she got involved in working for quite a few charities. She was particularly interested in helping childless women. At first, it had nothing to do with the fact that she was childless herself. She was very young and we had no idea that she would be unable to conceive, although we never practised any kind of birth control.

"Eventually, when we'd been married for several years, she went to see a doctor. He carried out some tests and discovered that she had leukaemia. As you can imagine, we were horrified. Of course, I was able to pay for the best specialists and the disease then seemed to stabilise. It isn't the death sentence that it used to be – not always, anyway.

"Her illness was, however, responsible for her infertility. I was desperate to have an heir to carry on the businesses and she craved a child just as badly. IVF was out of the question – no legitimate provider would have helped a woman with Joanna's medical problems and even if they had it would have been irresponsible to try. So we agreed we would adopt a child, though I have to admit that for me it always seemed a second-best option. Joanna disagreed; she said she knew right from the start that she could love an adopted child as much as if it had been her own.

"We were both surprised to find that no UK adoption society would help us. We were still only in our early thirties. We obviously had the means to support a child. And Joanna's medication was working. She'd been stable for several years by this time. But we were told that the societies wouldn't allow a child to be adopted unless they believed that both parents would live to see it reach adulthood. We believed we could fulfil this requirement; they disagreed. We tried every argument we could think of, but it was of no use. We were devastated – Joanna, particularly. I was worried that the disappointment might have a detrimental effect on her health.

"During the same period, de Vries Industries was expanding rapidly. As well as enlarging the existing food-packing and canning plants, we'd opened a new canning plant and one for chilled and frozen foods. There was always a glut of seasonal work in the main harvesting periods – from May to September – and we were beginning to exhaust the supply of regular local workers. There was some student labour available during the summer, but not enough, and most students didn't want to work for the whole of their vacation. We employed some gangs of land-women, but they were notoriously unreliable and could be disruptive: there were sometimes fights in the plants between rival gangs.

"We already had an arrangement with the Maltese government by which we employed about fifty women on a seasonal basis. We paid their fares and provided them with Portakabin accommodation close to the Spalding packing plant. We also paid some of our own employees to take Irish students as lodgers for three months in the summer. Both of these schemes proved to be quite successful. Sentance suggested that he should build on them by trying to recruit seasonal staff from Eastern Europe. He mentioned Romania and Albania particularly. I should have smelt a rat then, because I've always operated on my grandfather's principle that a fair day's work is worth a fair day's pay, so if I'd thought about it I'd have realised that we'd have been as likely to attract staff from within the EU as from outside it. Anyway, I can only conclude that I didn't pay enough attention. I was probably distracted by the whole adoption thing. I gave Sentance permission to go and suss it out.

"When he came back, he asked if he could visit us at Laurieston. He didn't come to the house as much then as in recent years, even though I got on much better with him at that time. I was a bit surprised, particularly as he made it clear that he wanted to see Joanna as well, but we agreed to see him.

"He told us he'd been to an orphanage in Romania. There would be quite a lot of red tape involved, but he thought he might be able to come to an arrangement with the authorities to take girls who'd reached the age of sixteen who had grown up in orphanages there. There might be some boys as well, but from what he'd seen the girls were more tractable and more likely to make good workers.

"I was dubious about this. We've always employed school leavers, but to put whole groups of young teenagers on the payroll, especially if they couldn't speak English and were from a deprived background, struck me as rash and probably unworkable. What would happen if they proved not to be suitable employee material? Who would be responsible for them while they were still officially minors?

"Sentance danced around the point quite a bit in that ingratiating way he has. He was wringing his hands nervously. I could see he was directing his comments much more at Joanna than at me, even though she had little to do with the day-to-day running of the businesses. He finally blurted out that he had been appalled by the conditions he'd seen in the orphanages; that there were little babies lying in cots all day, some of them in filthy conditions, all of them underfed and under-stimulated. He was watching Joanna's face all the time. Once he'd mentioned the babies, he had her rapt attention.

"He said, knowing that we were interested in adoption, that he'd made enquiries, but he'd been advised it would be extremely difficult. There was a lot of red tape involved. It could take three years, possibly more, to get a child out of a place like that legally; even if it happened, which it might not, by then the damage would have been done. He said he'd made some 'reliable contacts', who had offered to help. He asked us if we'd like him to use these contacts to 'spirit a child away', as he put it. Of course, these contacts would have to be paid. They'd be taking a big risk for us, and they'd have to put in some painstaking work in order to succeed.

"I was very angry. I told him I was furious he'd come to our home in order to suggest that we should commit a crime and even more incensed that he'd dared to raise Joanna's hopes in this way. I suppose it was inevitable that Joanna took a different view. She asked me quite abruptly to stop shouting at Sentance, pointing out that he was only trying to help, while he cast down his eyes and grovelled and muttered that no offence had been taken. He said that he quite understood my concerns, but that he would 'leave it with us'. If we should change our minds, the 'door was still open'. You may have noticed that Sentance loves trotting out these platitudes. They make my blood boil.

"As soon as he'd gone, Joanna began to work on me. She said Sentance had our best interests at heart: we should be grateful that he was prepared to run such a risk for us and that we should take his offer seriously. It might be our only chance ever to have the child we longed for and it would save at least one orphan from an appalling childhood.

"It took a long time, but, to cut a long story short, eventually I gave in. Archie was the result. He was a beautiful baby and we had a few happy years with him before he began to display symptoms of being unwell. He was diagnosed as severely autistic. At about the same time, Joanna's condition de-stabilised again and has been volatile ever since, though it was only during the last year that we were told her case was hopeless. When Archie was five, it became obvious that he would not be able to attend an ordinary school. Until we went to St Lucia, he was a weekly boarder at a special school in Sleaford. He's now been a full boarder for the past two weeks, but I've just removed him from the school. I intend to obtain specialist support to help look after him myself."

To my surprise, as I finish my story and look DI Yates full in the face, I see that his eyes are moist with compassion. It is a dangerous moment. It won't take much to make me break down. He swallows.

"Thank you, sir," he says. "I realise that it took a huge effort

278

for you to tell me all of that, and I appreciate it. Of course I have questions, but most of them will keep. There's just one thing I'd like to know now."

"Yes?"

"What kind of relationship does – did – Tony Sentance have with Mrs de Vries?"

"You mean, after he brought Archie to us? Joanna was always prepared to overlook Sentance's faults. I don't think that she liked him, any more than I do, but she tended to show him respect. I always wondered . . ."

I hesitate. I know that I shall loathe myself forever if I sully Joanna's name, whether justly or unjustly.

"Please go on, sir. It might help us to apprehend Sentance."

"I always wondered if she enlisted his help to get babies for some of the other women involved in that charity."

"How much did you pay Sentance and his 'contacts' for Archie?"

"£50,000, initially. But Sentance has had free access to an account that was specially set up to provide Archie with regular papers. Although he's nine now, we still haven't managed to do this. Sentance keeps on saying that there are hitches. Every time one of these 'hitches' cropped up, Joanna was terrified that we would lose Archie. Sentance was always told that we would pay whatever it took. Sentance is a signatory to most of the business accounts, too. Those are the ones that Jean has just barred him from."

Jean nods. "And from the special one, too. I thought you would want me to do that."

DI Yates cuts in. "Romania is now an EU member."

"I know that – and now that people from Romania and Bulgaria have the freedom to work where they like in Europe, we have plans to develop a small capsule workforce from there and see how it goes."

"So nothing came of the idea of employing teenage girls from the orphanages?"

"No. It was too risky."

"The forged passports couldn't have been intended to help such girls get into the country?"

Jean doesn't give me time to answer.

"You can't expect Kevan to comment on that, DI Yates. He's already told you he knows nothing about the passports."

"Quite. Just one last question. Do you have any idea at all where Tony Sentance might be at the moment?"

"No. But if I were him, I'd be heading for Hull, for the ferry. If he is in serious trouble with the law, I'd say his best chance would be to head as far East as possible, quite possibly using our own transport on a regular route of ours."

FORTY-NINE

Sitting up in bed, Juliet pondered all that she knew about Frederick Jacobs and tried to surmise what had happened to him. Frederick had assumed the veneer of a gentleman – Juliet guessed he was the first of his family to aspire to that condition – but all the evidence suggested that he was a weak, base man. She imagined him sniggering like a schoolboy during his smutty-minded exchanges with Rhodes. She suspected that his proclivities predisposed him to fawn on certain members of his own sex, not only because he found them attractive, but because he was drawn towards the power they could command: true power, not just the passive deference that he was able to require of an unsophisticated agricultural community because of his social position. Cecil Rhodes exuded power. He was an important figure on the international stage: a colossus, a man who bestrode the last unconquered continent, a man whose talents even Queen Victoria herself had acknowledged, and at whose flattery and fine compliments she had smiled and allowed herself to unbend.

Although Frederick was evidently indifferent to women, he did not appear to find them repulsive. His wishy-washy character probably wasn't capable of any strong feelings of repugnance. He had not, therefore, put up much of a protest when his mother had pushed him into marriage; in fact, he might have recognised that a marriage to a woman who was not his social equal could offer him some very positive benefits.

Ostensibly, he had accepted his mother's argument that it was his duty to marry and produce a son who could then inherit his considerable fortune. Privately, he had colluded with her when she'd chosen his future bride. There was a tacit understanding between them that Florence was too uneducated and too stupid to realise where Frederick's sexual orientation lay and that, if she had her suspicions, she'd be so bowled over by her great good luck in having been liberated from a servant's life of drudgery that she wouldn't dare to protest about or draw attention to his prolonged absences and close male friendships. Correction, Juliet told herself: single close male friendship.

They had mostly been correct in their surmises: Florence was never anything other than dutiful and cheerful; she always supported him demurely when they were together; always made herself look pretty and neat. Nevertheless, he had known that attempting to plan out Florence's life for her was risky, but, if he'd thought that he might get his comeuppance, he had never imagined that it would proceed from such an unexpected quarter. He could never have predicted the intensity of the love that his mother had grown to feel for Florence. She might herself have been caught unawares by it. From pressing him to marry in order to continue his line and, probably (though of course she would not say so), to avert scandal, Lucinda had gradually moved to treating Florence as if she were indeed her own daughter. She had come to resent fiercely any perceived slights to or neglect of Florence on his part.

Frederick had found his formidable mother difficult to deal with even when she had been on his side. When she had ceased to put him first, his life became both complicated and uncomfortable. It might have been to alleviate this discomfort, or it might have been something he could not help, but over time he, too, had developed a fondness for Florence. It would never be a grand passion: he did not thrill to the sound of her voice or shiver when she touched him, but he came to admire her resilience and her unfaltering but not undignified wish to please.

FIFTY

Andy Carstairs had been holed up in a lay-by near the de Vries plant at Sutton Bridge for almost half an hour when he received the call from Tim Yates.

"Andy? I'm sorry it's taken me so long to call. Sentance didn't show up. Apparently he's now vanished. Are you at the plant now?"

"Yes. Does that mean you don't want me to go in?"

"No, I do want you to. But I think you should wait for police back-up. I'll get Spalding to send a car straight away. I can't tell you all I've just found out at the moment, but I'm pretty certain Sentance has been running some kind of racket that involves young girls and I think some of the staff at de Vries are mixed up in it, too. You remember how tense you said that meeting with the supervisors was? Willingly or not, I think they're in on whatever it is Sentance is up to."

"Do you think he killed the girl who was found at Sandringham?"

"Probably not personally, but I think he may have been behind it. That's why I want you to take care. Don't put yourself or those who come to support you at risk if you can help it. And play it all by the book, even if it's frustrating. I'd better get a search warrant organised, in case you need it."

"You don't want me to wait for a warrant?"

"No, see how far you can get without it. I'll make sure it's there as soon as possible. But do wait for the uniforms to arrive."

Andy continued to sit forward in his driver's seat, drumming his fingers impatiently on the steering-wheel. He found it impossible to relax. He had the sense that valuable minutes were slipping past because of the DI's strictures about prudence. He glanced across the road as a green Mondeo passed the lay-by and turned into the entrance to the packing plant; there was absolutely no doubt in his mind as to the identity of the driver – he'd seen enough of Miss Nugent to recognise her anywhere. Was it just coincidence that when Sentance had disappeared she found it suddenly important to be at Sutton Bridge?

He'd been waiting for a further ten minutes when one of the distinctive blue de Vries vans drove past him. Nothing unusual about that – in fact, on reflection he was surprised that he hadn't seen more of them since he'd been sitting there – but something made him look at the driver's face as he flashed by. The driver stared back at him and looked quickly away. Andy thought that he speeded up deliberately at the same moment, but he could have been mistaken: after a series of twisting bends, the road opened out into a long, straight stretch just beyond the lay-by. He thought that the driver's face was familiar, but he couldn't quite place it.

He spent the next twenty minutes thinking about it. It wasn't like him to be unable to put a name to a face and his failure to do so didn't improve his mood. He was still racking his brains when a police car pulled into the lay-by and parked behind him. Giash Chakrabati climbed out and nimbly ran the few yards that separated them.

"PC Tandy and I have been sent by DI Yates. He said you'd brief us."

"Hello, Giash. I don't know much more than you do. I interviewed the supervisors at the de Vries plant here a few days ago in connection with the girl that was murdered at Sandringham, and DI Yates has asked me to see them again. Individually, this time, and without anyone else present. Tony Sentance, their FD, was with them last time. Have you met him?"

"Yes. Slimy character."

"I agree with you there. It looks as if he might be the chief suspect, too. He's just pulled off a disappearing act."

"How do you want me and Verity to help you?"

"It's probably best if I talk to you both together. Go and get her, would you?"

Fifteen minutes later, Giash had driven into the approach road to the de Vries plant and halted at the security check. Verity Tandy sat beside him. DC Andy Carstairs was seated in the back of the car. He'd left his own car in the lay-by. Roberts, the security guard who'd checked him in on his last visit, emerged from his hut. He seemed not to be in such a genial mood today. He frowned at Giash.

"Can I help you?"

"I hope so. I've brought DC Carstairs to see Miss Nugent." Giash gestured behind him. The guard craned his neck to look through the open window at Giash's passenger.

"Oh," he said. "I remember you. Got an appointment, have you?"

"No. But I think Miss Nugent will want to see me."

"I'll check," said the guard gruffly. "Hang on."

He returned to his hut. They could see him using the telephone in there, gesturing at them and turning his back when he saw them watching. He put the phone down and strode across the tarmac towards them.

"She's not here."

"Are you quite sure about that? I thought I saw her car when I came past earlier." Andy saw Roberts' face register the stark reality that he'd been caught in a lie. "I'm here on urgent police business. It's an offence to be deliberately obstructive."

The guard looked uncertain.

"Yeah. Well, the receptionist says she can't find her at the moment."

"That's OK. We're happy to come in and wait." Giash switched on the ignition as Andy spoke. Still frowning, the guard returned to his hut and raised the barrier. Andy noted that on this occasion he offered no parking instructions. But the really important question was whether or not he'd been warned about their visit in advance. Had he been told to stall for time? If so, by whom, and how had they found out that Andy would be calling?

"Unpleasant guy," said Verity Tandy.

"Just doing his job," said Giash.

"I think that might not be the last time that we hear that sentiment this afternoon," said Andy.

Three quarters of an hour later, they were still waiting in reception. The receptionist had brought coffee and water. She'd offered them old copies of *de Vries Monthly News* to read. She'd turned on the flat television that was mounted on the wall. Andy had little doubt she'd been told to delay them as long as possible. She'd done a good job, but he was exasperated with waiting. He would get a lot tougher with her if she didn't now do as he asked.

"Thanks for the hospitality," he said. "It's appreciated. But we really need to see Miss Nugent immediately. If you can't help us further, I'm going to have to insist that you page her so I can speak to her myself. And we'll need to search the premises."

As if on cue, Margaret Nugent suddenly appeared from a door to the right of the receptionist's desk.

"DC Carstairs," she said, extending her hand. "I'm sorry I've had to keep you waiting so long. A staffing difficulty. Would you and your colleagues like to follow me to my office?" Andy thought she was as effusive as the security guard had been hostile: a strange about-face from his last encounter with her.

He accompanied her along the dingy corridor, Giash Chakrabati and Verity Tandy following in their wake.

"Now," she said, eschewing her rather grand desk and instead choosing to seat herself companionably at the small table in her office which just about accommodated four people. "Would you like some tea?"

"No, Miss Nugent, that's very kind, but we wouldn't. What we need to do with some urgency is to interview all the supervisors I saw last time I was here, not all together, but individually. But I want them all to gather in the same room before we start, so that the ones who have yet to be interviewed can't compare notes with the others. If you supply the room, PC Tandy will look after them. PC Chakrabati will assist me with the interviews."

"It's rather difficult to release all of them together ..."

"I'm aware of that, Miss Nugent, because Mr Sentance pointed it out last time. However, he managed it then, and I'm asking you to do it now. What's the matter?" he added. He thought she had paled visibly when he mentioned Sentance's name. She recovered her composure quickly.

"Nothing at all. I'll see what I can do. Some of them may have to be called from home, though it's shift-change time, so you may be lucky. I assume you have a warrant?" she added, a glint of her old steeliness returning.

"Not yet. There's one on its way. If you insist on waiting for it, I can demand that the supervisors are kept together in the same room until it arrives. Otherwise we can start now. Your choice."

"Well, I suppose there's no point in wasting time in that way." Her face said the opposite. Andy concluded that she dared not oppose him further. She wasn't as formidable when Sentance wasn't there to back her up. He decided not to mention the man yet, but he would stake his pension that she knew Sentance had gone.

"Thank you. We appreciate your co-operation."

"Will you wait here while I try to find them?"

"PC Chakrabati and I will wait here. I'd like PC Tandy to come with you, if you have no objection. She may be helpful to you, if the supervisors are too inquisitive. I'd like you to tell them as little as possible before we interview them."

"I can't tell them very much when I don't know myself why you're here."

"Correct. But PC Tandy will come along anyway."

"Let's go, then," Miss Nugent said gracelessly to Verity.

"I'm still worried that she'll manage to brief them in some way, even with Verity there," Andy said to Giash after the door had closed behind them.

"As she said, she doesn't know enough to cause much damage. Besides, Verity will keep close tabs on her. She's quite capable, you know. She's grown on me. I think she's a good copper."

"I'm pleased to hear it, although she'd have to be quite a bad copper for you to say so. But if you really mean it, tell DI Yates. He's not been very impressed with her so far."

"He goes too much by appearances and first impressions."

"I don't think that you . . ."

Andy's mobile gave the two short pips that indicated that

he'd received a text message. It was from Tim: *Call me when you can.*

Andy stood up and crossed to the window, so that he was as far from the door as possible.

"Give me a nudge if you think you hear someone coming," he said to Giash. "Sir?" he said to Tim.

"Where are you?"

"I'm in Miss Nugent's office, waiting for her to fetch the supervisors. Giash is with me."

"Is Nugent on her own?"

"No. Verity Tandy's with her."

"Oh, God, is she?" There was a pause. "Well, when you get in there with the supervisors, don't let Nugent stay with you. But do make sure she doesn't make any calls, or otherwise communicate with anyone else. And don't mention Sentance at all."

"OK," said Andy, a little aggrieved that he had actually already thought of most of the things Tim had told him to do. "Have there been any new developments, sir?"

"Just one. Jackie Briggs has told us that she doesn't know where her husband is. She says it's 'out of character' for him not to tell her where he's going, even though he goes away quite a bit. Personally, I wouldn't trust him as far as I could throw him, but she's upset about it, obviously. He may just have failed to mention what he's doing, but there's a chance he might have gone somewhere with Tony Sentance as well. Officially he's unemployed, except for the odd jobs he does for the de Vries family, but he may have some connection with whatever else it is that Sentance is up to his ears in. You'll remember it was Briggs who alerted Sentance when Laurieston House was first burgled."

"Yes . . ."

"Someone's coming," Giash whispered.

"I think Margaret Nugent's coming back, sir. I'll have to go now."

"Remember what I said."

"I will," said Andy. He terminated the call as abruptly as he could.

FIFTY-ONE

Andy Carstairs and Giash Chakrabati were having a frustrating afternoon. One by one, they had interviewed the supervisors at the Sutton Bridge de Vries plant. Each interview had followed the same pattern. Andy had introduced Giash, offered the supervisor concerned water or tea (which were always declined) and said that the police had had a tip-off that the girl who had been murdered had had an association with the plant. He'd agreed with Giash that he couldn't reveal more without running the risk of putting Dulcie Wharton in serious danger.

Each interview had been more or less a duplicate of its predecessor. The supervisors were less truculent than they'd been when he'd first met them. He thought that each in his or her own way was making some kind of a stab at courtesy. Nevertheless, his questions were clearly being stone-walled. The supervisors were united in being adamant that they could not recognise the girl from the photographs they'd seen, the least distressing of which he'd asked them to look at again. They were certain she had not worked at the Sutton Bridge plant. If she had, they would all have recognised her. Because shift patterns changed regularly, they all knew all of the staff.

Andy had asked Giash to observe the interviews. It was, of course, prudent for him to have another police officer present, but he had another reason. He wanted Giash to look out for two things: signs that the supervisors had been briefed to tell the same story and any evidence that he could detect that one or more individuals was either lying or showing signs of nervousness. He had a quick debrief with Giash between each interview.

"I think they've been quite clever if they've agreed beforehand on what to say," said Giash after the sixth interview. "They've all given you the same information, but they haven't put it in the same words. Some of them have volunteered extra stuff, like telling you about the shift patterns. And the only one who seems nervous is Eric Saunders. But he's got a pronounced nervous tic, so it's probably just how he behaves, anyway."

Andy nodded.

"I agree with you. We'll see what happens when Dulcie Wharton comes in. I don't know whether I should be worried that we haven't seen her yet. It may just be coincidence that she's one of the last. Or maybe she's held back until the end deliberately. We haven't seen either of the two female supervisors yet, come to think about it. I'll get Verity to send in the next one. It's bound to be one of them now."

Miss Nugent had allocated the first aid room to the police for the interviews. Verity and the waiting supervisors were in the canteen. It hadn't originally been his intention, but after the first interview Andy had decided to send them back to the canteen afterwards, as well. He didn't want them out on the shop floor talking about his visit just yet.

Verity texted: *Last one now*.

That was strange, thought Andy. There must be two interviews left to go, the ones with the two female supervisors. Perhaps Verity meant the last one after this one?

There was a brief rap at the door before Molly Cartwright entered. Andy had marked her down as a hard case on their first meeting. One look at her face convinced him that he'd been right. A large, unattractive woman, she came in hatchet-jawed and unsmiling.

"Mrs Cartwright, thank you for co-operating with us again. Please take a seat. This is PC Chakrabati."

Molly Cartwright met Giash's eye boldly before she gave him the briefest of nods. Giash had met her type before, though not often. She was barely bothering to conceal her dislike of his race. No doubt she thought of him as a 'Paki' and beneath her contempt. She looked away and took the seat that Andy offered her.

"Would you like some tea?"

"No, thank you," she said, as if he'd affronted her.

"Well, if you want water, there's some on the table. Please help yourself."

She barely acknowledged the offer. Andy produced the photograph.

"Mrs Cartwright, do you remember that when I first came here it was to investigate the murder of the girl in this photograph?"

He held it in front of her. She didn't take it from him.

"Of course I do, yes."

"Have you had any further ideas about who the girl might be? Has anything jogged your memory? You'll remember that unfortunately some of the photos I showed you were quite unpleasant. I saw you looking over Dulcie's shoulder at them. You must have been thinking about them since."

"Can't say I've thought about them a lot," Molly Cartwright said. She sat back in the chair and folded her arms, then unfolded them again, perhaps sensing that Andy would interpret the gesture as aggressive. "I might of been more troubled if I'd of known her. But as I told you – as we all told you – she didn't come from here." She met Andy's eye with an unblinking stare. She was lying, he thought. But he'd have a hell of a job on to break her story. He took a moment to gather his thoughts. He'd try a different tack with her from what he'd used with the others.

"Mrs Cartwright," he said, "you'll remember that your colleague, Dulcie Wharton, seemed to be a lot more upset by the photographs than the rest of you. Do you know why that was?"

Molly Cartwright fidgeted in her chair. It took her a while to reply.

"You'd have to ask her that. She's not at work today, though."

Giash's head jerked up. He looked pointedly at Andy and frowned. Andy didn't need the cue. The alarm bells were already ringing loudly in his head.

"Oh? Do you know why that is?"

Molly Cartwright shrugged.

"She's off sick, I think."

"Well, Mrs Cartwright, if you can't help me any further, I'd like you to accompany me back to the canteen now, please."

"Why's that? You haven't 'accompanied' (she put on an affected voice) anyone else there."

"No, but yours is the last interview and I'd like to see you all together now."

"Back up?" Giash mouthed at him as they left the room. Andy raised his thumb.

"PC Chakrabati," he said to Giash out loud, "Perhaps you wouldn't mind finding Miss Nugent and asking her to join us as well. And ask her for Dulcie Wharton's address, will you?" Andy was trying to sound as casual as possible, but he sensed that the woman beside him was feeling his fear. He wondered if she was afraid, too. He turned to look at her, but the hatchet face betrayed nothing.

Tim responded immediately to Giash Chakrabati's call. Its

urgency didn't surprise him – he'd had an uneasy feeling about Dulcie Wharton ever since their conversation had been so abruptly curtailed. He was extremely worried now. Perhaps he shouldn't have sent Andy to Sutton Bridge. If he'd responded in the wrong way, he knew that it could have put Dulcie in danger. She'd certainly been at work when she'd rung him that morning.

After some prevarication (stuff about data protection which the HR manager herself must have known was nonsense, given the circumstances), Giash had succeeded in worming Dulcie's address out of Miss Nugent and texted it to Tim. Tim rang Spalding, asked them to send a squad car to join him at Dulcie's home and got them to arrange with Boston for immediate back-up at the Sutton Bridge plant. He called Ricky Mac-Fadyen and told him to get to Laurieston House as soon as possible. He rang Jean Rook, who was still at Laurieston, to ask her to remain with Kevan de Vries and, on being passed to de Vries, told him that they must stay inside the house until Ricky arrived and not to let anyone except him inside. Although privately he thought that the possibility was slight, he told de Vries that he and his son could both be in danger if they didn't do as he said. To his surprise, he seemed alarmed and thought, if that were so, he would be unlikely to disobey. Not for the first time, Tim wondered exactly how far his involvement in Sentance's activities had gone. When he asked to be passed back to Jean Rook, he found that she seemed pleased, probably because she'd been asked not to let de Vries out of her sight. She also gave further proof of her renowned presence of mind.

"What about Mrs Briggs?" she asked.

Tim had forgotten about Jackie Briggs. He had never doubted his original impression of her, that she was a pleasant, straightforward woman married to a bastard – a view endorsed by Juliet. But Jackie was now the wife of a man on the run and had always demonstrated unswerving loyalty to her husband. He didn't know whether she could be trusted not to help Harry if he made a secret reappearance to ask for her help.

"Is she still there?"

"No, I think she's gone home. As you know, she's worried about her husband. She may be trying to reach him. She said she'd come back later, before Archie wakes up."

"She can reach him from there, can't she?"

"She doesn't have a mobile. You know what she's like. She won't want to take liberties by using Kevan's landline."

"Could you call her and ask her to come back and stay there with you? I don't think she's at risk, but I'd rather not take any chances. Try not to alarm her."

"All right," said Jean.

"I doubt if she'll be able to reach Harry Briggs on his mobile. We've tried the number and it appears to have been switched off. But if she does ask to use the phone, could you try to dissuade her until DC MacFadyen is there?"

"Yes," said Jean, "Although I must say I hardly expected to find myself in loco custodis."

Tim grinned inwardly. He was almost relieved that she'd got some of her bite back.

"Thank you. I must go. Remember, wait for DC MacFadyen."

Tim raced along the A17, hoping that a local patrol car wouldn't try to stop him for speeding. The address that he'd been given was Flat 2a, Nene Meadows. The satnav told him that the location was not far from the main road through the town, close to the river and a pub called the Nene Meadows Hotel. He'd travelled the seventeen miles from Sutterton in just under twelve minutes. As he drew into the kerb next to a small and unassuming block of flats, he saw a police squad car in his mirror. If it had come all the way from Spalding, it must have been travelling at a similar speed to his.

He jumped out of his car. The two PCs in the squad car also hopped out and walked briskly towards him. He saw immediately that one of them was Gary Cooper. He didn't know the other – presumably it was Cooper's new sidekick. He was glad to see Cooper – it would save a lot of unnecessary explanation.

"DI Yates," said Gary Cooper, "this is PC Brian Smith. We've been asked to meet you at this address. Is it a disturbance?"

"No," said Tim. He looked across at the block of flats. Quiet as the grave, he thought, and shuddered inwardly. Definitely no disturbance in evidence. "A witness in the de Vries case lives here – or rather I should say a potential witness. Her name is Dulcie Wharton. She made a call this morning that was cut short. She was at her place of work at the time, but wasn't there this afternoon. I'm concerned for her safety. If she has come to harm, I've reason to think that the people who've harmed her are ruthless. They're almost certainly responsible for the death of the girl whose body was found at Sandringham. So we need to be careful."

There were no gardens to the flats, not even a shrub or a tree. The three-storey building rose up from a small tarmacked car park. The entrance was on the right-hand side, a sturdy-looking door with a porch-style canopy over it. Tim tried the door. As he'd expected, it did not yield. A pad for swiping electronic cards was affixed to the wall under a row of bells.

Tim pressed the bell marked '2a'. He could just hear it ringing, deep within the building. There was no response. He waited a few moments, then pressed it again. Nothing. There were six flats in the building altogether. Tim systematically pressed all the bells, one by one. He could get no answer from any of them.

"Do you think they saw us coming and they just want to keep out of the way?" said PC Smith.

"Possible, but doubtful," said Gary Cooper. "Somehow, you can always tell when people are at home. This place looks shut up. I guess that everyone's at work."

"I think you may be right about the others," said Tim. "But we know that Mrs Wharton isn't at work. Let's just hope that she's out on an errand or something."

Tim was debating whether to force the door when he turned to see an elderly woman plodding purposefully towards him. She had a plaid shopping trolley in tow. Her feet were splayed and her legs bowed as if by childhood rickets, but she was moving quite fast. She wore a heavy green coat that fell in a bell shape from the shoulder. It was deeply pleated at the back. Tim remembered that his grandmother had such a garment – a 'swagger coat', he believed it was called. This woman must have owned it for the past sixty years at least.

She stopped immediately in front of him, making an uncomfortable invasion upon his personal space. When he first noticed her, he thought that he recognised the type: anxious to help and nosey about what was going on. He couldn't have been more wrong.

"What do you want?" she demanded, peering up into his face and fixing him with hostile steel-grey eyes. "We don't want no cops round here."

Tim tried to turn on the charm.

"Good afternoon," he said. "I'm DI Tim Yates, of the South Lincs Police. Do you live here?"

"What if I do?"

"We're trying to contact one of your neighbours. Mrs Dulcie Wharton. Do you know her?"

"I might do. Why?"

"I'm sorry to bother you, Mrs . . . I'm sorry, I don't know your name."

"Me name's Elsie."

"Right. Thank you. Elsie, we want to speak to Mrs Wharton and we can't raise her. Have you spoken to her today?"

"No, but I saw her leave for work this morning. That's where she'll be now. Works at de Vries."

"Thank you. I know she was at work this morning, but she's not there now. She reported sick. That's why we're concerned."

The old woman looked yet more suspicious.

"Go chasing after everyone who goes home poorly, do you?"

Gary Cooper stepped forward.

"Look, Elsie, love, we've got reason to be worried about her. Do us a favour, will you, and just let us in?"

"Who might you be?"

"I'm PC Cooper. Gary Cooper."

Elsie let out a short burst of cracked laughter.

"Go on with you! You're a caution. Now I don't believe any of you are who you say you are. You'd better clear off before I call the real police."

Tim and Gary Cooper both produced their identity cards.

"Well, I never. Well, all right, I'll let you in. But just this once, mind. The landlord's warned us about strangers hanging about."

She produced her swipe card and flicked it deftly across the metal pad. The door clicked. She pushed it open. Tim and the two PCs followed her in.

"Me flat's just here," she said in an exaggerated whisper, indicating the first door they came to. "She's upstairs. Don't say it was me let you in, will you?"

She brushed past them, dragging the tartan trolley after her. She unlocked the door she'd indicated and disappeared beyond it.

Tim waited until she'd gone before he ran up the stairs. The two PCs followed him. He knocked gently on the door of Flat 2a and waited. He rapped a little louder. Still there was no reply.

"We're going to have to force the door," he said. He and Gary Cooper took a few steps back and ran at the door, bracing their shoulders to take the impact. The door was made of cheap pine and began to yield after the first blow. Another run at it caused it to swing open brokenly.

The flats had probably been built within the last ten years, but, inside, Dulcie Wharton's existed in a time warp. Into the tiny hall had been squeezed a Victorian hat and umbrella stand. A matching oval mahogany-framed mirror had been hung above it. There was barely room there for the three police officers. The door into the living room was open. Tim tapped on it lightly and went in, the others following him. The room was neat but gloomy. A huge mahogany sideboard, ornately but hideously decorated with scrolls and carved fruits, was jammed against one side of the fireplace. On the other side was another ugly piece of furniture which he believed was called a chiffonier. A massive dark red moquette sofa had been planted squarely in front of the mock-flame gas fire. It was piled with cushions worked in multi-coloured tapestry wool, painstakingly done but, to Tim's eyes, hideous. A small rectangular coffee table had been placed between the sofa and the window. It was probably the only item in the room that had been manufactured since the Second World War. A half-empty mug of coffee was standing on one of the dried-flower coasters that had been placed on the table's surface at accurate intervals from each other.

"Christ!" said Gary Cooper. "This stuff must have belonged to her Mum and Dad."

Tim put his forefinger to his lips to indicate that they shouldn't speak.

"Mrs Wharton?" he said. "Anyone at home? We're police officers; there's no need to be alarmed."

It was obvious that there would be no reply. He'd just felt obliged to call out as a courtesy. He hoped against hope they'd find the flat was empty. He was only too aware of the likely alternative scenario.

The flat had a curious design. The other door in the living room was close to the window. Tim opened it to reveal a small kitchenette, its surfaces all immaculate, all utensils apparently in their place. He touched the electric kettle briefly with the back of his hand. It was still warm.

He hadn't noticed a second door in the hall, but realised there must be one. He retraced his steps. There were no windows there, but when he approached the hall from the living-room the other door was obvious. Tim drew on a pair of latex gloves. He took a deep breath and wrenched it open.

Dulcie Wharton was lying on her back on the bed. Her body was twisted unnaturally – her legs were curled into the foetal position, but her blank face gazed up at the ceiling. She was still wearing her shocking pink de Vries Industries overall. Tim hastened across to the bed to check her pulse, but he had known the moment he saw her that she was dead.

"Call for an ambulance!" he said to Gary, who was peering over his shoulder. "Get this flat cordoned off as a crime scene. I want interviews set up with all the other tenants. And I'd better give Professor Salkeld another call."

FIFTY-TWO

The tense silence that had descended upon the canteen as soon as Andy had escorted Molly Cartwright through the door had lasted more than twenty minutes. Andy had expected the supervisors and Miss Nugent to be hostile and even, perhaps, aggressive, when he'd insisted on detaining them, but they'd merely seated themselves in two adjacent groups at the shabby tables and stared either at their feet or into space. No-one spoke. It was difficult to try to gauge their mood: panic, resignation, defiance? It could have been any or all of these. The strangest thing about them was that they seemed to act as one: whatever their attitude was, it appeared to be shared by them all. There was no attempt to break ranks, no indication that one of them was itching to get away from the others.

Verity and Giash had stationed themselves at the two exits. Like Andy, they were obviously finding the situation oppressive. Probably, also like him, they were desperate for the back-up team to arrive or for someone to issue further instructions, so that they could be released from this odd vacuum.

Andy was relieved when he finally received a text from Tim. *I need to speak to you. Call me when you are alone*. Glad to have a legitimate pretext for leaving the room, Andy escaped through Verity's exit – he acknowledged her wry smile as she opened the door for him – and walked several feet down the corridor, until he was certain that he was out of earshot of the canteen. He checked the offices to his right and left. Both were empty.

Tim was as brief as possible.

"We've just found Dulcie Wharton dead in her flat. She probably died within the last two hours. Almost certainly murdered. I haven't had a chance to interview the neighbours yet – most of them are apparently out at work. No obvious suspect, unless you count Sentance. It could have been him, I suppose, though I think it's unlikely. Are you holding all the supervisors in the same place?"

"Yes. In the canteen."

"Is there a chance that it could have been any of them?"

"Doubtful, but not impossible. It depends on the exact time of her death. We were kept waiting a long time before Miss Nugent let us see them."

"Did she give you a reason?"

"She said it was 'a little staffing difficulty'."

"We're going to have to find out exactly what she meant by that. I take it that back-up has yet to arrive?"

"PC Chakrabati, PC Tandy and I are still here on our own."

"How did the supervisor interviews go?"

"They were reasonably polite, but none of them claimed to know anything that could help us. Even though I knew nothing about Dulcie Wharton's death, I was convinced they were hiding something. But they're going to be difficult to break and, as Giash says, they're being quite clever about it. They may all be singing from the same hymn sheet, but their statements aren't clones of each other."

"What's their general attitude now that they've been detained?"

"Sullen, but not obstructive."

"Well, we'll have more opportunity to put the screws on now. When back-up arrives, I want them all to be brought in for questioning. Get them taken to Spalding nick as soon as you can."

"All of them?"

"What do you think? You say that they're all singing from the same hymn sheet. Unless they're all innocent, which neither you nor I believes, that must mean that they're all guilty. Exactly of what, though, is what we have to find out."

FIFTY-THREE

Tim decided not to wait for Stuart Salkeld to arrive at Dulcie Wharton's flat. He was concerned about Andy and the two PCs he had with him. He knew they would be outnumbered if the supervisors cut up rough and he had no idea what kind of support the police could expect from the other workers at the de Vries plant. Zilch would be his guess. He was only a few miles from the plant now. He hoped the back-up team he'd told Andy to request would have arrived, but, either way, his presence would bring extra help. He was also curious to see the reaction of the supervisors when they were told that Tony Sentance had done a runner. He was intrigued by the strange solidarity that he'd been told they all exhibited. He wouldn't have described Sentance as a particularly charismatic character, yet all these people, and evidently also Miss Nugent, felt compelled to do his bidding. Not to mention Kevan de Vries, who by no stretch of the imagination could be called a pushover.

As he halted at the checkpoint of the Sutton Bridge plant, he saw that a large blue police van had just been admitted. The driver was motoring up the drive at as brisk a pace as its narrowness permitted. The security man, a rough-looking character, came out of his sentry-box, but was obviously in no mood to be obstructive. When Tim flashed his ID, the man nodded and opened the barrier without a word. There was a look of resignation on his face.

The police van halted in front of the main entrance. The last of the eight policemen it contained was climbing out when he drew in behind it. He hastened to talk to them before they could enter the building. They'd assembled in double file. He went and stood in front of them. They were all from Boston; he didn't think that he knew any of them personally.

"Who's in charge?" he asked.

"I'm Sergeant Dobson," said one of them, stepping forward.

"DI Yates," Tim said. "Thank you for getting here so quickly. DC Carstairs is holding eight people in the canteen here. Seven of them work as supervisory staff at the plant. There's also a senior manager with them. We believe that one or more of them are involved in the death of the woman whose body was found at Sandringham. We've also found another body in a flat in the town this afternoon. I intend to place under arrest all the people DC Carstairs is holding and we'll need your help with that, but there's something I want to talk to them about first. I'd like you to wait in the reception area until I, or DC Carstairs, comes to fetch you. If you hear any kind of disturbance or I call Sergeant Dobson's mobile, I want you to come in immediately. Is that understood?"

"Yes, sir," said Sergeant Dobson. Quickly he gave his mobile number to Tim, who keyed it into his phone.

Tim hurried through the glass door.

"Where's the canteen?" he asked the receptionist.

"Down that passage. Keep going until the end," she said. She looked terrified.

Tim ran down the corridor until he reached the double doors of the canteen. He could hear no sound coming from within. He peered through the one of the glass portholes. The sight that met his gaze was uncanny. The supervisors were sitting at two tables in the middle of the room. All were looking down at the table-tops, as if at something of interest. Andy

Carstairs was sitting at a table at the top of the room, like a teacher supervising a class. He, too, was silent. He could just make out Verity Tandy, sitting on a chair near to the far exit. He couldn't see Giash Chakrabati, but guessed he was stationed near the door that Tim himself was looking through, out of his line of vision. A tall, well-built woman wearing a white overall was standing near the window with her back to the others. All were motionless, as if deliberately creating a tableau.

Tim tapped on the porthole. Giash Chakrabati appeared from his left to look through the glass from the inside. He opened the door.

"DI Yates," he said in a low voice.

"What's going on here?" said Tim, also keeping his voice down.

"Nothing at all at the moment, sir. They all say that they can't help us; that they don't know anything. DC Carstairs is keeping them here until back-up arrives."

"He was following instructions. Back-up's here now. Could you ask him to come and talk to me for a minute? Take his place over there while he's with me."

"Haven't you managed to get anything at all out of them?" asked Tim, when Andy had joined him in the corridor.

"Not much. A bit of padding about the way that this place is run. The Nugent woman's also indicated that they want Tony Sentance to join them. She says it's because he's their boss."

"Interesting. I wonder why they really want to see Sentance? To advise them, do you think, or give them a cue on how to handle this?"

Andy shrugged.

"I guess so. Or to accuse him, maybe?"

"I can't see that, myself, though you could be right. From all that you've told me, he seems to have a hold over them. Let's see if we can break it by telling them that he's scarpered."

"You're going to do that now?"

"Yes. I want to spring it on them as a surprise. It might help us to find out more. It may even show us that they're not all involved, though I doubt that."

"What about back-up, if it turns nasty?"

"Back-up's here now. Eight cops from Boston. So we out-number them. Are you ready?"

Andy nodded. He followed Tim back into the canteen. Margaret Nugent swung round to face him.

"Good afternoon," said Tim. "I'm DI Yates. I'm sorry that we've had to keep you here for so long. I understand from DC Carstairs that you've been fairly co-operative and I'd like to thank you for that. But DC Carstairs also thinks that you might be keeping something back." He surveyed the faces in front of him. All eyes were fixed on him, all expressions hostile. "Perhaps," Tim added, "out of a mistaken sense of loyalty for someone? Mr Sentance, for example?"

"Where is Tony?" asked the only woman seated with the supervisors. "Have you got him somewhere else?"

"No such luck," said Tim, watching her carefully. "I'm afraid Tony Sentance has absconded."

"Come again?" said one of the men.

"He means he's cleared off," said the woman. "It's probably a trick, though." But her cheeks had reddened and there was uncertainty in her tone.

"It's not a trick," said Tim, "though if he's your leader I can see why you might think it. But policemen don't usually play tricks when they're talking about murder."

"We don't know nothing about that young girl," said another of the men. "She didn't work here, despite the overall."

"We haven't got to the bottom of that yet," said Tim. "But I wasn't thinking about her. I was thinking about your colleague, Dulcie Wharton. I found her dead in her flat about an hour ago."

He was watching them closely. None of them over-reacted, but they seemed unsettled. There was some shuffling in their seats, even some indication of distress, but mostly, he thought, they looked afraid. All except the woman, whose face remained devoid of all expression.

"But she can't be dead!" said the beefy one with the red face. "She was working this morning. I saw her."

"She went home sick," said the woman laconically. "Must have been properly ill but we didn't realise."

Tim's eye travelled along the whole row of overalled individuals seated before him. He noticed that the man sitting at the end was having difficulty in controlling his emotions. His jaw was working and he was taking some very deep breaths.

"Are you all right . . . Mr . . ?" He turned to Andy to ask for the man's name.

"I think it's Douglas," Andy whispered.

Tim moved closer to where the man was sitting.

"Douglas?" he said. "Is that your name?"

The man nodded. He seemed close to tears.

"He didn't have to kill her," he said. "The bastard!" Andy realised that he'd heard these identical words on his first visit.

"Shut up!" hissed the man sitting next to him.

"Don't take no notice of Douglas," said the woman. "He gets some strange ideas sometimes."

Tim looked along the row again. He sensed that it wouldn't take much to break them now. He thought it probable that only the woman would hold out when they started the proper interrogation.

"I don't know who you mean when you say 'he'," he said to Douglas, before turning to address all of them, "but I'm guessing that it's Tony Sentance. Just remember that, whatever misplaced loyalty you may feel you owe him or whatever influence he may have over you, he isn't here to support you now. He's gone. He's trying to save his own skin without any thought of what might happen to you. Rest assured that we'll catch him, too. It'll only be a matter of time. So the sooner you start talking, the better it'll be for you."

"I don't believe that Tony killed her," said one of the other men. He was spare-limbed, with a grizzled beard and an incipient pot belly that looked incongruous against his otherwise athletic build. "He wouldn't have done that. He shouldn't have trusted Harry Briggs in the way that he did. I bet he asked Harry to take her home. He never knows when to stop, does Harry."

"Will you shut up?" said the woman viciously.

"What's your name?" Tim asked the man.

"Wayne. Wayne Stanley."

"Thank you, Mr Stanley; what you've just said is extremely helpful. Now I want to know when Dulcie went sick. What time did she ask to go home?" He looked at Margaret Nugent.

"I'll have to check my records . . ."

"No, Miss Nugent, you won't. You've got a mind like a steel trap. I know you know when she left."

"Some time between eleven and twelve."

"You can be more precise than that."

"It was nearer to twelve," said Wayne. "It was almost dinner-time. She came to ask me to keep an eye on her gang until the break."

Tim beckoned to Giash.

"Back-up's waiting outside. I'd like you to ask them to come in now." He called Verity Tandy over and spoke to her and Andy. "We need to caution all of these people and arrest them. Take them to Spalding. Put them in separate cells when we get them there. I'll come as soon as I can."

Verity moved immediately to caution Margaret Nugent.

"You surely can't mean to include me?" she called across to Tim.

"I certainly do, Miss Nugent. Why did you think you might be exempt?"

It might have been his imagination, but he thought that he saw a small flicker of triumph cross the faces of more than one of the supervisors. Otherwise, they seemed dejected, even broken. None of them tried to resist arrest. Arranging strong back-up had been prudent, but in the end had proved unnecessary.

FIFTY-FOUR

Juliet stepped out of the taxi into Acacia Avenue, the rather faceless street where she lived. She felt quite weak, as if she were walking on slippery, treacherous glass, but her mood was euphoric. It seemed as if she had been away for a million years. She took out her purse and paid the driver, adding a substantial tip.

"Thanks very much, duck. You stand there and I'll bring your bags round. Do you want me to carry them up the steps for you?"

He leered at her in a way which made her feel uncomfortable. He had a large wad of gum in his mouth which he was chewing noisily.

Normally she would have disdained such an offer, especially from such a character, but today she could not trust her powers of balance. Although she only had a small suitcase on wheels and an overnight bag, she was worried she might not make it up the shallow outside stairs flight without stumbling. She forced a smile.

"Thank you."

He scrambled up the steps, a bag in each hand, and dumped them in front of her doorstep.

"There you are, my darling. Anything else I can do for you?" He winked.

"No, thank you," said Juliet firmly. She waited until he'd got back in his car before searching for her key and inserting it in the lock. She might still be a little frail, but she could recognise a perv when she saw one. The man would have had no inkling of her police training, so he might have thought of trying it on. She'd have been ready with the pepper spray she kept in a special zipped pocket in her bag. Despite her weakness, she thought she could probably have managed one of the arm grapples she'd learnt on the kick-boxing course she'd gone on when she joined the force. However, there was no need: the taxi driver reversed to the end of the road and roared away, giving her an ironic little wave. He had ducked his head under the sun-shield so that he could grin at her. He reminded her of someone, but at first she couldn't think who. Suddenly it came to her: Harry Briggs. It wasn't him, of course, but the resemblance probably explained why she'd taken such a dislike to the driver.

Juliet turned her back on him and let herself in, dragging the case and the bag with her and dumping them inside the door. The flat felt warm and there was a pleasant smell. She turned from the tiny hallway into the main room and saw there was a vase of roses standing on the table. Her fruit bowl had been filled; her mail had been neatly gathered into a small pile to one side of it. A plain postcard had been propped up against the fruit bowl. The gas fire had been turned on and switched to a low setting.

Juliet pulled out one of her dining-room chairs and sank on to it gratefully, dropping her handbag to the floor. She picked up the postcard.

Hi. Hope you're feeling OK. Sorry I couldn't fetch you from hospital. I'll drop by tonight. There's food in the fridge and a bottle of wine! Regards, Nick.

She let the postcard fall again. Nick Brodowski was the neighbour who had found her when she'd collapsed and who'd called the ambulance. He was a large, plain man in his mid-thirties, but she'd always been quite drawn to him. She found his kindness engaging and, although he was often shy and reserved, he could be extremely witty once he'd managed to relax. She'd thought for a time that they might try dating, but both had been too reticent to be the first to suggest it and now the idea had somehow lost its appeal. She pushed the thought away. She hoped Nick hadn't gone to too much expense on her account. She knew that he was a draughtsman. She'd no idea what kind of salary that meant he could command, but she suspected it was quite modest.

She hauled herself to her feet again and tottered the few steps to her kitchenette. She was amazed at how light-headed she felt. She'd make herself some tea.

She opened the fridge and saw it had been stacked to the gunnels with food. Milk, water, wine, butter, salads, cheese, cold meats and a packet of chicken breasts all sat, neatly arranged, on the shelves. She'd have to pay Nick for all of this stuff; she couldn't accept it as a gift, on top of the flowers and fruit. She knew it was churlish of her, but she realised she didn't actually want to accept it from him. What was it she'd read about gifts? That they never actually came free?

She filled the kettle and put it to boil. A glance at her kitchen clock reminded her that it was time to take one of her antibiotic tablets. She moved slowly back to where she'd left the bags and opened the valise. The box of tablets lay at the top of the bag. She lifted it out. Immediately underneath was Florence Jacobs' journal. Juliet took that out, too. She'd been discharged so quickly from the hospital that Verity Tandy hadn't had time to pick it up to take it to the Archaeological Society. Juliet peered at the small patch of protruding yellow paper once again. She was impatient to get to the bottom of this mystery. She'd call Katrin after she'd drunk her tea – or perhaps it would be better to call Tim. She didn't think it would be appropriate for her to get in touch with Jackie Briggs without clearing it with him. The request she wanted to make wasn't related to any of the current de Vries investigations, after all. She knew Tim would give her the go-ahead if he possibly could, but he might have some reason for not allowing it. Superintendent Thornton's thick-set figure loomed in her imagination.

She felt better after she'd drunk the tea. She picked up her phone and dialled Katrin's number.

"Juliet? Sorry! I meant to call you earlier. There's been a lot happening. Are you at home now? How are you?"

"Yes, I've been here about half an hour. I'm feeling a bit shaky, but otherwise OK. It's I who should apologise, because I haven't managed to get the journal back to you. I hope Verity Tandy didn't have a wasted journey. I haven't called Jackie Briggs, either, because I thought I ought to ask Tim if it was OK first."

"I'm pretty certain that in the end Verity wasn't asked to pick it up. I don't know if you'll be able to get hold of Tim at the moment, but you could give him a try. He probably won't want you to talk to Jackie Briggs, though. I understand her husband has gone missing – and Tim thinks he's involved in some way in whatever it is that happened at Laurieston House."

"That wouldn't surprise me in the slightest. Harry Briggs probably isn't the shiftiest character I've ever met in my life, but he certainly strikes me as one of the most unwholesome. I certainly won't bother Tim if he's dealing with a crisis. Pity, though. I'm desperate to find out what's under the cover of the journal. And I thought your idea of asking the Archaeological Society to help was a good one."

"Well, as you know, I'm champing at the bit myself, but I think we're just going to have to wait. How soon can we meet?

I'd really like to see you, not just because of the journal! Have you got the all-clear now?"

"I'm still taking antibiotics. I'll check with my GP – I think she'll visit me tomorrow. My guess is that she'll say I should finish the course before I see you. But I'll ask."

"I'd better go. I've got a terminally boring job to do at the moment, but I need to get on with it."

"OK. Take care."

The antibiotics were making Juliet feel thirsty, as well as light-headed. She debated whether to make more tea, but decided she couldn't be bothered. She poured herself a glass of water and sank down on the sofa.

Two hours later she was awoken by the sound of a key turning in the lock of her front door. She'd been asleep on the sofa, her legs tucked up on the cushions, her head and neck resting on the arm at an awkward angle. She swung her feet to the floor and tried to sit upright. Her neck was aching and her head felt muzzy.

"Juliet?" It was Nick's heavily inflected voice. "Are you there? Can I come in?"

"Hello, Nick. Yes, of course. In here."

He came padding into the room. He was still wearing his jacket, an old-fashioned thigh-length quilted garment that her father would have called a 'car coat'. His heavy black square-framed spectacles accentuated the flabbiness of his face and its apparent absence of bone structure. Juliet reflected that nevertheless he did not at this moment look unattractive, largely because his features were lit up by a broad, ear-to-ear smile.

"Juliet? You are better?" He stooped to peck her shyly on the cheek.

"Getting there," she said. "But, Nick, I'm so grateful to you for all that you've done for me – warming the flat and buying everything that I need. You must let me pay for the food, though."

"It is out of the question," he said, still smiling, but with a warning note in his voice. "It is my pleasure to do this. I should be insulted."

"The flowers and the fruit are wonderful gifts and I'd love to accept them. But it's over the top to let you pay to fill the fridge as well."

He shrugged.

"The fruit is nothing. The flowers I did not buy."

"I don't believe you! Who else could they be from?"

Nick shrugged again, clearly struggling not to appear to be offended now.

"I do not know. I took delivery of them this morning. They were brought to your door when I was getting ready for work. I heard the delivery man and came out to get them. There is a small card to say who they are from. Look, I will show you."

He poked gently among the flower stems for a few seconds, then scrutinised the glass vase from several angles. Then he flipped through the pile of mail, dealing the letters and cards into a fresh pile.

"It is strange. The card is not here. It was a small mauve card."

Juliet decided that he had determined to cover up his generosity in order to persuade her to accept all of his gifts. She could see that he would be both humiliated and offended if she pursued the point further.

"Don't worry about it. I'm sure that it will turn up. And thank you again for everything. I don't know what I would have done without you when you called the ambulance. And today, as well."

The smile returned.

"I will make you a cup of tea?"

"I'd love one. But I should be making it for you. Have you come straight from work? You must be tired."

Nick held up a hand.

"Today I am in charge. Tomorrow, perhaps, you can make tea for me. After I've made tea, I shall prepare supper for us both." He was grinning properly again now.

Juliet felt a great wave of happiness wash over her. Just for today, she'd forget about being independent and shelve her great dislike of being beholden to anyone. She could see that Nick wanted to look after her and suddenly she realised that she not only needed but wanted to be looked after. She lay back against the cushions and returned his smile.

"What will you cook?"

"Chicken breasts in breadcrumbs. It is a Polish dish. You will like it?" he added anxiously.

"Yes, I'm sure I shall." She closed her eyes again for a few minutes.

"There is your tea," said Nick. "Should I put it on the table?" he added as she tried to focus, her eyes still filled with sleep.

"What? Oh, yes, please, I'll drink it in a few minutes, when it's a bit cooler."

He found a mat and carefully placed the mug of tea on it. "What is that book?"

Juliet was struggling to wrest open her eyes.

"Uh? Oh, you mean the journal. There's a bit of a mystery attached to it. It was written by a young woman at the end of the nineteenth century. Or perhaps it wasn't. I've been trying to get to the bottom of it while I've been in hospital."

"Now you're confusing me. But I would like to hear the story, I suggest when we have eaten. Did the young lady perhaps come from Africa?"

Juliet was wide awake in a moment.

"Whatever makes you think that?"

Nick shrugged again.

"That flower on the cover. It's very pretty – and distinctive. There's probably no connection – it may just be a pretty flower that the young lady took a fancy to. I don't know how easy it would be to get it in nineteenth century England. But she may have had relatives who travelled. Brothers, perhaps."

"Her husband certainly travelled, and in Africa, too. But tell me about the flower. Is it some particular type? As you say, it is very pretty, but I thought that it was just decorative, an invention of the manufacturer of the visitors' book, which is how the journal started out in life."

"It's an Eryngium Planum. A few years ago I spent some time in South Africa, working for a construction company, and while I was there I visited Zimbabwe. They grow everywhere there. When they bloom, they're really beautiful. I think it's the country's national flower now. I don't know about in the nineteenth century."

"The country was called Rhodesia then," said Juliet absent-mindedly. She was trying to think what significance Nick's identification of the flower might have.

"At the end of the century," said Nick, with rising indignation, "it was called after an individual who was not a monarch or one of the ruling class, purely for his own self-aggrandisement."

"Cecil Rhodes. You seem to know a lot about him."

"I studied politics and history at university. I'm interested in colonialism, in all its forms. The so-called Iron Curtain countries, like Poland, were colonies of a kind."

"I suppose they were. I hadn't thought of that," said Juliet. Nick's mood had darkened considerably.

"Would you mind passing my tea? I'm very thirsty."

His gently courteous demeanour returned as quickly as it had disappeared.

"Yes, of course. Here you are. I'm sorry; I got side-tracked. Now I will go and cook."

Juliet could hear a lot of banging about in the kitchen and the opening and shutting of cupboard doors as Nick searched for crockery and utensils. She decided to leave him to it; she'd probably only irritate him if she tried to interfere. She spent the next half hour luxuriating on the sofa, flicking through the journal and re-reading some of the passages in it. Skimming through it in this way pointed up its falseness more than reading it straight through. The uniformity of the writing and the ink, the recurrent use of certain words and phrases over what was ostensibly a period of several years, all suggested that it had been written during a much shorter period of time than the carefully-inscribed dates indicated.

Nick came in from the kitchen, his face red and dripping with sweat. He was bearing white wine, which he had poured into one of Juliet's only two delicate crystal glasses. They'd been a present from the one serious boyfriend she'd ever had.

He peered at her anxiously.

"You are fully awake now? Are you allowed to drink wine? I didn't think: perhaps your pills don't allow it."

"I don't know. I'll have a look."

Juliet cast around for the antibiotics and finally found them on the floor, almost hidden underneath the sofa. She must have knocked them down when she'd been sleeping. She inadvertently picked up something else when she was retrieving them. It was a small mauve card with a loop of silver ribbon threaded through its top left-hand corner. She dropped it again deliberately and, with a surreptitious flick of one finger, sent it scudding under the sofa. It looked as if Nick had been telling the truth about the flowers, but she certainly didn't want to revisit that conversation again. She'd take a look at the card when he'd gone home.

"It doesn't say anything about alcohol," she said, turning the packet over and scrutinising the tiny printing on the label. "I think I'll risk it. I feel like a glass of wine!"

"Well done!" Nick pressed the glass gently into her hand and went back into the kitchen, returning instantly with the other glass. He clinked it very carefully against hers.

"Cheers!" he said.

"Cheers!" Juliet responded, rather more quietly. Her feeling of euphoria was evaporating. She was now apprehensive about where all of this might be leading.

In fact, Nick's supper proved to be very enjoyable. The dish that he produced was rather like Wiener schnitzel, but made with chicken. It was accompanied by a potato salad, which he had also made, and a large green salad. They laughed and talked while they were eating. Juliet was astonished to see that by the time they had finished eating they had also polished off the whole bottle of wine.

"Do not worry, I have another bottle in my flat," said Nick. "I will go to fetch it."

"Certainly not," said Juliet, laughing. "I may not have been told not to drink alcohol, but I'm sure my doctor didn't mean me to get drunk on my first night at home."

Nick shrugged, but good-naturedly.

"As you wish. I think that a bottle of white wine is not much, but I don't wish to encourage you in bad ways. Let me make coffee instead and you can tell me about your journal."

Juliet recounted what she knew of Florence's journal as briefly as she could: where it had come from, what it contained, why Katrin had sent it to her, her suspicions about its authenticity and her conviction that Cecil Rhodes was involved in some way with Florence's husband. Nick was spell-bound all the time that she was talking. She almost told him about the skeletons in the cellar at Laurieston House as well, but decided against it. There had been no public announcement about the skeletons yet and, since nothing that she'd read in the journal linked them to Florence, she realised that to tell him would be an uncalled-for indiscretion on her part. She was equally careful not to mention Jackie Briggs, except in passing. She identified Jackie as the owner of the journal, but didn't say that she couldn't get in touch with Jackie at the moment because of Harry Briggs' disappearance. Instead, she concluded her tale by explaining to Nick that she was hoping that someone at the Archaeological Society would be able to help her to discover what was sandwiched in the cover of the journal without damaging it too much.

"But I can help you with that!" Nick cried. "There's no need to involve the Archaeological Society. I have craft knives and my hand is very steady."

Juliet looked doubtful.

"I don't doubt your skill," she said, "but I'm not sure that we ought to tamper with the journal until we have Jackie Briggs' permission. It could get my boss into trouble if it goes wrong."

"But that means you do doubt my skill!" said Nick with a grin. "Let me fetch my craft knives. I will just try to lift a tiny piece of the paper. If it doesn't work, we'll leave it. You want to know what is under there, don't you? And I would like to know myself, now that you have told me the story."

Still dubious, Juliet sighed but nodded her head slightly.

"All right. You've persuaded me. But promise me you'll stop if I ask you to."

Nick was gone before she could change her mind.

FIFTY-FIVE

Nick Brodowski returned to Juliet's flat within a few minutes, bearing three craft knives, a paperknife, a wooden board, some sheets of blotting paper, scissors, a tube of glue and another bottle of white wine.

"We may be in for quite a long evening," he said. "But you must tell me if you are getting too tired, and I will leave and return tomorrow." He raised the bottle. "You will have another glass of wine?"

"Yes, but only a glass," said Juliet. "The doctor is coming to see me tomorrow. I really don't want to be hung over."

She watched as Nick seated himself at the table and placed the journal on the board and opened it.

"Could you sit beside me?"

"Certainly. What do you want me to do?"

"Just hold the front cover as flat to the board as you can. Hold it down firmly with both hands."

Juliet seated herself next to him and tried to do as he asked.

"That's fine, but you need to place both your hands away from where the edges of the cover have been stuck down. Put that hand there, in the middle of the cover, and that one there." He gently rearranged her hands. "I shall have to come quite close to you with the craft knife, but don't worry, I won't let it slip."

Juliet watched, fascinated, as he carefully prised the paper away from the thick board of the journal, making tiny insertions with the craft knife. After an hour, he had levered up almost half of the top edge of the cover. Juliet's fingers were aching and she had cramp in the back of her hands from holding them in the same position for so long.

"You would like a rest? Or perhaps to stop now? We can leave it for tonight if you like."

Her whole body was screaming out for sleep, but she fought off its demands.

"I'd like to finish this today if we possibly can. It's too exciting to want to give up on it now!"

"A rest, then. Drink some wine."

She sat back in her chair, flexing her fingers before she picked up her glass and took a couple of sips.

Nick drained his glass and poured himself another. The alcohol seemed to have no effect on his hand-eye co-ordination.

"Ready to start again?"

She nodded. It took the best part of another hour to separate the paper from the whole of the top of the cover. They paused for another break.

"I'm sorry it is taking so long. The glue is very old and stubborn. We're lucky that the paper is good quality. If it had been cheaper it might just have flaked into powder. Then you would certainly have told me to stop!"

Juliet laughed.

"Yes, I would! Are you ready for another go?"

He nodded. He took hold of her hands and positioned them differently so that he could start work on the side of the cover. Was it her imagination, or had he given her fingers a fleeting caress as he'd guided them into place? She saw that he'd made no further inroads into the wine. She pushed the bottle to one side.

Now their heads were bent so close together that at times

they touched. The first time it happened, Juliet drew away gently. She noticed that Nick flinched and decided not to do it again. After a few more minutes, he relaxed completely, completely absorbed in the task.

"I think that this will be a little easier," he said. "There doesn't seem to be as much old glue here."

He was working at it intensely now, his movements rapid and sure.

"That's half of it," he said, straightening up and wiping his forehead. "I think we might be able to get at the paper now. Do you want to try?"

"No, you do it," said Juliet. "You have nimbler fingers than I do. Please be careful, though."

"Here goes!" he grinned. "What do you bet that this will just be scrap paper that's been used as padding?"

He pushed the loosened paper up so that it formed a kind of envelope and grasped the wad of yellow paper inside it. He was unable to extract it. A fine film of yellow appeared on his fingertips, as if he'd been collecting pollen.

"The paper inside isn't such good quality. I'm afraid it might disintegrate if I pull too hard. It may also be stuck to the bottom of the board, or wrapped around the whole of it, on both sides."

Juliet thought for a moment.

"Jackie Briggs doesn't know about the yellow paper," she said. "She won't be upset if we damage it, whereas she might be if we damage the cover of the journal. I think we should risk putting a bit more purchase on it. At least we'll then be able to tell whether you're right. Then we'll know we need to do more work to lift the covering."

"Do you have some tweezers? And a bulldog clip?"

"Yes, I'll fetch them."

When she brought the tweezers, he used them to open

out the envelope a little more. Carefully, he dug down to the bottom and ran the tweezers around it and the closed side. He took the bulldog clip and clamped it to the top edge of the wad, causing a small cloud of the pollen-like dust to rise into the air and fall on the board. Gritting his teeth, Nick yanked at the paper.

It slid halfway out before the bulldog clip tore off, taking with it a ten-pence piece sized fragment. Nick reattached the clip and pulled again. This time the whole of the wad emerged. The yellow paper was speckled brown in places and smelt musty, like old hymn books.

"It's been folded over several times. Unfold it as carefully as you can, while I glue these edges down again. The sooner I do it, the less damage there's likely to be; I'll leave a gap for some padding refill."

Juliet took the wad of paper from him. It seemed at first that it consisted of several sheets stuck together, but there were folds on two sides. Gradually, she managed to open it out, taking off the surface in some places but not actually tearing any holes, until she had spread out in front of her two foolscap-sized sheets of paper. Time had stuck them together, but not firmly. Juliet took one of the craft knives and gradually eased the sheets apart with it. Laying the two sheets side by side, she saw that each was a separate but almost identical document. She was looking at two printed forms, each of which had been written on sparingly in a neat hand in brown-black ink.

"Have you got something interesting there?" Nick looked up from what he was doing. "I'm glad that the pages aren't just blank, anyway. Do they seem to have any kind of meaning?"

"I'm not sure yet," said Juliet slowly. "Give me a few minutes to read them."

"Sure." He returned to his task. He had cut some blotting

paper so that it formed a wad of similar size and thickness to the one that he'd removed and slid it into the envelope. Now he was easing tiny lines of glue on to the edge of the board before smoothing down the cover paper with the flat blade of the paperknife.

Juliet studied the first sheet. Some of the writing was indecipherable or worn away by age or the more recent damage inflicted by herself, but she could read enough of it to see that the document formed some kind of report.

"Louisa Jameson," she read. "Age: thirty-three. Height: Five feet two inches. Weight: ten stones. Physical features: Strong. Good worker. Excellent teeth. Does not tire easily. Large breasts and buttocks. Neat enough for the house. Illnesses: None recorded. Slight limp. Demeanour: Pleasant. Cheerful. Obedient. Personal hygiene: adequate." The next printed word was difficult to make out. Pediment? Parchment? The written words offered no clue: they consisted merely of a series of dates. The first one of these was 9th August 1870; the last 24th December 1894. There were about a dozen dates in the list, each one followed by the letters 'btg'.

"That should do the trick," said Nick. "We just need to leave a weight on that for twenty-four hours now. Are you having difficulties with that? I'm going to wash my hands. Then I'll take a look, if that's OK?"

"Please do," said Juliet. She glanced at her watch. Ten minutes to midnight! She felt deathly tired now, but she was determined to see this through, get as far as she could with it.

Nick came back.

"Have you come to any conclusions yet?"

"Not exactly. It's some kind of form. I'm convinced that it belongs to the period of the journal – late nineteenth century. It's set out like a school report, but it reads like a cross between a doctor's notes and the kind of stuff that's written about models in modern celebrity magazines. It could be a kind of checklist for a servant's reference, I suppose, but it seems less . . . respectful than that, even for the period. Almost as if it's a prize cow that's being described. And there's a word that I can't make out, with a list of dates written against it."

"Let me see."

She handed him the paper. He scrutinised it for a few minutes and whistled.

"Jeez!" he said. "Do you know what I think this is?"

"I'm sure you're going to tell me!"

"I think it's some kind of slave indenture. Unfortunately the bottom of the sheet is too damaged to read – but my guess is that the owner had signed it. Possibly signed the person concerned over to a new owner."

"The woman's name is European."

"If I'm right, and she was a slave, the surname is almost certainly that of her white owner. He'll also have given her a European first name."

"But slavery had long been abolished in England in the late nineteenth century."

"There's no proof that she was a slave in England – or where she was from, for that matter." Nick looked at Juliet curiously. "Unless there's something else you know?"

Juliet avoided meeting his eyes. "Nothing for sure. I've got a few theories, but probably all too far-fetched."

"Oh, OK. Well, let's have a look at the other sheet."

The second piece of paper was lying forgotten on Juliet's knee. She handed it to him without looking at it.

"This one's more damaged than that one," Nick said, holding it up towards the electric light and frowning. "I can certainly make out the surname, which is also Jameson. I can't read the first name properly, but it looks as if it might also be Louisa."

"Is it just a copy, then?"

"No, I don't think so. The age given here is sixteen, the height five foot five inches. And there is a date on this one: it's January 13th 1896. Both the forms seem to have been filled in at the same time, even though we can't see the date on the other one."

"If there were two separate women, why would they have identical names?"

"The second one might be the daughter of the first one. But if they were slaves belonging to the same household, it wouldn't have been unusual for them to have been called by the same name. There'd have been some way of distinguishing them in everyday life – they might have been called Little Louisa and Big Louisa, for example."

Juliet held out her hand for the paper.

"I suppose there's a list of her 'qualities', too, though it's been rubbed out. But the word beginning with P is clearer on this one: I think it says 'Punishment'."

Nick stooped to peer over her shoulder.

"You're right."

"The list of dates is longer, but the entries cover a shorter period of time. They only start in 1889. What do you think 'btg' means?"

Nick paused. Juliet looked up at his face. It had contorted with the effort of trying to manage powerful emotion.

"I'm afraid that it stands for 'beating'. I think that these women were physically chastised, perhaps for trivial offences, perhaps for some more sadistic reason."

Juliet sat, silent, for a long time. She struggled to prevent it, but her eyes were filling with tears.

"I have over-tired you and I should know better," said Nick gravely. "You must go to bed now. Try to forget about this until tomorrow."

He stood up slowly and began to gather his possessions. Juliet knew that if she stood, too, he would kiss her good night. She remained seated, with the result that Nick merely brushed the hair back from her face and gave her another circumspect peck on the cheek.

"Goodnight. I will call in tomorrow evening. We may find out a little more when we look again. Promise me that you will not brood over the papers in the meantime."

Juliet nodded.

"Good night, Nick. And thank you. I really mean it."

As the door shut behind him, she stooped to retrieve the little mauve card from under the sofa.

Welcome home. Best wishes from Dr Wu and Dr Butler.

The card had been written in ballpoint, in the nondescript handwriting of the florist's assistant, not Louise Butler's precise and elegant hand. Nevertheless, Juliet was now in no doubt about who had really sent her the flowers.

FIFTY-SIX

It was two days after Nick had helped Juliet to release the indenture documents. She'd divided her time between resting and searching the Internet for more information about Cecil Rhodes. She'd read with fascination about the Jameson Raid in which he was involved, but at first couldn't understand why Rhodes might have wanted to name his slaves after such a fiasco. The Jameson Raid had been a foolish plot to overthrow Paul Kruger, the political leader of the Transvaal, and seize Johannesburg's reserves of gold by force. Of all his exploits in Africa, it had come closest to discrediting him. But, by following further links, she discovered that Dr Leander Star Jameson (some name!) was one of Rhodes' oldest friends and also the doctor who attended his deathbed. The slaves might have 'belonged' to Dr Jameson or Rhodes might have named them in his honour.

Technically speaking, there were no slaves in the Cape in the second half of the nineteenth century. The indenture forms did not specify the status of the women; they were similar to the contracts drawn up for servants, with one glaring omission: neither of them specified a wage or any of the other entitlements – such as new sets of clothing – that were usually part of such contracts. This and the fact that they had identical names persuaded Juliet that these women had been slaves in all but name.

If two of the skeletons that had lain for a century in the

cellar at Laurieston had belonged to the two Louisa Jamesons, how had these women come to be in England? Juliet didn't know the answer to that. She could only guess that she and Katrin had been correct when they'd surmised that Frederick Jacobs and Cecil Rhodes were friends and that somehow this accounted for it. There was plenty of evidence to show that Frederick Jacobs had spent long periods of time in Africa and travelled extensively there. Cecil Rhodes was known to have made lengthy visits to England on several occasions in the 1890s, including 1896, the year in which Frederick Jacobs had married Florence, but there was nothing that actually proved that he'd ever been a guest at Laurieston, even though an imaginative reader might believe that the journal hinted at it. It was true that Rhodes' Aunt Sophy had lived in Sleaford and likely that both he and Frederick Jacobs had attended the school and possibly been treated at the sanatorium there, so they probably knew each other, but it was doubtful that Juliet would ever be able to prove that Cecil Rhodes had not only visited Laurieston, but also arrived there accompanied by three black women. Although this was the only explanation she could think of for the presence of the skeletons, even to herself it seemed far-fetched. The rural Lincolnshire of the period was not only intensely conservative – as witnessed by Florence's journal – but very short on news and gossip. More than a hundred years later, local people were still calling Laurieston 'Sausage Hall' after its first owner. It beggared belief that the presence of three black women in a village the size of Sutterton had failed to provoke comment or some kind of record in local folklore.

Most of Cecil Rhodes' biographers seemed to think that he was a closet homosexual. There was little doubt in Juliet's mind that this description also fitted Frederick Jacobs. Was either of them attracted to women? Whatever his sexual preferences, Frederick had managed to fulfil his mother's notion of duty by marrying Florence and siring a son. Tucked away in one of the accounts of Rhodes' life she'd found a footnote that said that one of his friends had asserted that Rhodes had liked 'low-life females'. It would be fair to assume that in that period of South Africa's history it was probably a way of referring to black women. Another acquaintance, speaking many years after Rhodes' death, had said that he liked 'rough' sexual encounters. Was it conceivable that the three black women had been sexual prisoners? That they'd been taken to Laurieston in secret and held there in order to fulfil Rhodes' brutal sexual fantasies? Had his friend Frederick Jacobs also participated in them? It would not have been possible for them to hold the women there when the house had contained other occupants. Even Florence, the ever-obliging wife, would have been unprepared to turn a blind eye and Lucinda Jacobs would have sent Rhodes and his unwelcome companions packing at once. But, according to the journal, Lucinda and the pregnant Florence had spent several months at the seaside in 1896. And Frederick had left them there and gone to meet Rhodes; had they both returned to Laurieston House for their own illicit purposes? And how had the indenture documents come to be hidden in the journal, which had eventually been given to Jackie Briggs by her grandmother, Florence's last housekeeper?

Juliet remembered that Kevan de Vries and Jackie Briggs had both met Florence Jacobs when she was a very old lady. She wondered if either of them had memories of Florence that might help to solve the mystery. Bothering de Vries was out of the question while he was still mourning his wife and helping Tim Yates with two murder enquiries. Jackie was likely still to be upset by the possible arrest of her husband. Nevertheless, returning the journal to her was long overdue and would give Juliet the perfect excuse for calling on her.

She was still taking medication and, on balance, a little shaky, but she decided she felt well enough to drive. It would be easier than taking the bus and much less stressful than ordering another taxi. She arrived in Sutterton a little before midday. She was intrigued to see two police cars parked in the drive at Laurieston House and even more curious when she spotted Patti Gardner's small white van, but technically she was on sick leave and acutely aware that she had no official business there. She parked her car in the lay-by on the green, removed the bag containing the journal and walked the short distance to 1 Laurieston Terrace, hoping that none of her colleagues would emerge from the de Vries house and spot her. She opened the wrought-iron gate and walked up the narrow pathway that bisected the neat garden as briskly as she could, glancing nervously at the small stream to her right as she went. It was a bright day and there were no rats in evidence.

Jackie Briggs opened the door almost as soon as she'd pressed the bell. She was wearing her pinafore dress, the high neck of her blouse once again primly fastened with the large brooch.

"Hello!" said Jackie with forced brightness. "I thought it was you. Are you feeling better?"

"Much better, thanks," said Juliet.

"Would you like to come in? I expect you've come to ask me some questions about Harry." The smile vanished and Juliet glimpsed bleak misery in the woman's eyes before she lowered them. "He didn't do it, you know. Oh, I'm sure that he was mixed up in some of those things – too easily led, too fond of the betting-shop, and he always looked up to Tony Sentance – but Harry's no murderer."

Juliet stepped into the cool, dark hall. The smell of lavender polish was as strong as she'd remembered from her previous visit.

"I haven't come to talk to you about your husband, Mrs Briggs," said Juliet quietly. "I'm not back at work yet and I'm no longer part of the case. I'm sorry for you, whatever the outcome. I know how unhappy you must be feeling."

"Yes, well, fine words butter no parsnips," said Jackie Briggs brusquely, a catch in her voice. "If it's not about Harry, why *are* you here?" She'd turned to face Juliet now, as if barring the way further into the house.

"I've come to return this," said Juliet. "You kindly lent it to DI Yates and he asked me to take a look at it while I was in hospital. It's fascinating. Thank you."

She handed over the bag containing the journal, deciding in a split second that she wouldn't tell Jackie about what she and Nick Brodowski had found concealed under its covers.

"Oh," said Jackie, taking the bag from her and looking inside it. "The diary. I'd almost forgotten about it. Myself, I didn't think it was particularly interesting, except that it gives you a glimpse into what life was like in those days."

"You told me that you met Florence Jacobs when you were a child. Can you remember her?"

"I saw her quite a few times when my grandmother was working there. Not every time – sometimes she was ill, or had visitors. She was bedridden by then. Her room was where the drawing-room is now."

"What was she like?"

"Dull. Sullen. She didn't say much. She had white hair in tight curls – permed, probably. And one of those pouchy faces that women get when they've put on weight and then lost it again."

"But did you form any impression of her? Of her personality, I mean?" Juliet persisted.

"Like I say, she struck me as dull. You'd have thought she was not too bright, except that she had that shut-in look that people have when something's made them wary."

"You think that there was some tragedy in her past?"

Jackie shrugged.

"There might have been. She didn't have much to be happy about. She'd been a widow for a long time and her son, Gordon, rarely visited. My grandmother would lose patience with her sometimes. Said that she gave herself airs and graces because she'd come from a poor background; that real ladies didn't behave like that. But she could be kind enough when she wanted to be."

"Why do you say that?"

"Sometimes I'd be sent in to see her and she wouldn't say anything. I'd try to talk to her and she'd just lie there for half an hour or so until my grandmother rescued me. But occasionally she'd show more interest and odd times she'd talk to me – just a few words – and give me things, too. She had several boxes and purses in the cabinet next to her bed. This brooch was one of the things she gave me," said Jackie, fingering it. "She said that it had been given to her by a very bad man. I took her to mean that it was someone who'd made a pass at her, or worse. It was hard to believe then, but she'd been quite a looker in her day. You could see it in the photographs she had by her bed."

"May I see the brooch?" asked Juliet.

"Yes, but be careful with it. The stone is solid enough, but the gold is delicate. It gets bent out of shape easily. Silly idea, making a brooch in the shape of a spider, but I'm attached to it. It's just costume jewellery, but you don't get anything like it nowadays."

Juliet took the brooch and turned it over. A tiny assay mark had been engraved on the pin. The large, brilliant cut stone was pale pink. Juliet walked to the still-open door and stood on the step, holding it up to the light.

"Mrs Briggs," she said. "I may be mistaken, but I think that this stone is a diamond. A very large, pink diamond. I think you should get it valued. If I'm right, my guess is that it's worth a great deal of money."

And if I *am* right, thought Juliet, it was almost certainly Cecil Rhodes who gave it to Florence Jacobs. A very bad man, indeed.

FIFTY-SEVEN

Despite the fact that the tip had come from Kevan de Vries and was therefore slightly suspect, Tim was convinced that he'd been correct in suggesting that both Sentance and Harry Briggs were headed for Hull. He believed they were almost certain to try to leave the country and that getting on a ferry from Hull was their best option; they might well be travelling, hidden by the driver, in one of the de Vries lorries, which took the North Sea crossing on a daily basis. The alternatives would be to risk going further to another port or airport, or holing themselves up in the Fens somewhere. Given what he knew of both men, he thought that their choosing either of these possible courses of action was unlikely. Sentance, in particular, would want to escape with the money. No doubt Harry Briggs had made sure of his own hefty cut and, as Sentance was physically afraid of him, Harry was probably calling the shots.

Tim thought that they'd try to meet, either en route somewhere or once they'd boarded a ferry. He made a number of phone calls to the Humberside police and the transport police who patrolled the docks at Hull. He asked Ricky MacFadyen to get a photograph of Harry from Jackie Briggs and had it scanned and emailed to the police at Boston and Hull. Ricky had established that Harry had a passport which Jackie could not find. Although she'd said she didn't know where to look for it, the fact that she couldn't lay hands on it only served to confirm Tim's suspicions.

Tim felt restless. He couldn't decide whether to go to Hull himself, purely on a hunch, or drive back to Spalding to take part in interrogating the supervisors. He realised with a pang of guilt that he'd barely seen Katrin during the past forty-eight hours and gave her a call. She seemed quite calm.

"How are you feeling?"

"A bit better, at last. Juliet came out of hospital a couple of days ago. She thinks she's made some kind of breakthrough with Florence Jacobs' diaries. She needs to talk to you about it."

"Great. But it's going to have to wait until tomorrow. We've just made some arrests and I've got another suspect on the run. Could you call her and say I'll be in touch tomorrow? And I'll catch you later. I'll come home for dinner, but it might be late. Don't wait for me."

"OK. I love you."

But Tim had already gone.

On balance, he decided not to go to Hull, much as he enjoyed the thrill of a chase. Given the levels of vigilance that he'd now instigated, he knew it was unlikely that Sentance and Briggs would be able to embark unnoticed on one of the ferries from Hull. Interviewing the eight staff from the Sutton Bridge plant would be a much trickier operation than hanging around in Hull. He was certain that they'd all instruct solicitors before they agreed to say anything at all. The evidence against them was still only circumstantial. He'd had the Sutton Bridge plant shut down and police from Boston and Spalding were combing it for clues.

His decision to return to Spalding was timely, because, when he arrived, Superintendent Thornton, whose normal demeanour exhibited reasonable but impatient testiness, was indulging in one of his rare out-and-out rages. On approaching his office, Tim could hear him storming at Andy Carstairs.

"You'd better speak up, DC Carstairs! Why have you arrested all these people? And what's happening about Kevan de Vries? I hope that you haven't been troubling him with your enquiries . . ."

Tim tapped at the door and walked in.

"Yates! Would you kindly tell me what is going on?"

As soon as Tim had explained that another murder had taken place on the Lincolnshire side of the county boundary and that it was probably linked to the Norfolk murder, the superintendent quietened down. He shot Andy a baleful look.

"You could have told me that, Carstairs," he said. "It would have saved a lot of trouble. Well, get on with it, both of you. I'm still dubious about bringing in so many suspects all at once. I hope you know what you're doing. Just make sure you handle it carefully. Give them legal help if they ask for it. And, Yates, I still expect you to debrief me later about what is going on in the de Vries household."

In the event, the interviews went even more smoothly than Tim could have wished. The supervisors were terrified of being charged with murder and opened up without too much difficulty when they were interrogated separately and under caution. Some even said more than advised by the solicitors appointed to safeguard their interests. Only Molly held out for a while before giving her own, sparser, account, but all their stories tallied and this time Tim knew they had not been able to collaborate in advance; on the last occasion they'd met alone they'd had no intention of admitting their guilt.

When all their accounts had been pieced together, Tim realised that the police already held much of the information they disclosed. It had been given to them in snippets by Sentance and by Kevan de Vries himself. Whether or not with de Vries' permission – and Tim suspected that he would never know the truth on that point – Sentance had pursued his idea of recruiting young women from Eastern Europe to work in the ever-expanding de Vries plants. He'd encountered much more red tape than he'd expected. The solution that he'd come up with was to supply them with bogus British passports.

When they'd arrived in the UK, the girls were vulnerable and completely dependent on the company. Some of them were very young and few could speak English. Most were also pretty in a waif-like, underfed sort of way. They were clearly attractive to men and Sentance had shelved his original plan to board them with any employees who were willing to take them and had instead boarded some with specially-selected employees, others in the caravan park on the edge of the town. None of the girls was officially employed by the company. They were treated as casuals, like gang women, and paid much lower rates than 'real' employees. They were offered the option of earning extra money 'in other ways'. The supervisors had to have been in on it, of course, and probably Margaret Nugent as well. The extent to which the other employees realised what was going on was open to question. They were used to working alongside gang women and other casuals, so their innocence may have been genuine. What was not in doubt was that Sentance had set up a syndicate with the supervisors to enable them to make money from the girls' immoral earnings.

Although no-one was identified, the supervisors said that some of the clients were wealthy, influential local people. A few of the most promising girls were groomed for 'special services', which were usually supplied at the container 'village' that Andy Carstairs had stumbled upon. There was some talk of a more exclusive location that catered for the wealthiest and most privileged clients, but the supervisors were vague about this. They said that only Sentance knew about it. It flashed through Tim's mind that the 'special location' could have been the cellar at Laurieston House. He thought of the vicious-looking hook on which Giash had injured himself. The hooks had been there for many years, perhaps since the time of the bankrupt butcher, but the furniture in front of them had been disturbed quite recently.

The young woman who'd died had been one of the 'special' ones. None of the supervisors would admit to knowing how or why she'd died. On balance, Tim felt inclined to believe them. Thinking about Stuart Salkeld's conjectures, Tim suspected that her death had been the result of a rough sex game that had gone wrong. The client had probably called Sentance in a panic and Sentance had more than likely told Harry Briggs to get rid of the body. Although the supervisors didn't know the details, Harry was clearly in up to his neck and getting a substantial cut of the proceeds.

There were many questions still to be answered. Most important and most urgent was the need to understand what happened to the women when they grew too old to be useful. The supervisors were unanimous in asserting that all those who'd been exploited were in their teens and twenties, yet this racket had been going on for at least ten years. There must have been a constant exodus of spent prostitutes, their numbers roughly matching the influx of new young women. Tim fervently hoped that when the girls grew 'too old' they'd been sent back to Eastern Europe, perhaps with some kind of gratuity to keep them quiet. The alternative would be too horrific to contemplate.

Tim had yet to understand the nature or extent of Margaret Nugent's role. It was unclear whether she, too, was making money out of Sentance's exploits, though somehow

Tim doubted it. He thought it more likely that she had some 'extra' covert relationship with Sentance, or alternatively was hoping for one. He guessed that Molly was in a similar position: it would explain the animosity of the two women towards each other.

Finally, there were the passports. The supervisors claimed to have no detailed knowledge of how Sentance had forged the passports for the girls; they just knew that he'd done it. Tim was inclined to believe this, too, but it didn't explain why the five partially-completed passports had been found in the cellar at Laurieston. Why would Sentance be concocting passports there, unless Kevan de Vries was involved in some way? Or Joanna de Vries, of course. Tim thought back to de Vries' story about Archie and how he thought that Joanna might have continued to help other childless parents. If she and Sentance were working together to 'import' orphans, that could explain why the passports were being forged in her cellar. And Joanna de Vries had not wanted to go to St Lucia. Kevan de Vries had suggested, and Tim had accepted, that this was because she was reluctant to leave Archie, even though she didn't want him to see her in the last stages of her illness, a reluctance that she'd overcome because the desire to hold him again had been stronger. But perhaps she'd had a further reason for returning. It would take many hours of police time to delve into all the illegal immigrant stuff. He suspected that if Sentance were not apprehended they would never get to the bottom of it.

There was another question nagging away at him. How guilty was Kevan de Vries? As things stood, he could be accused only of bringing a child into the country without the correct papers: a venial sin, especially if he could produce evidence that that child was an orphan rescued from very disadvantaged circumstances. Tim had warmed a little to Kevan de Vries as he'd seen more of him and he certainly pitied the man for the loss of his wife and the many years of bearing the trauma of her illness that had preceded it. Something about him still didn't quite ring true, even so. All of the crimes, from the break-in and discovery of the passports to the murder of Dulcie Wharton, had been played out against the backdrop of the de Vries empire and Kevan de Vries, its boss, was surely too shrewd an operator to have let all that happen unnoticed under his very nose. Several of the key events had actually happened in his house. Could he really be as innocent as he claimed? If the answer was yes, despite not usually having truck with superstition, Tim would be forced to conclude that 'Sausage Hall' was indeed jinxed.

Harry Briggs' van was apprehended by a police car on the A15, near Horncastle. A search of the van produced two holdalls, one packed with clothing and the other with £100,000 in twenties. He was carrying a one-way ticket for a foot-passenger on the Hull to Rotterdam overnight ferry. He was arrested, cautioned and taken to Spalding police station to be interviewed.

Briggs demanded to be provided with a solicitor and would speak only when the latter had arrived. He denied any involvement in the deaths either of the woman whose body had been found in Sandringham woods or of Dulcie Wharton. He said that the money that he'd been carrying was to pay for materials for a 'back pocket' construction job that he'd been offered in the Netherlands. He refused to provide contacts to corroborate his story. He denied that he'd failed to tell his wife about his departure, saying that 'she must have got confused'. When asked if he knew the whereabouts of Tony Sentance, he appeared to be extremely agitated, but would only answer: 'No comment.' Thereafter, this was his standard response to all of the questions that he was asked.

Police road blocks on all the routes to all East coast ports and extensive searches carried out on vehicles and foot passengers at the ports themselves failed to reveal any trace of Tony Sentance.

FIFTY-EIGHT

Two months had passed. Under further questioning, Alan revealed that the name of the girl in the woods at Sandringham was Ioana Sala. She'd been living at the caravan site, where she was known as Joanna Sale. That she had the same name as Kevan de Vries' wife was an irony not lost on Tim Yates. When the police visited the caravan, they discovered two other girls living there. They took away Joanna's hairbrush and some items of clothing, as well as a passport in her name. DNA tests on hairs from the hairbrush confirmed that the body in the woods was Joanna's. The two girls, who were both very young, were taken into care by social services. Further enquiries and searches produced about twenty other girls, some living in caravans, some lodging with de Vries employees. All were in their teens or early twenties. Tim continued to hope that Sentance had devised some kind of repatriation scheme for the girls as they grew too old to be commercially useful, but Sentance had covered his tracks with almost preternatural efficiency. The police could find no trace of evidence relating to the girls or their clients, either at his house or at any of the de Vries plants. Margaret Nugent's files held records only for the girls they had discovered. There was no folder for Joanna Sale.

Professor Salkeld had managed to detect fingerprints on the skin of both Joanna and Dulcie Wharton. They were an exact match with Harry Briggs', which the police already had on record from minor crimes that he'd committed in the past. Briggs was charged with the two murders. Tony Sentance had still not been found: he seemed to have vanished into thin air. Tim spent many hours interrogating Briggs and told him repeatedly that he believed that Tony Sentance had masterminded the whole project. He pointed out that Sentance had deserted him and asked him why he was being loyal to the man who had betrayed him. If Briggs would help the police, they would ensure that his co-operation worked to his own advantage. On more than one occasion Briggs grew very agitated, but he continued to refuse to say a single word about Sentance. Finally Briggs' solicitor stepped in and asked Tim not to harass his client.

Tim and his colleagues began to prepare a case against the supervisors, but they knew it was flimsy. There was no evidence that they had kept a brothel. Although Tim was certain that they must have been in it for financial gain and therefore had been profiting from immoral earnings, he could find no evidence of unusual payments into their bank accounts. Sentance had taken money from several of the de Vries accounts and presumably used some of this to pay Harry Briggs, but Sentance's own account also revealed no payments that couldn't be explained. As for Margaret Nugent, on the face of it she was as clean as a whistle. It came as no surprise to Tim that her bank account, although containing substantial savings, was fed solely by her salary and unless he could prove that she had falsified or destroyed staff records, she was in the clear.

The police had been stymied by a conspiracy of silence. The girls refused to testify against anyone. They didn't seem to be afraid of the de Vries supervisors; their demeanour towards them was rather one of gratitude to the people who had helped them. They seemed not to understand that they had been exploited, degraded and their lives put in danger by these same people. Conversely, conditioned perhaps by their experiences in their mother country, they showed to the police nothing but implacable hostility and defiance. Tim knew that he would have to prosecute them for travelling on false passports and that this would probably mean that they'd be deported, but that in itself seemed a very hollow victory. He would be forced to turn the victims into criminals.

He had no proof that the supervisors were involved in the passport forgeries and indeed he believed them when they said that they weren't. He was convinced that Sentance alone had engineered the forgeries, probably assisted by a professional forger who had long since melted back into London or one of the world's other great anonymising metropolises.

They had to arrest Sentance in order to make further progress. But where was he? In the whole of his career, Tim had rarely felt so frustrated.

FIFTY-NINE

Juliet stood in the chapel of the crematorium at Boston, her head bowed, as the three coffins were carried in. It was a very small congregation. Besides herself, there were two other representatives from South Lincs police, Giash Chakrabati and Verity Tandy. Katrin, now visibly pregnant, was also there, as well as Dr Louise Butler and Nick Brodowski. Juliet was grateful because she knew that the reason for the presence of all three was that they had come to support her. They knew how much she had invested in finding out who the dead black women were. Like her, they were also there to show respect for these victims of abuse who had died in unknown horrific circumstances so long ago.

Somewhat unexpectedly, Jackie Briggs had also crept into the chapel shortly before the service was due to begin. Juliet guessed that she'd come as the self-appointed representative of Laurieston House. She'd known that Kevan de Vries would not attend. He and Archie had left for the other Laurieston, the one in St Lucia, about a week before, but he'd made it clear that he would not have come even if he'd still been resident at 'Sausage Hall'.

They had been obliged to opt for a humanist funeral because no-one knew for sure which religion the three women had practised. However, Juliet knew that if she was right about who had 'owned' them, it was likely that they'd been brought up as Christians, so she'd asked an Anglican minister to give one of the readings. He and the humanist officiant brought the total number of mourners to nine, not counting the undertaker's men. Tim Yates had hoped to be present, but a few days previously Stuart Salkeld had released Joanna Sale's body and, by coincidence, her funeral had been arranged to take place at Peterborough Crematorium on the same day. Tim had decided to attend in the slim hope that the other mourners might offer him some further clue about how to find Tony Sentance.

Juliet had chosen the order of the service. She'd gone for simple, mainly secular music: *Morning Has Broken* and *Wonderful World*, but she'd decided to conclude with *Amazing Grace*. She'd been convinced that the women would have liked it. She'd followed her hunch that they'd have been dismayed not to have some Christian element included. For the same reason, she chose Walter de la Mare's *Silver* and Keats's *Ode to Autumn* for the two of the readings, but had asked the clergyman to give the 23rd Psalm as the third.

Perhaps it was because she'd been so ill, perhaps because she'd had a small but terrifying glimpse of the atrocities that must have gone on at Laurieston House a century or so before and had imagined the unknown details all the more vividly, that she felt consumed with grief. The tears rolled down her cheeks, unstoppable. Katrin, who was standing next to her, caught hold of her hand. Nick Brodowski, on her other side, awkwardly patted her arm. The experience was yet more harrowing because, in the absence of any other information, each of the three women had been given an identical name: Louisa Jameson. It was as if their very identity, every trace of their individuality, had been stripped from them as a result of the barbarous treatment they had suffered.

She hadn't wanted them to be cremated, but the local authority had been obliged to bear the brunt of the costs

(South Lincs police had also made a contribution) and it was the authority's practice always to choose cremation in such cases unless there was a very good reason for incurring the extra expense of a burial. She'd made a tentative approach to Kevan de Vries to see if he would be prepared to contribute, but he'd made it clear that the idea appalled him. In some odd, superstitious way he seemed to think that the undetected presence of the three skeletons in his cellar had been at the root of all his misfortunes. He hadn't even considered it appropriate to send wreaths: each of the coffins had borne just one modest wreath, these also paid for by the police.

One by one, the curtains closed round the coffins. Juliet had always hated this part of the cremation ceremony, considering it to be ghoulish and theatrical, qualities that were even more exaggerated when the identical procedure took place three times in quick succession.

Afterwards, the small group filed out slowly to the strains of *Amazing Grace*. As they emerged into the crematorium's small courtyard, they were enveloped in a burst of golden sunlight. It was far fiercer than usual for the time of year. Juliet felt her spirits lift. She felt as if she'd been sent a sign, some token of approval, from the deceased, perhaps even a message that they had been liberated from their dreadful limbo at last.

Nick Brodowski drew her quietly to one side.

"Well done," he said. "I know what this has cost you, but you've seen it through perfectly. It makes me very proud . . ."

Juliet's head jerked up sharply. She wasn't ready for such proprietorial behaviour. He read her mood instantly.

". . . to be your friend." He finished lamely. He took hold of her arm again. "You must be exhausted. And I've been working away from home, so I've not been able to drop in much lately.

I'm sorry for that. If you're not too tired, would you like to come for dinner this evening?"

"I . . ." Juliet glanced beyond his solid bulk and saw that Louise Butler had been standing close by. Now Louise turned suddenly on her heel and walked rapidly away. Juliet longed to run after her, to ask her to wait, but she hesitated and the moment passed. It wasn't in her nature to cause a scene or draw attention to herself, especially on this solemn occasion. She watched as Louise negotiated the next funeral cortège as it lumbered through the gates before marching on towards the car park.

"I think I am a bit too tired, to be honest, Nick," she said. "I've only been back at work for a couple of weeks and it's still taking it out of me. But thanks, all the same. It was a very nice idea."

Nick shrugged.

"No matter. Some other time, then. I'd best be getting back to work. Take care."

Juliet nodded. "Thank you for coming," she called softly after his retreating back. If he heard her, he didn't acknowledge it.

"Who was that?" said Katrin, coming to stand beside her. "I don't think I've seen him before." Her curiosity was almost palpable.

"Oh, that was Nick, my neighbour," said Juliet. She tried to sound casual, but she knew that the lump in her throat was putting a strain on her voice. "You must have heard me talk about him. He's the one who found me after I collapsed."

"Mm, yes, I do remember now," said Katrin. "He seems very keen on you." Her eyes twinkled.

"Nonsense!" said Juliet. "He was just being kind, that's all."

She hoped that Katrin had not noticed Louise Butler, or seen her walk off without a word. Without trying to analyse her feelings, she knew that this was the real reason that she was still upset. She was relieved that Katrin didn't mention it, though she knew that this might just have been tact on her part. Not much escaped Katrin's observant gaze.

SIXTY

The last few weeks have worked out better than I could have wished for in my wildest dreams. The police have accepted I had no part in the death of the girl at Sandringham. They've said they believe Sentance was responsible for the passport forgeries but that they can't build a case until they've found him. Professor Salkeld has said that although Joanna was certainly moved after she died, it could have been me when I was trying to revive her – I would have been so distressed that I wouldn't have realised what I was doing at the time. (I doubt it!) He's sceptical, after all, that anyone else was with her in the cellar when she died. (I'm convinced he's wrong, but I'll have my own way of dealing with that.)

They've found no endemic crime within de Vries Industries – its accounts are all in order. (They don't seem to connect this with the fact that Sentance was a painstakingly efficient FD – with all that that implies!) The supervisors were obviously conducting some kind of prostitution racket, no doubt masterminded by Sentance, but there's little enough concrete evidence of that and apparently the Crown Prosecution Service is still compiling its case. It's a moot point whether Margaret Nugent knew that the papers she was given were false. It appears that the twenty-odd girls they've found won't speak up. That doesn't surprise me. I know what women like that are like.

DI Yates is concerned that Sentance might have had some

nefarious way of disposing of girls no longer hot enough for the game, but I gather there's no evidence of that, either. And Sentance has left no trace at all of the identity of the girls' clients.

No doubt owing to compassion for my grief, I've apparently been exonerated of all wrongdoing. Squeaky clean! They didn't charge me with abducting Archie and they even agreed to fast-track the legal adoption papers and his passport. They understood that there'd be no possible chance of finding his real parents, who had abandoned him before Sentance first discovered him. Jean has been a great help with this. Her motives are suspect, of course, but I think she's beginning to understand there's no future for 'us'. God knows why I had that fling with her. Temporary madness when I found out about Joanna, I suppose. I need to keep Jean sweet for the moment, though, because I've had a bid for the company from our biggest competitor and I definitely intend to take it if the price is right. I'll need Jean to help me to see it through.

Best of all, I believe I'm getting somewhere with Archie. It's going to be a long process, but already he's speaking more and seems to hate me less than he did. I've hired a specialist doctor and a nurse to work with him. They're coming out to St Lucia to join us in a day or two. Archie and I will get settled in first. We're on the flight now. He's dozing against my shoulder. Partly it's the effect of his medication, but generally he's more placid, more prepared to try to enjoy his life. Neither of us ever mentions Joanna. Her memory will always be too dangerous a place to visit.

It's getting dark when we touch down in St Lucia. Derek is waiting for us at the airport. He's never seen Archie before, but he is as discreet as ever. He makes no comment about the boy as he greets me. He stows all our luggage in the four-by-four while I bring out Archie, who is now sound asleep, and fasten him into the back seat.

It's midnight when we arrive at the Caribbean Laurieston (I'm resolved to change its name as soon as I can). The house is in darkness, but I see that Derek has turned on the swimming pool lights.

"A drink in the cool of the evening, Mr Kevan, before you turn in?" he asks.

"Thank you, Derek, that would be excellent," I say. "Just let me put Archie to bed and get changed; I won't be very long."

I carry Archie up to the suite of rooms that belonged to Joanna. He's never seen them before, of course, but I'm still fearful that some trace of her might unsettle him. I check that the sheets have been changed as I ordered. I take off Archie's outer clothing and settle him in the bed. He barely stirs. I open one of the wardrobe doors and note with satisfaction that it has been emptied, again as I directed: the hangers swing free; her clothes are all gone. Archie will be fine here.

I think I hear a sound – a footstep on the polished floor, an arm brushing the wall? I listen again, but there is only silence. It must have been the trill that rippled through the coat-hangers. It lingered longer than I thought. I am not expecting anything to happen tonight. Not yet.

I make my way to the swimming pool, pausing only to wash my face in one of the rest rooms as I go, pulling the robe around me. Derek has dimmed the poolside lights now, so that they cast a deep turquoise glow over the water. It is so tranquil, so restful, so full of peace. Archie and I will stay here until he is quite well. Perhaps we will stay here forever. Just a little unfinished business now stands between me and a life of perfect blamelessness.

I sit down on a sun-lounger, recline against its tilted back. Derek comes across and draws over a small table. He is wearing his white jacket now and carries a white bar towel on his arm. He sets down a tray of canapés.

"May I pour you a drink, sir?"

I smile up at his broad black face. There is nothing complicated there: no irony, no sarcasm, no sense of treacherous double-dealing. He is the perfect servant: it shines out of him that he wishes only to please, to do his job well so that I will admire him and, as he also knows, reward him. Opa was right to buy this house. His mistake was to build his life and his business in Lincolnshire, to come here only for holidays. If he'd based the business here, how pleasant life would have been. I'd have been surrounded by straightforward folk like Derek; never have had to suffer devious pricks like Sentance.

I lie back and sip the whisky that Derek has handed me. I close my eyes. I open them again briefly to see Derek tip-toeing away. He dims the lights still further, but he doesn't switch them off. The night is very warm. Soon I am deep in sleep.

A noise awakens me. Someone has knocked against the table. I open my eyes. Sentance is there, standing over me. Standing very close. He's too close. I sit up, try to edge away. Sentance advances a step or two to the very edge of the lounger. I knew he would come and I am ready for him, but still I feel at a disadvantage, waking like this to find him standing there. He is much taller than I am, even when I'm standing.

"Sentance," I say. "I knew you would come. Not necessarily in the middle of the night. Do you want a drink?"

"No," he says, "*Mister* Kevan." The sneer in his voice is threatening. "I want nothing from you except money."

"You've already helped yourself to plenty."

"Five hundred grand, a hundred of which went to Harry Briggs to feed his gambling habit? Do you think that's enough to keep me for the rest of my life?"

"Why should I give more?"

"I think you know why. Whiter than white, aren't you, *Mister* Kevan? Not interested in girls. Knew nothing about what was going on at Sutton Bridge. Blessedly faithful to your lady wife. Marriage made in heaven. Distraught when she died."

"Of course I was distressed when Joanna died. She meant the world to me."

"She did, eh? What about that little peccadillo with the solicitor?"

"Joanna knew about that. It always caused pain between us, but we managed to move on."

"I see. And did she manage to move on from your visits to the caravan site?"

"I don't know what you're talking about."

"Don't you? Don't you really? Do you remember stopping off for a drink at the Bridge Hotel last winter, after you'd been to the plant?"

"Not clearly, no. I've been in there several times."

"Well, on this particular occasion you met Harry Briggs in there. Does that jog your memory? He introduced you to a couple of his friends. Young girls."

I swallow.

"You weren't to know that we were running those girls, of course. Nor that we had cameras set up in the containers."

He fans out several grainy black and white photographs on the table. The quality isn't good, but you can clearly see that the man with the girls is me.

"Joanna didn't like these pictures when I showed them to her. In fact, she hated them!"

"You showed these to Joanna! When?"

"I posted one to her as a taster while she was still here. I showed her the others more recently. On the night she died, as a matter of fact. Now, if you . . ."

I see red. There is a momentary look of horror before he

crumples, and my finger remains curled tight around the pulled trigger in my robe pocket.

"Sir!"

"It's all right, Derek. Just deal with this, will you? We don't want to hear any more about it."

I walk back into the house, secure in the certainty that there will be no visible stain on the paving or on the rest my life.

ACKNOWLEDGEMENTS

Authors often say that it would have been impossible to complete their books without the help of their family and friends. For *Sausage Hall*, this is literally the truth! Without the hawkish editorial eye of James Bennett and Annika Bennett's incredible memory for detail, *Sausage Hall* would not have seen the light of day. Thank you! And thank you both, Chris and Jen Hamilton-Emery, for your enthusiasm, encouragement, amazing good humour and, even more important, the faith that you always place in my work. I'd also like to thank four friends who have been unfailingly supportive: Pamela, Robert, Mandy and Sally. And Chris my son, for his pithy comments. And thank you to all my readers and friends, including my many 'virtual' friends across the globe. You enrich my life every day.